MOMENT OF TRUTH

"You don't have a farthing's worth of worldly sense, Beth, or you would not be here with me tonight."

Frustrated, Beth pressed curled fists against her hips. "I did not plan this, you know. But since we're both here, and alone, I'm going to speak of this . . . this *thing* that lies between us. I'm going to speak plain and clear and loud, since there's no one in the wide world to hear us but the toads and crickets." When Alex did not turn or reply, Beth continued. "We both know what's happening between us." A sob caught in her throat, and tears stung her eyelids. "I don't know how or why . . . and I don't know what to do!"

"Go inside, Beth. I implore you." Alex turned slightly, and a shaft of moonlight pierced the shadows to illuminate his profile. He walked swiftly away to lean one hand against the trunk of the tree, his head bowed. Beth followed until she stood just behind him.

"Tell me you don't love me, Alex. Then I'll go. Tell me you don't love me, and I'll leave you willingly . . ."

BELOVED RIVALS

DANICE ALLEN

DIAMOND BOOKS, NEW YORK

This book is a Diamond original edition, and has never
been previously published.

BELOVED RIVALS

A Diamond Book / published by arrangement with
the author

PRINTING HISTORY
Diamond edition / January 1993

ISBN: 1-55773-840-8

Diamond Books are published by The Berkley Publishing Group,
200 Madison Avenue, New York, New York 10016.
The name "DIAMOND" and its logo are trademarks
belonging to Charter Communications, Inc.

PRINTED IN THE UNITED STATES OF AMERICA

10 9 8 7 6 5 4 3 2 1

To Jerry,
one last token of affection,
from Cricket

Acknowledgments

Many thanks to my critique group and best friends, Lisa Bingham, Lyn Austin, and Sharilyn Cano, for listening to my first historical romance and sighing and crying in all the right places. Thanks to my family—Allen, Chris, and Aaron—for eating frozen TV dinners and order-in pizza when I was deeply immersed in early-nineteenth-century Cornwall and too busy to prepare a meal. Thanks to my agent, Jane Jordan Browne, for her faith in my ability as a writer and her positive attitude. Thanks to Judith Stern, my editor (and fellow Anglophile), for loving my characters as much as I do and for her friendly professionalism and consistent enthusiasm.

BELOVED RIVALS

CHAPTER
one

Cornwall, England—June 1821

"DO YOU THINK he'll come, Zach?" Elizabeth Tavistock slipped her arms around the tall young man, stood on tiptoe, and rested her chin on one of his shoulders. Together they looked out the mullioned windows of the library toward the moor. A lock of her rich chestnut hair tumbled over the lapel of Zachary's coat of black superfine. Leaden clouds rumbled in. Another storm was headed for Pencarrow.

Zachary Wickham pressed her little hand, but his gaze never strayed from the scene outside the window. "Yes, damn 'im! He sent word ahead that he'd arrive in time for the reading of the will. Mr. Hook could have arranged to meet him in London later on. I don't know why he's coming here. Richer than a nabob, I've heard, so he can't be that eager to hear of the possibility of inheriting money. I'm sure he knows as well as I do that it'd be devilish queer if Grandfather left him a single groat when the stubborn old clutch-fist refused even to acknowledge his existence all these years. And he's not coming out of respect, I'll wager."

Zachary shrugged away and dragged slender fingers through his thick, straight hair.

"Maybe he's coming to see you," Beth suggested, watching anxiously as he paced the floor and pulled at his thatch of wheat-golden hair.

1

"Why would he wish to see me now, when he's not wished to see me these seventeen years?"

Beth bit her lip, hard. Pain knifed through her at the depth of anguish in Zachary's voice. He'd seemed so calm just moments before. But that was Zachary—outwardly a placid pool, inwardly a deep, raging sea. And, as with his every thought, every joy or trouble, Beth felt Zachary's pain as if it were her own. She reached out a hand toward him, beseeching, "Please calm down, Zachary. It won't do any good to put yourself in a taking. Mayhap this will be an opportunity for the two of you to work things out. Then you can be friends, be as brothers should be to each other."

Zachary stopped pacing and fixed his strange tawny eyes upon her. Beth's heart wrenched at the look of agony reflected there. Dressed all in black as he was, his bright hair and gilded eyes were all the more striking—like Adonis in mourning.

Yet Beth knew that he did not really mourn his grandfather's death, for that event had been expected for some time now, and she knew from watching her own dear father's slow demise from a consumptive disorder last year that lingering illnesses tended to blunt the edge of grief.

In truth, it would have taken a determined heart to cling to an affection for Zachary's grandfather, the reclusive Chester Hayle. He had scorned any display of emotion and seemed to dare anyone, including Zachary, to love him.

Beth knew the main reason Zachary was so distraught at the moment was the loss of his brother years before, a traumatic event of childhood he was driven to relive from time to time. He would feel that loss dearly today when they faced each other for the first time since their separation.

"As well you know, Beth, my father did not want me," Zachary said bitterly. "But for many years I was foolish enough to believe that my brother regretted the separation as much as I did. When I never heard from him, I thought that our father must have forbidden him to write me. But when he did not come to me even after our father died, I was forced to admit the truth.''

Despite his two and twenty years and the usual manly horror of giving in to emotion, Zachary's voice broke. With a grunt of self-loathing, he turned away and moved to stand by the mantelpiece, resting his head against the cool marble and grasping the edge with white-knuckled hands.

Beth took a deep breath and pushed back a dark curl that had sprung loose from the combs holding her heavy mane of hair. The damp, storm-charged air hung oppressively around her. A rumble of thunder bowled across the moor.

Beth knew the story well. Indeed, it had surfaced many times during the years she'd known Zachary. And just as a best friend would do, each time she'd helped him deal with the resurgent feelings of loss, rejection, and finally resentment. But this had been the only real sorrow to mar their otherwise blissful childhood, for they had grown up together as surely as if they'd been raised in the same house, though she lived three miles away at Brookmoor Manor.

Beth had always had mixed feelings about Zachary's estrangement from his family. If he had not been rejected by his father and sent to live at Pencarrow, she would never have known him. And she could hardly conceive of such a thing. Her childhood would have been dull indeed without his lively presence in the neighborhood. With just one other child in her family—Gabrielle, a sister much younger than she—Beth delighted in the entertainment and adventure of a boy three years her senior supplied. He'd become the center of her life, and she knew him as well as—or better than—she knew herself.

Now Beth recognized that what Zachary needed most was a diversion. Dwelling on the problem would only make him feel worse. Once started, he could brood for days, and Beth was determined to forestall a fit of moodiness from him, even if she had to dance a jig naked! But not as yet convinced that such a drastic measure was necessary, she decided that a gallop on the moor would be just the thing. Now if only she could convince him. She moved to stand beside him and pressed her cheek against his arm, saying in a cajoling whisper, "Why don't we ride out on the moor, Zach?"

He grunted, never lifting his head.

"There's still time before Mr. Hook is due here. Come!" she coaxed him, pulling on his arm.

"Good God, Beth, I hardly think it the most respectful thing to do on the very brink of Grandfather's funeral," argued Zachary, but Beth could see by the returning light in his eyes as he lifted his head to look at her that he was weakening.

"Pooh! As if your grandfather would wish you to be moping about like this," she returned, laughing. "In fact, if he were here, he would very likely give you a blistering setdown for pulling a long face. 'Vulgar,' he'd say." Beth mimicked old Mr. Hayle's gruff tones. " 'Zachary, you're being vulgar!' "

Zachary straightened up and turned about completely. His shapely lips quirked in that winsome Wickham smile that had all the village lasses pining for him, and he said, "It's raining, you idiot. Or hadn't you noticed?"

"It isn't raining yet. 'Tis only thundering. You aren't such a pudding-heart as to be put off by a little thunder, are you?" she taunted him.

"You fancy dodging lightning, do you?" he inquired dryly.

Grasping both his hands, she pulled him toward the door. "I fancy many bright, exciting things, my dear boy," she said saucily. "I'm betrothed to you, am I not?"

The witticism earned her a shout of delighted laughter and the gentleman's complete cooperation. They left arm in arm.

Alexander Wickham, Lord Roth, was devilish tired. After fourteen straight hours traveling from Surrey through everlasting thunderstorms, he found the damp confines of his coach suffocating. His dog, Shadow, a huge mixed breed that had somehow managed to inherit a coat of pure white, lounged against the opposite squabs.

A musty smell had invaded the spotless traveling chaise, as had the distinct odor of wet canine, and the cloying stickiness of humid air pressed the viscount's slate-gray pantaloons to his muscled thighs.

But Alex dared not rap his cane with its golden lion's head against the ceiling to catch the attention of his cloak-shrouded coachman. If they stopped in this damnable moor so that he might stretch his long legs and breathe some freshness into his lungs, the horses might not be able to drag the narrow wheels from out of the raw, rich mud of Cornwall. Remote Cornwall, he mused. The back of beyond. The setting for many of his childhood nightmares.

Shaking himself, Alex returned to the uncomfortable present, which was marginally more comfortable than his faraway past.

He again weighed the possibility of halting the carriage but concluded that it was wishful thinking at best. Shadow might take a notion to jump out if they stopped, and the blasted cur was wet enough, thought Alex, ruffling the dog's wolflike head affectionately. And once Shadow made up his mind about something, it was a stronger man than he who could change it.

Alex turned his gaze to the fast-streaming rivulets of wind-driven rain sheeting his carriage windows. Turning back, he scowled at Shadow until the dog whimpered and moved restlessly on the cushions.

"Oh, never mind me, Shadow," Alex apologized. "It's not you I'm fretting over. I just wish I could get out of this damn coach! But even if I dared stop in such a storm, I would not dare to get out. I'd be drenched of a certainty! And Dudley would be vexed, wouldn't he?"

Shadow had begun to look sympathetic, but at the
mention of Alex's fastidious valet, the same valet who
would not ride in a coach that carried a dog, he lifted his
drooping upper lip in a slight sneer.

"Sorry I mentioned Dudley, old boy. Go to sleep now."
The dog complied.

Alex sighed heavily. He was generally a patient man, and
he withstood inconveniences with more good humor than
most noblemen would. But this day and this trip were
different. At the end of his journey, he expected to find
nothing but misery.

This was not to be a house party with the usual diver-
sions. There would be no alfresco luncheons, riding parties,
gay dinners, impromptu dancing with the rugs rolled up
against the walls, and, as so often happened, a dalliance with
some luscious, lusty widow or bored wife. No. At the end of
this journey there was nothing to greet him but an old man
four days dead and a younger brother who must surely
despise him.

Zachary. The wine-colored squabs and the huge white
dog blurred as Alex returned in memory for the thousandth
time to the day he was separated from his five-year-old
brother. He'd adored Zachary. Since his father had paid
scant attention to the tot except to glare resentfully at him
from time to time, Alex had supplied the child with the
affection he was being denied through no fault of his own.

A lad of eight when the boy was born, Alex had only
vaguely understood that Papa was mad at Zachary because
Mama died while giving him birth. His father was never the
same after his mother died. But with a childish and innate
sense of justice, Alex thought it terribly unfair for Zachary
to suffer as a result. Alex had desperately missed his
mother, too, and seemed to draw comfort from his closeness
with Zach.

So Alex was there in the nursery when Zach first smiled
and when he first sat up. He had held the sturdy, towheaded

toddler's hands and set his fat little feet on top of his boots and walked him about the room until Zach got the idea and took his own first steps. Alex was there to watch and cheer him on. When Zach mouthed his first word, Alex was delighted to hear his own name—or at least something that sounded very much like it. Then, when Zach was five, Grandfather Hayle had come and taken him away.

Alex would never forget the tall, silver-bearded man with the stern mouth and black eyes—and he'd never forget the look of betrayal and bewilderment on Zach's little face when he was thrust inside the carriage and driven away.

When Alex turned to his father for an explanation, Lord Roth had advised his eldest son, then thirteen, to leave off thinking of "the child." His very existence, the galling sight of him day after day, had served only to remind Lord Roth over and over again of the loss of his precious Charlotte. They were all better off, he'd said, with Zachary tucked away in the wilds of Cornwall. Now they could rest much easier.

Alex smiled crookedly, bitterly. Easier, indeed! Perhaps his father was made easier, but many months passed before Alex could go to bed without crying himself to sleep. He was deeply ashamed of what he perceived as a womanly weakness, but he could not seem to help himself.

Alex wrote faithfully to Zach, and his father relented so far as to frank and post the letters for him, but there was never a reply. Even later, when Zach was old enough to pen his own letters, Alex never heard from him. There was the *one* letter, of course, the reply to a letter Alex had written to him after their father died. Zachary's missive was brief and to the point: He wanted nothing to do with his older brother.

Bitter disappointment and a sharp repetition of the grief he'd felt when Zach was first taken away had threatened to overwhelm him, but Alex was a survivor. He immediately set about trying to fill the void in his life. And by all appearances, he succeeded wonderfully well. He had not earned the name "Wicked Wickham" for nothing. If the possession of money, the attentions of women who were not only accommodating but enthusiastic, and the adulation of the ton were indications of one's happiness, well then, he supposed he was happy.

Suddenly the carriage lurched to a stop, and Alex shuddered free of the vexing thoughts that plagued him when he was too tired to resist.

Barely discernible through the fogged carriage window was a rumbling, terra-cotta stone building. Alex knew it must be Pencarrow, his grandfather's estate, which stood just this side of Bodmin Moor. Its occupants undoubtedly were considered the reigning gentry of the nearby village of St. Teath. Huge wooden doors, solid to withstand the erosive sea-salted winds and frequent rainfalls of Cornwall, seemed, to Alex's doubting heart, barred against visitors as well as inclement weather.

Through a slightly open carriage window Alex watched as his portly but spry coachman, Joe, jumped down from the carriage and moved to the door. Water dripped off Joe's wide-brimmed hat in an endless stream as he banged the brass knocker against the door for the third time. No one came. Joe turned and gave his master an apologetic shrug.

"By God!" muttered Alex, reaching for his tall beaver hat and an umbrella lying next to him. "I haven't come this far to be put off, damn 'em!"

To his well-trained servant, who not only took great pride in his job, but held his employer in considerable affection, the sight of Lord Roth's most imposing figure stepping unattended out of the carriage and into the muck of the courtyard filled him with horror. But he did not attempt to run forward to let down the steps, for, though he was spry, he knew he couldn't possibly compete in speed with the athletic Lord Roth.

With two long-limbed strides, Alex joined his coachman at the door of the house, popped open his umbrella, and gave the knocker such a battering against the door as to rattle the teeth of anyone within a one-mile radius. Predictably, Shadow followed and had pressed himself against his master's elegant pantaloons to avoid as much of the rain as possible.

Joe eyed his master while pretending to snatch a glimpse at the horses who were prancing about, impatient to be settled in a dry stable and to dine on a bucket of oats.

Alexander, Lord Roth, was not your average viscount. He had not the look of smooth symmetry usually attached to generations of careful inbreeding. He was not pale and delicate with a long nose, thin lips, and heavy-lidded eyes of a vapid hue. He was tanned, his nose seemed sculpted after some ruler's noble profile on an unearthed ancient Greek coin, his lips were shapely and sensuous, and his jewel-bright eyes were large almond crescents of deepest jet. From the tip of his obsidian hair to the toes of his polished Hessians, he was as glossy and black as a raven's wing.

Tall, broad-shouldered, lean-hipped, dusky-eyed, and swarthy, indeed, had it not been for the excellent cut of his clothes, which bespoke the elegant Spartan style of Weston, Lord Roth might have been mistaken for a bloodthirsty highwayman or a Gypsy rogue.

But it wasn't just Lord Roth's physical attributes that set him apart from others. He had an energy about him, a virile intensity that sent many a susceptible maiden into an exquisite shudder when he turned his keen black gaze upon her. Joe had seen it happen many a time.

Presently one of the massive doors creaked open just a little. A faded, cataract-clouded eye peered distrustfully around the casement, blinking against the gusts of rain to observe the gentleman whose vigorous handling of the knocker had made him drop a rather expensive crystal decanter on the stone floor of the kitchen.

"How may I help you?" the butler inquired icily.

Alex, driven to exasperation by hours of thought-burdened inactivity, dreadful, uncomfortable weather, and the incivility of a servant who would keep someone standing thus in the rain, sharply returned, "I daresay you might begin by letting me in! Mr. Wickham is expecting me."

"Mr. Wickham is not about the house," the butler informed him. "And he never told me about any expected visitors, sir." His cold eye flickered over the huge white dog with muddied paws and the jolly-looking red-faced coachman. With a moue of distaste, he began to close the door.

Alex ground his teeth together. He was astonished by the insolence of the servant. No butler of his would ever refuse an obvious gentleman admittance to the house. By God, his servants wouldn't even turn a dog out on such a day! He thrust his foot forward, lodging it in the crack before the butler could shut the door in his face.

"I don't care what Mr. Wickham did or did not tell you," Alex retorted with caustic, quelling authority. "I was sent for by a solicitor, Mr. Hook, for the reading of the late Mr. Hayle's will. I am Lord Roth, Mr. Hayle's *other* grandson. And if you don't admit me into the house this minute, I will very likely strangle you with the first convenient bell rope I should happen to see when once I'm inside."

Awakened to the fact that this was not a congenial situation, Shadow growled.

The butler's mouth dropped open like the jaw piece on a metal helmet. Alex could even imagine the noisy clank it might have made if the butler were indeed a suit of armor standing sentry in the hall. But the revelation of who he was, or perhaps the threat and the growl, had done the trick. The butler stepped aside, opening the door wide.

Joe and Shadow followed Alex inside, and the butler hurriedly closed the door behind them. A swelling puddle of water quickly formed around each new arrival, and the butler, an aged, emaciated-looking fellow with sunken eyes and cheeks, stared at the sullied floor in dismay.

Perceiving that the butler had to be intimidated into proper behavior, Alex assumed his loftiest mien. "Summon someone to help my coachman with the horses and then make sure he is provided with warm accommodations and a good meal. Do I make myself clear?"

"Yes, my lord," muttered the butler in a grudging tone, his mouth disappearing into the puckered lines of his rawboned jaw. Then, while the ill-mannered, ill-featured fellow took care of Joe, Alex took stock of his surroundings.

So this was the house his mother had grown up in. . . . Alex surveyed the lofty hall and the massive oak staircase that dominated one end of the large room. In a moment all other chafing thoughts became secondary to an overpowering surge of longing for his mother—for he could picture her here. Whatever grim associations he'd attached to the place evaporated for a time as he imagined his mother gliding gracefully down the stairs, her slender fingers sliding along the ornately carved banister. The Tudor furnishings were solid and reassuring compared with the spindly gilt chairs and Egyptian couches cluttering the houses of the fashion-mad ton. Pencarrow's furnishings were comforting, as his mother had been.

To squelch this disturbing tide of childish yearning, Alex determinedly turned his thoughts to his grandfather. He knew that Chester Hayle had been a landowner with some considerable holdings, and his land was pocked everywhere with tin mines. Although much of the tin had already been mined, he had accumulated enough wealth to keep his progeny flush in the pocket for some time, if they were careful. Of course Grandfather had ever been a careful man. Indeed, he was a God-fearing, prudent man, which was precisely why he so hated the frippery fellow his daughter had chosen to marry.

Jared Wickham *was* a frippery sort of fellow when he met Charlotte Hayle. He gambled and wenched, got himself foxed at every opportunity, and generally led a most dissipated life. But when he met Miss Hayle at a rout in London, he fell in love with the speed and depth of a plunging boulder.

While Charlotte reciprocated his passion with equal feeling, her father considered the viscount unfit for marriage and forbade her from ever seeing him. Charlotte did what any besotted girl would do. She defied her father and ran off to Scotland to be married. Thus began the rift between father and daughter that endured till her death. And beyond her death, thought Alex grimly.

Impatient with his nagging thoughts and desperate for some distracting activity, Alex looked about for the butler, but that fellow seemed more intent on supervising the two maids who were mopping up the mud and water off the floor than with settling him comfortably in a room. Besides his mental discomfort, he felt chilled standing in the drafty hall, so he decided to trouble the butler no longer and find himself a chair near a fireplace somewhere.

He dropped his hat and umbrella on a table and opened the first door off the hall to his right. Good God, what a mistake. It held the coffin! Since dead bodies did not hold up well in warm rooms, there was no fire, the draperies were shut, and only a single candle held vigil as it gave off an eerie glow at the head of the richly varnished casket.

Alex stood frozen. Here was Grandfather Hayle, the man who'd stolen the joy out of his boyhood. Harmless, now. Dead. Then, while bitterness and sadness boiled together in his stomach, a most unlikely sound drifted across the hall. Laughter, a man's and a woman's—his a clear, true tenor, hers a throaty contralto.

Trapped on one side by death and darkness and on the other by vibrant sounds of human joy, Alex still did not know which he preferred to face just now. He knew with certainty that it was Zachary's laughter he'd heard, although he had not seen his beloved little brother in seventeen years. Despite the voice of reason that advised him against allowing it, unbidden hope welled up inside him to mix with his apprehension.

There were footfalls in the hall, and suddenly the laughter stopped. Alex turned slowly around and came face to face with his past. Black eyes locked with golden-sorrel swirls. He recognized those odd eyes, but that was all he recognized of his little brother in this man who matched him in height, if not perhaps in strength. He had a lean, tanned, unlined face with an aquiline nose and arched golden brows. God, how ironic. He was the image of their father!

"You didn't alert your butler that I was expected," Alex said at last, clawing past the throbbing lump in his throat to break the screaming silence between them.

"I wasn't sure if you were coming," Zachary replied, his tone even and impassive to match his expression.

"I said I would come, and I'm not one to break my word." Alex reached deep inside for the strength to speak calmly. His face ached from the fierce effort it took to keep from showing the myriad raw emotions he felt.

Then—had he imagined it or did Alex detect for just a moment a reflection of his own anguish in Zachary's eyes? But he must have imagined it because those queer eyes were shuttered now against scrutiny and held a distant expression that reminded him all too exactly of his father.

"What a beautiful dog!"

Jolted out of his turbulent musings, Alex suddenly remembered the feminine laughter and looked down to see a slender young woman kneeling quite unselfconsciously by Shadow. Unlike the generality of delicate females, this one did not recoil from the smell of a wet dog. In fact, she had wrapped one arm about the mangy cur and was scratching him behind an ear. Shadow looked completely conquered.

Indeed, in Shadow's place, thought Alex distractedly, with such a comely arm wrapped about his neck and such a lush bosom pressed against him, he'd have been conquered, too! God's teeth, her skin was like fresh-skimmed cream,

ivory and flawless. Ripe-berry tints feathered her high
cheekbones and inviting lips.

But what thoughts to be having at such a time! Alex was
appalled at the unexpected quickening of his body from just
looking at the chit. He could only suppose that his tumbled
and fevered emotions at meeting his brother again were
affecting all his reactions, for it was with quite an effort that
he at last wrenched his gaze away from the dark-haired
beauty. But it was not before he'd observed that her
dusky-fringed eyes were aqua-blue.

When he turned his gaze back to Zachary, Alex got the
distinct impression that his brother's uncanny golden eyes
had not left his person for even a moment.

"Aren't you going to introduce us, Zach?" The girl stood
up and shook out her skirt. Such a simple, everyday
feminine gesture, shaking out one's skirt, but Alex found
himself beguiled by the girl's natural grace.

Then, bemusedly, Alex realized that both she and his
brother were wet. Not drenched, of course, but large spots of
rain covered their black mourning clothes. He must have
been riding at the front of the storm all along, and these two
had just missed a thorough soaking. He wondered what
they'd been doing outside at such a time and with such a
sober event as a funeral about to take place. Curiosity and
something else—disapproval?—stirred within him.

"Lord Roth," his brother said very formally, "this is
Miss Tavistock, a friend of the family."

Alex took Miss Tavistock's outstretched hand and
sketched an elegant bow. Her fingers were cool and soft,
and he desperately wished to feel them on his pounding
forehead, stroking the tension away.

Lord Roth! Zachary had called him Lord Roth with about
as much warmth as a coffin nail! He realized how foolish
he'd been to allow himself to hope that seventeen years of
estrangement could be swept under the rug at first meeting.

"How do you do, Miss Tavistock?" he said, grateful for

the few seconds he could avert his face. He released her slim fingers reluctantly.

"I do very well, thank you," the young lady replied brightly, "except, of course, that I'm chilled to the bone."

Alex lifted startled eyes to hers. An enchanting mix of humor and understanding lit the aqua-blue depths. But such a prosaic comment was exactly what he needed. It brought him firmly back to reality. "Indeed, Miss Tavistock, of course you would be cold in those damp clothes. How thoughtless of me to keep you standing thus. I daresay you ought to go home and change."

"I shan't bother to do that," she returned matter-of-factly. "Sadie'll help me out of this dreadful bombazine and dry it by the fire. In the meantime I shall just have to sit about in my petticoats."

Alex had had many flirtatious references to underthings whispered in his ear, but he'd never heard the feminine objects spoken of so freely by a gentlewoman. And Miss Tavistock had to be that. The black bombazine she was about to discard was fine. Her enunciation, in that lovely husky voice, was perfect, and though her hair was a bit disheveled at the moment, the shiny mahogany curls that fell well below her shoulders were held together by exquisite ivory combs. She was an artless enchantress, he concluded, discovering and admiring a single dimple in her right cheek.

"Sadie'll have your hide, Beth. She has enough to do today without rescuing you from yet another scolding from your mama," Zachary advised her in an affectionate but weary tone, as if he were speaking to a trying but adorable child.

"Sadie's used to me, Zach," she retorted pertly. "By now you ought to be, too."

Obviously quite a close family friend, thought Alex, for they spoke to each other like brother and sister.

"Perhaps I'm not used to you yet, Beth, but we've time," Zachary replied with a grudging smile.

Somehow the girl had managed to pry a smile out of the fellow, thought Alex with ready admiration. But what did Zach mean when he said, "We've time?" Surely they weren't . . . ?

Beth turned to Alex. The question foremost in his thoughts must have been reflected in his expression. She arched a dark brow and said, "If your brother won't tell you, Lord Roth, I shall. Zachary and I are more than family friends—we are betrothed."

Despite his suspicions, Alex was stunned. Their manner toward each other hadn't seemed the least bit loverlike. And, even more shocking, Alex found himself profoundly disappointed that the beautiful Miss Tavistock was taken.

God, how could he possibly covet his brother's betrothed? He'd just met the girl. And the Lord knew that the most important thing to Alex right now was reestablishing some kind of relationship with Zachary, mending old wounds, not embarking on a new flirtation. His own notions of honor dictated that he firmly suppress every amorous thought of Miss Tavistock. Now that he knew she was to be his sister-in-law, that was imperative. After all, of what importance was another comely chit to add to his list of conquests?

"Beth!" Alex was surprised by Zachary's suddenly stern tone. "I thought we agreed not to announce our betrothal until Grandfather was decently buried."

"We agreed not to tell anyone outside the family," she said pointedly.

Alex and Zachary both stiffened at this bold reference to their relationship. Yes, they were brothers, but Zach seemed as ready to ignore the fact as ever. The fact that he had not chosen to reveal his engagement was just further proof of the chasm between them. Alex's chest constricted, as if heavy chains bound him. He was suddenly desperately tired.

"Allow me to extend congratulations to you both," he said at last, forcing a smile. "But do not linger out of politeness, Miss Tavistock. I would feel bad if you caught cold. I'm retiring to my own room, anyway." Then, turning to Zachary and dredging up as casual a tone as he could muster, he added, "That is, if I can bully your butler into giving me one."

Zachary smiled with what Alex bleakly suspected was a certain enjoyment at his expense. "Stibbs was well taught by Grandfather to discourage visitors," he explained simply, "especially people he's never clapped eyes on before." The tawny eyes bored into him.

Alex frowned at his brother. Indeed, Zachary acted almost as though Alex rather than Zach himself had cut off the relationship. It was damned irritating!

Confused, impatient, and wild to be alone so he could organize his disordered thoughts, he growled, "Well, I would be vastly grateful if you'd bring the old griffin to a comprehension of his duties and have a bedchamber prepared. I would like to change my clothes before the solicitor arrives."

"Of course," Zach returned with cold courtesy. "But are you quite sure you've done with paying respects to Grandfather?" His gleaming eyes flickered toward the open door behind Alex.

"Yes, quite sure," Alex answered, strangling the urge to tell his brother exactly how he felt toward their grandfather.

Zachary inclined his head, then turned to approach the butler, Stibbs, who was still standing over the maids as they mopped the floor.

Alex watched Zachary walk away, a new despair squeezing his heart. He had spent these many years regretting the loss of his five-year-old brother. He had always visualized him so very young, even though his rational mind told him he was growing up day by day. The child was gone forever. He must cease to grieve for him. But he could not suppress the hope that in the grown man Zach had become there was still a possibility of reviving the closeness they'd once had.

"God, what a fool I am," he muttered beneath his breath.

"Perhaps not," came a whispered voice from across the hall. Beth stood on the bottom step of the massive staircase. She had been watching him, and he judged from the gentle understanding in her expression that she had heard his mutterings and divined the contents of his foolish heart.

Embarrassed to have exposed his vulnerability to this perceptive woman—his brother's fiancée, he reminded himself—Alex pretended not to understand her. In a bracing tone, he exclaimed, "Indeed I am a fool, Miss Tavistock, to have thought my valet would get here shortly after my own arrival. He probably has the coach stuck in a mire by now, so determined is he to travel slowly and safely." Then he added rather lamely, "Thinks he'll break his neck, silly fellow."

"Indeed, Lord Roth," she replied guilelessly, "none of us want to get hurt, do we?" She turned and left him to ponder her words.

CHAPTER

two

"LOR', MISS, YE look like one of them mermaids Pye Thatcher's always telling tales about. Ye're wet as one!"

Beth pulled off her sturdy half boots, then plucked the ivory combs out of her hair and shook the chestnut curls loose about her shoulders. "Nothing the fire won't fix, Sadie. How long do you think it will take my gown to dry?"

The gangly middle-aged maid bobbed her head, her frizzy gray-blond hair peeking out from under the ruffle of her mobcap. "Won't dry at all, miss, 'less ye take it off. Here, let me help ye."

Beth stood close to the fire in the bedchamber she'd come to think of as her own special retreat at Pencarrow. Many times she'd been led there by Sadie or gone there on her own to tidy herself up and straighten, mend, clean, or change her clothes. She and Zachary seemed always to find the greatest fun in doing things that got them both dirty and disheveled.

While this unladylike behavior did not exactly suit Mrs. Tavistock's notion of what was proper, Beth's mother put up with it in the hope that one day her daughter would marry Zachary. The events of the last month, commencing with the betrothal of the wild couple and ending with the death of Mr. Hayle and Zachary's certain inheritance of Pencarrow and the wealth attached to it, had fulfilled Mrs. Tavistock's loving ambitions for her elder daughter most satisfactorily.

Sadie untied Beth's dress, and the high-waisted, long-

sleeved, modestly cut dress slipped past her slender hips to
the floor, followed in short order by a petticoat. Beth
stepped out of the pile of black bombazine and ruffled
muslin, sorely tempted to prance about the room in her light
shift. It felt so good to be free of the heavy, sober gown!

"Sit by the fire, miss, or ye'll likely catch yer death,"
commanded Sadie, correctly interpreting the liberated light
in Beth's eyes. "Yer mum asked me to watch out fer ye here
at Pencarrow, and I'm bound to keep my word. I'll fetch ye
a blanket."

Beth sat down in a high-backed purple velvet wing chair
and assumed a most obedient air. Sadie hung the damp dress
over a broad rocker near the fire and dug a blanket out of a
heavy chest at the foot of the bed. She covered Beth from
her neck to her toes, taking care to tuck the brown woolen
blanket snugly about her icy feet.

"Thank you, Sadie," Beth said demurely.

Sadie cast Beth a suspicious look, but only asked,
"When's yer mother and Miss Gabrielle coming, miss?"

"Mama and Gabby are coming with Vicar Bradford. I do
hope the rain lets up soon," she added, glancing worriedly
toward the dark windows. A persistent drizzle still fell
outside, and a brisk wind blew in from the sea. "It will be
a wet procession to the gravesite and, I fear, an even smaller
congregation than we expected."

"'Twill be small enough," Sadie predicted sourly. "A
good man in his own way was the master, but folks
hereabouts won't shed nary a tear for 'im." Sadie sighed
heavily and shook her head, but soon shrugged off her
dismal thoughts and settled a keen gaze on Beth. "I can't sit
here and watch ye, Miss Elizabeth, but I hope ye've sense
enough to stay by the fire. I'm wanted in the kitchen.
Cook's all in a pucker, feedin' a viscount and all."

"Tell Cook to calm herself, Sadie," advised Beth. "The
viscount's very nice."

Sadie snorted. "Nice is as nice does, miss. Why ain't he

been to see his little brother in all these many years, I ask
ye?''

Beth's smooth brow furrowed. "I don't know, Sadie. But
somehow I think there must be a good reason. I'll find out,
of course." Beth gave Sadie an arch smile. "I've my ways
of getting to the bottom of things, you know."

Sadie gave her opinion of these proceedings with yet
another snort. "Meddlin', Miss Elizabeth, don't bring
nobody nothin' but bad luck. Ye'd best leave well enough
alone."

With those words Sadie left the room. Beth's smile faded
as she stared into the fire. Indeed, she thought, how could
Sadie advise her to leave well enough alone? In her opinion,
things just weren't well enough to leave alone. Zachary
would always wonder why his brother hadn't answered his
letters or come to see him after their father died. She felt it
very much her wifely duty to help Zachary come to some
kind of understanding with his brother.

The viscount's figure came promptly to her mind's eye.
Beth vividly recalled the tall, elegant gentleman called
Alexander, Lord Roth. In looks he and Zachary were
nothing alike. In fact, Lord Roth looked exactly like the
Hayle side of the family. She suspected that somewhere in
the ancient Hayle lineage a little Gypsy blood had tumbled
in. Those eyes of his were as brilliant and black as wet coal.

The fire crackled companionably as Beth contemplated
Alexander Wickham's Gypsy eyes. She'd studied him
thoroughly during the few minutes they'd stood together
outside the parlor that held the mortal remains of his
grandfather. She'd watched the emotions flash in his eyes
even while his facial muscles remained unmoved. He had
striven valiantly to hide his feelings, but his eyes told all.

A surge of compassion flowed through Beth, along with
some other warming sensation she couldn't quite peg.
Suddenly she felt oppressed and hot beneath the heavy
woolen blanket and thrust it off and onto the floor. She

tucked her legs beneath her and tugged her thin shift down to cover her ankles.

Now the firelight shone on bare skin, and Beth could feel the heat seep into her bones, just as if she'd been swimming in Brookmoor Pond and had lain on the sunny bank afterward to dry herself. Her shift dipped low over her full breasts, exposing two pale mounds that were pinkening in the glow from the fire. Beth reveled in the free, sensual feel of firelight licking against her skin.

Blushing, she tried to understand the feelings and subtle changes that had besieged her lately. Not physical changes, really, because she'd developed breasts earlier than most girls and had at first deemed them merely a nuisance. They'd crowded her gowns and gotten in her way whenever she took a notion to climb a tree or scramble on her stomach down a hill. And they'd been embarrassing. Everyone had noticed them. Especially men.

But when Zach had finished his schooling, grown tired of traveling about the gay postwar continent, and was casting about for a suitable wife to settle down with, Beth's respect for her breasts increased tenfold. Suddenly she very much liked having a womanly shape, because Zach looked at her with new eyes.

It had been Beth's intention to marry her childhood friend since she was six and he was nine and they'd enacted a marriage ceremony down in Dozmary Cove. She loved Zachary dearly and was determined from that date forth to secure him as her husband.

She certainly couldn't think of anyone she'd rather spend her life with. They were so very comfortable together. But through reading this and that and listening in when her older cousins came to visit, she'd discovered that men demanded something more than comfortable companionship from a wife. Passionate beasts, obviously, they had to feel a certain eagerness to crawl into bed with their life's companion. As her mother informed her, however—shuddering delicately as she did so—genteel, proper, *respectable* women were not required to feel anything during the marital joining. In fact, they were better off if they didn't.

Beth had taken her mother's word as gospel. Indeed, who would know better than her mother what constituted a happy marriage, since it was obvious that her parents had loved each other very much? But lately Beth had been having second thoughts. She was glad that Zachary desired her. That alone gave her a certain gratification that bordered on the sensual. But she wanted more. She knew instinctively that there was something more to be had between a man and a woman. Her curious mind and her quickening body told her so.

Moving restlessly in the chair, Beth thought about the village lasses. She'd seen the way they looked at Zachary whenever she rode into town with him. Obviously they found him attractive. Some even looked as though they'd gladly lift their skirts for him in return for just one of his smiles. Beth puzzled over this and couldn't understand what one's station in life had to do with physical desire. If the village lasses were aroused at the sight of Zachary, dimpled and blushed under the influence of his teasing gaze, why didn't she?

Perhaps, thought Beth, she just hadn't gone about things properly. Well, "properly" probably wasn't quite the most precise word to use in this case. In fact, maybe she'd been *too* proper.

"Knock, knock. I'm coming in, Beth."

Beth started guiltily when she heard Zachary's voice at the door. It was almost as though she had willed him to come to her chamber while she sat in her near-nakedness shamefully contemplating carnal lust. She got up on her knees in the chair and observed him from over the back of it. He was raking his hands through his hair again, a sure sign he was agonizing over something. And of course Beth

knew exactly what that something was—Alexander Wickham.

As always, Beth left off thinking of herself when she
knew Zachary needed her. Heeding time-proven methods of
lifting Zachary's mood, she proceeded to tease him out of
his sullens. She smiled mischievously.

"Sadie'll beat you senseless, Zach, if she catches you in
here. Remember that time when she chased you about the
house with the broom?"

"I was a mere boy then," retorted Zachary, glowering.
"She wouldn't dare thrash me now that I'm master of the
house."

"But that's just the point," Beth continued, lowering her
voice to a sultry softness. "You're no longer a boy, and
with me like this . . ."

Judging by the alert way Zachary's head reared up and
the glow in his golden eyes, Beth knew she had succeeded
in diverting him from his troubled thoughts. But after a
moment of staring at her intensely, his eyes shifting away
only once to note her black dress drying on the rocker, he
moved to the door and locked it with a key that had been
lying nearby on a chest of drawers. Now Beth really began
to suspect her own motives. She wondered if she was truly
trying to divert Zachary's mind from his troubles or if she
had some brazen experiment in mind.

Her conscience told her that proper women didn't do such
things, but her more adventurous self reasoned that if she
could please and beguile her husband-to-be just a little now
and then, where was the harm in it? And if in the course of
pleasing and beguiling her betrothed she discovered
whether or not she had a single passionate bone in her body,
well, that was all right, too, wasn't it? She'd never let him
see her nearly naked before, however—at least not since
they'd matured into adults—and he'd never locked them
alone together in a room. She trembled a little at her own
boldness.

With just a few long strides, Zachary stood by the chair.
Beth instinctively pressed herself against the back cushions
in a belated show of modesty. Zachary's eyes moved
purposely over her tousled hair, along her long neck and
shoulders, and down to the swell of her breasts. Cheeks
flaming under the fire in his eyes, she tried to analyze
whether she was blushing as a result of rising desire or if she
was merely embarrassed.

Then, following Zachary's gaze, Beth glanced down and
discovered that pressing against the cushions to shield her
breasts from his eager view had actually accomplished the
opposite effect. They only looked all the more enticing,
she supposed, thrust up that way and gleaming white against
the deep purple velvet of the chair.

"You're a fetching little baggage, Beth my love,"
crooned Zachary, dropping one hand below the curve of the
chair and lightly trailing a long slim finger over the mound
of one breast, dipping into the cleavage, and then continuing
along the mound of the other breast.

Beth shivered. It pleased her to please him. And it was
exciting, in a way; she'd never been touched so intimately
before. She swallowed and brazened it out, hoping to please
him yet a little more and still succeed in sending him away
while keeping her virginity intact. And maybe, just maybe,
her breath would quicken like Zach's, and her pulse would
beat frantically just as Zach's was doing. Since his cravat
was undone, she saw how the hollow of his throat pulsated
as his heart beat a reckless tattoo. Why didn't her heart beat
thus?

"I want to make you happy, Zach," she whispered,
determined. She lifted her head and parted her lips slightly.

Zachary's gaze was riveted to those full, inviting lips. His
hands grasped her shoulders firmly, and he bent low till she
could feel his breath on her face. "You shall, my love," he
said.

His lips came down on hers, softly at first, then harder

and more insistently. Suddenly she felt herself being lifted out of the chair, her feet dangling inches above the floor. When her feet finally connected with the hearthrug, Zachary was pressing her so close to him that Beth could hardly breathe. He was firm and lean and smelled of sandalwood soap, and she supposed she ought to feel light-headed with desire by now. But when Zach's tongue slipped into her mouth, all Beth felt was blind panic. In her opinion, the experiment had gone quite far enough—and so had the pleasing and beguiling! At the first lessening of Zachary's embrace, she squirmed away and scampered around to the other side of the chair.

"Zach, I said I wanted to make you happy," she reprimanded him playfully, though her heart beat fearfully fast. "But not *now*!"

Zachary seemed dazed. He blinked several times, then cupped his chin and ran his lean fingers along his jaw. "By God, Beth," he said at last, "I believe you've turned into something of a flirt. You don't invite a man into your bedchamber while you're half dressed, love, without making the poor fellow think . . . Well, you know!"

As Zachary strove to recover his composure, Beth's confidence returned. After all, it was only her dear Zachary gone slightly berserk. She returned to her former teasing manner. "First of all, this is not my bedchamber—"

"Will be if you wish it," interrupted Zachary, moving forward a step, embers of passion showing in his tender expression, ready to ignite with the least encouragement.

"And second of all, I didn't invite you," she finished, flashing him an impish grin before snatching the blanket off the floor and wrapping herself in it, Indian style.

"Dash it, Beth, we're as good as married. I don't know why you're being so skittish," he complained, plowing through his hair again with impatient fingers.

"I know you men, Zachary Wickham. No one buys the hen when the eggs are free," she stated roundly, lifting a slender white arm from out of the folds of the huge blanket and wagging her finger in his face.

Zachary laughed out loud, and Beth could see the tension easing out of his body. As she watched him, she felt a foolish, happy smile curving her lips. Oh, she *did* love him. So what if he never sent her into a passionate swoon? After all, what was passion compared to true, abiding affection? Then he surprised her by catching her up in his arms and twirling her in a circle till her head was spinning.

"Beth, Beth, my wicked little wife-to-be, you'll pay for this when I've got you for my very own," Zachary warned. And judging by the bright glimmer of his eyes when he said it, Beth was quite sure he meant to keep his promise. She shivered again and still did not know why.

"Now go on, Zach, before Sadie catches you," she told him as he set her feet on the floor again.

"Yes, Hook will be here within the hour," he said, his arms draped loosely about Beth.

She noted with approval that Zachary seemed to anticipate the reading of the will and another encounter with his brother with more calmness than his earlier demeanor had seemed to predict. She felt safer now in approaching the subject that she knew was foremost in both their minds.

"He seems very nice," she ventured.

"The word 'nice' is too all-encompassing and at the same time quite inadequate and vague," argued Zachary. Then he sighed, adding, "Besides, you've only just met him. How can you know?"

"I know what you used to tell me about him, the things you remembered . . ."

"Well, perhaps I was remembering with the inaccurate wishfulness of a child," countered Zachary on another sigh.

"Still, I don't think he—"

"Good-bye, Beth." He cut her off, pressing a brief kiss against her brow. "See you at the funeral." Then, just as he reached the door and had the key in his hand, he turned with

a thoughtful expression, saying, "Or do you want to come
to the reading of the will?"

Beth's face lit up. "Might I? I must admit I'm curious."

"Well, you *are* to be my wife, and mayhap if you hear
firsthand just how rich you'll be, you'll be more *grateful*,"
he suggested playfully.

"Don't wager on it," she tossed back, grinning. "But I
shall come to the reading!"

"I had, er . . . words with Stibbs, my lord."

Alex lay on the bed, shirtless and bootless. He'd crossed
his long legs at the ankle and flung an arm across his face
to shield his eyes from the brace of candles his valet had
placed on a rosewood table by the bed. "I knew you would,
Dudley," he replied dryly, never moving.

Apparently even such an unencouraging comment was
enough to get Dudley started. Without looking, Alex could
picture precisely his high-strung valet with his hands on his
hips and his face screwed up into an expression of offended
disdain. "He's an insufferable thimble-wit! A disorganized
sap-skull!" he declared theatrically. "Kept me standing in
the rain and then in the hall for nearly half an hour! How
difficult is it, I ask you, to summon a pair of footmen to tote
baggage? And whilst I waited, never once was I offered a
drop of ale—nay, not even a glass of water—to wet my
parched throat. And parched it was, my lord, for I was
frightened near out of my wits driving through that hellish
storm!"

Alex slid his arm up to rest it on his forehead. He lowered
his black brows and stared speakingly at his valet.

Dudley straightened up and endeavored to gather his
dignity. His carrot-red hair shone bright in the candlelight,
and his heavily freckled face, youthful for a man nearing his
fortieth year, looked properly contrite. "Of course, my lord.
You're quite right!" he said stiffly. "I needn't fly into one
of my pelters. Beg your pardon. Lost my head! It's just that

I can't abide an ill-managed household. Stibbs ignores essentials while he fusses over trifles!''

Alex raised a brow, a half smile quirking his lips. Perceiving his master's expression, Dudley confessed, ''Yes, yes, I know! *I* fuss over trifles, too. But you must admit, my lord, that I do not at the same time ignore essentials!''

''I daresay, Dudley, that I'd be hard pressed to discover anything you ignore,'' Alex drawled, pushing himself up and swinging his long legs over the side of the bed. ''I believe nothing escapes your critical eye. You're quite a fusspot, you know.''

Dudley looked deeply pained by the mild reproof. He cast Alex a baleful look and without another word returned to his task of unpacking.

''Now, Dudley, don't get peevish,'' Alex taunted. ''If all you're going to do is fret and complain, I might as well have brought Aunt Saphrona.''

This time it was Dudley's turn to raise a brow. Alex understood his meaning and retorted, ''Yes, you're quite right. You have much the better way with polishing my Hessians and pressing my breeches than Aunt Saphrona does. But I do hope you'll try to get along with the staff as long as we're compelled to stay here at Pencarrow.''

Despite himself, Alex couldn't help the tired edge that crept into his voice. Blessed with dynamic stores of physical energy, he knew the tiredness he felt had more to do with his flagging spirits than with his body.

As perceptive as a woman, Dudley immediately detected and analyzed the weariness in his master's tone and turned to closely observe him. ''And how long, might I ask, my lord, are we to stay at Pencarrow?''

Alex avoided Dudley's questioning look and said simply, ''I don't know.''

Dudley seemed about to say more, but stopped himself and continued his task. Alex was grateful for his valet's

restraint in this instance. He couldn't always count on
Dudley to hold back when he had something to say.

Alex moved to the dressing table and poured the warm
water Dudley had ordered for him into a pewter basin. He
threw a washcloth into the water, wrung it out, and lathered
it with a bar of spice-scented soap. He thoroughly bathed his
upper torso, relishing the cool air as it hit his damp chest and
arms. Then he bent over the basin, cupped some water, and
rinsed his face several times. He picked up a towel lying
nearby and dried his face. As he emerged from the fragrant
towel, he caught Dudley staring worriedly at him by the
reflection in the mirror. Perceiving that he had been
observed, Dudley quickly looked away.

Alex sighed, inwardly chastising himself for letting his
frustration over Zachary show. His valet was a worry-worm.
And he especially worried about Alex.

Dudley had joined the staff at Ockley Hall five-and-
twenty years ago when Alex was still in short pants. His
father, Lord Roth, had found Dudley through a domestics
registry office in London and employed him as a footboy.
Dudley was only thirteen then, and having reached his adult
height already despite weeks of near starvation, he looked
more like a lamppost with a red bird's nest perched atop it
than the youthful orphan he was.

His mother was a widow who earned her living as a
midwife. When she died during a sudden fit of the ague, she
left Dudley and his several siblings to make their way in the
world as best they could.

Through the years, Dudley had worked his way up the
ranks of the household staff from footboy to postilion to
under-coachman to footman and finally to valet. His eye for
detail and his uncompromising standards, which demanded
perfection in everything he touched, had recommended him
for each new job. They were womanly qualities, unusual in
a man but highly useful in his various tasks.

Along with the benefits of Dudley's decidedly feminine

nature came the drawbacks, however. He often reminded Alex of a maiden aunt—fussing, fretting, moralizing, nagging, and showing a most troubling and sometimes meddlesome interest in his master's personal welfare. But since Alex had a fondness for the fellow and found his talents indispensable, he put up with the personality quirks that came with him.

"Are you ready to dress, my lord?" Dudley asked him now, hanging the last of Alex's waistcoats in the wardrobe.

"Yes, Dudley," growled Alex, tossing the towel down. "But I shan't let you assist me if you continue to eye me pityingly as if I were the sacrificial lamb. Never fear. I shall weather this storm just as I have weathered every other storm that has blown my way."

"Of course you will, my lord," Dudley replied soothingly, easing the sleeves of the fine lawn shirt over the viscount's powerful arms. "I daresay Master Zachary will come about."

"Who said anything about Zachary?" snapped Alex, turning away as he buttoned up his shirt.

"Why, I'd be an absolute simpleton if I didn't know why you were in such a twitty mood, wouldn't I?" Dudley calmly observed, reaching for one of several neckcloths he'd laid out on the broad back of a wing chair. "If you please, my lord," he said, pulling a chair out in front of the dressing table and motioning with an elegant wave of his hand that his lordship should be seated.

Alex scowled at his valet and sat down, facing the large oval mirror. Dudley handed him the neckcloth. "Might I suggest the Mail Coach, sir? 'Tis a fitting style for so sober an event as a funeral. Now where was I?" He ruminated briefly while he tenderly draped two more neckcloths over his left arm. "Ah, yes. Zachary. Being taciturn, is he?"

Alex grunted noncommittally, his long fingers impatiently flinging and twisting the ends of the starched muslin neckcloth. With his brows lifted and his lips slightly pursed,

Dudley watched his master, usually so deft, pull the neckcloth into a hopeless knot.

"Damnation!" Alex snarled, jerking the knot loose none too gently and throwing the sadly wrinkled neckcloth onto the floor.

Dudley calmly handed him another. "Zachary was ever stubborn, you know," he continued, as if Alex welcomed his chatter and didn't look as cross as a bear with a sore ear. "But indeed, my lord, you always knew how to handle Master Zachary. As I recall, you teased him out of his sullens many a time. Nurse's mild scoldings were quite ineffectual, and Lord Roth paid the boy no mind at all. But you used to vex him till he was all on end! And then, when he was ready to pop your cork, as they say, you'd get him to talking. Out it would all come in a tumble! In no time at all you had reached a solution!"

"If you're suggesting that I can treat Zachary just as I used to do when he was five years old, Dudley," grumbled Alex, "you are quite out! Drat, hand me another neckcloth!"

Dudley handed him the requested item, saying, with servile deference, "Well, I'm sure you know best, my lord. Just thought I'd put a little flea in your ear. Can't fault me for that, can you?"

Alex glowered into the mirror at his valet's blandly innocent expression. "I can certainly fault you for a great many things, Dudley, if I choose." Dudley stiffened. "But I won't," he ended with a grudging grin. "Frankly, except for your damned meddling, you are a jewel and quite indispensable to my comfort."

Dudley unbent and preened himself at Alex's lavish praise. Then, thinking himself bound to keep his tongue in return for such kind words, Dudley helped his lordship complete his toilette in utter silence.

Despite his valet's impertinence, Alex had to admit that Dudley's words had set him to thinking. Mayhap Zach did need to be pricked and needled till he spoke his mind. Mayhap all that was needed to restore their friendship was an honest discussion between brothers, an airing of feelings, a sharing of thoughts. Alex's black eyes glimmered and narrowed, and he clenched his jaw as he planned out his strategies.

Dudley saw the determined expressions flit across his master's handsome face, dispelling the grimness, and was satisfied.

The cabinet clock's heavy pendulum swung through the humid air, the great "tock" at the end of each swing reverberating through the otherwise silent library as they waited for the solicitor. Alex sat at one end of a long, well-stuffed sofa with Shadow lounging at his feet, the dog's massive head resting on outstretched paws.

Zachary was at the other end of the sofa, and his charming fiancée leaned over the back, absently smoothing the sleek straight hair at the nape of Zach's neck. Alex now and then snatched a look at those slim white fingers threading through his brother's hair and tried to suppress the envy that expanded alarmingly in his chest. Damn, she was a distracting wench! But he had plans to put into motion. Plans that involved his brother. He needed an opening, and Zach was being mulish.

"It lacks only twenty minutes before the vicar will be here," said Zachary all of a sudden, his tone irritable. "Where can Mr. Hook be?"

Ah, here was an opening. "Are you speaking to me?" Alex feigned surprise.

"I wasn't speaking to any person in particular," growled Zachary.

One of Alex's brows lifted a jot higher than the other. "No *person* in particular, eh? Then perhaps you were speaking to Shadow?" The dog raised his head from off his paws, fixed his adoring gaze on Alex, and waited.

"Why would I wish to talk to that blasted animal of yours?" spat Zachary. "Haven't taken leave of my senses, you know."

"Oh, I wouldn't be the least bit alarmed if you talked to Shadow," Alex assured him, reaching down to pull one of Shadow's long ears through his curled fingers in a gentle caress. The dog's eyes drifted shut, and his face reflected canine ecstasy. "You see, I talk to him all the time."

Alex heard a muffled giggle and turned his eyes toward Beth, who had hiked one shapely thigh over the broad sofa arm and was leaning an elbow on Zach's shoulder. The giggle dissolved into a cough when Zach turned to eye her suspiciously. Seemingly satisfied, Zachary turned back, but Alex wasn't deceived. Beth's face was a picture of demure mischief. She seemed to be waiting expectantly, eager for more thrusts and parries in this verbal fencing. Suddenly Alex knew that Beth understood exactly what he was trying to do, and approved. He was surprised to discover himself immeasurably encouraged by her approval.

"If I wanted to talk to somebody, I'd talk to Beth," Zachary returned at last, challenging Alex with a smoldering glare.

"Why, Zach, I'm flattered," Beth said brightly. "But you haven't even talked to *me* since we sat down near an hour ago. You've been as silent as Sunday."

"I've had nothing to say."

"Civilized people certainly don't let that sort of thing stand in the way of conversation," observed Alex.

Zachary stiffened. "Are you implying that I'm not civilized, Alex . . . Lord Roth?"

Alex noted the slip and inwardly rejoiced. He couldn't help darting an exultant look toward Beth. Her wide smile expressed how he felt. His plan to irritate and annoy his brother as a means of chipping away at the ice fortress he'd surrounded himself with seemed to be working.

Withstanding with seeming insouciance the darkling gaze

Zach was hurling at him, Alex stated pleasantly, "Dash it, you Cornish are a sensitive lot! But never mind. At any rate, I would be deuced surprised to discover your conversation directed toward me. If I had something to say and was confronted with the decision of whom I should say it to, and if the room held a brother, a dog, and a beautiful woman, there would be no question as to whom I would choose to converse with."

Alex was quite sure Zachary meant to make a pithy retort, probably saying something about Lord Roth being most likely to talk to the dog. But Zach seemed suddenly to realize that he was being baited. He clamped his mouth shut and folded his arms across his chest in a gesture of pure stubbornness.

Alex's heart jerked. Zach was ever a stubborn child! He could remember him sitting just so many times when Nurse tried to feed him vegetables. Thrusting away the memories, he persisted with his strategy.

"Ah, but I can understand your annoyance, little brother," he said on a ponderous sigh. "It doesn't seem quite reasonable that it would take Mr. Hook this long to travel from Exeter, even considering the storm."

He paused for a moment or two, just long enough for Zachary to think he intended to retreat once more into silence. But as soon as he observed his brother unfolding his arms and sitting back in a more relaxed attitude against the sofa cushions, he said conversationally, "Ah, yes. Cursed annoying waiting for someone. Why, just today . . ." He interrupted himself to buff the nails of his right hand on the taut fabric covering his thigh, then lifted them close to his face for inspection. Out of the corner of his eye, he saw Zachary sitting up again, as rigid as ever.

"Today," he continued airily, "I had to wait a full hour for Dudley—he's my valet, you know—to catch up with me here at Pencarrow. We left Ockley Hall at precisely the same hour yesterday. But Dudley's such an old fusspot.

Makes the coachman drive like a schoolroom miss." He leaned confidingly toward Zachary. "Worries about everything. As squeamish as a maiden aunt. I daresay he's got as many quirks and niceties as he has freckles. Dudley's freckled, you know."

"I really couldn't care less about your manservant's freckles or any other detail, however fascinating, of his person, Lord Roth," snapped Zachary. "And why you should suppose I'd have the least interest in any of this prittle-prattle, Alex . . . Lord Roth, is beyond my understanding."

At Zach's second slip, Beth clapped her hand over her mouth, her eyes peeking merrily over her fingers, slanted in a smile. Barely able to contain himself, Alex was constructing a fitting rebuttal when the door opened and a short, stocky man in a black coat and baggy black trousers bustled into the room.

"So terribly sorry to keep you waiting, sir," he murmured apologetically, bowing deeply to Zachary. "Your servant, Miss Tavistock," he said with another, deeper bow. Then, spying Alex, he hurriedly added, bowing lowest of all, "And you, too, my lord. You *are* Lord Roth?"

"Yes," said Alex. "And you, of course, are Mr. Hook. Don't bother to explain your lateness," he advised the harried solicitor. "It will only take time, a commodity we have little of at present. The how-do-you-do's have already taken a goodly amount of time, what with all the bowing. The funeral begins in a quarter of an hour, and you have a legal document to read, which we in turn must decipher. I hope it isn't long?"

Mr. Hook, a swarthy fellow with a nose so large and curved it made one think his name all too accurate, seemed relieved to be spared the necessity of making excuses. He pulled a chair across the carpet and sat down in it directly in front of the sofa the two brothers occupied, with Beth still perched on the arm. Then he rummaged in a large scuffed-leather portmanteau and came up with several sheets of paper.

"Indeed, it is long, Lord Roth, but it really isn't necessary to read it just now. The intentions of Mr. Hayle in the distribution of his property can be quite easily summed up."

"What do you mean?" inquired Zachary, sitting forward.

"I mean just this. He left everything to you, Mr. Wickham—his money, his properties, all his personal belongings—"

"I'm not surprised, Mr. Hook," Alex interrupted. "That is as it should be. But why, then, did our grandfather require *me* to be present at the reading of his will?"

"He left everything to Mr. Wickham—except this." Mr. Hook then dived again into the vast portmanteau. He extracted a large, bulging envelope and handed it to Alex. "Now, if you will excuse me, I will go to the kitchen and avail myself of the hot tea I was offered as I was coming in." Mr. Hook, barely noticed by the others, bowed and left the room.

Alex stared at the package. "Good God, dare I open it?" he exclaimed. He glanced at Zachary and noticed him eyeing the package curiously. "You haven't a clue as to the contents of this package, either, do you?"

"No, I haven't," Zach answered, then said impatiently, "Aren't you going to open it?"

"Perhaps I should wait till after the funeral," Alex suggested warily.

Beth moved around to the front of the sofa and squeezed herself between the arm and Zachary. Her eyes were wide aqua pools of blatant curiosity. "Oh, *do* open it now, my lord," she implored him, fully expecting to be included.

Who could resist such a plea? In answer Alex immediately pulled loose the seal holding the flap closed at the top of the envelope, then dumped its contents onto the sofa between himself and Zachary. There were two bundles of letters and a sheet of parchment, folded once. After staring confusedly for a moment at the two heaps of letters, he realized that one string-tied bundle contained the letters he'd sent to Zachary over the years, ever hoping for an answer, and the other bundle held letters Zachary had sent to him. Or, more correctly, they were letters Zach had written to him which were never posted!

"Good God, the old man deceived us," he muttered, more to himself than to Zachary. Alex lifted his eyes to his brother, who was sitting as still as death, staring at the bundles with the same horrified look. "You never saw my letters at all?"

"No, never!" Zachary choked out. "And you never saw mine?"

"No. That is, only the one." Alex winced at the memory of that hated letter. "The one you wrote to me after Father died."

"I never wrote you after Father died!" Zachary exclaimed, standing up, mobilized by the torrent of emotions surging through him. "I was waiting for some word from you. I thought that if he'd forbidden you to write to me before, there was nothing to stop you after his death."

Alex stood up, too. "But I got a letter. In it you said you didn't want anything to do with me!"

Zachary reached down and extracted one of his letters from the pile on the sofa, fumbling and jerking at the string with shaking hands, and thrust it toward Alex. "Did the handwriting look like this?" he demanded to know.

Alex snatched the letter and examined the writing. "No. But why—"

"Because I didn't write the letter you received. Grandfather must have written it. By God, what's been done here? It must all have been Grandfather's doing. Our father at least posted your letters to me."

"Good heavens, quit speculating," urged Beth, bouncing with excitement. "Read the letter!" When the two gentlemen stared at her, then down at the dozens of letters on the sofa, she grabbed the folded parchment sheet lying unattended on the sofa and waved it in front of Alex's nose. "This letter, you loobies! It must be from your grandfather explaining everything. Do read it and end this wretched suspense."

Alex did as he was bidden. The letter from his grandfather was indeed an explanation. In a low voice, with only the cabinet clock's ponderous tocking and the patter of rain in the background, he read it aloud:

Lord Roth,

You're probably damned mad at me right now, and rightfully so, I suppose. But I'd do it again if I had to. In exchange for allowing me to raise Zachary, your father made me promise on my honor as a gentleman to intercept the letters you wrote to Zachary and the letters he wrote to you. I don't regret it; Zachary would have had a hellish life with your father. There have been times, however, when I have deeply regretted the necessity of enforcing a separation between two brothers. It seemed unnatural. Especially after your father died, I was tempted to bring about a reunion, but I'd given my word. Most of all I beg pardon for the letter I wrote to you then. But now that your father and I are both dead, there's no point in perpetuating the lies. It gives me great pleasure to disoblige your father. I hope he's spinning in his grave.

Chester Hayle

"So 'twas Father after all," Zachary said rather dazedly. "He hated me that much. But why was I denied my brother, too? I can understand *him* not wanting to see me, but—"

"Well, *I* don't understand why he didn't want to see you," Alex rasped. "By God, you were his own flesh and blood. You couldn't help what happened to our mother."

"But I had come to believe that you felt the same hatred for me, Alex. At least I thought you had willingly forgotten we were brothers. All along, all through these years, you *have* thought of me!''

"And you of me."

The room grew still. Even the rain stopped its persistent splattering against the windows for a time. No one spoke, as if everyone felt the importance of this enlightening moment. For Alex there *was* no one else in the room. He had his brother back.

Without knowing or caring who stepped forward first, suddenly he had Zach clasped against his chest in a manly embrace. After a fierce hug, they thumped each other heartily on the back. Then, pulling away with a rather self-conscious grin, Alex declared, "We have a lot of catching up to do, little brother."

Beth watched, tears of joy smarting against her eyelids. She was very happy for Zach and Alex. Then, observing their boyish grins and the light in their eyes, she felt something else creep into her heart, something dark, disturbing, and unwelcome. She felt excluded. She was jealous.

CHAPTER
three

"WHERE DID THEY go, Stibbs?"

"I'm sure I don't know, miss."

"Did they drive or were they mounted?"

"I've been in the kitchen, miss. I never saw how they left the premises."

Beth sighed with frustration. "Mayhap they didn't even leave the house, then. Are you sure they're not in the library? Zachary told me to meet him here at half past noon!"

"One of the footmen said he saw them leave right after breakfast, miss," Stibbs persisted.

Beth eyed the taciturn butler with obvious annoyance. She was sure that behind his facade of respectful forbearance he was sneering at her. And who could blame him? she thought, turning away and stomping out into the sunshine of the front courtyard where one of the stable hands walked her saddled red gelding. This wasn't the first time in the past month that Zachary had failed to show up when he'd said he would.

The wide skirt of Beth's royal blue riding habit swung about her legs as she impatiently paced the graveled drive, her bonnet swinging from her hand by its ribbons. She shielded her eyes from the sun and peered across the lawn toward the moor, then turned and looked in the opposite direction toward the sea. They could be anywhere, she thought bitterly. Alex had expressed a desire to see the

Cornish countryside, and Zach seemed determined to indulge his older brother's every whim. In fact, in his
devotion to Alex he reminded her of an adoring dog. He had
become another Shadow.

Beth signaled to the stable hand, and the young man
brought her horse around to the front of the house. "Thank
you, Henry," she said, managing a tight smile for the
servant, who stared at her worshipfully. "That will be all."
Henry turned toward the stables, but not without another
adoring look back at her. Too bad Zach no longer cherished
similar feelings for her, she thought wryly, reaching up to
stroke Ginger's long nose. Ever since Alexander Wickham
came upon the scene and the two brothers reconciled their
differences, Zach had taken about as much notice of her as
a gnat on the wall.

She had wanted them to reconcile very much, but she had
not imagined that it would so effectively deprive her of
Zach's company. Zach and Alex seemed to be trying to
make up for the seventeen years they'd been kept apart by
the maneuvering of their unforgiving father. But Beth
couldn't help but feel abandoned. Even if they included her
in their plans, she felt like an intruder.

One day, during a moment of extreme exasperation, she
had fleetingly considered the desperate strategy of catching
Zach's attention away from his brother by disrobing and
arranging herself in a suggestive pose. But she'd discarded
that idea after imagining how mortifying it would be if he
told her to quit being a goose and put her clothes on.
Besides, Beth had no intention of indulging in intimacies
with Zach before marriage. She would just have to find
another way to compete with Zach's fascination with Alex
Wickham.

Beth could not deny that Alex was interesting. His
travels, his education, his stint as a captain in the Royal
Dragoons warring against Napoleon on the Peninsula, his
circles of friends and acquaintances in London and around

the world supplied material for many diverting stories. But even if he had nothing more to say than that the wind seemed coolish that day, or that the pigeon pie was turned to a nicety, he commanded one's attention easily. Alexander, Lord Roth, had a compelling personality. At times she became irritated when she found herself listening as avidly as Zach did.

"Well, Ginger," she said, pulling herself easily atop the horse and putting on her bonnet, "I'm not about to give up! Zach has been my best friend for seventeen years, and he's to be my husband for the next forty, God willing. Alex Wickham may have had Zach first, but Zach's more mine than his."

Then, just as she was about to urge Ginger into a canter and set out to find the inseparable brothers, her sister, Gabrielle, darted out from behind the stone walls that surrounded the kitchen garden. Long honey-blond hair, frizzed by the humid air, tumbled down the young girl's back as she ran toward Beth. In her blue gown, straw poke bonnet, and striped spencer, she looked like a smaller, fairer version of Beth.

"Beth, where are you going? Where's Zach? I thought you were going riding with him."

"I'm meeting him somewhere else," Beth lied, avoiding her little sister's keen eyes.

"Posh! He's gone off without you again, hasn't he?" Gabby surmised, looking much too wise for her eight years. "In that case, won't you take me home now?"

"I'll be back for you later, Gabby," said Beth impatiently, holding back her eager horse with difficulty. "Run along and play with the puppies! That's why I brought you, you know!"

"But I've seen the puppies," Gabrielle returned petulantly. "Their eyes are still closed, and all they want to do is snuggle against their mother and eat. They're not cute at all. They look like rats! I thought they'd be furry and playful.''

"I told you it was too soon," Beth reminded her in the superior tone of an older sister. "Go find Sadie. Maybe she'll let you muck about in the kitchen till I come back for you.''

Gabrielle put her fists on her small hips and pushed out her full bottom lip. "I'm not a baby, Lilibet! I don't want to squeeze my fingers in the bread dough anymore or make gingerbread men! Oh, I wish Mama had let me ride my own horse.''

"If you minded better, Gabby, Mama wouldn't have to restrict you so often. She was afraid you'd take off on another of your adventures and get yourself lost again.''

Gabby stamped her foot. "Oh, you're such a fusspot, Beth. I don't know why Zach wants to marry you anyway!'' Then, with her back as straight as a Maypole, Gabby thrust her nose in the air and huffed away, as indignant as a wet hen.

Beth couldn't help but chuckle at Gabby's theatrics. Depending on which approach would be most effective, Gabby could be as sweet and irresistible as a sticky bun, as feisty and unapproachable as a cornered alley cat, or, as now, as haughty and high-handed as royalty displeased. If Gabby ever had to fend for herself in the world, Beth speculated, she could do very well treading the boards, holding her own with the greatest of actresses.

But for a girl with Gabby's genteel upbringing, marriage was the only respectable outlet for her talents. God help her future husband, Beth thought with amusement. He had better have a strong will of his own, or she'd run roughshod over him in a pig's whisper.

And speaking of future husbands . . . Beth urged Ginger into a trot. Once she passed through the lodge gates and reached the lane just past the boundaries of Pencarrow, she reigned in and pondered which direction to go. It was such a beautiful cloudless day that she guessed they might have ridden over to Dozmary Cove to look at the view. She and Zachary used to play there for hours as children, building miniature Camelots in the sand and speculating on the magic legends of King Arthur and his lovely Guinevere. She turned her horse north, toward the sea.

Leaving the lane, Beth followed the well-worn trail through low gorse bushes and shrubs of feathery tamarisk till the ground turned to sand strewn with rocks that had been chipped from the dark cliffs by salt spray and Atlantic gales. Several minutes later she found herself at the top of a granite cliff overlooking the ocean. A mild breeze lifted her hair and cooled her neck. The cove below was hidden from view and accessible only by a narrow, sharply descending footpath that hugged the rugged wall of the cliff. But if they were down in the cove, where were their horses?

As if in answer to her unspoken question, she heard a whinny close by. There, just yards away, were the two horses, Zach's dapple gray and Alex's black stallion, tethered to a tree sheltered by a rock overhang. Beth felt a thrill of pride and a fierce possessiveness. She had known exactly where Zach would go. She knew her Zach better than Alexander Wickham would ever know him, better than anybody would ever know him!

Spurred on by this much needed affirmation of her connection to Zach, Beth rode over to the horses, dismounted, and tethered Ginger to the tree. She took off her bonnet because it was hot and confining, caring not a jot that the faint freckles on her nose would surely multiply with the exposure to sun and wind. Then, looping her skirt around her arm and exposing a goodly amount of bare leg above her riding boots, she started down the steep path to the cove.

Before she could see the cove, Beth heard Zach's and Alex's voices rise for a moment above the noise of the surf. They were laughing, obviously enjoying themselves hugely. Zach's slightly higher pitched bell-like tones blended musically with Alex's velvet baritone. Now their voices dissolved into low conversation, and she strained unsuccessfully to hear what they were saying, feeling the veriest fool, so eager, so desperate to be a part of their camaraderie that she would stoop to eavesdropping!

Her breath came swift and shallow as she hurried down the rough trail that was hardly a trail at all. She slipped on a loose rock and scraped her ankle against a sharp edge, biting back her impatient exclamation of pain. She didn't want them to see her climbing down the cliff with her skirt hiked up to well above her knees—it would have been too undignified, and they'd surely have laughed at her—so she had to be as quiet as possible. She hoped Shadow would not sniff her out and expose her.

Finally she reached the bottom and had only to round a jutting, contorted wall of granite to be on the sand and in clear sight of them. Struck with sudden shyness and a lowering realization that perhaps they wouldn't be best pleased to see her, Beth hesitated. First she would watch them from behind the cover of the cliff wall and then, unless her courage failed her at the sight of them so happily occupied with each other, she would make her presence known.

She inched one eye to the edge of the wall and peeked. Beth gasped and fell back, turning to support herself against the rock wall. They were naked! They must have been swimming and now were sunning themselves on two large flat rocks near the shore, just yards away. She bit her lip, wondering what to do, her heartbeat as loud and heavy as a tin miner's sledgehammer. They were talking to each other, but she couldn't hear what they said. Her ears thrummed with the rush of blood through her veins.

She knew what she ought to do. She ought to leave this place straightaway. She had no business gaping at her fiancé and his brother as they lounged stark naked in the sun. But despite the voice of conscience and the natural fears of an ignorant virgin who'd never clapped eyes on a naked man before in her life, Beth was curious. She wanted to stay; she wanted to *see*.

Besides, she told herself as she carefully poked her head around the corner again, Zachary would soon be her husband, and she would no doubt see him time and again without his clothes on. But it wasn't Zachary her gaze was riveted to when the two men came into view. It was Alexander, Lord Roth, the titled Gypsy, the elegant rogue, who caught, claimed, and absorbed her complete attention, his white dog sleeping beside him a perfect complement to his dark beauty.

It seemed odd to call a man beautiful, but he was. Alex was tanned from tip to toe and everywhere in between, as if he sunbathed regularly. His long legs were lightly furred with dark hair and as sinewy and leanly muscular as his fitted pantaloons had suggested. His broad chest and shoulders were not the result of a clever tailor, but his by right of birth. He rested on his side, facing Beth, one taut arm holding up his head and the other draped casually over one slim hip, luckily—or was it unluckily?—shielding his manhood from her view.

His waist was narrow, his stomach firm and flat. A triangle of curling hair began just below his stomach and disappeared behind his draped hand. Her eyes traveled lingeringly up the length of him again and paused for a mesmerized moment as she examined his face. She'd seen him nearly every day for a month now and had been keenly aware of his dark attractiveness, his strong, straight features, his sensual mouth so often curved in a teasing grin. But today, with his tumble of black hair windblown into tempting disarray, he was . . . irresistible.

Beth fought the word, fought the feeling. Irresistible? Surely no one was irresistible. But then why was her mouth so dry? Why was her breath so hard to catch and control? Why were her nipples taut and heavy? Why did sensation flood hotly through her veins and pool low in her stomach? Why did she tremble?

Beth tore her eyes away and rested her feverish forehead against the cool rock. She was a fool! Of course she was trembling. She was nervous and excited because she was doing something that went strictly against her straitlaced upbringing. Surely any naked man would bring about the same response. Determined to test her theory, she looked again, this time at Zachary.

He was turned away from her. He was light-skinned but equally as stunning as his brother. Though not as muscular, he was still beautifully sculpted with broad shoulders, narrow hips, and taut buttocks. Golden hair, as golden as the thick, straight thatch on his head, lightly covered his legs. He looked just like an Apollo. He was just as she had imagined him.

But where were those disturbing sensations she'd felt when she looked at Alex? Observing Zachary had been similar to examining a painting or a statue. Stirring in its beauty, lovely to behold, but . . . But what?

No longer able to help herself, Beth looked at Alex again. Oh, *he* was no statue, no painting! He was flesh and blood. The sight of him made her ache with a longing she'd never experienced before. She yearned the way she wanted to yearn when Zachary kissed her. If only Alex could kiss her, she thought, her mind fogged with a vision of long, sweet, slow, deep kisses and tangled arms and legs.

Then he moved his hand. Beth swallowed. She was sure she was going to faint then and there. He was beautiful. All of him. Beautiful and irresistible.

Alex felt good, so damned good. With the sun seeping into his bones like heated honey, he felt he could lie on this rock forever. The ocean was calm and blue, stretching out below the congenial summer sky like a glistening amethyst.

''What are you thinking?''

Zach looked just as content as he did, Alex thought. Like a big golden-furred, golden-eyed tomcat stretched out on the porch. "I'm thinking how glad I am that I came to Grandfather's funeral," replied Alex, grinning. "But we've discussed this before."

"Yes," agreed Zach, grinning back. "Actually, I was hoping you were thinking about . . . something else."

Alex raised his brows inquiringly.

"Why don't we go into St. Teath tonight, Alex?" Zach suggested eagerly. "There's a chit there I've been seeing for some time now. Tess, she's called. I've put her up in a little cottage and everything. She's bound to be wondering what's been keeping me away for so long. I'm sure she could set you up with a friend, Alex. I imagine you must be feeling a little randy yourself after a month in the wilds of Cornwall, as you so love to put it. What do you say?"

Alex's grin disappeared. It was a perfectly natural suggestion and shouldn't have surprised him in the least. He'd never supposed that Zach was celibate, and he'd certainly never been so himself. But coming unbidden, unexpected, to Alex's mind was the question of why Zach could want anyone else with such a delectable fiancée like Elizabeth Tavistock waiting in the wings.

"Speaking of neglecting people," he began, a slight frown creasing his brow, "don't you think Beth's been a little mopish lately? You know, it's quite understandable that she might resent me a little, considering she had you all to herself till I came along."

Zach waved a dismissive hand. "Pooh. Beth's a Trojan. She doesn't mind. Besides," he added with a cocky grin, "we'll be married soon, and she'll have me all to herself every night."

"Every night?" Alex gave his brother a keen, questioning look. "Does that mean you're giving up the chit in St. Teath?"

"God, no," said Zach. "I've quite an affection for Tess.

I don't expect Beth'll be enough for me by and by. And when she's breeding, she won't want to have anything to do with me, I suppose. What's a man to do? In my opinion, a mistress is the only answer.''

"Perhaps when the marriage is loveless, passionless," Alex suggested. "But Beth's a taking little thing, and you love her, don't you?" Why was he holding his breath?

"Lord, yes, I love her," Zach admitted with a disarming crooked smile. "Always have. To tell the truth, I think I'd rather make love to her than to Tess tonight. Something new, you know. And as you said, she's a taking little thing, and full of passion, I'll wager. But she won't let me touch her till that blasted golden band's on her finger. Women, eh?''

Alex released the breath he'd been holding. "Then why don't you set the date for the wedding?" he asked, his tone even and expressionless. "No one will fault you for not observing a year's mourning period for your grandfather. You were engaged before he got ill, and people aren't such sticklers for propriety 'round here that they'd take offense, are they?''

"You'd be surprised how stiff-rumped people can be, brother," Zach returned ruefully. "I've got myself quite a reputation for wenching already. And only by doing what comes natural to a man!''

"But back to Beth . . ." Alex was about to bring up the date of the nuptials again, to try to urge an earlier wedding. The sooner Beth was married to his brother, perhaps the sooner he could pry her constant image out of his thoughts and dreams. But a movement over by the rock wall that jutted out from the cliffs, just where they'd climbed down from above, drew his attention. Was someone spying on them?

Without appearing to watch, Alex kept an eye on the rock wall. He continued to converse with his brother but steered the topic away from Beth and women and to another area of

mutual interest—horses. Zach didn't seem to notice or mind
in the least.

There it was again! Though he was several feet away
from the wall, he did not doubt that what he saw was a long
lock of chestnut hair flying out from behind the rock on the
wings of a sea breeze. There was no mistaking whom the
lock of hair belonged to. He'd memorized the rich, glossy
color long ago. Beth was watching them. Beth was seeing
them—*him*—naked!

He ought to cover himself, he supposed. Unobtrusively,
of course. He didn't want to embarrass her by revealing that
he knew she was hiding there, watching them. But somehow, God help him, he didn't want to cover himself. He
liked the idea that Beth hadn't run away when she'd caught
them without their clothes on, that she was curious enough
to stay and look and perhaps enjoy what she saw. It meant
she wasn't missish. Lord, it probably meant she was as
passionate as Zach hoped she'd be.

The thought was too much for Alex. He felt himself
quickening, tightening, growing rigid. Determined not to
show Beth more than she'd bargained for, or to inadvert-
ently reveal that he was aware, achingly aware, of her
nearness, he stood up and dived into the water. After
breaking the surface, he discovered Zach staring down at
him.

"Take a sudden notion for another dip, Alex?" inquired
his brother, his expression one of genuine puzzlement
mixed with amusement. "I was right in the middle of a
sentence, I'll have you know, when you—"

"Sorry, Zach," interrupted Alex, darting a glance toward
the rock wall. He had stirred Shadow from sleep when he
dived into the water, and the dog was looking up the cliff
wall, wagging his tail. She was gone. "Just got a little hot
lying in the sun like that. Come on in! We've time for
another swim before tea."

If he kept Zach swimming for another thirty minutes,

Beth would have plenty of time to get home, or to Pencarrow if she chose, and compose herself before she was compelled to meet them again. It would give Alex time, too. Time he needed badly, he realized, as his body continued to want her.

"I'm glad we're staying for tea, Lilibet," Gabby said as she fidgeted on the settee in the drawing room. "I helped Sadie and Cook make the scones. They've bilberries cooked in 'em, just the way Zach likes 'em."

Although Gabby had earlier insisted that she had no desire to squish her fingers in bread dough, her floured appearance when Beth returned from the cove had testified to the contrary.

"I'm sure they'll be delicious, Gabby," Beth said, absently patting her sister's shoulder. She'd been in a sort of daze since her experience at the cove. The attraction she'd felt for Alex over the past month, so easily dismissed and explained away as a natural and harmless admiration for her fiancé's brother, had blossomed into something frightening. Her resentment of Zach's devotion to Alex was more complicated than she had at first supposed. It seemed she was just as resentful at being denied Alex's company as she was at being denied Zach's. Lord, what *did* she want, anyway?

The trouble was that Alex made her experience the special emotions she wanted to feel when she was with Zach. But she loved Zach. She'd always loved Zach. Could she be so fickle? To her way of thinking, there was only one solution to this muddle. She and Zach had to get married as soon as possible! She was sure that once they were married, all her yearnings for Alex would disappear.

"Heigh-ho, my love! There you are."

Beth's heart skipped a beat when Zach and Alex entered the room. They looked healthy and glowing, exhilarated by their day spent outdoors. She rose, offered her cheek for

Zach to kiss, and met Alex's gaze over Zach's shoulder. His eyes were luminescent pools of velvet ink. Fathomless pools a silly girl could drown in, she told herself. He was dressed in a wine-colored jacket and a shiny black waist-coat. She remembered that his shoulders were all his, with no buckram wadding to enhance their breadth. She remembered all of him, every detail, from tip to toe. . . .

Forcing her eyes and her thoughts back to the matters at hand, Beth confronted Zach and skewered his middle waistcoat button with an accusing finger. Determined not to be a nag, she tempered her severe words with a playful smile. "You had an engagement with me, Zachary Wickham, which you failed to keep! I was here at half past twelve, just as we arranged between us. But where were you, pray tell?"

"Yes, Zach, where were you?" Gabby echoed from behind Beth. "I knew you were off with Lord Roth again, though Lilibet lied to me quite shamefully and said she was meeting you somewhere."

Zach had the grace to blush, saying, "Dash it, Beth. I'm devilish sorry. I forgot all about it. You will forgive me, won't you?"

"On one condition," Beth said, arching a brow.

"Anything, Lilibet," he declared, charmed by her play-fulness.

"Marry me at summer's end, you rogue!"

Beth kept her gaze fixed on Zachary, smiling determinedly. She dared not look at Alex for fear that she would lose her resolve.

After an astonished pause, Zach said, "You're that eager to marry me, are you, love? And I don't suppose you care a fig about what the tattle-tongues in the surrounding villages and towns will say about having a wedding so soon after Grandfather's funeral?"

"Not a fig!" Beth assured him.

"Not a fig!" repeated Gabby, squeezing herself between

them. "We love you, Zach, and we want you to marry us—I mean, marry Beth—*right away*."

Laughing, Zach bent and picked Gabby up to straddle his hip. "Then it shall be done in a trice. With my best man already in residence, the timing couldn't be better. How long can you stay, Alex? You won't go away till I'm safely married to this lovely girl—I mean, these lovely *girls*—will you?" Zach pinched Gabby's cheek, which brought on a delighted squeal.

Beth watched Alex closely. He seemed different, or did she just see him differently? The way he looked at her—it was almost as though he knew why she was pushing for an earlier wedding date. But that was impossible, wasn't it? She felt the warmth creep up her neck.

"I shall be delighted to extend my stay here till the wedding, brother," Alex assured him, "but only if it *is* by summer's end. I've business that will compel me to visit London in September."

Zach looked surprised. "You've business in town? You never said a peep before."

"I never saw the necessity till now," Alex explained. "I wish I could stay longer," he added with mock gravity, "but three on a honeymoon would be deuced inconvenient. I'm delighted to have reclaimed you as a brother, Zach, but I'm quite sure you will agree with me in this case that brotherly love has its limits, too."

"Do you mean that I can't go on the honeymoon, either?" demanded Gabby, obviously highly incensed. "Why must Lilibet have Zach all to herself? 'Tisn't fair. She has all the fun!"

"You'll understand by and by, little one," soothed Alex, winking at Gabby.

Gabby did not reply, casting Alex a look designed to wither.

Alex could hardly keep from laughing out loud when Gabby leveled him with that blistering, scornful stare. She'd never liked him. But considering her childish infatuation with Zach, it was easily understandable that she would resent Alex's domination of Zach's time recently. But Gabby's comical attempt at a setdown was the only thing Alex had felt the urge to laugh about that afternoon.

Perhaps infected by the festivity of setting a wedding date—August twenty-first, Beth's birthday—Zach impetuously invited Beth to stay to dinner, quite forgetting that he'd planned to go to St. Teath that evening. Then, adjusting his plans, he left for St. Teath as soon after tea as he could politely manage. He assured Beth and Alex that he would return with time to spare for dinner. He said he wouldn't make such a point of going to town in such haste, but he wanted to buy Beth a small token in celebration of the occasion.

Alex watched Beth during Zach's little speech and wondered if she suspected anything. He fervently hoped she hadn't overheard those parts of their conversation at the cove concerning Zach's mistress. He did not think so. As soon as he noticed her hiding behind the rock, he'd quickly changed the subject, but it was hard to tell anything about Beth today. Her usual animated manner was now subdued.

Alex was especially curious to know how the scene Beth had accidentally come upon in the cove had influenced her decision to set the wedding date. Now that he knew that Zach had missed meeting her for a riding engagement, he realized that she'd probably been looking for him, angry and resentful that Zach had quite forgotten her and was with his brother again. Mayhap she thought that if she hastened the wedding, he'd soon be gone and out of their lives for a time. Or mayhap the sight of Zach naked had made her eager to be bedded by him. Jealousy stung like a viper's bite. Alex much preferred the first explanation.

Gabby was sent home—quite against her will, of course—driven by one of the servants in Zach's cabriolet, and word was sent to Mrs. Tavistock that Beth would stay at Pencarrow for dinner and needed a particular dress. Then Beth removed upstairs and remained there till the dinner hour.

But the dinner hour had come and gone. It was eight o'clock, and still Zach had not returned from St. Teath. Sitting in the drawing room alone with Beth was proving to be a nerve-shattering experience. Alex had dressed carefully, ruining five neckcloths in the process. It did not help, either, that Dudley had noted his agitation and commented that his lordship hadn't ruined so many neckcloths in one sitting since that first day at Pencarrow.

Was it vanity that made him so nervous, so anxious to look his best? But then, he'd always striven to dress well. Lately, however, he suspected his own motives. It was ridiculous, too, to be uncomfortable around Beth. They'd spent so much time together in the past month and had sometimes been alone. She, of course, was suffering under the acute embarrassment of having seen him naked earlier. But since she had no idea that he knew she was at the cove that day, there was no reason why *he* couldn't act as natural as before. Having talked himself into a semblance of calm, he began their conversation.

"You know, we ought to go ahead and eat without Zachary. I suspect he ran into an old chum and is chirping merry over his sixth tankard of ale."

"Do you think that's what happened?" Beth looked as though she'd welcome a reasonable explanation for Zach's continued absence. "I'm a little worried about him," she admitted.

Anger toward his brother, a singular feeling, quite new and unexpected, flared up in Alex. "I'm sure he's all right. I wish you wouldn't fret about him. In fact, I could almost guarantee you that Zach's in good hands and has merely lost all sense of time. Then, if he does notice the time, he will think it too late to return for dinner and may even stay the night.''

Beth looked hopeful. ''I do believe you may be right. I feel much easier now. Perhaps we should have our dinner. In truth, I'm dreadfully hungry.''

Alex was glad he was able to assuage Beth's worries over his irresponsible brother. It irked him no end to have to lie to the girl. He was quite sure, however, that Zach *was* in good hands. Tess's hands, to be exact.

If the chicken was a little tough from being too long on the spit, Alex did not mind in the least. He sipped liberally of the wine that was served and found himself relaxing. After all, he was sitting across from the most enchanting of women. And since he would have no opportunity for another tête-à-tête with Beth, surely there could be no harm in enjoying himself this once. He did not mean to seduce her; he would merely delight in her conversation and company for as long as the evening allowed.

She was dressed in pink tonight, a lovely deep rose that set off her ivory complexion to a nicety and made her dark hair, which was swept up off her neck, look even darker. The bodice was low-cut, more daring than the dresses she usually wore, probably because she had thought of tonight as a celebration. Her delicate shoulders were bare and her pale, creamy breasts peeked above the white ruching that edged her neckline, gleaming like pearls in the candlelight. He tried to decide if he thought her nipples were as pink as her dress, then he tried to forget that he'd ever thought about nipples in the first place.

''Tell me about your family, Beth,'' he said suddenly, as the servants removed the dishes for the last course and set a decanter of port in front of him.

Beth looked surprised, then pleased. And it pleased him to see her shed her shyness for the first time that evening as she began to speak. ''Well, you've met Gabby and Mama and can see how thoroughly alike they are. I've often thought either of them would do quite well on the stage, but alas, we are too genteel for that."

"What about your father? Zach said he died not too long ago."

Beth's eyes glistened. Alex was ready to kick himself when her eyes cleared and her face kindled with emotion. She smiled reminiscently. "Dear Papa. I loved him so! But then, perhaps I'm being a little vain to say such a thing, since everyone assures me that I'm just like him in every way but sex. He loved life. He lived with a passion and was never satisfied with the ordinary. He was always reaching for"—Beth puckered her lips in concentration, looking for the right word—"more," she said at last, shrugging her shoulders.

Alex pulled his gaze away from her lips, which looked so inviting. "Zach said he was a philanthropist. He butted heads with Grandfather over conditions in the tin mines owned by the Wickhams, I hear."

Beth's face reflected displeasure. "Indeed, the conditions were worse than you can possibly imagine." Her expression softened. "But Papa convinced Mr. Wickham at last. Your grandfather wasn't a bad man," she hastened to add, "just very stubborn and not easily convinced of anything."

"So I gather," Alex said grimly. "Not unlike my own father." Then, eager to avoid that unhappy topic, he said, "I understand there are a lot of abandoned tin mines in the area that are really rather dangerous. Zach means to board them up so livestock won't wander into them and get lost or caught in a collapse. He says there's quite a lot to do about the estate because our grandfather was a little . . . close with money."

"Yes, there is. Zach said he'd see to setting things to order right after your grandfather's funeral, but he's been so . . ." Beth stopped, embarrassed.

"Preoccupied with entertaining his brother," Alex finished ruefully.

"But that's perfectly understandable," Beth quickly assured him. "You deserve time together. I'm so happy you've been reconciled. Zach was always so miserable about your estrangement."

Alex couldn't help himself. Her hand was lying on the table between them. He covered it with his own. It was small and delicate, warm and soft. "It's been difficult for you, though. Sometimes I imagine you wished me at Jericho. Zach hasn't meant to neglect you. . . ."

Then he remembered where Zach was at that very moment and he could say no more. Keenly conscious of the strong desire to lift her palm to his lips and follow that chaste salute with a much more intimate exploration of her lips and the satin warmth of her mouth, he released her hand.

When he looked up, he saw she was trembling. Her lips were slightly parted, and her eyes were misted and dark, like a late summer's gloaming. God, if she weren't his brother's betrothed, he'd have hoped—nay, believed—that what he saw reflected there was desire. Desire for him.

"Please, Alex . . . Don't . . ."

CHAPTER
four

STILL HE SLEPT. His head was nestled against a plump goose-down pillow, his face turned toward Tess. She sighed and lifted a hand to trace an adoring finger along the square, sun-kissed line of Zach's naked shoulder. He said he'd been swimming in the cove that day, and when they'd made love, Tess had felt the residual heat in his skin and breathed the fresh brine scent of the sea in his hair.

He'd pushed down the bedclothes so that they draped the narrow span of his waist; one long leg had escaped the coverlets and was thrown over Tess's hip. His leg had grown heavy in the past hour, but she relished the weight of it, just as she relished every moment she spent with him. His arms were tucked close to his body, his hands aligned together in an almost prayerful attitude. In sleep his face had the peaceful innocence of a choirboy's.

Tess smiled. He had not behaved like a choirboy hours earlier when he'd thrust open the door of her small cottage and descended upon her with a wide grin and glistening gilded eyes. Her smile widened. And she had not responded like a nun.

Tess had just finished weeding her garden, and he had come upon her while she scrubbed the fresh black dirt from the callused pads of her fingers—fingers toughened by years of work as a seamstress for Mrs. Turley, the local dressmaker. Zach had rescued her from the drudgery and tyranny exercised by Mrs. Turley and had given her the first and only taste of heaven she'd ever known.

Balmy lavender dusk was unfolding over the moor now, melting into the small window opposite the bed, throwing caressing shadows over Zach's straight aristocratic features. Funny that the likes of her should be sharing a bed with the likes of Zachary Wickham, she thought, dropping her hand to mold her palm over his firm, sculpted breast and small brown nipple. But her mum, dead of the pox for over a year now, had always said that someone would pluck her like a dew-petaled rose and keep her plump and pretty for his own pleasure. When she reached the age of seventeen, her beauty became her fortune at last. In the six blissful months as Zach's kept woman, she had learned to hope for nothing more.

Zach stirred, his arms unbending in a languid, awakening stretch of muscle. His eyes blinked open, and Tess basked in the sultry golden flame of his gaze. A slow, sensuous smile tilted his mouth, and he eased a warm hand under the coverlet and splayed his long fingers over her softly rounded stomach. Spears of pleasure stabbed through her at his touch, and her heart thrilled at the simmering passion in his eyes.

"Tessy," he breathed softly, deep satisfaction resonating in his sleep-husky voice. "Lord, I've missed you." He pulled her close—as close as a miser kept his gold—fitting her small slender body against the hard length of his.

"Then why'd you stay away so long, Zach? I missed you, too." She gasped as his hand cupped her breast.

"I told you, didn't I?" He nuzzled the wisps of yellow hair at her temple.

"You never told me anything, Zach. We've been abed since you came. And then you fell asleep."

Zach's brows furrowed slightly. "Thought I told you, Tessy. M' brother came to Grandfather's funeral. We're friends now. I've been spending time with him. Good man, Alex.''

"I've heard about your brother. 'Tis the talk of the town. I'm glad for you, Zach. But I wasn't sure if that was why you weren't coming to see me, or if there was another reason. I was afraid . . ."

Zach pulled back and searched Tess's face. "Afraid of what, love?"

Tess lowered her lashes, frightened that her eyes might betray how much he meant to her. She'd been warned that the gentry didn't like their light-o'-loves to become too attached, too possessive. "I thought maybe you didn't need me anymore. Didn't want me . . ."

Zach chuckled deep in his throat, the warm tones comforting to Tess's troubled heart. "I can't imagine ever not wanting you, Tessy," he told her, forcing her to look at him by tilting her chin with a nudge of his slender forefinger. "You're my sweet Tess, as sweet as the scent of honeysuckle from your garden that still clings to your guinea-gold hair." He buried his face in a fistful of crushed curls and breathed deeply, then slid his hand along the curve of her waist and hips. "And you bring me such pleasure, love. Such pleasure." He lowered his head and took her nipple in his mouth, twirling his tongue around the pink bud, sucking. . . .

Tessy was glad, glad to bring him pleasure, as he brought pleasure to her. Perhaps that was enough. Perhaps he would not be angry if she told him.

"You're plumper," he said, lifting passion-hazed eyes to hers and cupping her full breasts with both hands. "Do you pine so for me that you must resort to eating apple tarts to alleviate the boredom?" he teased.

Tessy stiffened. "Does it displease you?" He had noticed the heaviness of her breasts, the slight swelling of her stomach.

"I like your body a little plumper," he growled, capturing her mouth in a hard, quick kiss. "I've more to love. Just don't puff out to the size of Mrs. Turley or our good King George."

"No, I won't, Zach. I want to please you," she said, her lips tingling from his kiss.

"And so you shall, even after I marry Beth."

Before the twisting pang of jealousy that always came at the mention of Zach's betrothed had had time to dampen Tess's spirits further, Zach lifted his head abruptly, saying, "Ye gods, what time is it? I'd forgotten all about Beth. She's waiting me dinner!"

Zach pushed himself up, swung his legs over the side of the bed, and stood. Tess sat up, too, and clutched the coverlet in a wad beneath her chin, feeling suddenly bereft. Her breasts still throbbed from the teasing imprint of his tongue, and need coiled in her stomach. Yet Zachary was leaving. He strode to the pile of clothes discarded so eagerly and carelessly when he'd arrived that afternoon and dug through them to find his stockings.

Zach couldn't imagine how he'd let the time pass without noticing the lateness of the hour. Beth would be in a pucker. She was a fiery little baggage, not complacent and biddable like Tess, and not too missish to give him a rare trimming for his tardiness. He sat on a narrow reed-bottomed chair and commenced the process of dressing himself without the aid of a valet, Tessy watching with big sad eyes.

Her large calico cat, Tom, had jumped up on the bed as soon as Zach got up, snuggling his fat, furry body against Tessy's thigh. Tom's slanted feline stare seemed strangely accusing, too, and Zach turned away.

He was still hard and aching with renewed passion, but Zach knew he had to get back to Pencarrow before nightfall and try to explain his lateness. Thank God he'd bought Beth's bauble before visiting Tess, or he'd still have that to do. He had stuffed the tiny satin box that contained Beth's gift in his trouser pocket.

"You *have* to go, Zach?"

Zach glanced hurriedly at Tessy, trying to ignore the fetching, come-hither picture she presented with her hair in a tumble about her alabaster shoulders, her finely etched ethereal features dominated by large cornflower-blue eyes, her lips kiss-swollen and parted.

"Yes, I have to go," he grumbled, a barbed edge to his voice as a result of the passion he was striving unsuccessfully to suppress. "Today Beth and I . . ." His voice trailed off as he wondered how best to put it and finally decided that straightforward truth was the kindest course in the long run. "We've set a date, you see. We're getting married in August, on her birthday. I ought to have been home hours ago."

He darted a quick glance at Tess and caught in her expression the flash of pain that he'd expected to see after announcing his impending nuptials. Tess was a tender-hearted creature, but she knew he was going to marry Beth. She'd known it for months. He'd always made it quite clear that she was his mistress, and he had been honest about their arrangement from the beginning. Sharing him with a wife was something Tess would grow used to. The pain would ease when she realized that marriage wouldn't alter their cozy arrangement in the least.

He tugged his stockings on and reached for his shirt, which was wrinkled past help. He had better contrive to get up to his bedchamber by the servants' back stairs and change clothes before he saw Beth and Alex. One would have to be a simpleton not to recognize that his clothes had been discarded hastily and tossed on the floor. Alex would understand his dilemma, but Beth assuredly would not.

"But your body's still quickened and ready for . . ." Zach lifted his eyes from his task and observed Tess's flushed face, her keenly interested examination of his arousal. "Won't it hurt when you straddle your horse?"

Zach laughed. He couldn't help it. Despite her pain over

Zach's coming marriage to another woman, she was still so
sweet, so charmingly blunt and direct. "I shall manage,
Tessy. Don't worry about me. I shall take great care,
however, not to neglect you, or my need for you, for such a
length of time again."

"But I hate to see you leave in such a state," she
persisted quite seriously, scooting seductively to the edge of
the bed.

"I haven't time to remedy my . . . er, state," Zach
insisted, eyeing Tess suspiciously and reaching for his pants
before he'd even finished buttoning his shirt.

She stood up, and the bedclothes fell away from her into
a heap on the bed. The sight of her firm breasts, fuller now
than they used to be, the nipples proud and deep pink,
considerably weakened his resolve. He had raised a leg to
shove in his trousers, but stopped midway to stare at
Tess—sweet Tessy—as she moved toward him, innocently
seductive, so eager to please.

"I won't come back to bed," he told her sternly, looking
her square in the eye to avoid the increased desire sure to
result from looking at the rest of her.

"You don't need to come back to bed, Zach," she said,
now standing directly in front of the chair he sat in. "I've
come to you."

Then he watched—helpless, speechless, marveling,
mesmerized—as she braced her hands on his shoulders and
eased her slim legs around his, sitting astride him, sheathing
him in her sweet, tight wetness. Zach moaned, the trousers
falling from his clasp, his hands reaching up convulsively to
circle her small waist.

"Lord, Tessy," he gasped, watching her eyelids droop
with pleasure as she began to slowly rock against his
muscled thighs. "You're an enchantress!" Then he began
to move with her.

Beth realized her mistake the moment she'd uttered the
words. Alex mustn't touch her, but more important, he

mustn't know how very much the sensation of his large, elegantly tapered hand closed over hers had affected her. If she acted like a frightened peagoose every time he touched her, and if she then begged him not to do it—

"Please don't do what, Beth?" Alex prompted her softly, his keen dark eyes compelling her to speak the truth.

A warm sea breeze belled the Venetian lace curtains at the open window, bringing with it the heady fragrance of clove pinks and roses from the garden. A bead of wax, like a creamy teardrop, sidled down the slender taper that flickered at their end of the table. The servants had withdrawn long since, and silence hung about them like an intimate shroud.

Beth pulled her hand away and laughed, the false trill of amusement jarring the quiet and breaking the confiding mood that had developed between them. "Don't worry about Zach neglecting me," she said gaily, bracingly. "I'm made of much sterner stuff than you give me credit for. I don't resent the time you spend together," she finished with a bold-faced lie.

Alex continued to observe her silently, his wide, shapely lips tightly and grimly compressed, as if he knew of her falsehood and was sorry for it. Why did she feel as though he knew her very thoughts?

"I admire your attitude, and I'm grateful for it," he offered finally and with a remote politeness that pricked at her pride. How could he have known that she was lying? He smiled then, a smile as false as her own, but dazzling nonetheless. He had probably conquered the hearts of many of the eager chits who populated the marriage mart during the London Season with just such a smile. But she much preferred his other smiles, especially the one that lit his face with warmth and sincerity.

"Why don't we go into the drawing room?" she suggested, afraid yet eager to resume their former friendliness.

Perhaps if they avoided the topic of Zach they would do
better. "Unless you wish to drink some port?"

Alex's mouth slanted with mild distaste. "I seldom drink
alone. And I'm not so egotistical that I would enjoy my
solitary company for any length of time. No, I shall
accompany you to the drawing room," he said, then added
wryly, "Zach may still honor us with his presence." Alex
pulled a gold watch from an inner waistcoat pocket and
observed the time with a frown. "'Tis ten o'clock. When
does your mother expect you home?"

"She is attending a musical party at the Smiths' in
Camelford. She said 'twill be an early evening and she will
bring the carriage 'round for me about twelve."

Two hours. He had yet two hours to resist her, thought
Alex, tugging at his collar as if it were a shackle about his
neck. He had loathed the necessity for her dishonest
response to his question earlier, but he ought to have been
glad of it. Too much truth between them could be dangerous. Of course she resented his intrusion into their lives. She
would have had to be a saint not to resent Zach's constant
attendance on him. And Alex knew she wasn't a saint.
Saints did not spy on naked men. The trouble was, that dash
of deviltry only made her more alluring.

Now if only he knew that what he'd seen in her eyes
earlier was really desire. Or would it be better if he didn't
know? Either way, divining Beth's thoughts was an exercise
in futility. She belonged to Zachary, his beloved brother.
But his beloved brother was a damned fool who didn't
recognize and appreciate the jewel Beth was.

He stood and pulled out her chair, cursing the hell-
spawned temptation that made his gaze linger on the white
swell of her bosom. Then he followed her into the drawing
room, his eyes resolutely fixed on the portraits of stern-
faced ancestors lining the walls. Their dark Hayle eyes seem
to mock him, saying, "Just like your father's side of the
family, you have a Wickham's callous disregard for Zach's

tender feelings. She's soon to be his bride, you scoundrel!''

Beth sat down on a gold brocade settee near the fire, but Alex did not join her there, choosing instead to dispose himself in a chair opposite her, his legs negligently crossed in an attitude of languid elegance. If he could not deny the wrenching, growing knot of longing for her, at least he would not show it outwardly. The imagined accusations of his pursed-lipped ancestors echoed in his brain. He would not hurt Zach, as his father had done. No, he'd never hurt Zach.

Perched on the edge of the settee, Beth looked as uncomfortable as he felt. She smiled tentatively and opened her mouth to speak, only to be forestalled by the appearance of Stibbs.

''Yes, Stibbs?'' said Alex, raising a deliberately haughty brow at the hatchet-faced butler. Even after several weeks at Pencarrow, Alex was still forced to intimidate Stibbs into appropriately butlerlike behavior.

''Mr. Wickham has instructed me to tell you that he will be joining you shortly, after he has rid himself of the dirt of the road.''

Beth pivoted in her seat, a radiant smile wreathing her face. ''He's back, then? He didn't meet with an accident, I hope?''

Stibbs looked much put upon to be required to make a reply to such imbecilic questions. ''I believe he would have been bloodied or bruised if such had been the case, miss. He is neither, and I can only surmise that he did not meet with any sort of mischief on his journey.'' Then Stibbs bowed, minimally, and left the room. As he passed into the hall, Shadow eased through the opened door and pranced eagerly to Alex's side. Alex dropped his hand over the arm of the chair and stroked the dog's thick white coat.

''Oh, I'm so relieved that he's back and safe!'' said Beth, her blue eyes dancing. ''I can't wait to hear what kept him

so long. Zach attracts adventures the way flowers draw
bumblebees!''

"I can't wait to hear, either," drawled Alex, his black
eyes slitted in a fair imitation of drowsy ennui. Anyone
who looked closer, though, would have wondered at how
brightly the inky orbs glittered behind the drooping eyelids.

Zach was in a rare tweak. He had looked everywhere, but
the small satin box that contained Beth's cameo pin was
nowhere to be found. He'd even sent servants to the mews
to scour the straw scattered on the stable floor. Maybe it had
fallen out of his pocket when he dismounted his horse. Or
maybe he'd lost it somewhere between Pencarrow and St.
Teath! Tess had distracted him so thoroughly that he hadn't
even checked for it when he finally left the cottage.

Damn! He had thought of using the gift as an excuse for
his lateness. He had considered telling Beth that he'd spent
the entire afternoon searching for the perfect gewgaw to
bedeck her fair self. He hadn't picked up the first piece of
jewelry he saw, either, but the moment he clapped eyes on
the simple, elegant cameo brooch he had known it was
eminently suitable for Beth. And that was within fifteen
minutes after he'd walked into Mr. Bean's Emporium of
Fine Jewels, a tiny shop that belied its grandiose appella-
tion.

Zach paced the thick Aubusson rug that covered his
bedchamber floor, stroking his chin in thought. He'd bathed
and changed hurriedly into a crisp white shirt and cravat and
a brown frock coat. His champagne-colored pantaloons
were stretched taut along the smooth length of his legs. He
supposed he could tell Beth that he'd discovered the gift
missing before leaving St. Teath and had spent hours
looking for it there. It seemed as likely an excuse as another,
though he hated the idea of telling her an out-and-out
whisker.

Omission of certain facts—such as declining to discuss

one's mistress—spared a delicate female's sensitivities, but outright lying stuck in Zach's craw like a piece of fetid meat. He would tell her the truth, he decided finally, but in such a way as not to expose himself.

He descended the stairs with a slow step-pause, step-pause, practicing his opening lines like the impassioned orators who walked the vaulted halls of the Houses of Parliament before each session, practicing their speeches to the Lords. Then, when he entered the room and saw Beth standing expectantly, happily, to greet him, guilt swooped down like a hungry vulture. She wasn't even angry.

"Zach! We were worried about you! Why are you so late? Did your horse throw a shoe? Did you meet a friend in town?"

Beth stood before him, her small hands clasped together in an unconscious gesture of lingering anxiety. A tiny frown marred the smoothness of her brow. She waited trustingly. She would believe anything he told her. He had worried for nothing. Yet her trust in him compounded his guilt.

Over Beth's shoulder, Zach saw Alex lounging in a chair, his gaze averted. A niggling feeling of irritation swept over Zach. Alex ought to be helping him out of this muddle. What were brothers for if you couldn't count on them when you found yourself in the suds?

"Well, Zach?" Beth prodded him, genuinely concerned.

Zach stepped forward and took Beth's clasped hands in his, untangling the fingers and pressing her palms together between his own. He locked his gaze with hers. "I've a number of reasons for being late, Beth, each one insignificant in itself, but all of them together proving to be deuced annoying. I met with a friend, a friend I hadn't seen for an age, and spent entirely too much time in . . . this friend's delightful company. Then, in my haste to get home for our celebratory dinner, I managed to lose the gift I bought for you at Bean's Emporium. Alas, my love, I fear it's gone for good. I'll have to buy you another when next I visit Mr. Bean's establishment.''

"Oh, dear, what an unlucky day you've had," she said, ready sympathy springing to her eyes. "But tell me, Zach, what did you buy me? I know it's lost, but I'd still like you to describe it to me. They say it's the thought that counts!''

He noticed that Alex's keen gaze was riveted to his face; he was watching to see if Zach had indeed bought something and lost it or was completely making up the part about the jewelry. That Alex suspected him of being so selfish as to forget Beth's gift entirely tore at Zach's pride like a jagged knife.

"It was an ivory cameo, Beth. Creamy white and pale peach, with a delicately wrought silhouette of a woman whose profile reminded me of you, love, and laced all about with golden filigree. It was a brooch to wear at the throat of your redingote or on the bodice of your dress. It was lovely, and I wish I hadn't been such a noddy and lost it. Do you forgive me?''

Beth's eyes warmed to the balmy blue of a summer's day. "Of course I forgive you. I was just concerned that something might have gone amiss with your horse or that you were set upon by footpads on the road.''

"Footpads in Cornwall?" Alex questioned, a wicked black brow climbing to a roguish peak. "They could hardly hope to ply their trade with much success in these rural realms." Zach watched as his older brother stood up and sauntered over. His cool assessment of Zach was unnerving and too much like the way he'd looked at him on that first day. "I'm glad you're back and safe, brother," drawled Alex, at last a little warmth apparent in the sardonic humor winking in the depths of his obsidian eyes.

Zach returned his brother's smile hesitantly. He hardly knew what to make of Alex's attitude. Despite the brotherly love they'd built on throughout the past month, despite the warmth and caring he still felt emanating from beneath

Alex's mocking welcome, Zach sensed strong disapproval. Alex apparently disapproved of his arrangement with Tess. Wicked Wickham, with one of the worst reputations for wenching in London, disapproved of his keeping a mistress? Why?

Tess sat at her dressing table, smoothing her hair with the silver comb Zach had given her for Christmas. She'd sponged away the heat of the day and donned a nightdress of cool lawn. The night would be humid and hot. She wished she could bathe yet still keep the lingering essence of Zach's masculine aroma that clung to her after their lovemaking.

He'd said that he liked the scent of honeysuckle in her hair, so she was determined that from then on she would fill the house with the essence of honeysuckle by setting bouquets about the room and by steeping dried petals on the hearth. Anything to give him pleasure.

She smiled sadly, bittersweetly. If only she were a great lady, someone of social standing in the community. Or even, perhaps, if she were rich. Maybe with wealth she could buy her way into the circles of the gentry that excluded her now. The daughter of an underservant at a local inn, fathered by a rag peddler who'd been passing through one summer eighteen years ago, Tess had no illusions about her squalid obscurity. She was lucky she was pretty, or else Zach would never have noticed her walking down the street that chilly December eve last year.

She replaced her comb carefully on the glossy rosewood surface of her dressing table, then touched the exquisite ivory and peach cameo that lay in resplendent elegance in the small satin box that had fallen from Zach's trouser pocket as he rushed out of the door that evening. She had tried to call him back, but he couldn't or didn't choose to hear her. He was hastening away to Beth.

Elizabeth Tavistock had the bloodlines Tess craved. She

was pretty, too; Tess had seen her many times. And Beth had Zach, or would have him in the space of a few weeks. No matter how much bedding they'd done or would do, Tess was just Zach's light-o'-love, his kept woman, his doxy. She'd never measure up to the status of a wife.

Wife. How Tess wished she could be that to Zach. A militant gleam suddenly sparked in her eye, something quite inconsistent with Tess's meek, yielding, patient character. But if she could not have Zach, she would take what she could. Tonight she'd wear the cameo he'd bought for Beth. She lifted the brooch, admired its smooth luster in the candlelight, then pinned it to the tucks at the placket of her nightdress. Somehow the mild act of rebellion soothed her aching heart a little. She would pretend that she was Mrs. Zachary Wickham and dream of life at Pencarrow, surrounded by sons and daughters.

Tess pressed a hand against the barely perceptible swell of her stomach. She was increasing day by day with Zach's child. She had tried to be careful. She'd used the potions and creams Granny Harker had sold her that were supposed to prevent babes from taking seed in the womb. But she was already five months along, though she didn't show. Her mother had carried her babies low and flat, and no one was the wiser till she'd neared her seventh month. Apparently Tess carried the same way.

She wondered how Zach would react to the news that she was carrying his child. She wondered if it would make a difference to him in the days that would surely come when he'd tired of her. She hoped that by bearing him a child she'd carve a permanent niche in his heart, a place in his life till death did them part, just like married folks. She knew she could never be a wife, but she would settle for second best. Dear God, she thought, please let me at least be granted second best!

CHAPTER
five

MRS. TAVISTOCK WAS a social being, and despite the recent demise of her closest neighbor, she could not resist the urge to invite her friends to a dancing party in honor of her daughter's betrothal. Now that the couple had actually set a date just a few weeks hence, the news could no longer be confined to the family circle. Having released such information, Mrs. Tavistock felt quite sure that the expectations of a celebration of sorts would arise among their acquaintances.

Zach had enthusiastically supported the idea, knowing full well that his grandfather would have thought them a parcel of hypocrites had they postponed their merrymaking simply because he'd lately stuck his spoon in the wall. Beth agreed but begged her mother to keep the guest list to a tasteful few.

Mrs. Tavistock opened wide her fine blue eyes in an expression of bewildered innocence. "Of course, my dear," she said in a dulcet tone. "Not above a few close friends, I assure you!"

Beth was skeptical and stared hard at her mother, who did not flinch in the least. Sitting on an ivory satin settee in her bedchamber, which was decorated in soft, ripe peach tones and creamy whites, Louisa Tavistock looked almost too youthful to be Beth's mother. She'd kept her figure over the years and showed only a trace of gray in the dark hair at her temples. Yet she had not Beth's beauty. Her features were too sharp. What she lacked in beauty, however, she made up for in an animated style and conversation.

Mrs. Tavistock was a favorite about the neighborhood for she could always be depended upon to enliven even the dullest gathering with her light, nonsensical chitchat. Above attending a party, Mrs. Tavistock's keenest pleasures came with the experience of hosting a party. Even a *small* party.

A few days later Beth watched from her forward-facing bedchamber window as carriage after carriage pulled up to the front of the house, disgorging well-dressed couples and groups of people till it was no longer possible to keep count of them. No doubt some would be spending the night, since many of them must have traveled from as far north as Exeter.

That her mother's modest plans had increased on a daily basis had not escaped Beth's notice, but the steady stream of guests was beginning to make her feel a trifle giddy. She'd never had a coming-out ball or spent above a fortnight in London. And though she was naturally of a self-composed disposition, the idea of being belle of the ball with every eye upon her as she took her place at the top of the stairs was a tad discomposing.

The women would stare at her gown and calculate the cost of the fabric from which it was made. They would examine her complexion, speculating on whether or not the bloom in her cheeks was real or the result of subtle cosmetics. They would admire the luster of her hair or deplore the lack of it, then judge her abigail's skill at the latest style of coiffure lately come from France.

Such an examination by people Beth hardly knew, and who, in her estimation, would be quite shallow to base their opinion of her merely on outward appearance, ought not to have troubled her in the least. Beth's brows drew together thoughtfully. Perhaps her state of discomposure was based on her reluctantly acknowledged wish to gain approval and

admiration from one person in particular—Alexander Wickham.

Frustrated, Beth turned and moved from the window to
the cheval glass next to her dressing table. She had
dismissed her abigail and was alone in her chamber.
Suspecting a bit of vanity to be the reason for her inclination
to return repeatedly to the mirror to inspect her appearance,
Beth felt more and more guilty with each anxious appraisal,
but she could not seem to help herself.

"What a goose you are," she scolded herself aloud. "To
base your entire happiness on the evening simply on the
hope of seeing a certain pair of black eyes all alight with
admiration at the sight of you is excessively stupid!"

Beth held the skirt of her gown between the forefinger
and thumb of either hand and turned from side to side,
observing herself from all angles. Her dress was white,
since her mother deemed the virginal color most acceptable
for one of Beth's age and inexperience. Her mother also
favored white because it became Beth's complexion nearly
as well as the rose-pink she often wore.

Styles had changed in the last year. The Empire-style
gown, inspired by French fashions during the Revolution,
was modified. Bodices were longer, and the blue silk sash at
the front of Beth's gown was tied just inches above her
natural waist. The gauzy puffs of soft lace that barely
sufficed as sleeves perched atop her shoulders like naughty
angel wings. The décolletage was low, exposing Beth's
bosom in a manner she considered slightly risqué. Her
fashion-conscious mother assured Beth, however, that she
was quite the thing and not at all beyond what was proper.

A slip of blue showed through the white lace overdress
and a pair of dainty pearl-seeded blue silk slippers peaked
out from beneath her skirt. Her hair was styled à la Sappho
in a riot of thick ringlets falling from a single twist of hair
at the crown.

Beth shook her curls ruefully. "All dressed up for my

betrothal dance and not thinking one whit about my betrothed,'' she chided herself. Lately Alex's image seemed
constantly before her, and in her vivid imagination that
image was most often unclothed. Would she ever be able to
forget how he'd looked that day at the cove? Not an hour
passed that she didn't wish she could relegate her feelings
for him to that safe category called sisterly. But Beth was
honest enough with herself to know that her feelings were
far from sisterly and unfortunately growing stronger day by
day.

In the hopes of developing a revulsion for Alex, Beth had
tried to discover imperfections in him to dwell upon. She
realized how dire was her situation when his imperfections
did not trouble her but rather made him more human, more
attractive. Drat Alex Wickham! The man was the *perfect*
imperfect man!

Her only hope, she finally decided, was that her attraction
to Alex would cease as soon as he left Pencarrow for
London. By the time she next clapped eyes upon him, she'd
have been married to her dear Zach for a while and would
be quite naturally besotted with her husband, perhaps even
increasing with child. Or so was the plan.

Beth had thought about discussing her attraction to Alex
with her mother. She would have welcomed some advice on
how to deal with such distracting feelings, would at least
have drawn comfort from someone telling her that she
wasn't losing her mind or her morals. She had no girlfriends
she felt like confiding in. In fact, she had never trusted
anyone with her innermost thoughts except Zach, and she
could hardly discuss this particular subject with him!

She suspected that her mother would be quite troubled by
such a confidence, since Mrs. Tavistock had been planning
Beth's marriage to Zach since they were children. She might
begin to see Alex as a threat to a dear and long-held dream.
Beth didn't want Alex to be viewed in an unfavorable light
simply because she was having inappropriate thoughts and

feelings for the man. No, this was her problem, and she would have to deal with it alone.

Suddenly the door opened, and Mrs. Tavistock bustled into the room, in fine trim in a gown of yellow sarcenet with a matching turban decorated with a jaunty jeweled aigrette. "Dearest girl! Lizzie, why are you still in your bedchamber? The guests are arriving, and you must join Zachary and me at the top of the stairs to greet them as they pass into the salon."

"Zach is here, then?"

Mrs. Tavistock surveyed her daughter with exacting thoroughness, plumping a sleeve here, twitching a crease out of her gown there. "For an age, my love."

Beth averted her eyes as she pulled on her white net gloves, which extended from fingertips to above the elbows. "And Lord Roth came with him, I suppose?"

"He did not, which surprised me at first, till I thought about it. Zachary said Lord Roth wasn't ready when he was, and Zach was compelled to leave him behind. Then I considered the possibility that Lord Roth may be of a mind to be fashionably late, a tonnish habit acquired during frequent stays at his London town house, I daresay. But whether he is late or not, your betrothal party gains considerable cachet by his simply being part of the crush. Now, don't be offended, Lizzie, if he does not stay for the whole affair. I'm afraid this sort of party might seem a bit countrified for his tastes. Turn around, child, and let me look at you."

Beth obediently twirled for her mother's inspection, but her heart had plummeted to her slipper straps. It was a lowering realization that her enjoyment of the party would be postponed till Alex arrived and would possibly be curtailed if, and as soon as, he made an early exit.

She had never considered the possibility before. . . . Did Alex think of them as countrified? Did he think of her as an awkward little country chit? She had never perceived that Alex felt himself above his company. But why hadn't he come to the party with Zach? Where *was* he?

"You're such a lucky girl, my dear," said her mother, standing back to gaze with fond complacency at Beth. "Zachary is a wonderful young man, so handsome, so wealthy! You'll be very happy together."

"I hope we are," said Beth with a pensive smile.

Her mother beamed. "There can be no question of that, my love."

Alex cursed the necessity of steady hands to execute a neatly tied cravat. Once again he'd entertained Dudley with an awkward display of neckcloth demolition, and now, en route to Brookmoor sitting quite solitary in his own carriage, he could not remember feeling more chagrined. Late to his own brother's betrothal party! And certainly not for the sake of elegance, since he would never presume to put on citified airs at the risk of offending his brother and Beth. There was no telling what they would think of him, and all because he could not command the use of his damned fingers!

The gentle swaying of the carriage, the companionable jingle of the traces, the muted luster of moonlight against the window glass, the fresh air of a mild July evening in Cornwall . . . none of this could soothe his shattered pride. Even in the throes of his first passion he had never felt so out of control, so at the mercy of his own emotions! What was he so nervous about? Was he afraid he'd expose his mixed feelings about celebrating Zach's betrothal to the only woman Alex had felt a stirring of interest in for years? But with Beth it was more than a stirring of interest. He was fast becoming obsessed with her.

To add insult to injury, Dudley had even offered to help steady Alex's nerves by mixing up one of his personally concocted remedies, consisting of a pinch of this, a pinch of that, and a stiff amount of good scotch whisky. Alex had taken the whisky without the medicinal herbs, informed Dudley that he wasn't the least agitated, only a trifle ham-handed, and wasn't he allowed the luxury of an occasional fit of clumsiness? And even if he was agitated about something, even if the very hounds of hell were nipping at his heels, he'd never quack himself like some rubber-kneed, dandified, fribblesome court card!

Dudley took this verbal thrashing in stride and helped his lordship into his black cutaway coat with only a slightly wounded countenance. Such forbearance only made Alex more irritated, and he left Pencarrow in a foul mood indeed. He only hoped that the short journey to Brookmoor would lend him sufficient time to compose himself and reclaim a bit of his old sangfroid.

After all, he'd sat at table with Prinny himself, the two of them exchanging witty repartee. Without a misstep he'd danced at Almack's with innumerable society misses, each Season's diamonds of the first water, under the eagle-eyed scrutiny of Sally Jersey. He'd played macao at Watier's for incredible stakes without blinking an eye. Now he was reduced to an absolute clodpole by a slip of a girl named Beth because he did not think he was capable of hiding his feelings from her or from Zach much longer.

If only Zach paid her a little more attention, appreciated her as she should be appreciated, he would not feel such an urge to give Beth the kind of relationship he knew she craved. Beth was passionate and loving. He could meet her passion with equal intensity. Maybe he could even love her. . . .

Alex abruptly forced his thoughts to mundane matters. He examined the buttons on his jacket sleeve and thought of ledger sheets, the need for new paint on his crested carriage boot, his aunt Saphrona's pet raccoon—everything, anything but Beth.

Now they were passing through the lodge gates of Brookmoor. He'd been there in daylight hours and had observed with appreciation the modern building that was erected in the classical style of Robert Adam, though Alex knew Mr. Tavistock himself had overseen the design and building of the house. White stucco, Doric columns, bay windows, and graceful balconies made up a dignified front to a gracious manor home that was reached by way of a long drive lined with beech trees. Alongside the drive a brook percolated and splashed over a rocky, reed-bottomed bed.

Tonight the house was all ablaze with candlelight, every window winking a bright invitation. But Alex could see the multitude of carriages huddled together in the stable yards and could well imagine the squeeze of people inside. Just like the parties he'd attended ad infinitum in London, this one would be hot, stuffy, tedious, and quite boring.

Alex much preferred quality over quantity and would rather have spent the evening with a small group of people he sincerely cared about. But for the sake of Zach and Beth he'd go inside and make himself disgustingly agreeable. But it would not be easy, especially since he must play the proud and happy brother-in-law to a woman he constantly imagined lying naked and eager beneath him.

The carriage stopped, and the footman opened the door for Alex to alight. He walked up the steps with his public smile firmly in place. He entered the house and found himself in the large entrance hall at the bottom of a wide oak staircase. There was a line of people ascending at a pace most excruciatingly slow. He skimmed the plumed, turbaned, bejeweled, bewigged, and pomaded heads of the gaily garbed line of guests till he saw Zach and Beth on the landing that led into the grand salon.

Then Alex's heart did a dreadfully disloyal thing. It pounded with joy at the sight of her, at the sight of Beth. As if she'd heard the telltale heartbeat above the din of wagging tongues, Beth turned and looked down the stairs, down past all the people, directly at Alex.

Even from a distance Alex saw how Beth's eyes lit up. He

responded with a genuine smile reserved for private happiness, the sort of smile one did not display in a roomful of strangers. He glorified in her obvious delight in seeing him, but he soon sobered, considered how he must have disappointed her by coming late, and decided that the delighted expression she wore was merely the result of profound relief. After all, what would everyone say if Zach's brother had not even bothered to attend his betrothal party? Relief and gratitude were the logical explanations for Beth's happiness in seeing him. He would try not to hope for any other explanation.

He wasn't about to wait in the reception line, so Alex weaved his way through the crowd, ignoring the curious stares as he politely nudged his way down the hall to the library. Just as he'd hoped, the dim, book-lined chamber was empty. He closed the door behind him and leaned against it with a sigh. A single brace of candles shed a circle of light near the fireplace, and Alex spied a brandy decanter on a table situated just to the right of the mantelpiece. He immediately walked to the table, poured a moderate amount of liquor into a goblet, and drank down most of it in the first hasty gulp.

Just then he heard a slight stirring behind him and turned around to discover himself not alone as he'd thought. A young man with a flushed face, a slack jaw, and a disheveled cravat lay unconscious on a sofa that faced away from the door. He appeared to be inebriated. A half-filled goblet on the floor in front of the man seemed to support this theory.

"Poor wretch," Alex grumbled to himself. "Driven to drink by some wilesome woman." He realized how utterly unfair he sounded, but he wasn't in the mood to be judicious and he sat down in a chair opposite the pathetic-looking fellow to nurse what was left of his own drink. Perhaps he was not in the mood to be judicious, but he would not embarrass his brother by casting up his accounts in the middle of the dance floor. No, while he could not *think* moderately, he could at least *drink* moderately.

"Yes, old man," Alex addressed his dormant companion, leaning back in the chair and crossing his outstretched legs at the ankles. "What a comfort it is to have someone to talk to. You must realize how difficult it is for me to be harboring the most scandalous feelings for my brother's betrothed, and no one about to confide in, though I've never really wanted to tell my deepest thoughts to anyone except Zach. And I bloody well can't tell him." Alex frowned. "I think my valet suspects something's afoot. The fellow must be fey."

The man turned on his back with a grunt. "Exactly," Alex drawled. "So commonplace these sins of the flesh." Alex rolled the stem of his goblet between his fingers, watching the play of candlelight on the glass. "Only thing is, I sometimes think there may be more to my attraction to Beth than wanting to bed her. Frightening thought, eh?"

Naturally the man did not reply, and Alex finished his drink, set down his glass on the table, and stood up. "Time to face the throng of well-wishers, my good fellow. I'd join you if I could in your state of blissful, unthinking inertia, but duty calls!"

"Alex?"

Alex lifted his head and saw Beth standing at the open library door. Light from the wall sconces behind her bathed her in a golden aura. Dressed in white and sky blue, she looked like an angel. Saints, angels. He was always comparing her to ethereal beings, but she was flesh and blood, like him—only flesh and blood. Right now his flesh tingled, and his blood boiled at the sight of her. After what seemed an interminable pause, he commanded his tongue to speak. "I was waiting for the line to diminish. I'm sorry I'm late. Rude of me. But I couldn't seem to—"

"Who were you talking to?" she interrupted, looking

curiously about the room. "Are you alone in here?" She stepped forward and closed the door behind her.

If it had been any woman but Beth, Alex would have suspected a feminine trick to catch him alone. And if the woman were comely, Wicked Wickham would have obliged her with a kiss. To be sure, this woman was comely. But, alas, there could be no kissing tonight.

Beth moved into the circle of light and smiled up at him, the dimple in her left cheek begging to be touched. "The line has finally disappeared, and they are about to strike up the music for the first dance."

In that moment Beth's enjoyment of the party was ensured. She could float through the rest of the evening simply from the euphoria she felt as she stood close to Alex. She had hoped he would admire her, and he did. She could see it in his eyes. She could feel it, like a warm caress.

She wondered if he could read her eyes, too. She hoped not, for his handsome image that evening would be imprinted on her brain till she'd breathed her last rattled gulp of air. Clothed or unclothed, the man was devastating. He stood just beyond the reach of the candles' light. The outline of his superfine jacket, brocaded waistcoat, and smoothly sensuous pantaloons—all black—blurred into the shadows of the dark room behind him. His white cravat contrasted blindingly with his tanned face, his glossy hair, and the luster of his dark, fathomless eyes. Desire swept through her like a banshee—frightening, wild, and unearthly.

Alex raised his brows. "If the first dance is about to commence, Beth," he said in a strained, low voice, "then hadn't you ought to be upstairs? I imagine you and Zach must lead out the set."

Beth clasped her hands nervously in front of her. "Zach said—and I agreed with him—that you should be there before the actual dancing begins. He . . . he wants to introduce you 'round to some of the guests. We both started looking for you, and I—"

"And you found me," Alex finished with a sudden brilliant smile that made her heart convulse with yearning. "Clever girl! You knew I'd be hiding out in some quiet corner, away from the crowd."

Beth's happiness dissipated like mist on the moor. "Oh dear! Mother was right. You *do* think this whole affair too countrified, not as elegant as London. I know you're used to something different, and I'm sorry you feel compelled to—"

Alex caught Beth by the shoulders. She could feel his lean fingers pressing into her skin beneath the wisps of material serving minimally as sleeves. "Dear girl, you misunderstand me! This party is *too* like London for me. Every bit as elegant, every bit as . . ." He seemed to be struggling to find the right words.

"Every bit as boring and stuffy," Beth finished with a tremulous smile. How alike they thought! "But I suppose we must attend to make Mother happy, mustn't we?"

Alex smiled his relief at her understanding. "Generally I don't dislike parties and dances, Beth. It's just that I vastly prefer quieter evenings with people I really care about. For too long I had so few people I truly wanted to spend a quiet evening with. As a result, I was continually attending these sorts of affairs. Then I came to Cornwall and found . . ." Once again he hesitated. His fingers were gently kneading her shoulders.

"You . . . you found your brother again," Beth suggested with a little encouraging nod of her head, which made her long ringlets brush against Alex's knuckles. "You were reunited with Zach."

Alex did not reply. He just kept looking at her, the tender—and strangely stricken—expression in his eyes hypnotizing. Then his gaze shifted, and he was staring at her lips.

"So there you are! Beth, you found him in the library, of all places, when I was so sure he'd be in the billiard parlor!"

Startled, Beth took a guilty step backwards as Zach strode quickly into the room. He was all smiles, spruce and handsome in his black evening clothes. If he'd noticed that she'd been standing quite close to his brother, it apparently didn't bother Zach; his cheerful expression did not waver in the least. "Alex, we can't start the dance without you! And I've the prettiest girl in Cornwall to introduce you to." Zach caught Alex's elbow and nudged him toward the door, pulling Beth along by the hand. "Her name is Lydia, and her father's a rich viscount from— Good Lord, is that Charlie?"

For the first time, Beth noticed the man lying on the sofa. It took just a glance to ascertain that the man was intoxicated, completely knocked out from too much drinking. He must have come directly to the library the minute he'd arrived at the house, because Beth could not remember meeting him in the reception line.

"Who is he?" she asked as Zach leaned over the man and peered into his face, slapping him lightly on the jowls. "Goodness, why did he bother to come to the party if he was planning to cuddle up to a brandy decanter and snooze away the whole night?"

"It does seem a bit irregular," commented Alex. "Cupshot so early in the evening bespeaks an unsettled mind."

Zach straightened and sighed deeply. "Charlie's got an unsettled mind, all right. Charles Laughton, Viscount Benbridge, is his name, Beth. I had not thought his state so bad as I'd heard or I'd not have troubled him with an invitation to our party. You see, he's been reduced to this lump of pickled flesh as a result of an infelicitous marriage."

"How dreadful," said Beth, sincerely sorry for the man. "What happened? Was he forced to marry someone his parents chose for him?"

"No," Zach returned dryly. "He chose his bride of his own free will. But I've no time now to repeat the sordid tale." He reached for a quilted throw that was folded over

the arm of a nearby rocking chair. "We'll make him
comfortable and return to our party. I'm afraid old Charlie
won't be dancing tonight." Zach unfolded the throw and
pitched it over his friend, tucking it securely about his
unshod feet.

Beth was curious about Charlie and his ill-fated marriage,
but she agreed that they should return to the salon immediately. Her mother would be anxiously looking about for
them. Perhaps sometime during the night she could dance
with Alex. She cast him a surreptitious look from beneath
lowered lashes. He returned her look, but this time she could
not tell what he was thinking.

The grand salon was lit up like Vauxhall Gardens during
a fireworks display. Alex walked into the crowded room and
was greeted by the usual odor of melting wax and a
sundry—and slightly nauseating—mix of perfumes.

"This is Richard Long, Alex," Zach was saying as he
moved his brother smoothly through the crowd. "Richard,
my brother, Lord Roth."

"How do you do, Lord Roth?" The stout auburn-haired
man bowed respectfully. Alex thought he heard a corset
creak.

"Very well, thank you," Alex replied with a smile. "A
pleasure to meet you." Alex darted a look over the man's
shoulder toward the chair where Beth sat next to her mother,
surrounded by girls her age, all of them laughing, simpering,
preening. Many of them were staring at him boldly. One
flirted openly, a petite blonde who batted her lashes from
around the curve of an Oriental fan. He sighed.

"And this is Lady Edyth, our nearest neighbor to the
north."

Alex recalled his attention to the matter of introductions,
and he found himself being thoroughly scrutinized by a tiny
wizened woman of an incredibly advanced age.

"Lady Edyth," Zach addressed the woman in a loud

voice, "this is my brother, Alexander Wickham, Lord Roth, from Surrey."

Alex took the woman's cronelike hand and bowed. "Enchanted to meet you, Lady Edyth," he murmured.

"Eh? What did you say?" she cackled.

"Enchanted to meet you," he repeated much louder, speaking succinctly as he looked her straight in the eye.

Lady Edyth appeared pleased, smiled broadly, and nodded her head in a jerky acknowledgment. "Posh! Enchanted? I doubt it, but the thought's pleasing to an old woman." Her words were muffled, and Alex realized that she was using plumpers, cork stuffing worn inside the mouth to fill out the cheeks. This fashion had been the mode some thirty years ago, but along with her powdered wig, Lady Edyth apparently had not abandoned it.

Then, suddenly and miraculously, the blonde who had been some thirty feet away not more than a minute ago, was directly before Alex, hanging on the arm of a tall, stately man. After meeting her father, Viscount Hedley, Alex was introduced to "the prettiest girl in Cornwall," Lydia Elmstead. At this point Zach suddenly decided that enough introductions had been made, and the small orchestra, ensconced in a corner of the oblong room, struck up the first serious chord at the nod of Zach's head.

The set quickly formed for dancing. Alex asked Miss Elmstead for the first dance. It was expected; in fact it would have been grossly impolite of him to behave differently, since the young woman stood resolutely beside him. The selection was a cotillion, and since Alex and his partner were almost at the bottom of the set, he had plenty of time to become acquainted with her before they actually danced.

"So, Miss Elmstead," he began, setting his mind to the task of conversing in an attempt to refrain from ogling Beth as she skipped lightly through the steps of the dance, "are you a close neighbor to Pencarrow?"

Miss Elmstead tapped Alex's shoulder with her fan,

saying with an arch smile, ''Indeed, my lord, I suppose you are asking me that because I do not exactly fit your idea of the country girl from Cornwall? I am—how do the French say it?—*mal à-propos*?'' She threw back her head and laughed affectedly. ''You may be honest with me, *n'est-ce pas?*''

Alex immediately perceived that Miss Elmstead was as false as her laugh. This, perhaps, was the result of a weak intellect subjected to profuse flattery and indulgence. Too pretty and not wise enough to balance beauty with brains.

Alex gritted his teeth, determined to get through the dance without uttering an uncivil word. ''Then I must infer, Miss Elmstead, that you are a neighbor but do not exactly feel comfortable in your native surroundings? You prefer London, I suppose?''

Again Miss Elmstead tinkled a laugh. ''I would like nothing better than to be a habitué of London, and next spring I will be going there for my Season.'' She did not say her first Season, since she probably expected to need only one Season in London to snabble herself a well-breeched, titled *parti*. Her blue eyes slanted in a sultry smile. ''If you are in residence, will you come to my coming-out ball, or am I parvenue to be so bold as to ask you?''

Alex smiled his public smile. ''Indeed, Miss Elmstead, if I find myself in London in the spring, I shall be most happy to attend your ball.'' Alex decided then and there to make quite sure that next Season's genteel society would not count him among its numbers. What French phrase would she employ in her next sentence? he wondered.

Several sets later, as Alex dutifully danced with young girl after young girl, with an occasional turbaned matron thrown in for good measure, he retired to the refreshment table for a glass of punch. The beverage was as unspirited as he'd expected it to be, but it was at least wet, and he tossed it down quickly.

Then he cast his eyes about the room for Beth. They were

well into the ball; supper would be served in an adjoining room within the hour. It would not be remarked in the least if he now sought out his future sister-in-law for a dance. Ah, there she was, sitting in an alcove with only two other females. And, conveniently, she was looking his way. She smiled. He advanced.

It would not have been fair to say that all of the women he'd danced with that night were as vapid and shallow as his first partner. Three or four of them had been sensible enough, attractive enough, entertaining enough, actually quite likable. But they were not Beth.

Finally he stood before her. He bowed. "Miss Tavistock," he intoned formally, "would you do me the honor of joining me for the next dance?"

Beth stood up and extended her hand while her friends looked on smiling. Alex sincerely hoped he'd danced with them already, but he couldn't remember. He couldn't think straight just now.

"I should be delighted, Lord Roth," she answered him demurely, but those mischievous eyes of hers twinkled merrily.

They moved to the edge of the dance floor and waited for the music to begin. When it did begin, they looked at each other, startled. It was a waltz, the second of the evening, and Zach had quite appropriately partnered Beth in the first one.

"Perhaps I should ask Zach's permission? Maybe he wants you to save all your waltzes for him," Alex suggested reluctantly.

"Well, I don't see Zach anywhere," said Beth. Then she smiled, melting Alex's reservations like cream on a hot scone. "Besides, you're soon to be my brother. Next to Zach, you've the most right to dance the waltz with me, don't you think?"

"If you say so, Miss Tavistock," Alex answered, beguiled by her teasing. Lord, if she knew how his body quickened at the mere thought of holding her in his arms even in full sight of a huge roomful of people, she'd think twice about who had the most right to claim her for a waltz! But Alex had no desire to relinquish such rights and ceased to look about the room for Zach.

He placed a hand on her slender waist and took her right hand in his, palm to palm. He led her onto the circle of waltzing couples, and they began to dance.

Beth had been waiting for this moment all evening. And just as she'd hoped, it was bliss dancing with Alex. She hadn't expected a waltz, and the fact that she was gliding across the floor exclusively with him in as close an embrace as she could respectfully hope for was just icing on the cake. Sweet, mouth-watering icing.

His scent was still fresh and clean despite hours of dancing. Her head came just to his chin, and when she looked up at him, the first thing she saw was that wonderful cleft of his. Then his smile—friendly, confiding . . . tender?

"You like to dance, don't you, Beth?"

She lifted her gaze to Alex's eyes. She was drowning but she didn't care. "It's the best part of these dull affairs," she admitted.

"You do it admirably well," he said, finding the compliment the easiest he'd uttered the whole evening, since he had said it with absolute honesty.

"I find that enjoying something makes one do that something much better, don't you?" she offered with a serious little quirk of her eyebrows.

Alex found himself wondering in quick succession whether she enjoyed kissing, if Zach kissed her often, if it would be different if *he* kissed her. But he knew it would be different, at least for him. It would be earthshaking.

"Hold on," he said suddenly, "we're going to twirl a little faster." Then he pulled her closer and spun her with dizzying and graceful precision. He could feel her thighs lightly brushing his. She could feel the muscles in his shoulder flex as he masterfully swept her about the room.

Beth's musical laugh drifted across the floor to Zach, who was watching from the doorway. He'd been to see Charlie.

"They dance well together," opined Mrs. Tavistock, who'd just walked up to stand beside him.

"Yes, they do," said Zach, but his mind was still full of Charlie, the unhappy wretch he'd just taken strong coffee to. Too bad the poor man had been so unwise as to marry his mistress. Bad ton, that. But some men were unable to think with their pants down. Zach shook his head dourly, vowing then and there to keep his wits and his dignity, with or without his trousers.

CHAPTER
six

ONLY A FEW days had passed since the betrothal ball and all its attendant busyness, but Alex had never seen Zach so restless or so nearly foxed as he was tonight. Beth and Mrs. Tavistock and Gabby had joined them for dinner at Pencarrow that evening and had left the men to their port a good half an hour before.

"Don't you think we ought to join the ladies?" Alex lifted his brimming glass and took a small sip, eyeing his brother over the rim. He had no doubt that Zach's skittishness, and his overindulgence in Grandfather's best cellar stock, had everything to do with the fact that it had been two weeks since last he'd seen his mistress.

Alex hadn't said a word against Tess, but perhaps Zach sensed his disapproval. Whatever the reason, Zach had stayed at Pencarrow despite a desire to be elsewhere—at Tess's, to be precise. Alex realized now what a testimonial it was to the importance of their reunion that Zach had gone a whole month without visiting the chit directly after Alex's arrival. It was obvious she had quite a hold on him.

Zach heaved a sigh and hunched forward in his chair, propping his elbows on the white damask tablecloth and cupping his chin in both hands. He stared hard at the minuscule amount of port left at the bottom of his own glass as if the claret-red swallow of wine held in its shallow depths the answer to Alex's question. "I s'pose," Zach drawled at last.

Alex set down his glass, his mouth twisting in a sardonic smile. "Your response is overwhelming, brother. Do I detect a note of reluctance in your voice? Mrs. Tavistock is a charming women, though a trifle excitable. I find your future mother-in-law's conversation rather diverting."

"Wouldn't if you'd been listening to it since you were in leading strings," Zach assured him, lifting his golden eyes to stare owlishly at Alex.

"You've had too much to drink." Alex reached over to remove Zach's glass and the near-empty decanter of port from his brother's side of the table.

Zach watched Alex's movements with a bemused unconcern, a half smile tilting his lips. "You're right. I'm bosky. In my altitudes t' be sure. Maybe a brisk ride in the cool night air would sober me up a bit. What d'ya say to that, Alex?" Zach looked hopefully at his brother.

"If you didn't break your neck, I'm sure you'd somehow lose your way and end up in St. Teath at a certain young woman's cottage. Beth and her mother and sister are awaiting us in the drawing room. You don't want to disappoint them, do you? I'll have Stibbs serve tea at once, and if the tea doesn't sober you up, that grim specter of a butler standing sentry by the tray surely will."

"Oh, very well," Zach conceded with another ponderous sigh, tugging at his cravat with impatient fingers till the intricate knot his valet had painstakingly created was in total ruin. "Damned dull business, all this courting folderol! I'd as soon have Beth to m'self without you, her mother, her little sister, and half the servants at Pencarrow hovering about like mother hens!"

Alex stood up and moved to Zach's side of the table. "Naturally you would wish to be alone with your fiancée," he said in reasoning tones. "But though I loathe to remind you of it, you are in need of a chaperon. As you told me yourself, Beth doesn't intend to relinquish her . . . er, maidenhood before the two of you have tied the nuptial knot. In your present state, brother, Beth needs all the protection she can get.'' He pulled out Zach's chair and assisted him to his feet with a firm hand under the elbow.

Zach stood up, weaved, cursed, then sat down again. ''Worse than I thought,'' he mumbled.

Alex clicked his tongue. ''Perhaps you *could* use a little fresh air, but I daresay we need only go so far as the garden. Come.'' Alex pulled Zach to his feet once again and led him toward the French doors that opened to the formal gardens, taking a small three-tapered girandole with him. Zach tried to compensate for his lack of balance by walking with overcareful exactness, his steps precisely placed, his shoulders rigidly pulled back, his head held unnaturally high, and looking for all the world like a wooden marionette on the end of a jerky string.

Alex was torn between amusement and irritation. Zach was like a favorite puppy, one moment charming you with its youthful exuberance and the next moment wetting on your boot. You wanted to either cuddle it or kick it, depending on its latest antic. Currently Alex was having difficulty refraining from the latter method in his dealings with Zach. Though he'd stayed on the premises, Zach had continued to forget appointments with Beth and seemed distracted even in her company. All this, despite Alex's frequent reminders. He also continued to dodge any attempts by the steward or Alex to address the needs of the estate, particularly in the boarding up of the abandoned tin mines. He seemed too restless to get down to any sort of serious business.

Alex led Zach to a low marble bench sheltered on one side by tall, sculpted yew bushes and helped him to sit down. After ascertaining that Zach was capable of sitting up without assistance, Alex lit a cigarillo he'd plucked from an inner waistcoat pocket, then set the girandole next to Zach on the bench. He moved a few feet away to lean against an ancient, thick-trunked oak tree and drew a few relaxing puffs of the aromatic mixture of Indian tobacco, lifting his face toward the star-spangled ebony sky.

The night was balmy and softly lit by a three-quarter moon. Night-scented stock drenched the air with a heady clove and almond fragrance. Moor crickets strummed their tunes, and sea gulls cawed in the distance. It was a glorious night, a night to share with a woman as soft and dark, as fragrant and lovely, as the night itself.

"Don't you ever want a woman, Alex?"

Alex was startled by the question—a question so well timed to his inner musings that it was uncanny. He stared hard at Zach, his brother's slightly fuddled expression clearly illuminated by the candlelight. He decided that Zach was still too inebriated to be very serious about anything. He relaxed and said, "Why do you ask?"

Zach seemed to be concentrating, collecting his thoughts. "Because you never go to town, you know. You haven't laid a finger on any of the maids, either. At least not that I know of." Then his eyes widened. "Or have you?"

Alex chuckled. "No. I've no desire to dally with the servants. It only brings them grief in the end, no matter how willing they profess themselves to be."

Zach nodded sagely. "'Salways been my policy, too. Hands off the servants. But don't you . . . ?"

"I'm very particular, Zach. I don't tumble into bed with the first comely chit I see. In the meantime, if I feel . . . romantic, and there's no one about whom I've an inclination to be romantic with, so to speak, I busy myself with as many physical activities as I can find to do." He drew another puff of his cigarillo.

Zach's tawny brows dipped in a deep frown. "But sometimes that just don't meet muster, you know. Especially when you're thinking of one woman in particular, it's hard to be satisfied by anything but . . . well, *that* woman."

"Are you talking about Tess or Beth?" Alex studied Zach's face.

Zach cocked his head thoughtfully. "Right now, I suppose I'm talking about Tess. I love Beth, but since I've never bedded her, I can't ache for her as I do Tess. Do you understand what I mean?"

Alex understood, and yet he didn't understand. He understood how a man could want just one woman, but he didn't understand what not bedding Beth had to do with not aching for her. He'd never made love to Beth, but he ached for her night and day, every hour, every minute. Right now!

"What did you think of Lydia Elmstead?"

The question surprised Alex. Beth's betrothal party had come and gone like a shooting star. It brightened Mrs. Tavistock's conversation for several days before and after, but it had very little lasting impact on their quiet lives. The most memorable event of the evening for Alex was dancing with Beth. But he'd tried to forget how right she'd felt in his arms. As for Lydia, he hadn't given her a second thought.

"She's pretty, but not my sort," Alex replied at last.

"What is your sort, brother?" Zachary prodded.

A contralto laugh shimmered across the garden from the house. Alex turned and saw Beth's slender silhouette at the open drawing room window, etched against the candlelit background. At dinner he'd had to continually pry his eyes away from her end of the table. She wore a lustrous silk dress tonight, the butter-cream color of it giving her skin the soft, beautiful patina of fine porcelain. Suddenly he had to go inside. He had to see her, even if he couldn't touch her. A bitter kind of bliss, but all he had.

"No more questions, Zach! You've had enough fresh air, haven't you?" he said briskly, flicking his cigarillo into the closely scythed grass and crushing it with the heel of his boot. Then, not waiting for an answer, he said, "Topped off with some strong tea, you ought to be in prime twig in no time and easily able to tolerate Mrs. Tavistock."

"Lord, Alex," Zach complained, dragging a hand down his lean jaw and grimacing. "Sometimes I think you haven't a thimbleful of sympathy for me. I *have* to see Tessy. I *need* to see her. I promise you I shall attend to my estate business as soon as I return. But I can't concentrate on anything till I see Tessy. Are you made of stone, man?"

Alex wished he was made of stone. A part of him did have sympathy for Zach. But another part of him recoiled at the thought of condoning his trysts with Tess because if Beth knew of them, she'd be hurt and angry. Wouldn't she? Would she loathe to share Zach with another? If Beth were his fiancée, he wouldn't want her to feel anything less than furious if he spent time with another woman.

"I've never said anything to you about staying away from your mistress. I've never spoken a word against her," Alex told him.

"You've never said anything, but I've felt your disapproval," Zach quickly interjected. "And I can't fathom it in the least. You've had your share of mistresses, I'll wager."

Alex did not rise to the bait but kept his voice cool and emotionless. "Do you love her?"

Zach looked startled. "Tess?"

"Yes, Tess."

Zach grimaced. "She's my mistress, Alex. I'm not stupid enough to cherish that kind of feeling for her. It would be bound to complicate things if I loved her. M' friend Charlie—you know, the drunken fellow who passed out on Beth's library sofa?—he loved his mistress too damned well! He married her."

"So that was the case, eh?"

"Yes, and I'll not make the same mistake! And I've never told Tess I love her, either. I believe in being honest with the chit."

"Well, you're your own master now. You don't have to answer to anybody but yourself and your conscience."

"My conscience is quite clear," Zach answered defensively.

"Then do as you will, brother." Alex forced a smile. God, he didn't want to fight with Zach! Their renewed relationship was too precious, too fragile. "But don't let us come to fisticuffs over it. I won't tell you how to live your life, but I would be less than a brother if I didn't occasionally try to counsel you on matters in which I've had more experience. I'm older than you by several years."

"Are you advising me to quit seeing Tess?" Zach persisted.

"Have I said so?"

"Not in so many words, but—"

"Just don't neglect Beth," Alex interrupted, lifting a hand in protest to a continuation of the subject. "That's the advice I give you." He hesitated, set his jaw determinedly, and added, "She will respond to your attention like a flower to the sun. She needs a man's . . . She needs your attention, Zach. And pay heed to your responsibilities about the estate. You will surely regret it if you do not. You sow what you reap, brother," he finished wryly.

Zach seemed relieved by Alex's smile and lighter tone of voice, despite the serious advice he'd just offered him. "I'll tend to business directly upon my return from St. Teath tomorrow, Alex. Or by the next day without fail, since I *could* return quite late in the evening from Tess's," he amended. "Believe me, I shall be in much better mettle once I've bedded my Tessy a time or two. As it is, she's all I can think of."

Zach stood up, tottered only slightly, tugged on his waistcoat to straighten it, and combed his long fingers through his disheveled locks till he'd achieved a semblance of order. Cheered, he said, "Well, then, let's go inside, shall we?"

"As soon as I've straightened your cravat," Alex said, pulling and prodding the limp muslin into a more respectable appearance. As for going inside, Alex was only too ready to comply. He'd had enough of advising his brother. He wasn't at all objective about anything that concerned Beth, and he didn't trust himself to advise Zach fairly. Should Zach give his mistress the congé, or would that make him all the more eager to bed Beth? But why should *he* care if Zach made love to Beth before they were married? After all, he'd made love to her *after* they were married of a certainty. What difference would a few weeks make?

Hell and damnation! Alex cursed vehemently beneath his breath as he picked up the girandole and strode quickly toward the house, practically dragging a still unsteady Zach. How he wished he'd never met the girl!

Candlelight flickered in every corner of the drawing room except one. There in the darkness sat the droll-teller in a ruby-red wing chair, his hoary head bent over a mug of cool cider. His white mane of hair hung well past his shoulders, and his beard rippled like a snow-flecked stream over the front of his patched and sun-faded jacket almost to the last chipped button. His trousers were the same washed-out dun color as the jacket, baggy and obviously mended time and again. His boots were scuffed and worn thin at the soles till his bare feet shone through several holes. He would have to visit the cobbler soon and spin him a tale in exchange for a pair of shoes.

Beth knew Pye Thatcher well. She had seen him in the village and about Brookmoor and Pencarrow since she was no bigger than a flea bite, peddling his drolls in return for food and clothing. But she had been ten years old before her father had allowed her to sit in on one of his stories. Papa had said that Beth's imagination was of such a lively and vivid variety that it was unwise to expose her to Pye's Cornish faerie-tales about piskies, spriggans, mermaids, and knackers. She wouldn't sleep for a month, he'd said.

Papa had been right. Even at the mature age of ten, Beth

had lain awake for many nights imagining piskies in the shadows of her bedchamber, wigs of gray moss hanging down to their shoulders, a pointed red cap atop each elfin head. They were short, no bigger than moor hares, with wide sloped shoulders and bloated bellies. Piskies were basically friendly, but it wasn't lucky to catch one or even catch sight of one by accident.

Spriggans, however, were mean elves who crept about the countryside after nightfall. They were skinny with sun-crinkled skin and twiggish legs that ended in flat, broad feet. Their arms dangled to their knees, and their heads were large and odd-shaped, with jutting brows and eyes that glowed like searing embers.

Pye said that spriggans were as wicked as they looked. Old Bloody Bones, an especially horrid spriggan, would come and snatch naughty children from their beds at night. Naturally Beth feared spriggans most of all. She did try harder to be a good girl—at least for a little while.

As an added precaution, she had fastened an old horseshoe above her bedchamber window, a practice that Pye said was quite effective in scaring off stray spriggans. She also never failed to shoo toads from her doorstep if one should happen to squat there, since toads were known sometimes to consort with bad spriggans. Lastly, she kept a glove, turned inside out, on her bedside table. If a spriggan managed to sneak in, she had only to throw it at him quickly and it would send him on his way.

Pye Thatcher had advised her in these matters all those years ago. Now, watching him down his brew and think and mutter to himself over the tale he was about to tell, Beth knew with an awful certainty that Gabby should not be allowed to listen. Gabby's imagination was every bit as lively and vivid as Beth's had ever been. She was more precocious than Beth, especially since their father had died and Mrs. Tavistock had had the sole responsibility thrust upon her of raising and disciplining such an adventurous and rebellious child. Gabby was a taking little thing, much too engaging for her own good.

Mrs. Tavistock disagreed with Beth about sending Gabby to sit with Sadie till Pye was through. She insisted that Zachary, being the master of the house, ought to be applied to for advice. She would defer to him in this matter. Gabby had thrown Beth a triumphant look from the settee, which she shared so companionably with her mother.

Beth fervently believed her mother's confidence in Zach to make the decision concerning Gabby was sadly misplaced. Zach had been drinking liberally during dinner, and he and Alex had sat in the dining room for another half hour after the ladies withdrew. Besides, Zach had little resolution against Gabby's childish wiles. He spoiled her shamefully.

Beth's brows furrowed with worry. Zach had seemed so restless and inattentive over the past two weeks, and it was unlike him to drink that much wine with dinner. She hoped he wasn't regretting his decision to wed her in August. Perhaps he was having second thoughts about marrying so soon after his grandfather's death. She determined that she would find out his true feelings as soon as possible. But tonight she must somehow prevent Gabby from twining him about her dainty little finger.

It would not be an easy task. Beth almost wished she'd refused to let Pye in when Stibbs announced his arrival. But she sympathized with him, knowing that he was probably tired and thirsty after walking across the moor. He lived to tell tales and would be hurt to be turned away from a house he had visited regularly over the years.

There were footfalls nearing the door. Beth turned eagerly and watched Zach and Alex enter the room. Predictably, her traitorous eyes fixed themselves on Alex. He was impeccably dressed as usual, his Devonshire brown jacket and white cravat complementing his swarthy complexion and dark eyes, as deep and black as midnight. Champagne-colored breeches hugged his muscular thighs.

And as he leaned his shoulder against the mantelpiece and crossed his legs at the ankles, his gaze met hers with a lingering, unreadable expression. The look was intense but shuttered, disguised.

What did he think of her? she wondered. What did he know about her that she wished to hide—from him especially? Could he tell she was drawn to him, shamefully drawn by desires that ought to be tamped down till Zach—till her husband—bedded her? Had he revealed her overwhelming attraction to him that night at her betrothal party when they'd danced together?

"Zach!" exclaimed Gabby, bouncing off the settee and running to throw her arms about Zachary's waist. His hands dropped naturally to enfold her small shoulders. She lifted her face to look up at him, her expression full of melting supplication. "Oh, please, *do* please let me stay and listen to Mr. Thatcher! Mama says I may if *you* say I may, though Beth says I'm too young." She threw Beth a look rife with childish resentment.

Zach laughed and pressed a caressing palm to the top of Gabby's burnished golden head. "Mr. Thatcher's here, is he?" Zach narrowed his eyes and scanned the room till he saw Pye sitting in the shadows. Beth thought Zach seemed to be having difficulty focusing. Obviously he was still feeling the effects of the wine he'd consumed that evening.

"Good evening, Mr. Thatcher," Zach called across the large room. "Are you come to tell us a droll?"

Pye's mumbling ceased, and he lifted his head, the firelight catching in the jewel-bright sharpness of his blue eyes. He peered at Zach from beneath thick white eyebrows as tangled as the nest of an untidy bird and nodded soberly. "Aye, sir," he said in his low, gritty voice. "This eve I've come t' tell ye about the knackers."

"The knackers? Those little mine-dwelling sprites? How capital! I've not heard a tale of knackers for an age!" Zach

exclaimed, much animated. "Come, Gabby, let us sit and
listen."

Gabby's face lit up. She had won easily—too easily, by
Beth's estimation. Beth stood up and walked to Zach,
clasped his arm and pulled him to one side. She tried not to
feel self-conscious about Alex's intent observation of her
movements. She felt, rather than actually saw, his keen
watchfulness. He had watched her during dinner, too. She'd
hardly been able to swallow her food and had left most of it
untouched on her plate.

Zach weaved a bit, and Beth allowed him time to steady
himself while she sternly eyed Gabby from around the curve
of his broad shoulder. The little girl's arms were akimbo,
and her usual piquant expression had turned thunderous.
Returning Gabby's glare unflinching, Beth whispered in
Zach's ear, "Do you truly think it wise that Gabby be
allowed to stay? You know how her imagination sometimes
runs amok."

Zach cocked his head and grinned at Beth. "Lord, Beth,
how I love it when you breathe in my ear. Do it again, won't
you?"

Beth frowned and pinched Zach's arm, hard, just as she
used to do when they were children and he teased her.
"Don't be a ninny, Zach. I'm quite serious."

Zach grimaced and rubbed his arm where she'd pinched
him. "Well, I think you're acting like a fusspot, Beth."

When she opened her mouth to heatedly debate this
unfair description of her concern, Zach raised a restraining
hand and continued. "'Tis an unflattering name, I know,
and Gabby has been saying it to your face lately, which is
quite wrong of her, I admit. But—beg pardon, Beth—it's
true. You worry too much. I want her to stay. It won't hurt
her, I promise you."

"I thoroughly disagree with you," Beth replied stiffly,
stung by his name-calling. Did he think it was all right for
him to call her a fusspot, though he admitted that Gabby

should not? "But since this is your house, I suppose I must do as you say."

"There's a good girl, Beth," he soothed, patting her on the back and allowing his hand to slide farther down till it settled briefly on her bottom. "It's good practice to agree with me, y'know. I want a biddable wife."

Beth was surprised and flustered by the intimate caress, especially since he did it in full sight of a roomful of people. And his condescension was insufferable! Embarrassed, she let her gaze dart to Alex. Their looks collided, held, then jerked away. He was scowling, lines of disapproval grooved deep on either side of his mouth.

"Don't put yourself in a pet, Lizzie," her mother scolded, no longer able to restrain herself from speaking, and apparently unmoved by Zach's familiarity with Beth's bottom. "You're making a mountain out of an anthill. I know if I were Gabby, I'd simply *die* if I were denied such a treat," she declared with her usual tendency to overstate. "Now sit down and quit being such a Friday face. I'm just as eager as Gabby to hear Mr. Thatcher's droll."

Beth moved woodenly to a chair on the far side of the room, at some distance from the others. She was angry and felt abused by those from whom she thought she deserved a little consideration. She stared at her feet, concentrating all her ill feelings on the ivory slippers embroidered with pink rosettes. She half expected the blossoms, fashioned from silk thread, to wilt and wither from the intensity of her darkling glare.

No one seemed the least aware of her feelings, though. Zach had settled on the settee with her mother and Gabby and was listening raptly to Gabby prattle on about the puppies. Pye was finishing the last dregs of his cider and was wiping his lips on the sleeve of his dirty jacket in preparation for the telling of the droll.

But then there was Alex. She hadn't looked his way—she had forced herself to look anywhere but toward the mantelpiece against which he'd propped his wide shoulders—but she felt his black eyes upon her. A rill of awareness shimmied over her skin, compelling her to look at him.

The movement was as slow and halting as a falling drop of dew clinging to a leaf, but she turned. This time when their eyes locked, neither looked away in embarrassment, though there was more than enough naked emotion reflected in his eyes—and probably in hers, too—to cause embarrassment. She saw compassion reflected there, certainly, but overshadowing, *overpowering*, the sympathy was . . . patent desire. He wanted her as much as she wanted him!

Beth's stomach twisted, leaped, writhed with need. Her breasts felt heavy, flushed, longing for his touch. Her lips throbbed with anticipation. But all to be denied! All to be subdued and saved like a sacrificial offering for another man, a man she loved but didn't desire. God help her. What should she do? Despair slipped cold fingers around her heart and squeezed.

Alex felt violence course through his veins, violence spawned by thwarted passion. In all fairness, he could hold no one responsible for the dilemma he found himself caught up in, so he turned the violence inward, allowing it to scorch his insides like a raging inferno. He stood rigid, unmoving, stifling his urge to carry Beth away, out into the freedom of the dark, concealing night where secret passions could unfurl beneath the vastness of the heavens.

In this room—this cramped, confining room filled with obligations and commitments—he was fettered, caged. This stifling chamber represented all his pent-up emotions, everything he felt for Beth. Beth . . . Beautiful, beloved, and *betrothed to his brother.*

He pulled his eyes away from hers, rejoicing yet despairing in the sure knowledge that she felt the same depth of emotion for him. God help him, what should he do?

"I thought you were going to order tea, Alex."

Alex was stirred from his troubled reverie by Zach's prosaic comment. He focused his eyes on his brother, who was staring at him as if he were a Bedlamite, and mentally struggled to form an appropriate reply. But tea and other such everyday rituals dimmed in the wake of this new revelation. Beth wanted him.

"I forgot, Zach," he managed at last, digging deep inside himself for a convincing semblance of composure. "I suppose we had better have it served before Mr. Thatcher begins his droll or wait till he's through. I'm not familiar with the process, but I imagine he doesn't like to be disturbed once he's begun his story. Are you feeling more the thing, brother, or do you still need tea?"

"Why don't we wait till after the droll, Zachary?" Mrs. Tavistock suggested, wringing her hands dramatically. "Indeed, I don't think I can wait another moment to hear Mr. Thatcher's story."

"Neither can I, Mama," Gabby added, imitating her mother's hand-wringing display. "I should think I might fall into a swoon if I wait *much* longer!"

Zach laughed and softly flicked Gabby's cheek in an affectionate gesture. "We don't want Gabby swooning and skinning her pert nose on the floor, do we?" he said, winking across the room at Beth. Then he turned to Mr. Thatcher and said, "Commence droll-telling, my good fellow. We're all ears!"

The spell had begun. The droll-teller's deep, rough voice softened and lowered to the soothing cadence of a wide river's easy tumble—flowing, mellifluous, carrying its listeners along on a lazy raft to parts unknown. But their gentle passage was fraught with tension—delightful, teasing tension.

Gabby felt it right down to the tips of her toes. A cool waft of sea breeze skimmed across the floor, and gooseflesh rose on her arms. Pulling her feet up and under the hem of

her skirt, she snuggled close to Zach and listened to Pye
Thatcher spin his tale.

"Bob Lovell was a lad—about yer age, lass—what didn't
believe in the knackers," he began, staring hard at Gabby
from beneath his wildly snarled eyebrows, "though his
dadda was a tinner, and his granddadda before 'im. Tin run
in their veins like blood runs through yers and mine." He
swept a gnarled hand about the room and finally rested it,
palm down, against his sunken chest. He leaned forward.

"But the knackers are there whether ye believe in 'em or
not, down in the mines, workin' away each day 'cept
Christmas and Easter. Then ye kin hear 'em singin' carols
deep below the earth. But few has seen the knackers, only
heard the tap-tappin' of their tiny picks in the far chambers
of the mine.

"Knackers be friendly creatures, 'less they be spied on.
They don't like t' be spied on, nor do they fancy bein'
disbelieved in, like Bob Lovell disbelieved. The knackers
worked the best parts of the mine, and if a tinner be wise, he
followed the sounds they made as they worked and played
games deep below, and he'd find the richest veins and be the
richest tinner in all o' Cornwall.

"One day Bob's dadda took him along with 'im, minin'
fer tin. Bob didn't want to go, 'cause he didn't like how dark
it was in the mines. The miners wore stubs of candles on
their caps t' guide 'em through the long, twisting passages.
The mines were damp, and water dripped from the ceilings,
sometimes snuffin' their candles and leavin 'em in the dark
and the quiet. On this day the water dripped on both their
caps at once, and Bob and his dadda found themselves in
dark what were as black as a witch's heart."

Pye's eyes widened and glistened like sapphires. "And
remember, down below there be no sound—no wind in the
trees, no mother's voice callin' ye t' dinner, no birds singin'.
It be as quiet as the grave."

Gabby shivered, and Zach's arm eased around her,

squeezing her reassuringly. She looked up and was comforted by Zach's smile and wink. She snatched a glance at Beth, wanting to share the frightening delight of the story with her sister, but Beth was staring out of the window, as if she wasn't listening at all. Her eyes seemed fixed and dull. Gabby frowned. How oddly Beth was behaving lately! Lord Roth, too. He looked so grim tonight, so stern, as he, too, stared out of the window. She shrugged and turned back to Pye.

"As they stood there in the dark and Bob's dadda fumbled fer his tinderbox to relight the candles, they heard a sound nearby, like pebbles kicked by fast little feet, and sly giggles and snickerin'. Bob felt his dadda's hand squeeze his shoulder. At least he hoped it was his dadda's hand grasping him there in the thick, black bowels of the earth.

"'Did ye touch the horseshoe four times afore ye come down here, Bob, like I told ye to do?'

"'No, Dadda,' Bob confessed, trembling like a cornered moor mouse. Bob hadn't done it 'cause he didn't believe in knackers.

"'Did ye tip yer cap in all directions afore ye picked up yer ax?'

"'No, Dadda,' Bob said again.

"'May the good Lord be with us, then, Bob, 'cause we've knackers all about us and we've not done as we ought to do fer tinner's luck.'

"Bob was afeard now and stood shivering while his dadda lit first Bob's candle, then his own. Bob squeezed his eyes shut, not daring t' look at whatever it was he felt crowdin' against him.

"'Open yer eyes, Bob,' said his dadda, 'and pull out yer sack of dinner yer ma made fer ye.'

"Bob opened his eyes and started to reach into his bundle for his dinner, just as his dadda had told him to do, but his hand froze in place. He could do naught but stare at the ghastly creatures that stood all about, leaning on their wee tools and staring at him and his dadda. They were old, wrinkled elves with broomstick legs and apelike arms that hung to their boot tops. They'd no necks, just huge heads like pumpkins with greasy red curls poking out. Their eyes were tiny, squinty slits, and their toothless mouths stretched from cheek to cheek in a hideous grin.

" 'Bob,' said his dadda. 'Take out the pasty yer ma made ye and break off a piece. Crumble it on the ground in front of ye fer the knackers. 'Tis said that if ye share yer dinner with 'em, they be pleased. Do it now!'

"Still Bob was too afeard to move. When the knackers saw how frightened he was, they all began at once to waggle their long, hookish noses with their thumbs, taunting him. Then they turned their backs to 'im, stooped over, hung out their tongues, and grinned at him from between their knees.

" 'Bob, do as I tell ye,' hissed his dadda.

"Still Bob didn't move, and one of the knackers crept close and pinched his leg. Then another crept forward and kicked him sharply on the ankle. The others, some thirty of 'em, took a step or two toward 'im. Then Bob realized he'd better move or else be pinched and kicked black-and-blue by these squatty little sprites. He reached inside his bundle and pulled out the pasty his ma had made, full of mutton and fresh turnips from the garden, tore off a piece, and crumbled it on the ground in front of 'im. The knackers scurried and squawked like a flock of distempered peahens, snatched the crumbs up, then disappeared into the far shadows of the cave. Bob and his dadda together heaved a big sigh of relief.

" 'Do you believe in 'em now, son?' his dadda asked him.

" 'Aye, Dadda, that I do,' Bob told him. 'But kin we be through with tinnin' for today, Dadda?'

"Bob's dadda chuckled deep in his tinner's throat. 'As long as ye promise to do as I tell ye next time I bring ye down to the mines. Now leave the knackers a few more crumbs afore we go and drip a bit of candle grease on the floor. The wee fellows scoop it up and make their own small lights. If ye befriend 'em, as I've done over the years, they'll bring ye luck, Bob, and won't begrudge ye comin' and working in their mines. Let's go home now, son.'

"And home they went," finished the droll-teller, leaning back in the chair, his eyelids dropping slowly down to shutter the mesmerizing brilliance of his keen blue eyes.

"Is he asleep?" Gabby whispered to Zach when Pye continued to sit completely still with his eyes shut.

"No, I don't think so," Zach whispered back. "He always rests after a droll. It seems to take a great deal of his strength. He'll stir by and by, and then he'll leave. Here." Zach reached inside his jacket pocket and pulled out a shinny new guinea. He reached for Gabby's hand and pressed the coin into her small palm. "Put it in Mr. Thatcher's coat pocket, love. He's a funny old fellow, and he likes to pretend that we don't pay him for these delightful visits."

"Then why do we, Zach?" asked Gabby, confused.

"Because he's dreadfully poor, Gabby," chided her mother, gesturing in Pye's direction. "Can't you see his ragged clothing?"

Gabby looked at Pye as if for the first time. She'd noticed his lined face, his thicket of silver hair, his piercing eyes as blue as Dozmary Cove on a clear day, but she had not seen his poverty. Now she saw it because someone had brought it to her attention. A dull pain tugged at her heart. She stood up and moved to stand next to the chair Pye sat in. He smelled of moor heather and dirt, sunshine and sweat. She pitied him and wished that she had a small mite to give him, too.

She reached over and gently hooked a finger in a pocket of his coat, gaping it slightly so she could ease the coin inside without disturbing him. Her deed done, she straightened and looked into his face. His eyes were open. They shone gimlet-bright. He smiled, deepening the wrinkles in his withered cheeks. "Don't worry about me, child," he said, so low only she heard him. "I be rich beyond *their* wildest dreams. Rich in life. Rich in story. Are ye a believer, lass?"

Gabby smiled back. "Yes, Mr. Thatcher, I believe."

CHAPTER
seven

BETH SAT ALONE on a blue quilted coverlet on the sand, her arms wrapped about her knees, and watched the late morning sun arc across the sky to its twelve o'clock zenith. The wide-bottomed skirt of her yellow walking gown was tucked around her ankles, her feet were bare, and her straw bonnet hung by its jonquil ribbons against her back. The air was pungent with sea salt, and the tide swelled and foamed low and quiet, tugging at the shore as gently as a bridegroom might tug at his virgin wife's modest nightdress on their wedding eve.

Would Zach be as gentle? she wondered, an unexpected sharp dread digging at her, bone-deep. She squeezed her eyes shut, trying desperately to dispel the thought of lying naked in Zach's arms. All she managed to do was replace Zach's straight butter-gold hair with waving locks as black as a Stygian night and change the color of Zach's blue eyes to a dark Gypsy brown. She shook her head. This image— the image of herself lying naked in Alex's arms—was even more disturbing.

She'd brought food to share with the gulls, but no pang of hunger tempted her to open the basket and pull out the fruit and cheese wrapped in clean white cloths. Not even Cook's special crusty bread with fresh salty butter seemed appetizing to her. She was hungry for something—someone—quite beyond her reach.

Last night during the droll-telling she'd seen an echo of

her own desire reflected in Alex's eyes, but she dared not investigate the meaning or intent of that desire. And today, in the sobering brightness of daylight, she supposed she must have imagined much of what she saw, or thought she saw.

After Pye was done telling the droll last night, she'd pleaded fatigue and somehow managed to persuade her mother to end the evening early. In the flurry of departure, Beth had not once looked Alex in the eye, even when he bade her good night. Whether his desire for her had been a fleeting spark or an imagined folly of her own fevered mind, her responding look had bared her own feelings shamefully. What must he think of her now?

Beth's common sense told her that Alex Wickham, Lord Roth, was accustomed to engaging in flirtations with women, and she did not flatter herself that his attraction to her—if he truly felt an attraction—was anything special. Even if he did cherish feelings for her beyond physical desire, they were destined to be left unexpressed, unexplored. Alex loved Zach, perhaps as much as she did. She'd have to be blind and deaf to believe otherwise. They could never hurt Zach by succumbing to a passion that might diminish or dissipate within moments of fulfillment.

A gull fluttered down just a few feet away from the blanket and strutted back and forth, advancing gradually. "Oh, all right, you pest," Beth addressed the bird good-naturedly, suppressing her troubled thoughts. "I'll get some bread out for you. But as soon as I do, all your friends will join us, and the lot of you will peck and pick at each other over every morsel!"

She opened the basket and unwrapped a round loaf of oven-browned bread, the rough crust glossy with the egg white that Cook brushed on before baking. Tearing off a portion and releasing the fresh, yeasty aroma into the air, she pulled it into small pieces and threw them on the sand. As she'd predicted, her blanket was soon surrounded by birds bickering and cawing excitedly, dashing and dueling for every crumb. Their silly antics made her giggle. The mirth bubbling inside her felt good, and she threw back her head and laughed out loud.

A splashing noise drew her attention, and she turned to look upshore where the trail led down from the cliffs near Pencarrow. A rider on a black horse, hoof deep in sea-foam, skirted the jagged shoreline followed by the white blur of a huge dog racing alongside. It could be none other than Alex. Her heart stopped for a moment, then resumed beating with a heavy thump she felt to the tips of her toes. As he drew near, she prayed he'd stop and she prayed he wouldn't.

He was easing his horse—a brute of a stallion Alex had tamed in the few weeks he'd been at Pencarrow—to a gradual halt. He was in shirtsleeves, cuffs rolled neatly to just below his elbows. She admired the sinewy strength of his forearms and his shapely sun-browned hands so capably handling the tethers. She imagined them twined about her waist, pulling her against his broad chest and felt herself blush.

She ducked her head and pretended to be engrossed in tearing apart another chunk of bread as he swung down from the saddle. The horse still pranced and threw his elegant head in protest against such a sudden cessation to the gallop he'd been enjoying. Shadow loped toward the blanket and scattered the last of the gulls who had not been scared away by the horse's thunderous approach.

"Down, boy!" said Beth, fending off several attempts by Shadow to lick her face, all the while trying fervently to calm herself. Why had Alex come? If he had just chanced by, why did he stop? She supposed he was simply being courteous by stopping a moment to say hello, and he would be on his way in the twinkling of a bedpost. Would their meeting be awkward for him, or had he already dismissed last night's moment of revelation as folly?

Finally Shadow settled on his haunches next to Beth, his

long tongue hanging out as he panted vigorously. Suddenly remembering that she'd kicked off her sandals, she shifted her legs to one side and rested on her hip, tucking her bare feet under the hem of her skirt. She looked up and saw Alex staring down at her, one hand grasping the horse's ribbons and the other curled into a fist and braced against his lean thigh. His hair was a windswept tumble of coal-black waves.

"Good morning, Beth," he said in his mellow baritone.

"Good morning, Alex." She lifted the corners of her mouth, attempting to form a natural smile, but her lips trembled with the effort. She needn't have tried so hard, though, because Alex wasn't smiling. He looked at her searchingly. She bowed her head and busied herself with the bread, anxious to hide the yearning that thrummed through her blood and quickened her body at the mere sight of him, at the vital, warm intoxicant of his nearness.

"Why do you come and eat alone on the beach?" he asked her.

"Why, indeed?" she replied quickly, lifting her head to show a flickering rueful smile. "Gabby is riding about the countryside with our groom, and Mama is still abed. As for Zach, he has gone to town to buy me another bauble," she finished dully. As soon as she'd said it, she recognized and loathed the peevish tone of her voice. But before she could speak again, before she could cover and dispel the disappointment she'd revealed by the careless intonation of her voice, Alex spoke.

"He's fretted about that cameo ever since he lost it, you know."

"Yes," Beth agreed, grateful that he'd either not recognized or mercifully ignored her peevishness. "Perhaps that's why he has seemed so agitated lately. Mayhap a trip to town will ease his restlessness."

"Yes, I should think it might . . . for a time."

Beth thought his statement rather cryptic but forbore to

question him, afraid that her resentment toward Zach and his neglect of her lately might show. Overshadowing this concern and every other thought and feeling was the need to know how Alex felt about *her*. She needed to know whether he truly had feelings for her or if last night's mystical aura of droll-telling had permeated her brain and made her imagine things as unreal as the knackers and spriggans of Cornish folklore.

His eyelids drooped over the black fathoms of his eyes, revealing nothing. His stance was tense, the angle of his jaw square and firm. Then he smiled suddenly, crookedly. "Do you think you can spare a bit of that bread or are you going to toss it all on the sand? The gulls are too frightened of Shadow to dare approach, and *he* doesn't fancy the stuff. I, however, am famished."

Taking her cue from this abrupt change of mood, this friendly, offhand approach, Beth replied lightly, "Then you must by all means join me for nuncheon. I've plenty of food and had much rather share it with you than with the gulls. They are ill-mannered, thankless creatures, never satisfied."

"So that you will not regret your invitation, I promise to eat my food with the fastidious nicety with which one eats the stale cake and drinks the weak ratafia at Almack's. I shall be *cloyingly* thankful and pretend to be satisfied even if I'm not," Alex assured her, his smile broadening as he inclined his head in a playful courtly bow.

Beth smiled back, her heart fluttering like a legion of butterflies. It was impossible not to respond to such a roguish grin. If he could converse with her so easily, tease her so naturally, he must not have recognized the shameful yearnings she'd felt were so blatant in her expression last night. Relief and disappointment tumbled and collided inside her till she hardly knew which emotion held the upper hand. Lord, this was too confusing!

"I'll tie up my horse and water him, then join you in a

moment," he said, casting about for some shrubbery or a
jutting rock on which to tether his horse. Apparently spying
a wind-blasted tamarisk bush several yards inshore, he
turned and led the animal away in that direction. Shadow
followed, no doubt anticipating a refreshing drink along
with the horse.

"I'll prepare the food," she called after Alex, but found
herself unable to do anything of the sort. She could do
naught but watch, mesmerized, as he strode across the sand,
his tall, athletic form shown to distracting advantage by the
tight-fitting buckskin breeches and white shirt tucked
loosely into the waistband. Without a coattail draped over
his backside, his narrow, firm buttocks were revealed to be
muscled and well defined. A tailor's dream come true, or a
lover's. . . .

Beth gasped at her own unmaidenly brazenness at gaping
at a man's pleasingly shaped derriere and, furthermore,
speculating on one's enjoyment of such a pleasing derriere
in the midst of heated lovemaking. Horrified at the turn her
thoughts had taken, Beth gave herself a stern shake and
concentrated on emptying the picnic basket. Fixing her eyes
on her task, she sliced the cheese and peeled the fruit with
the single-mindedness of a miser counting his coins.

Alex soon returned and eased his imposing frame onto
the coverlet next to her. Shadow remained behind to loll in
the shade of the tamarisk bush. Alex stretched out on his
side and propped his jaw against a clenched fist, unluckily
repeating the exact pose he had assumed that day on the
beach when Beth had chanced to see him sunbathing naked.
Memories of his bare sportsman's body pounded through
her every thought, caught at her every breath, and cleaved
through her composure like an ax.

She had scooted aside to make room for him on the
blanket, but he was still a mere arm's length away. At such
close proximity, it seemed inevitable that her gaze would
drift to the gaping neckline of his shirt and the hair peeking

just above the pristine white edges. The dark coils looked downy soft. She had a strong urge to insinuate her fingers inside the open collar of his shirt and lay her hand, palm down, against his chest.

"The food looks good."

Beth's eyes lifted guiltily to his. "I'm . . . I'm sure it is," she stuttered, thoroughly convinced she'd finally, truly, made him aware of her attraction to him. But his eyes were steady and guarded. "Please, don't stand upon ceremony. Help yourself to anything you see." Beth fluttered her hand over the food in an almost feeble gesture. That was just how she felt, too. Feeble and without defense against her own thoughts and passions.

Alex reached for a slice of cheese and a wedge of apple, stacked them, and lifted them to his mouth. Beth watched him like a devoted lap pug as he took a bite and chewed slowly. After he'd swallowed, she watched his lips curve into a grin. Startled, she raised her eyes to his and saw tender amusement reflected in the inky depths, his left brow elevated to a questioning arch.

"Aren't you going to eat something?" he asked her. "I'm hungry, but not such a glutton as to wish to have it all for myself. You can't assuage the pangs of hunger simply by watching your companion eat, you know."

Beth's lashes fluttered down. She was embarrassed to have been caught ogling him. "I'm really not very hungry."

"Eat something anyway," he coaxed, putting down his own food, then picking up a wedge of apple and lifting it to her mouth. "I can't really enjoy myself unless you join me."

Beth looked into those teasing black eyes and then down at the lean brown hand that was holding the slice of apple an inch from her mouth. Compelled to do as he asked, and frightened by the realization that she'd probably do *anything* he asked of her, Beth parted her lips.

Alex leaned forward and eased the juicy, sweet-tart piece

of apple between her lips, nudging against her teeth. "You're going to have to open wider, Beth," he said in a low, persuasive voice. Electrified by such a loverlike tone, she raised her gaze to his and obediently opened her mouth a little wider. He inserted the apple wedge, and she took a small bite, chewed it self-consciously, and swallowed. Alex's hand was still poised in the space between them. He'd been watching her eat with as much concentration as she'd watched him.

"More?" he asked, the word a caress, as he held the apple near her mouth again.

"I can feed myself," she said breathlessly, wrenching her eyes away from the seductive lure of his. Then, with trembling hands, she snatched a slice of cheese, pulled off a rounded corner of the bread, and proceeded to eat. But every bite she swallowed tore at her panic-parched throat. She turned toward the water and concentrated on the ebb and flow of the tide, trying to shut out all impressions but the sight of the tranquil sea. The sea could usually calm her, but Alex's masculine scent and the circle of warmth he radiated reached out to her, teasing her, tempting her.

Tempting her with an apple, she thought with a sudden secret burst of ironic humor. How ageless. How biblical! But the roles were reversed, and he was the seductress, Eve, and she the hapless Adam!

"You must be thirsty. I know I am," Alex said, his voice as smooth and silky as a houri's veil.

"There's wine in the basket," she said, grateful to be reminded of it, since her throat felt as dry as an Indian desert. As he reached for the bottle of wine wrapped in a serviette, Beth studied him. Surely her imagination was running amok, just as Gabby's tended to do. Alex wasn't tempting her or flirting with her or doing anything except being cordial and charming, she reasoned. He was a vital, attractive man who probably had the same effect on every woman fortunate enough to share food and conversation with him. He probably made them all feel beautiful, desirable and . . . willing.

Willing. Beth didn't like that word as a description of herself—since she was far from free to be willing—or as a description of the other women in Alex's bachelor existence. Jealousy rumbled and spit like the dark ominous clouds of a gathering thunderstorm.

"There's only one goblet, but I daresay we can share it," he said easily, uncorking the bottle and half filling the glass with plum-colored wine. "You first." He handed her the goblet.

Beth drank greedily, the sweet, fruity potable coating her aching throat. Then, chagrined to discover that she'd left a mere swallow at the bottom, she returned the goblet with an apologetic, shy smile, saying unnecessarily, "I was thirsty."

Alex received the glass with an amused and tolerant grin, refilled it, and took a languid sip. Beth squirmed restlessly, his apparent ease an abrasive irritant to her own disquiet, and toyed with the decorative tasseled edging of the coverlet.

"Tsk-tsk, Miss Tavistock," he said teasingly, gesturing toward her small pink toes peeking out from beneath the flounce of her dress. "You're barefoot and likely to catch an inflammation of the lung if you gad about so underdressed. What would Sadie say, hmmm?"

Beth's head jerked up defiantly. It was on the tip of her tongue to point out that *he* had, on at least one occasion, exposed himself to the elements a great deal more underdressed than she was! He returned her look with a challenging expression that almost made her believe he knew what she was thinking and what she was tempted to retort. But that wasn't possible, was it?

"They must be cold, so unprotected," he said, reaching over to slip his hand just under the hem of her skirt to cradle the exposed foot in his large palm.

Beth was rendered speechless and motionless by the

unexpected power of her reaction. He was hardly touching an intimate part of her body, yet the warmth of his strong fingers curled about the tender, sensitive pads of her foot sent spidery tingles of awareness from her toes all the way to her sun-warmed scalp.

She gasped, and her eyes flew to his face in time to see the careless grin slide away, to see his expression change from one that he might assume for the purpose of a drawing room flirtation to one of dangerously serious intent. The teasing facade, the guarded, superficial chivalry, disappeared. Last night had been no flight of reason, no wishful fancy. *He wanted her.* At that moment all thoughts, all feelings, became as distant and meaningless as the misty details of a dream. All that mattered to Beth was *now.*

"Beth . . ." Low and urgent, he whispered her name. Without removing his hand, he eased himself to a sitting position, one knee crooked and angled to the side, the other leg tucked under him Turkish style. Now he was so close that his wine-laced breath mingled with Beth's own. Locking her gaze with his, he slid his hand slowly, purposefully up to encircle her trim ankle.

Startled, breathless, Beth reached down to stay his hand from further wandering. "Alex, we can't! We mustn't . . . I don't want to—"

"You know you want me to touch you, Beth, just as much as you want to touch me. Touch me, Beth. Touch me."

Beth could not resist the invitation. For too long she'd wished to do exactly what he was asking of her, what he was compelling her to do. In a fever of anticipation, she found that her most pressing thought was where to start.

"Beth!" Alex ground out her name through clenched teeth, his black eyes snapping with emotion. "I need you to touch me."

Though a small, sane voice in a corner of her mind told her she ought to be alarmed by the near-violence of Alex's look and manner, Beth felt a soul-deep thrill, an urgency that rose to meet his. She lifted a trembling hand and traced with sensitive fingertips the lean planes of his face, from his forehead and the arch of those wicked black brows to the chiseled line of his jaw, around to the deep cleft in his chin and up to the sculpted, sensuous curve of his lips. All the while he watched her, his breath seemingly suspended, while Beth's breath came quick and jagged.

Then, driven by a hunger she used to wonder about and wish for in her relationship with Zach, she dropped her gaze to Alex's open collar and slid her hand inside, brazenly stretching her fingers to maximize the contact. He was warm, the thatch of dark hair springy and soft. She felt his heartbeat beneath her hand, like the wild rhythm of a pagan drum.

"Alex," she whispered hoarsely, terror and guilt crowding her throat as he bent his head toward her. "What's happening to us? You know we mustn't kiss. We mustn't do any of this! Zach . . ." Beth shook her head and pulled back, her hand fleeing reluctantly from the warm haven of his chest.

Alex straightened, grasped her wrist, and brought her hand to his lips, softly kissing the tender hollow of her palm, sending a shiver of pleasure up her arm. He lifted heavy, tortured eyes to hers. "Lord, Beth, don't you think I know that what we're doing is wrong? But, God help me, I can't seem to stop myself. When I saw you sitting on the beach, I thought I could spend a few moments with you, enjoy your company, without this happening. I deluded myself into believing that what I saw in your eyes last night was only wishfulness on my part. And I prayed that I hadn't exposed my own needs. Needs that blossomed the day I met you. Needs that have grown daily, insistently, with every hour I've spent near you."

Still clasping her wrist, he pulled her closer till her aching breasts pressed against his chest. "If you were indifferent to me, perhaps it would be easier to resist the urge to hold you in my arms. But I know you are far from indifferent. Would that it were not so,'' he rasped hopelessly, thrusting her gently from him and turning away.

Beth felt bereft, alone, wanting. He was so close, yet so unattainable. Her whole being ached for him, yet it could never be. Even now Zach was choosing an engagement present for her. But she did not want Zach as she wanted Alex, body and soul. *Why?* she asked herself. She loved Zach. She'd loved Zach since she was a tottering devoted child and he a sprig of boyhood, all platinum hair and gangly limbs! Surely all she was feeling for Alex was a transitory thing, a phantom thing that would fade away like the prismed colors of the rainbow—beautiful, but only a fleeting mirage.

And Alex had spoken only of needs. He had not spoken a word of affection, of respect or regard, of love. Would it make a difference if he loved her? Suddenly she had to know.

''Alex?'' she whispered.

He did not reply. His shoulder was turned to her, and all she could see of his face was the stark angle of a cheekbone, the lowered sweep of ebony lashes, the slash of a grim mouth.

''Alex, I need to know something,'' she persisted, stoking her courage, lifting her chin determinedly. ''I need to know if what you feel for me is just . . . passion or . . . or if you love me.''

Alex reared around to face her. He looked stricken, confused. ''Do I love you?'' he repeated, as if she'd recited gibberish.

Did he love her? Alex wasn't sure what he felt for Beth. An obsessive need to claim her for his own did not necessarily constitute love. He wished for her happiness; he cherished her compassionate and loyal nature; he relished her brightness, her curiosity, her wit; he was excited and enthralled by her passion. Was he in love with her? It was hard to know, because thus far in his fickle dealings with the fair sex he had never, to his knowledge, been well and truly in love.

As for familial love, that was another matter. He knew he'd loved his mother dearly, and he'd loved Zach the moment he saw the fragile whelp bound up in flannel and screaming from his cradle, screaming to suckle at the breast of his dead mother. God, poor Zach! Denied his mother, abhorred by his father, and separated from his brother, the only one who really loved him, till Beth. . . .

Alex plunged curled fingers into his tangled mass of hair. And now he would take away Beth's love? Nay, he would not!

"It doesn't matter whether I love you or not, Beth," he said, his voice as cold and hissing as winter's breath across the moor. "You are betrothed to Zach. We cannot allow this sort of thing to happen again."

Beth gasped, obviously wounded by his suddenly icy demeanor. "If you recall, Lord Roth, 'twas not I who clasped you about the ankle. 'Twas not I who implored *you* to touch *me*!"

"I spoke for both of us, Beth. You did not have to utter a word," he shot back, his tone as barbed as an arrow. "You tell all with your eyes."

The telltale eyes narrowed, simmering with anger. "Then I will take care henceforth, Lord Roth, to say as little as possible to you with my eyes or any other part of me, my lips included."

Lord, she looked so beautiful with her head cocked just so and her lips pressed together like the knees of an old maid. All Alex's resolve melted in the space of a mere moment. She was so proud, so prickly, so kissable! He felt the grim set of his mouth relax, his lips parting slightly. He leaned forward and watched her chin lower to a level with his, her

mouth soften from defiance to surrender—pouted, yielding—
her eyes mist with wonder and passion. . . .

"There you are, my lord! Hallo! Hallo?"

Alex started at the sound of Dudley's strident tenor.
Twisting around, he observed his manservant not twenty
feet away, trundling up the beach with the sluggish gait of
a city dweller. Anxious to preserve Beth's honor even with
the servants—even with Dudley, who would not say a
peep—Alex rose to his feet and stepped forward to intercept
his servant, leaving Beth some time and a little privacy to
pull herself together, a luxury he could not indulge in
himself.

"What is it, Dudley? Good God, it must be something
important for *you* to fetch me like this," he suggested,
assuming a casual attitude.

Dudley kept his eyes fixed on his master, apparently
sensitive to the fact that Beth was slightly discomposed.
Knowing Dudley, he'd probably seen it all. Too perceptive
by half. Just like a woman, keen-eyed and knowing.

"Begging your pardon, my lord, but you're quite right
about that," Dudley began complainingly, his breath la-
bored from the unusual exercise he'd been compelled to
take in the line of duty. "I'd have sent another servant to
scale these hideous dunes if things weren't in such a
hubble-bubble at the house, what with Mrs. Tavistock
kicking up such a dust. But I didn't dare trust those louts to
compose themselves sufficiently to track you down, my
lord. A more paper-skulled, beetle-headed bunch of Johnny
Raws I never hope to see again, my lord! It's just as I told
you from the start. Stibbs can't manage the house—"

"Dudley," Alex began repressively, "I know your opinion of Stibbs. Now out with the news, if you please! What
has Mrs. Tavistock got to do with goings-on at Pencarrow?"

"Well, it's like this, my lord. Miss Gabrielle is missing.

She went riding with the groom this morning and somehow played him a rig, slipping away suddenlike—''

''Gabby's missing again?''

Alex turned toward the blanket. Beth was standing now. She'd pulled her straw bonnet into place atop her rich chestnut hair and was tying the bow beneath her chin. Her tone of voice clearly implied that she was not feeling overly concerned about Gabby's disappearance. When she lifted her eyes from the task of smoothing her skirt, her gaze slithered past Alex and focused on Dudley. She was flushed but otherwise appeared cool and controlled. He suspected that her composure depended on avoiding the source of her aggravation—himself.

''Yes, miss,'' Dudley promptly replied. Alex could tell that Dudley liked Beth. She was one of the very few in Cornwall who'd received such a distinction. '' 'Tis more than an hour since your sister . . . er, lost her groom, and your mother is up in the boughs . . . I mean, she's beside herself with worry.''

''After all the other times Gabby's lost her groom, Dudley, I can't imagine why Mama frets so. My sister always returns by the afternoon, unless Zach finds her first and the two of them go off on some adventure. And it would serve best if Mama stayed at Brookmoor instead of descending upon Pencarrow and whipping the servants into a froth. I suspect I ought to return with you, however, and try to calm her, or Stibbs will be sadly out of curl for the rest of the day.''

''She expects *you* to look for Miss Gabrielle, my lord,'' Dudley hastened to add, turning back to Alex. ''In the past Master Zachary has taken it upon himself to search for the child, but since he's gone to St. Teath for the day . . .''

''I shall be happy to play a part in easing Mrs. Tavistock's mind, Dudley. But that will require that Beth and I return to the house as expeditiously as possible. You, my

poor fellow, must carry the blanket and basket back to
Pencarrow while I take Beth on the horse with me.''

"Oh, I don't think that will be necessary!'' cried Beth,
her cool demeanor shaken at the prospect of sitting a horse
with Alex, their bodies *touching*. "I walk very fast, you
know,'' she insisted. She dared not touch him again. He
went from frost to fever in a matter of seconds, and she
responded like a besotted concubine, ever ready to forget
her anger, her reservations, her commitments.

"Don't be a goose, Beth. It will take you three times
longer to walk. On the horse we'll reach Pencarrow in mere
minutes,'' he stressed, an underlying message behind his
innocent words. He was telling her that they'd be touching
for only a short time. And he was also implying that they
ought to be quite safe from temptation on the back of a
horse. Beth was torn between exasperation and a sort of
lunatic merriment at the idea of such an odd safeguard
against passion.

"Of course,'' she murmured, a strange inclination toward
hysterical laughter tickling the corners of her mouth. She
composed herself with an effort. Her obsession with Alex
was turning her into a Bedlamite. "I shall ride with you,
though I pity poor Dudley having to carry all this stuff and
trudging through the sand, too. If you're not used to the pull
of the sand on your legs, it can be quite tiring.''

"Thank you, miss, for your gracious concern,'' Dudley
intoned, flashing Alex a resentful look.

"I'll fetch the horse. You can begin gathering up the food
and cutlery to refill the basket, Dudley,'' Alex said, returning the man's glare with amused tolerance.

Dudley did as he was bidden, and Alex went for the
horse. All the seriousness of her situation returned in full
force as Beth watched Alex untether the stallion and stroke
the restive beast's shiny black coat, soothing him into
submission. Then he guided the horse toward Beth. With a
stroke of his hand, she thought. That was all it took to calm

the stallion, now that he was trained. Alex had a masterful way with animals . . . and women. For everyone's sake—hers, Zach's, Alex's—she had to be strong and resist Alex's all too masterful ways.

"Come, Beth, up you go!" Alex said as he twined his large, capable hands about her waist and easily tossed her onto the horse. "There. Wrap your knee about the pommel and grab hold of it. With me behind you as a prop, you'll be as steady as the squire's snore at Sunday service."

Beth smiled wanly at Alex's humorous repartee, then steeled herself for the impact of his body against hers as he mounted the horse. His muscled thighs pressed lightly against her hips, enfolding her. His chest was flush against her back, warming her. He reached around her shoulders to grasp the reins, embracing her. This was worse than she'd expected—the ride back to Pencarrow would be a most exquisite exercise in torture.

"Are you steady, Beth?" he asked her gently, his mouth mere inches from her ear, his wine-sweet breath fanning her cheek like a summer breeze.

"As I'll ever be, Alex," she said, sighing softly.

Dudley watched them ride away with Shadow keeping pace alongside. Dudley shook his head dourly. "There's fat in the fire, my feathered friends," he told the gulls, who were fluttering down again now that the dog had left. "You mark my words. Before the summer's over, those brothers are going to come to cuffs." Dudley heaved a resigned sigh. "Trouble is, I like them both, you see. What a pickle. What a pickle!"

Then he hung the basket from one elbow, tucked the folded coverlet under his other arm, and began his tedious journey back to Pencarrow and the vexatious household run by the bird-witted butler. But for once Dudley had more pressing thoughts to ruminate over than his disapproval of Stibbs.

CHAPTER
eight

GUILT WEIGHED LIKE ill-gotten gains, and Beth's heart was as heavy as thirty pieces of silver. Zach had gone to town to buy her a present, and in the meantime she'd been on the verge of kissing his brother. She'd nearly betrayed her fiancé with a kiss, and further intimacies might have occurred had they not been interrupted by Dudley.

"Lizzie, my head is throbbing," Mrs. Tavistock whined fretfully. "I begin to think I might need just a smidgen of laudanum in a small tumbler of wine. Perhaps it will relax me till Lord Roth returns with Gabby. You do think he'll find her, don't you?"

Beth's mother lay wilting on the couch in the blue sitting room at Pencarrow, one arm hanging limp to the floor and the other crooked across her bosom, a sodden handkerchief clutched in her fist. Her eyes were closed. Dust motes floated in the streamers of simmering sunshine that wedged their way through the slightly parted velvet draperies. The hot afternoon had dawdled by, and neither Alex nor any of the servants who'd been pardoned from their duties by Stibbs to participate in the search had returned with Gabby.

As she'd sat by the couch and nursed her mother's nerves with hartshorn and lavender water, Beth's mind had been preoccupied. Her thoughts dwelt not with her sister, however, but with the man who was seeking her. As the mantel clock chimed seven, Beth's brow furrowed. She was beginning to worry about Gabby, too.

"I'll have Sadie bring you some laudanum, Mama,"
Beth assured her, standing up to leave the room. She didn't
dare pull the bell rope, for Stibbs would appear and scowl
her down for requesting such a fribblesome item when there
was a dearth of servants about the house to run errands.
Stibbs cared not a whit for Mrs. Tavistock's nerves, for he
was well acquainted with them. And, as the saying went,
familiarity bred contempt.

"You're a dear, Lizzie," her mother whispered as Beth
left the room. Beth descended the stairs and walked down
the hall that led to the kitchen and the adjoining stillroom
where the medicines were kept. Sadie would be up to her
elbows in dinner preparation at this hour, and Beth did not
intend to disturb her; she would fetch the laudanum herself.
Her mother did not approve of Beth's willingness to run
minor errands when the servants were busy. She predicted
that Beth would never properly rule her own household but
would be taken advantage of at every opportunity. But Beth
could not conceive of sitting idle when she had a pair of
perfectly good legs and could walk about the house at will.

As she neared the kitchen, she heard voices, low and
urgent, all of them seeming to be talking at once. She
quickened her step, dread tugging at her heart like a needy
beggar. Something must have happened to Gabby! She
thrust open the door and entered the kitchen. Several stable
workers and Alex were conversing with Sadie and Stibbs.

"What has happened?" she asked abruptly, pausing just
inside the door, fear rooting her feet to the spot. All of them
turned toward her, their expressions startled, distressed,
wary. She could see now that all the men who'd been
searching for Gabby, Alex included, seemed to be covered
with a fine dusting of powder, such as the type that her
father had once worn on his wigs. Then she remembered
how the miners used to look when they trudged home from
work each day, covered with the silt that sifted down
through the acrid air of the tin mines.

Alarmed, she sought Alex's eyes. "Gabby?" she said, worry strangling her voice to a reedy whisper.

Stepping away from the knot of people who'd become dumbstruck at her appearance, Alex closed the distance between himself and Beth with two long strides. He gripped her elbow and pulled her through the open doorway and into the hall.

He closed the door behind them, turned her to face him, and clamped her shoulders with firm hands. "We think Gabby's lost in a tin mine, Beth. We found her horse nearby, and there's evidence of a recent entry. There are small footprints in the damp dirt at the front of the mine shaft. We went a few feet inside, but without torches it was impossible to see anything. I left a man there in case she appears, but the rest of us returned for equipment." Alex paused, seemingly waiting for a reaction.

After the initial shock and the wrenching surge of empathy she felt for her little sister's probable terror at finding herself lost in utter stifling darkness, Beth steeled herself and gathered strength to assist in Gabby's successful rescue. She would not entertain thoughts of any other possible outcome. And she would not dwell on the reason for Gabby's sudden desire to explore the depths of a damp tin mine. She suspected that the impressionable child had gone looking for knackers, but Beth ruthlessly suppressed the angry feelings that accompanied this thought. She would deal with all these feelings later, after Gabby was found safe and sound.

"Thank you for telling me the truth without a lot of beating about the bush, Alex," she said, lifting her chin determinedly. She thought she saw relief in his expression and was encouraged by his obvious approval of her unruffled manner. "What are your plans? I suppose the servants have told you that there are several tunnels belonging to each mine and that they meander for miles? And you must have observed that the walls are quite unstable from years of disuse.''

Though she'd meant to stay calm, acknowledging to Alex the problem of searching the serpentine tunnels that snaked through the earth in all directions, and the very real possibility of the walls collapsing, sent a shiver of misgiving down Beth's back. Poor Gabby could be anywhere by now, and she might be hurt!

Alex's hands still cupped her shoulders, and he must have felt the telltale shudder ripple her rigidly held spine. Squeezing her upper arms reassuringly, he said, ''We've as many servants as there are tunnels, and just to make sure no one else gets lost, we've devised a means of marking our way. It would be best if we could speak with the miners who worked this particular mine, since they would remember its various twists and turns, but so far I can't seem to—''

''Zach!'' Beth exclaimed, struck with a sudden inspiration. ''Zach used to play in the mines when he was a boy. Against his grandfather's strict orders, of course. He was punished more than once for disobeying that particular rule. Possibly he knows this mine and could help us reason out exactly where Gabby might be. At the least, he could make sure we don't miss some small chamber where she might have curled up in a ball and cried herself to sleep.''

''I had assumed you'd want Zach here, anyway,'' Alex said matter-of-factly, his expression neutral. ''I've already sent Dudley to fetch him.''

''Oh, you know precisely where he is, then?'' Beth said, surprised. ''At this hour I suppose he's eating dinner at the Nag's Head Inn. Is that where you sent Dudley?''

''I don't know *precisely* where he is,'' Alex said, his eyes averted from the searching look in hers, ''but I'm sure Dudley can locate him by making inquiries.''

Beth's brows drew together. ''Indeed, I can't think why he stays so long in town. It couldn't have taken him more than a few minutes to buy me a present and purchase new gloves for himself, as he said he meant to do. I suppose he's run into another friend, and as you said before, he's chirping merry over a tankard of ale—the wretch. But I shall be glad of his help, even though if it were not for him . . .'' Beth's voice trailed off. Criticizing Zach to Alex seemed disloyal.

"What about your mother?" Alex asked, changing the subject abruptly.

"I came downstairs to fetch her some laudanum to relax her. I will dose her liberally, and perhaps she'll sleep till Gabby's found. If she finds out what's happened, she'll become quite hysterical, you know. After she's dozed off, I'll leave a maid with her and join you at the mine. Please don't argue with me," she hastily added, impulsively laying her palms against his chest in a beseeching manner. "I want to be there. Gabby will have need of me."

Alex looked down at the small hands pressed against his chest, and despite the trouble they were presently caught up in, his memory tumbled back to that moment on the beach when Beth had slipped her warm, trembling fingers inside his shirt. She had been so innocently seductive in her tentative exploration, so curious, so sensual. He had responded as he'd never responded to any other woman, even a skilled courtesan.

Suddenly Beth removed her hands, and Alex lifted his eyes to her face and saw guilt imprinted on every delicate feature. Anger flared inside him—anger toward Zach, who was betrothed to this unusually sensitive and beautiful woman and had the gall to neglect her for the charms of a mistress. Did Zach truly deserve Beth's loyalty, Beth's love? And if Beth knew of Tess, would she still feel guilty?

"I must go to my mother right away," Beth said, interrupting the nagging questions that had plagued Alex constantly since their meeting on the beach. Beth kept her eyes averted. "If I'm gone too long, she'll work herself into a frenzy." She hesitated for a moment, snatched a furtive look at Alex, then walked past him toward the kitchen door.

"I'll have one of the men stay behind so that he can guide you to the mine when you're ready," Alex said to her back.

Beth's hand was on the doorknob, but she turned her head slightly, the sweep of lowered dusky lashes visible against her pale cheek. "Thank you, Alex." Then she was gone.

Dudley snapped the whip above the gelding's red-roan back and cursed fluently, the wind snatching his epithets and tossing them away. His coppery hair snapped in the gusting air like the flame of a torch. Sweat trickled down his forehead, and flying particles of dirt lodged in the corners of his eyes and mouth. He peeled a dead blood-bloated mosquito from his forehead and another from his cheek, then shuddered delicately as he wiped his sticky fingers on his white breeches.

This is not what a gentleman's gentleman does for a living, he told himself grimly. He ought to be home pressing his lordship's cravats in preparation for the evening's change of attire. But instead he was dashing hey-go-mad across the desolate Cornish countryside in the sweltering heat of an early summer's evening to fetch Zachary Wickham from the arms of a ladybird!

Dudley could not remember the last time he'd felt so unequal to a task. Or so thoroughly disheveled and unclean! But circumstances dictated that he drive the open gig with all due haste, and such haste was not conducive to an orderly appearance. But he could understand why Lord Roth had asked *him* to fetch Zachary and not trusted the errand to one of the Pencarrow underlings. Indeed, his chest swelled with pride at the confidence his master placed in him to carry a message to Zach and be relied upon not to repeat what he'd seen or heard. Too bad that such confidence had to be reinforced in such an uncomfortable manner.

Presently he entered the town and slowed his horse to an easy trot. Lord Roth could not be precise about the whereabouts of the cottage, for he had gleaned only a general idea of its location from tidbits of conversation with his brother. So Dudley would be required to further demean himself by stopping at the Nag's Head Inn to make discreet inquiries. Depending on the disposition and mood of the inn's proprietor, it could be a simple task to discover the directions to the little dovecote, or Dudley could be thrown out on his ear.

Once he'd obtained directions to the cottage, Dudley would still have to face the ordeal of interrupting Lord Roth's brother when he'd least appreciate an intrusion. God only knew what Master Zachary and his light-o'-love would be doing when Dudley knocked upon the door, but though he was only a mortal, Dudley could conjure up some alarming possibilities.

As it happened, the proprietor was a jovial fellow and readily and without question supplied Dudley with the information he needed. Encouraged by this success, Dudley headed for the cottage in a slightly more optimistic frame of mind.

Located on the northern outskirts of town, the cottage was a small Elizabethan structure surrounded by a flourishing garden that had been planted with picturesque disorder. Dudley jumped down from the gig and tethered the sweating horse to a rail of the neat picket fence that surrounded the cottage. He combed his carroty hair with skinny freckled fingers, gave his jacket lapels a straightening tug, and walked through the gate and up the cobbled walk to the door, which was overhung with trellised honeysuckle vines. Sighing deeply, he knocked.

Dudley waited, tapping an impatient rhythm with his foot against the flagstone porch. He heard bees buzzing lazily through the garden and a woodpecker applying his beak to a nearby tree. Calming sounds, but not today, and not for Dudley. When several moments had passed and no one came to the door, Dudley walked around to the side of the house, saw Zachary Wickham's dapple gray stallion standing alongside a white mare in the open stable, and returned to the door. He knocked again, this time harder.

As several moments passed again, Dudley began to chew on his bottom lip with energy. He had to speak with Zach. This was possibly a matter of life or death! If he was forced to climb through a window to accomplish his mission, he would do so, dash it! But perhaps the door was open. Dudley reached for the knob and turned it gently, carefully, to the right. Ah, it was unlocked! But— Good God, now what?

Suddenly the door squeaked open, and Dudley was sighing with relief that he wouldn't have to charge in upon an entwined couple in the throes of passion, when his breath caught at the vision before him. Hair like spun gold haloed a heart-shaped face of fragile beauty. Eyes as blue as cornflowers stared at him, shy, vulnerable. One dewy shoulder peeked above the bright flower-printed coverlet she clutched close to her body with pink, curled fingers— small, waiflike fingers.

"What do you want, sir?" she asked him in a soft, timid voice.

Dudley endeavored to collect himself. He had not expected the doxy to look so pure and innocent, to be so young and delicate. "I'm . . . I'm here to . . . to see Mr. Zachary Wickham," he stuttered, his eyes flitting past her distractingly bared shoulder to probe into the room behind her. But all was silent, and no small movement stirred the deepening afternoon shadows that fell across the muted purple tones of the rug that partially covered the floor. The girl lifted her chin slightly as though gathering resolve to tell a lie, to carry out her instructions and tell him her lover wasn't there. Dudley hastily continued, "I've an urgent message from his brother."

The young woman's eyes widened, her budlike mouth opening in surprise. Now there was sound and movement from behind her, a creak of bed boards and then the whisper of cloth as Zachary Wickham no doubt pulled on his trousers. "It's all right, Tessy, let him in," Dudley heard him say as she stepped back and opened the door wide, then padded away to curl up on the rumbled bed. Wrenching his eyes away from the ethereal creature called Tessy—an inadequate name, in his opinion—Dudley entered the house and turned to his master's brother, who stood by the bed buttoning his shirt. Dudley noticed that the scent of honeysuckle permeated the air.

"This had better be important, Dudley," he said, his hair a golden tumble, his aureate eyes glittering a warning.

"Oh, it is, sir! You don't think Lord Roth would send me here unless the matter was most urgent, do you? And even so, I feel devilish foolish, sir, and beg your pardon for bursting in on you like this while you're with a . . . er . . . friend," Dudley babbled, shifting nervously from foot to foot. "It's Miss Gabrielle. She's lost, sir, in a—"

Zachary's burst of laughter jarred Dudley's nerves and silenced him completely. "Good God, Dudley, is that all? Gabby's lost herself on the moor at least twice already this summer! I can't believe that Alex was so overwrought with worry that he'd fetch me away from Tessy when he knows that I . . ." His eyes narrowed. "Or can't I?"

Dudley did not like the skeptical look that transformed the younger man's face to a mask of suspicion. "Sir, you don't understand. This time Miss Gabrielle is lost in a tin mine. She's nowhere to be found on the moor, and her horse is tethered to a bush by the shaft of a mine. Her footprints were seen in the soft dirt near the entrance, leading into the—"

"Enough, Dudley," Zachary rasped, all color swiftly gone from his face, his features suddenly pinched and contorted. "I perceive the urgency of the matter and will leave immediately. Can you tell me which mine it is so that

I can go straight there?'' He dressed quickly now, every movement purposeful and economic.

Dudley's eyes strayed briefly to the bed to snatch a glimpse of Tessy. She, too, was as pale as the casing of her pillow. ''Lord Roth made up a map for you, sir. With your knowledge of the area, I'm sure you'll know exactly which mine it is from this sketch.'' Dudley delved into his breeches pocket, pulled out a folded piece of parchment, and handed it to Zachary.

Zachary grabbed the paper, unfolded it quickly, and scanned the hastily drawn map. He threw the paper down, saying grimly, ''Yes, I know it well.'' Then he sat on the edge of the bed to pull on his boots, muttering, ''Looking for knackers, I suppose. God curse me if she's harmed!''

Tessy lifted a hand to rest it consolingly on Zach's shoulder. ''You'll find her, Zach. Please don't blame yourself!''

''I've no one else to blame, Tessy.'' Zachary stood, his eyes meeting hers for a moment, so intense, so intimate, that Dudley turned away in embarrassment. Then Zachary walked swiftly past Dudley and through the open door without even bidding his lovely lady good-bye or good night.

Dudley knew he ought to follow without a backward glance at the girl posed like a frightened kitten on the bed. But he couldn't help himself. He'd just met her, but compassion and concern for her precarious position as a kept woman niggled at Dudley, poking at him like an accusing finger.

He turned to look at her. Her eyes were fastened to the door through which Zachary had hastily departed. Her unblinking, childlike stare radiated love, hope, dreams that she clung to despite the grasping hands of reality. Then she turned to Dudley, as if she knew he was watching her, and behind the infantile faith reflected in her expression he saw a bone-deep weariness for having to try so hard, for having to fight so fiercely for the mite she'd stolen from life's treasure trove of happiness.

Dudley's heart convulsed with sympathy, for something told him there would never be more than a mite of happiness for Tessy. Not with Lord Roth's brother. He was miles above her socially. She loved him; that was as plain as the freckles on Dudley's face. And possibly Master Zachary loved *her*. But love wasn't enough in a selfish world that spun around a complicated core of rank and money.

"'Twill be well in the end, sir," she said. Lost in his own thoughts, Dudley was startled by Tessy's gently spoken words. He focused his gaze on her face, saw a brave smile tug at the corners of her sweet mouth, and wondered if she was talking about Gabby's plight or her own.

"I hope so, miss," he replied, his sincere wish for a happy conclusion to both potentially dangerous situations lending conviction to his words. "I hope so with all my heart." Then Dudley spun around and marched to the door, cursing the very heart he'd hung his wishes on. He was too tender, too like a woman. And it hurt too much.

The mine shaft gaped like a ravenous mouth, ready to swallow up anyone who dared probe its damp, dark mysteries. Beth stood stiffly just inches from the entrance, her arms crossed in a viselike hug, as if she could hold in all the worry, all the fear. Henry, the stableboy, stood with her, both of them staring into the three- by four-feet entrance to the mine, which had been painstakingly pounded out of the granite hillock years ago by ore-hungry tinners.

Beth knew that just past the mouth of the man-made cave the dimensions widened and heightened, allowing a man of average stature to stand upright. Alex would have to duck his head to traverse the narrow, winding passageways.

When Beth and Henry had arrived at the scene, Jem, the last of the men who'd ridden out with Alex, had been waiting impatiently for them with instructions that they were not to enter the mine for any reason. If Zach showed up—an odd thing for Alex to say, Beth thought, for why wouldn't Zach come?—he was to wait till Alex reemerged before he conducted his own search for Gabby. He said Gabby might be found by then and on her way back to the entrance, and there was no sense in risking his life for nothing. Besides, Zach shouldn't undertake a search by himself. There was safety in numbers.

Beth acknowledged the wisdom in Alex's message, but she had no confidence in Zach's willingness to acquiesce to such a dictum from his brother. Zach adored Gabby and would not be able to stand idly by while a rescue mission was going forth, especially since he probably felt his knowledge of the tin mines would make him most apt to find her.

Night was falling rapidly now, a crimson stain from the dying sun edging the shadowy, irregular horizon of bracken-thick moor. Beth shivered and steeled herself against the chill of a creeping sea mist—and against her own resentful feelings toward Zach.

Why hadn't he listened to her? She had known that Gabby's head would be crowded with creatures from Pye Thatcher's droll and that the little girl would likely not sleep well for some time from thinking about the knackers. But even Beth had not expected Gabby to be so brave as to actually enter one of the dangerous mines to search out a gaggle of the netherworld elves.

Beth's mouth thinned. It was thoughtless of Zach to insist that Gabby be allowed to listen to the droll. No, it was downright irresponsible! It had been arrogant of him to so breezily disregard Beth's concern, to think of her as a fusspot. But lately Zach had been acting oddly. Indeed, his grandfather had demanded a certain amount of structure and responsibility from Zach; now that Chester Hayle was dead, perhaps Zach was feeling a heady sense of freedom and power he had not as yet learned to handle.

He'd been distracted, too, and groundless. Beth had begun to believe that Alex's visit to Pencarrow was not the only reason for Zach's restiveness. But whatever the cause, Zach's behavior was beginning to wear on her patience like a dog gnawing a bone.

Beth shook herself. She had made a promise not to dwell on that problem. The most important thing at the moment was Gabby. She must be found, or Beth could take no joy from any part of life. Grief would strangle all other emotions, even resentment and anger. Passion, too.

Disregarding Henry's curious look, Beth lifted her face to the gloaming sky and fixed her gaze on a faint first star striving valiantly to outshine the waning sun. If it had been a true wishing star, she'd have wished that the passion that rose in her at the sight of Alex, at the nearness of him, at the mere thought of him, would transfer its intensity to Zach. Zach, her betrothed.

But it was more than passion she felt for Alex. Just the thought of him inside the mine, surrounded by crumbling earthen walls supported by rotting timbers, made her blood run cold. With startling clarity she realized that if something happened to Alex, a part of her would die. . . .

Hoofbeats sounded in the distance, drawing nearer. She turned and saw a rider driving his horse hellbent for leather across the moor. His coattails flew in the wind. His pale hair caught the last rays of the sun and gleamed a strange pinkish gold. Zach.

She watched him approach, her mind in a muddle. She didn't know how to feel. She was glad he was there to help find Gabby, but she was angry, too. But no matter how angry she was with Zach, and despite the feelings that grew daily for Alex, she dreaded the thought of Zach entering the mine. Already two people dear to her had disappeared into the bowels of the earth. She hoped Zach would listen to reason and wait outside till Alex emerged from the shaft.

Zach reined in and dismounted, calling to Henry to attend

to his horse. Henry hurried forward, and Zach tossed him the tethers. Zach tugged off his coat and threw it on the ground as he walked quickly toward Beth, his face a mask of grim determination, his eyes narrowed and snapping with emotion. She recognized the most pronounced emotion: He was angry. At himself, she wondered?

"How long have they been inside?" he asked her, his voice harsh and clipped. He never looked at her, but stared instead at the mine shaft. His color was high from the hard ride across Bodmin Moor. Sweat shimmered on his upper lip, and his shirt clung to his damp chest. A part of Beth's anger relented, softened. Zach was obviously worried about Gabby and had come in a great rush. He stood close, and Beth noticed that he smelled like perspiration . . . and honeysuckle. Her brain registered the improbability of such a mixture of scents, then quickly dismissed it.

"They went in about an hour ago, I think. I've lost track of—"

"Bloody hell!" Zach cursed. "They're probably wandering around like a bunch of babes in a maze. I'm going inside. Henry, I'll need a torch."

Beth stepped in front of the mine opening, her hands on her hips. "Alex left word that you're not to go inside. He said if they find Gabby—"

Zach finally looked at her, but it was a look that implied she had suddenly taken leave of her senses, that she was a complete dolt to think she could physically bar him from entering the mine. "I don't care what Alex said; I'm going in. Step aside, Beth."

Her temper flared again, hotter than ever, fed by frustration and fear. She thrust her face to within inches of his. "You refuse to listen to anybody, don't you, Zach? Perhaps I can understand your unwillingness to listen to a mere *woman* like me, but Alex is a man, after all, and your brother, and a good deal older and wiser than you are!"

Zach's jaw clenched, and a muscle ticked in his cheek.

"You didn't waste a bit of time, Beth," he ground out. "You had to throw the blame for this whole mess right at my feet, didn't you?"

Beth raised a contemptuous brow. "If the shoe fits, Zachary . . ."

"I saw no harm in Gabby listening to Pye. I never anticipated this sort of thing happening—"

"I warned you, but you didn't listen."

"Don't tell me you thought she'd run off and look for knackers, for I won't believe you," he retorted.

"No, I never dreamed she'd do this. I didn't know what she'd do. But I had a strong feeling—"

Zach snorted. "You had a *feeling*. Humbug! If a man was to pander to a female every time she had a feeling, this would be a highly disordered world."

Beth stamped her foot. "Oh, why can't you give me a little credit? Why can't you admit I was right, Zach?"

"Is that what this is all about, Beth?" Zach demanded caustically. "If I say, 'Yes, Beth, you were right,' will you be happy?"

Beth felt the tension and fear rise to the surface as tears welled in her eyes. She swallowed hard, trying to rid herself of the aching lump that swelled in her throat. "Of course I won't be happy. I can't be happy till Gabby's found." Her voice quavered, and tears broke loose to stream down her cheeks. "I'm so worried and scared, Zach. I love her! What if she's lost to us forever? I couldn't bear it if—"

Through a salty veil, Beth watched Zach's expression change from belligerence to compassion, his golden eyes clouding with pain. He reached up to thread his long fingers through his hair—his usual gesture indicating mental anguish or turmoil—then his hand darted out suddenly to cup the back of her neck and pull her quickly, roughly, against his chest. Her cheek rested against his damp shirt, and she twined her arms around his waist. She clung to him like a frightened child and sobbed, a part of her ashamed for being so weak, another part of her immeasurably relieved to draw comfort from her childhood friend.

"There, there, Lilibet," Zach soothed as he stroked her hair with one hand and cradled her shoulders with the other. "We'll find Gabby. *I'll* find Gabby," he added, his voice firmer now, threaded with steely resolve. "I'll find her if it's the last thing I do!"

Beth didn't like the implications of such a pronouncement. It sounded foolhardy. She didn't want this to be the last thing Zach did, or the last thing anybody did.

Especially Alex, she thought, a sharp dagger of pain slicing through her.

She lifted her face to look Zach square in the eye. "Don't talk like that. You mustn't take unnecessary risks. Please stay here till Alex returns." *Pray God he would return!*

"I have to go in, Beth. Please understand." His tone was gentle but unquestionably full of determination. Beth's shoulders sagged. He would go no matter what she said or did. "Godspeed," she whispered, pulling out of his embrace to step aside and look at the ground, her fingers interlaced in a prayerlike grip.

He tilted her chin with a curled forefinger, his thumb tenderly brushing her single dimple. He compelled her to look at him. Their eyes locked. Shared worry and pain meshed and pulsated between them. Then he smiled that careless, charming grin of his. "See you soon, Beth." He turned to Henry. "I'll take that torch now."

Moments later Beth watched Zach bend and enter the mine. She stooped at the entrance and watched the torch's orange tip shrink to the size of a firefly and disappear, with Zach, around a curve.

It was cold, so cold. Gabby shivered and drew her knees up to her chest, resting her cheek against the soft, comforting velvet of her riding skirt. Her bottom hurt. The ground was hard and pebbled with small, sharp rocks. She squeezed her eyes shut and tried to ignore the shuffle of rats in the darkness. The thick tallow work-candle she'd borrowed from the pantry had been snuffed out long ago by a dollop of water that fell from the ceiling of the mine. She had no idea how far she was from the entrance, but in the pitch black she dared not try to find her way there.

She'd seen no knackers, no elves with jaunty caps and pickaxes smiling upside down and backwards at her between their legs. She'd seen only rats, the size of which she could only guess at by the darting shadows she'd seen by candlelight. They looked bigger than the puppies at Pencarrow.

Something brushed against her ankle, something long and prickly-soft like a rat's tail. She gasped and reared up, flailing her arms in the space around her. Connecting with nothing, Gabby wrapped herself into an even more compact ball than before.

"I'm not a coward," she said aloud, her voice oddly intrusive and defiant in the still musty air that cocooned her nearly to the point of suffocation. Her eyes stung with first tears.

"Zach, where are you?" she said. "I'm not afraid, really. Just worried, you know. You've always come for me before."

She lifted her head and stared into the darkness. "But I shall do as you told me when I was a bit worried about riding my horse for the first time. I shall say it now." She jutted out her chin determinedly. "I am Gabrielle Louisa Tavistock. I can do anything I set my mind to do because I'm an exceptional young lady. And I'm not afraid." Then louder: "I am not afraid!"

The words eddied in the dark, secret nooks of the mine. The mine, as still and black as the grave, Mr. Thatcher had said, where no birds sang, where there was no wind in the trees and no mother's voice calling you to dinner.

Mama! Oh, how she wanted Mama! Gabby pressed her face against her skirt again, tears sliding down her cheek. "Zach will come. I know he will. I'm not afraid," she whispered.

CHAPTER
nine

ALEX'S THROAT WAS coated with silt. He craved a quenching drink from a cool well. Hell, even the brackish water that guttered along the mine walls was beginning to look tempting. But the filth-infested liquid would surely kill anyone who dared drink it. He prayed that Gabby would have sense enough to leave it alone. His eyes ached from peering into the dark, and hope of finding Gabby sputtered as low as his torch.

"M'lord, we'd best head back," suggested one of the men. "Our lights're about done fer."

"I know," Alex replied on a deep sigh. "But are you sure you followed each tunnel to the end?" He fixed his keen gaze on each man in turn, looking for shifting eyes. If any of them could not return his questioning look straight on, he'd have to suspect that they'd been too afraid to follow the passageway to its conclusion because of the alarming fragility of the walls. Alex himself had been horrified to discover them so very tenuous. One false stagger against them would precipitate a collapse. But all the men appeared as concerned and sorry as he was.

"Trouble is, m'lord," said the same man, an older silver-haired fellow with some apparent authority among them, "we can't be sure all the tunnels was seen and searched. There be spots hid from view. There be pockets and holes in the walls a little bit of a girl like Miss Gabrielle

151

might squeeze into and find herself in another section of the mine. Could take days t' find her.''

"Blast it, man, we don't have days," Alex rasped. "She'll die of thirst—or something worse!"

"The master'd know where t' find 'er," piped up a man from the back of the group. "Master Zachary knows these mines like the back o' his hand."

"So I've heard," Alex said dryly. "Let's return to the entrance. I hope Zach will be waiting for us there. We can get fresh torches and commence another search under his direction. After we've told him where we've already been, it should be a rather easy task to know where to go next."

Following the markings they'd carefully carved into the timbers at intervals, and particularly at junctions where tunnels split and went in two directions, they returned to the entrance. Alex was looking forward to a drink of water and a glimpse of fresh English sky to fortify him for the continued search within the close confines of the mine. But he was not looking forward to telling Beth the bad news.

In the distance he saw the opening, an irregular pale gray circle suspended in a wall of dirt and rock. Just beyond, he observed a torch's blaze, its reddish-gold aura wreathing a woman's silhouette. It was Beth waiting there. Waiting for him? Worried about him as well as Gabby? His chest constricted joyfully, painfully, at the thought.

"Alex? Alex, is that you?"

Her low voice echoed through the tunnel, warming his heart, warming his blood. "Yes, Beth," he called back, his own voice gritty and strained.

"Good! Did you find her? Where's Gabby?"

They'd reached the shaft, and Alex bent to ease himself through the opening. He handed his torch to Henry, grasped Beth by the arm, and pulled her away from the curious stares of the other men. She'd held up wonderfully when he'd first told her that Gabby was missing, but could she continue to shore up her feelings? Could she continue to be so brave?

By now Beth surely knew that Gabby had not been found, but her eyes strained desperately toward the file of men climbing out of the mine, as if she might still see one of the Pencarrow servants carrying the child in his arms.

"Beth, we didn't find her." He didn't touch her, but he could feel the tremors of remorse rack her frame. He wanted to pull her into the circle of his arms and comfort her. She turned and looked up at him, her eyes tear-bright with barely suppressed anguish.

"But she must be inside . . . somewhere," Beth said hoarsely. "You're not quitting, are you?" Her hair was loose and tangled by the wind. Moonlight picked out honeyed highlights.

"Of course not," Alex swiftly assured her, his hands fairly itching to grab her by the shoulders and pull her close against him. But earlier that day when she'd touched *him*, she'd responded like a thief before the magistrate, guilt marking her every feature. He crossed his arms, burying his hands in the folds of his shirtsleeves. "Zach can help us now. Where is he?" Alex looked around. He'd been so caught up with concern over Beth's reaction to Gabby's continued disappearance that he'd almost forgotten about Zach.

"He's not here," Beth answered.

"He didn't come?" Alex had wondered if Zach might regard Gabby's latest runaway antic as a harmless and trivial lark, like the previous episodes. It would be especially hard to drag him away from Tessy, too, since they'd been apart for so long.

"No, he came. But he went inside the mine." Beth's voice was flat with resignation. "As usual, he would not listen to me."

"Or me," Alex added grimly. "The foolish jackanapes. Now he's in there alone, blast 'im!"

"He knows the mines well," Beth said hopefully.

"Yet he's not been in them, I'll wager, for many years. How can we assist him if he does not wait for us? Now there's no telling where he is or where we ought to go!"

"What are you going to do?" Beth's eyes were wide and fearful.

"After we've had a drink, I'll take a couple of men and go back inside."

"But you don't know where he is. Now you will be looking for Zach *and* Gabby." Beth reached out with both hands and grasped Alex's arm.

Alex's muscles convulsed under the light pressure of her fingers. His eyes met hers, and he saw the worry. She was fearful for *him* as well as for her sister and Zach!

"The mines are old, Alex," she went on. "Judging by the men's expressions and whispers, I suspect that the walls are in even worse condition than I thought, though you will not tell me the extent of their decrepit state for fear of alarming me. But I'm dreadfully frightened for all of you. Please, *please* be careful!"

Alex placed his hand over hers, stroking her small fingers tenderly. "Never fear, I shall be careful. I will find Gabby and that headstrong bantling brother of mine, and I have every intention of emerging from that hellish pit in prime twig. I've a great deal left to do in this life, and I'm not of a mind to leave it just yet."

Beth was electrified by Alex's touch and the determined tone of his voice. She felt certain that he would take no foolish risks, but she was confident that he was perfectly capable of accomplishing his mission anyway. There was a promise implied in his words, too, as if part of what he had left to do in this life concerned her. But she could not think of that now.

After Alex took a long drink from an oaken bucket of water, he took two men and fresh torches and went inside the mine. Beth sighed shakily. It seemed endless, this waiting. She felt so helpless. She supposed it was a woman's curse to wait while men placed themselves in peril, sometimes for the purpose of evil, like war, or for good, as in this case. If only they were not so essential to her happiness—Zach *and* Alex.

Zachary hadn't been inside the mine since he reached his majority, but its twists and turns seemed as familiar as if he'd been there the day before. He thought it ironic that Gabby had chosen this particular mine. It had been his favorite because of its unpredictable meanderings and its hidden chambers. But why would Gabby be drawn here over all the other mines? On the outside, it was no more remarkable than the others, yet she'd chosen this one above the rest to search for the knackers.

It was uncanny the way Gabby found danger, he mused as he quickly traversed the passageway, waving his torch back and forth to observe the unstable condition of the walls. Lord, they looked as though a hearty sneeze would send them tumbling down! If the Pencarrow servants knocked about carelessly, they'd all be entombed alive. A cave-in in one part of the mine could easily initiate a full-blown collapse.

Within minutes he'd reached his destination—the first offshoot from the main tunnel. It would have been indiscernible to all but the most practiced eye or to the eyes of an intrepid child. But it would take hours or even days for an average person to find the crack hidden behind the jutting rock that led to another smaller tunnel. He stuck the torch through the opening and tried to peer beyond it, though the glare made his attempts futile.

"Gabby? Gabby, sweeting, are you in there?" he called. There was no reply, but if she was hurt or asleep she might not be able to answer. He pulled the torch back and eyed the opening, wondering if he could still squeeze through. It looked like a close fit, but he was leaner and less muscular than Alex, who took after Grandfather Hayle. Zach smiled grimly. For once he was glad he took after his father and the Wickham side of the family.

He lifted one leg through, ducked his head under and in, then carefully eased himself into the narrow opening, scraping his chest and back as he went. He held his breath as dirt and rocks loosened and sprinkled him with a fine, powdery gravel. Last came his other leg and the torch he held in his right hand.

This tunnel was in worse condition than the others. Less timber had been used to shore up the walls. They looked fragile and extremely dangerous. The air was thick and dank. Water dripped from the ceiling and pooled along the sides, as it did in the stagnant sewers of London. His shadow loomed up and shuddered in the flickering torchlight, and rats scurried at his feet. God, poor Gabby! How frightened she must be. His heart ached for her.

"Gabby?" he called, turning down another corridor and then another. "Gabby, are you here?" Just when he was beginning to lose hope of finding her in that part of the mine, he heard her voice, muffled at first, then louder, more sure.

"Zach! Oh, Zach, you've come!"

And there she was. She would have been horrified to see the veritable herd of rats she shared her dark space with, their beady black eyes shining in the light of his torch. But Gabby seemed to see only him, a smile of tremendous relief and joy lighting up her pale, strained little face. She was huddled in the middle of the passageway, balled up like a porcupine under attack.

"Gabby! Thank God," he cried, bending on one knee to embrace her trembling form.

"I knew you would come," she mumbled against his shoulder. "You always come."

"I always shall, you little noddy," he assured her with rough affection.

"Don't scold me," she pleaded, lifting her face to look at him beseechingly.

"I won't, but Beth will," he predicted soberly. "And I shall be scolded, too. Justly so, I suspect," he added on a sigh.

Gabby looked at him, and Zach could tell she didn't understand what he meant. But that was just as well. Time enough for the poor little wretch to learn the complexities of mature relationships. Let her enjoy her innocence while she could.

"Let's get out of here. If you hold the torch in front of you—just so—I can carry you. Shall I carry you, Gabby?"

Gabby nodded gratefully. He lifted her, and they wended their way back toward the crack that opened to the main tunnel. Suddenly Zach stepped on a rat, and the nerve-shattering screech of the injured rodent sent him twirling around in surprise. He fell heavily against the wall, and a soft whoosh of dirt emptied onto the ground in front of him. Then, like blood spouting from a mortal wound, more and more dirt followed—mounding, building. Zach stood for one horrified, never-ending moment watching the wall dissolve.

"Damn!" he muttered, the mild epithet a monumental understatement for the mix of terror and anger that coursed through him. If Gabby died in this mine, buried beneath the earth as her sweet breath was crushed out of her, it would be his fault entirely. Gabby must have sensed the increased danger, for Zach felt her body stiffen.

Spurred on by Gabby's fear into desperate action, Zach hurried toward the opening. He could see it now, but he could also hear rotted wood straining and splitting. All the walls were crumbling. He darted a quick look behind him, but it was a senseless, instinctive gesture, for it was impossible to see anything. He could well imagine the sights hidden in the darkness, however, for he could hear the increased chatter and scurry of rats and the ominous gushing of heavy earth filling the passageway. Now there was a rumbling. The gravitational forces of nature were taking over. Soon the whole mine would collapse.

Zach ran. He stumbled on a rock and lurched forward, catching himself just before they both tumbled to the ground. Gabby squealed and dropped the torch. Zach could not stop to pick it up. Gabby wrapped her arms about Zach's neck and buried her face against his shoulder, whimpering softly in his ear. Lord, how was he to find his way out of there now? They were caught in utter darkness. But he had to try for Gabby's sake . . . and for Tessy's.

Suddenly Zach saw a light at the opening he was blindly approaching at breakneck speed. Someone was holding a torch through to light his way.

They reached the opening, and the torch withdrew. Zach peeled Gabby's clinging hands from about his neck and passed her easily through to waiting arms on the other side.

"Come on, Zach, hurry up!" It was Alex. His shadowed face appeared briefly, backlit by the garish orange aura of the torch.

"Take Gabby. Go on. I'll be along," he panted, hitching one leg through the opening.

"I've sent her ahead with the others. Hurry up! I'll not leave without you, brother!"

"More the fool you, brother," Zach retorted, though his heart swelled with love and a sense of kinship with Alex.

Alex thrust his hand through the crack. His muscular fingers tangled in Zach's shirtfront, the material wadding in his palm. He dragged Zach through none too gently, and none too soon. Zach fell against Alex, and a plume of dirt, like powder from a cannon blast, billowed through the hole. The noise increased to a deafening thunder as the walls inside the mine fell like dominoes. The ground shook like a harlots' den on Judgment Day. Alex pinned a dazed Zach against his side with an iron grip and propelled him toward the main shaft, hauling him to his feet when he stumbled.

Zach could see the shaft just ahead. The men were lifting Gabby through, and then Beth was reaching out for her, cradling her, welcoming her. Thank God Gabby was safe! But whether he and Alex would make it out was still very much in question. Clouds of dry, choking dirt filled the air, obscuring his vision, filling his lungs. The walls all around him were slipping, dissolving, the timber splitting, shifting.

Moments passed like years. Panic was replaced by deep, soul-wrenching remorse. He would not spend another night in Tessy's arms. Tessy . . .

Alex was determined they'd make it. Just a few more steps. Just a few feet stretched between him and Beth. He hadn't done with living. He would not go to his grave without kissing her, without loving her as a man loved a woman. *He loved her!*

Despite Beth's kicking and screaming, the men pulled her away from the mine shaft. It was too dangerous for her to stand so close, especially since she'd been leaning in to watch for Zach and Alex.

"Won't do ye any good standin' in harm's way, miss," said Henry, whose firm grip on her belied his gentle words. "If they're goin' to make it, they'll make it whether ye're standin' there or here. Watch and pray."

Beth prayed hard. She squeezed her eyes shut and promised God everything from her firstborn son to her own chastity. Then she prayed for the ability to keep her promises.

"They made it!" Henry's buoyant words ended her prayer on a note of thanksgiving. She opened her eyes and watched Alex and Zach stumble arm in arm from the mine to collapse on the ground, coughing and gasping for air. They were covered from head to foot in dust. She rushed forward, then stopped inches away. Her inclination was to go to Alex first, but it would not have been seemly for her to show affection for Alex in front of the servants. Indeed, it would not have been seemly in front of anyone to ignore her fiancé till she'd showered his brother with kisses.

So Beth stood there crying, aching to embrace them both, and embracing neither.

Beth stepped out of the copper tub and onto the glazed delft tile in front of the fireplace. A low-burning fire crackled on the grate. She'd washed her hair, and it streamed down her back in rivulets. Darkened by the water, it was more the color of walnuts than chestnuts. She picked up the towel Sadie had placed on the rocking chair and buffed her skin till it was pink, dry, and warm, then gently rubbed her hair and ran her fingers through it till it was damp-dry and fluffy. Untamed by the stern hand of her abigail and that lady's boar-bristle brush, Beth's hair fell in rippling waves about her shoulders. She reached for her white cambric night rail, pulled it over her head, and began the long process of buttoning up the front. She had no servant to assist her, having sent Sadie to bed after Gabby's bath.

Since they'd returned to Pencarrow, Mrs. Tavistock had refused to allow Gabby out of her sight. Even while Gabby bathed, she had hovered over her, wringing her hands and watching her younger child as if she were a precious jewel that might be stolen away at any moment. Now they were both asleep in the bedchamber across the hall from Beth's usual room. When Beth had last looked in on them, they'd been curled up together in the center of the bed, Mrs. Tavistock's arm draped over Gabby. It had been quite a shock to their mother when she'd awakened from her drugged sleep to learn that Gabby was missing in a tin mine, and the servants had had the devil of a time calming and controlling her till Gabby's return to the house.

Since everyone was miserably dirty and exhausted, Alex had deemed it best that Mrs. Tavistock and the girls stay at

Pencarrow for the night. Beth was happy to comply and Mrs. Tavistock too weak to protest even if she'd wanted to. Zach offered no opinion about this plan, nor did he comment on the fact that Alex—calmly issuing orders to the servants and returning something like normalcy to the household—seemed more the master of Pencarrow than he was.

In fact, Zach seemed so subdued and sorry about the day's happenings that Beth immediately and completely forgave him for the part his thoughtlessness had played in the near tragedy. He had gone to his bedchamber upon their return and had stayed there. Beth hoped he was making good resolutions. Gabby was quiet and submissive, too, but that could be attributed merely to exhaustion.

After Sadie had heated so many buckets of water and toted them up the stairs, Beth took pity on her and sent her to bed. Her mother would have disapproved, of course, but Beth knew she was perfectly capable of bathing and preparing herself for bed without a servant's assistance. She was glad to find one of her night rails tucked away in a drawer from another night she'd spent at Pencarrow.

The mantel clock struck midnight. Beth twisted a small, pearlescent button through each corresponding finely sewn hole as the chimes sounded through the quiet room, and still there were more buttons to fasten. Now the room was as silent as before, lit only by the brace of candles on the piecrust table by the tub and the low fire. The silence and darkness of the room ought to have been calming, relaxing. But Beth was restless. She padded on bare feet across the carpet to the window, still buttoning the night rail. A soft, cool breeze lifted her hair and toyed with the lace ribbons at her bodice. Beth breathed deeply. There in the night was life, a whole world of movement and sound.

The moon was nearly full, like a round of cream cheese with the barest sliver removed. The grass of the formal grounds below her window shimmered like fingers of light.

The fluttering leaves of the ash trees that shaded the topiary of an evening flashed like fobs on a dandy and rustled like tissue paper in a gift box. Beyond the gate the creek gurgled and splashed. Frogs and crickets sang their courting songs, and the distant cawing of sea gulls floated on a fine mist that blew in from the sea.

She ought to have been tired, but she wasn't. She ought to have been concerned about the changes that daily occurred in her feelings toward Zach, but she pressed that worry to the back of her mind to dust off and consider when she wasn't so attuned to the thrumming, living energy that stirred the night and stirred her blood, too.

Oh, how she wished she had an outlet for this odd sense of well-being, this strange urge to embrace each moment of life as if it were her last! Had today's near fatal accident brought on this renewed appreciation for her mere existence in such a perfect, imperfect world? Despite its beauty, it *was* imperfect, this world she was living in. If it were perfect, she'd be betrothed to Alex and not to Zach.

Beth shook her head and pressed her fingers against her temples. No! She would not think of herself as unlucky or as a victim of misfortune. She loved Zach—like a brother. In the truth-seeking part of her brain, those three words tolled like a death knell. *Like a brother.*

Beth could stand this restlessness no longer. She turned and left the chamber, determined to leave her vexing thoughts behind her as well. She closed the door and tiptoed quickly down the hall, down the main stairs, and around to the servants' entrance that opened to the kitchen gardens. She unlocked the door with a key that hung on the wall next to it and let herself out. With each step, the smooth, hard cobbles of the garden walkway gave the soles of her feet an icy kiss. How stupid of her, she thought on a giggle, to have come outside without shoes to protect her pampered feet. But she wouldn't go back.

She opened the ivy-covered garden gate and was surprised by a rusty squeak, a noise she'd paid no heed to before, but which now caught her attention quite effectively. She glanced up at the windows of the house. All was dark. No one would hear her or see her leave the premises. Where was she going? She didn't know. She didn't care. Something beckoned to her. Something as intangible as fairy dust, but as compelling as love's first embrace.

She walked past the flower beds filled with ghostly mock orange blossoms and the candescent globes of white roses and tobacco flowers. She left the formal grounds through a side gate that was always left unlatched at night—for Zach's convenience, she supposed. Here the grass grew tall and feathery, bending to the wind's will. Tonight the carpet of grass undulated like a soothed sea after a storm, still full of movement, but soft, soft. . . .

She made her way through this verdant sea at a leisurely pace, enjoying the tickle of the seed-tipped blades against her calves. The grass tugged at the hem of her night rail like an insistent child or an eager lover. But she would not succumb to this earthy invitation to sink down into a bed as soft as moss. She would go to the creek and sit beneath the ancient oak tree whose huge twisted roots writhed above the earth, seeking sunshine.

It was dark beneath the oak tree where the moon could not cast its light. Shadows from the leaves and smaller limbs of the tree danced on the ground below it. Then, when she was just a few feet away, another shadow caught Beth's attention. At first it seemed just a part of the oak's thick trunk, but it slowly separated and took on a life of its own. It moved toward her.

Beth stopped and stood deathly still, her exhilaration turned to panic. Had she been summoned by demons to her death? Had some creature from Pye Thatcher's store of fairy tales charmed her away from the safety of her home? But knackers and pixies and even water sprites were not so tall.

"Beth?"

Her heart lurched and twisted inside her. Alex! But while he still stood in the shadows of the tree, her fevered mind thought it might not be Alex but some creature masquerading in the form so beloved to her. Could fairies and witches conjure up so true a voice, so deep and melodious a tone?

He stepped into the moonlight. "Beth? What are you doing outside at this hour?"

Ah, here was substance—he was scolding her! "I'm walking," she said. She held her breath. He was beautiful, so beautiful. He was dressed in dark pantaloons tucked into boots, and his white shirt was half unbuttoned, the sleeves rolled up to just below his elbows. He looked very much the way he did yesterday morning on the beach, except more chest was showing. She remembered how it felt to touch him there, and she shivered.

"Foolish girl, you're cold," he said, stepping forward as if to lend her warmth. Yet how could he? He had no coat to lend her. He had only his arms. "Why are you gadding about in your night rail, Beth?" His eyes were averted, as if he'd suddenly realized how near naked she was. She looked down at her gown and saw how the moonlight filtered through the thin fabric and how the wind molded it to her body. She was oddly unashamed. And at the moment—for this bewitching night, perhaps—she felt no guilt.

"I don't know why I came outside," she answered, as puzzled as he was by her impulsive behavior, her total disregard for propriety. "It just seemed as though everything outside my window was alive and free, and everything within so dull and stifling." Her brows knitted. "I don't know why. I just came." Suddenly she lifted her chin, saying daringly, "Perhaps I knew you waited for me. Perhaps you beckoned me here. Have you been thinking of me, Alex?"

He studied her. They were separated by just two arms' breadth. His hair gleamed glossy black in the moonlight, blue lights threading through the waves that fell forward to skim his roguishly arched brows. So like a rogue he looked, except for his expression. He appeared deeply troubled. He did not share the moon-spawned ease of mind that loosened her tongue so, nor did he enjoy a similar relief from fetters forged by guilt.

"Go inside, Beth. Do it now!" he urged her, his tone harsh and insistent. He turned away and walked back into the shadow of the huge tree.

She stepped forward bravely. "Alex, we must talk. I'm so confused about my feelings for Zach, for you. . . . I need to—"

"You're not dressed for talking," came his brusque reply. Then, more gently, he said, "We've nothing to talk about."

"Nothing? That's a clanker if ever I heard one."

Alex chuckled, but a bitter note emerged. "Where'd you learn that cant phrase, gosling? From Zach, I'll wager."

"Where else? I've traveled little, you know," she answered defensively.

"Precisely." He hissed the word, enunciating each syllable. "You don't have a farthing's worth of worldly sense, Beth, or you would not be here with me tonight."

Frustrated, Beth pressed curled fists against her hips. "I did not plan this, you know. But since we're both here, and alone, I'm going to speak of this . . . this *thing* that lies between us. I'm going to speak plain and clear and loud, since there's no one in the wide world to hear us but the toads and crickets." She flung her arms in an all-encompassing gesture. When Alex did not turn or reply, Beth continued.

"We both know what's happening between us. We both know that I was more pleased to see you than Zach when you climbed out of that mine together." A sob caught in her throat, and tears stung her eyelids. "I don't know how or why. All I know, Alex, is that I've come to cherish you more than Zach. And I don't know what to do!''

"Go inside, Beth. I implore you." Alex turned slightly, and a shaft of moonlight pierced the shadows to illuminate his profile. He pressed the tips of his fingers, splayed and taut, across his forehead.

Beth stepped forward till he heard her approach and glanced over his shoulder. He walked swiftly away to lean one hand against the trunk of the tree, his head bowed. Beth followed till she stood just behind him. "Tell me you don't love me, Alex. Then I'll go. Tell me you don't love me, and I'll leave you willingly.''

Silence. She waited, but he did not move or speak. The crickets' chant sounded through the night, but its lulling rhythm was out of stride with Beth's fiercely beating heart. The leaves in the boughs above them rustled noisily, then calmed, ebbing and flowing with the wind's tide. Her breath came fast and shallow. Her skin was dewy and tingling with anticipation. It was as if she stood on the edge of a precipice, looking down, readying herself to jump. It seemed that paradise awaited her there, but she could not see it clearly. A cautious part of her feared purgatory waited instead.

Suddenly he turned, a low growl of anger or passion or resignation escaping his throat as he caught her waist and pulled her against him. His large hands were warm and strong and urgent, burning through the thin material of her night rail. Her breasts collided with his firm chest, soft curves melting and molding against masculine contours. She braced herself by grasping his upper arms. His mouth lowered and claimed hers.

Beth was stunned by the feelings that coursed through her as his lips moved over hers. This was no tentative, wooing kiss of a tender suitor. This was a bruising, savage kiss that demanded Beth's complete submission. It was pleasure so akin to violence that she ought to have been frightened, but a primitive part of her understood, submitted, and responded eagerly to Alex's passion. Too long! They'd been suppressing this need between them for too long. She cried out and in so doing opened her mouth to his.

Alex thrust his tongue into the wet, warm haven of her mouth, swirling and mating it with hers. Though Zach had kissed her, she'd never experienced anything so divinely intimate as this wonderful magic Alex was doing with his lips, his tongue. His hands stroked her back, his strong fingers kneading the tender dips below her shoulder blades and down into the subtle curve of her lower back.

Beth moaned and trembled, clasping him about the neck, pulling herself up on tiptoe to press closer, closer. . . .

"God, Beth," Alex groaned on an outflow of shuddering breath that warmed her ear. "Forgive me. I've wanted you so long, I'm an animal. I . . ."

Beth didn't care, didn't want to hear apologies for an all-consuming need she shared. She just wanted more. She kissed the curve of his jaw, stubbly with a day's growth, then his neck, and down farther till she found the hollow of his throat. He was still, so still she thought he must be holding his breath. She slipped her hands inside his shirt and fanned her fingers over his chest, the soft, dark, springy hair so sensually satisfying to her tender palms. She followed each exploring caress with a kiss, her face burrowed in his chest. He smelled so good, so musky clean.

She found his nipple, and not knowing or caring whether decently brought-up young women did such things, she acted instinctively and kissed him there, then slipped out her tongue to lave the puckering bud.

Suddenly she felt a gush of breath escape him. His hands slid down her back to cup her buttocks and lift her swiftly, surely against him, against the hard bulge of his manhood. Then he turned and pressed her against the trunk of the tree, pinning her between the abrasive bark and the rocklike urgency of his aroused body.

Beth gasped, her head falling back, baring her neck to

him. He uttered a snarl of pleasure, primal and male, as he devoured her neck with kisses. Her breasts were heavy and taut. His hands held her up just under her arms, bracing her against the tree. His thumbs grazed the fullness of her breasts, teasing, taunting. Then he suddenly lowered his head, and through the thin fabric of her gown he found the pebble-hard tip of her nipple and drew it into his mouth, sucking, enveloping, arousing.

Beth's head lolled back and forth. She was awash in sensations so strong and wonderfully delicious she could barely think. But over and over a thought emerged from the mire: This is right. This is how I want to feel about the man I'm pledged to share my life with.

But another voice intruded—that of her conscience nagging her, accusing her. She'd promised God that if Zach and Alex and Gabby escaped from the tin mine, she would not betray her betrothed with his brother. She would not give in to the need that grew heavier and more demanding day by day. But this need, like a breeding woman's nine-month babe, had painfully pushed its way, kicking and screaming, into full, flourishing life. She could not, would not stop, despite the sure knowledge that on the morrow she would regret her actions.

God forgive me, she silently pleaded. Zach, forgive me, she added, hardly knowing whom she sinned against more—Zach or the Almighty. But without Alex she was empty. So empty. Even if he went away and she never saw him again, if he loved her now, she'd have a part of him always.

"Alex," she murmured, tunneling her fingers through his thick silken hair. "Love me. Fill me, Alex. Please!"

CHAPTER
ten

ALEX LIFTED HIS head. It was dark in the shadows, but luminescent beams trickled through the pattering leaves, touching Beth's pale cheek and revealing her eyes to him, half closed and burning with passion. Alex's mind was fogged with desire. Had Beth truly begged him to make love to her, to *fill* her? It was what he wished most to hear and yet what he dreaded above all else. Taking Beth's virginity would be the ultimate betrayal of his brother. It would be unforgivable, the very essence of disloyalty.

God, but she was a picture of utterly innocent, utterly natural sensuality! Her head fell back against the tree trunk, her hair a satiny cascade. She clung to his shoulders, her fingers curled and tight. Her lips were parted and moist from his plundering kisses. Her night rail hung crooked, nearly exposing one white shoulder. The front of her bodice had a circle of wetness over one breast where he'd taken her peaked nipple into his mouth and . . .

Good Lord, he had her pinned against the tree! What kind of a man—nay, what kind of an animal was he? If she had not startled him with her beseeching, sweetly seductive words, would he have taken her like a savage, rending her tender maiden's body with the thrusts of a beast?

"I think I'm losing my mind," he whispered, gently easing her away from the tree and lifting her into his arms. Like a confiding child, she nuzzled her head under his chin, draped her arms about his neck, and sighed. Her breath was sweet, yet laced with the musky essence he recognized as his own scent. He swallowed hard. She was so childlike in her trustful, complete giving of herself, so unlike the jaded caution of experienced lovers who were afraid to give without first knowing what would be accepted. But her body was that of a woman—rounded of breast, slender of waist, subtly curved at the hips, and so responsive and ready for the gentle ministerings of a first lover. *Gentle*, he repeated to himself. Not pinned against a tree to be ravaged like a Drury Lane whore.

He carried her to the tall grass that bent in the soughing breeze and laid her down. He knelt beside her and sat back against his heels, his hands spread flat on his thighs. She'd thrown her arms above her head, the palms of both hands lying limp and open, her eyes slanted and heavy with need, yet patient, as if the two of them had all the time in the world, though Alex felt deep in his heart that they hadn't any time that wasn't stolen. An ache knotted in his throat, constricting his breathing.

The traitorous moon shone fully on her now, rendering her night rail diaphanous, exposing too clearly the dark thicket of hair at the apex of her thighs, the deep rose areolae of her breasts. His groin pulsated with need, need for Beth and only Beth. He closed his eyes, saying a desperate prayer. He had to resist this sweet madness, yet how could he do so without hurting and humiliating her?

Beth seemed to sense his turmoil. He felt her small fingers glide over his, then clasp his wrist. He opened his eyes and watched as she drew his hand down to tenderly kiss the ridge of his knuckles. "Alex, please don't think of leaving me now." She turned his hand and kissed the palm, the satin of her lips searing his flesh. "Don't think of anyone or anything but this." She tugged, gently urging him down to her, to her parted waiting lips, to her eager, compliant body.

Goaded beyond endurance, Alex lifted his face to the

star-studded canopy that separated man from heaven, cursing a God that would demand so cruel a test of loyalty: allegiance to a brother at the expense of true love's fulfillment. For it *was* true love he felt for Beth, a kind of worshipful devotion that made all his past dalliances with women a travesty. Every day, every hour of his life had been preparing him for this moment of awakening, for this sure knowledge of a perfect counterpart of self—spiritually and physically.

"Why must it be so?" he whispered, anguish cutting through his heart like a saber. "Why must I choose?" Then he bent to Beth, lowering himself atop her, balancing on his forearms to spare her the full weight of his body. In that moment he made his choice, silently begging Zach's forgiveness. Then he seized Beth's hot, sweet mouth with hungry, possessive kisses.

Beth had heard the tormented whispers, felt them tremble in the humid air all about her before they floated heavenward. Yes, why? But only God knew why. At this moment she had no patience for a soul-draining confrontation with deity concerning the trials required of mankind. For Beth, heaven and all its glittery promises paled beside the bliss of Alex's arms, Alex's body holding her to earth, to a paradise they'd create through their own giving and taking in the eternal sacrament of love.

Beth's arms tightened around Alex as he drank deeply from her mouth. She stroked the strong cords of his neck, then allowed her hands to roam freely over the smooth musculature of his broad back, then down, slowly down to his firm buttocks. Alex gasped in astonished pleasure, their panting breath commingling as their mouths broke contact.

"Beth, you've bewitched me," he murmured. "So full of passion and curiosity. 'Tis witchery, is it not?" He shifted a little to the side and slid one long, sinewy leg between her thighs.

Honeyed heat suffused Beth, and a sweet tension gath-

ered in her lower stomach like a brewing summer storm on
the moor, dark and rumbling, yet promising cool relief in its
aftermath. Her whole body ached, yearning to be closer,
flesh to flesh, with Alex. She arched, thrusting her breasts
hard against him. His right hand reached up to cup her
breast, kneading its softness in his warm palm, gently
tugging on the turgid nipple.

"T-too much. My gown . . . There's too much between
us, Alex," she murmured, grasping at the ribbons of her
night rail. "I want to feel you next to me."

Since realizing that he'd crushed her against a tree trunk,
Alex had tried to tamp down his fiery need. He didn't want
to hurt her, physically or emotionally, by going too fast,
though the throbbing tumescence of his loins demanded
release. But her words inflamed him. She was as eager as
he, as needful of the ultimate joining. He braced himself on
one elbow and scanned the front closure of her night rail
with desperate eyes. Damnation, she was shackled from
neck to ankle by a row of tiny buttons only the most patient,
dexterous pair of female hands could manipulate. Alex was
not feeling at all patient—or the least bit female, for that
matter!

"Hold still, love. I'm going to rip your gown," he
warned her in a tremulous voice that strove to be matter-
of-fact. Her eyes widened, and her mouth parted on a sharp
intake of breath, but she said nothing. With her silence she'd
given her permission and expressed her own impatience to
lie naked before him. His ardor fanned by this further proof
of her innocent passion, he grasped the placket of her night
rail and yanked, the sound of rending cloth a savage symbol
of their violent need for each other. As tiny pearl buttons
flew, winking in the moonlight like gossamer bubbles, Beth
gasped.

Alex rose to his knees and looked down at Beth. The
night rail was parted, exposing the white porcelain perfection of her body. Then, while he stared, awed, she slid her

arms out of the sleeves and patted down the night rail beneath her like a coverlet. It seemed so deliberate, so pragmatic a move, but she trembled like a fragile daisy in the wind. Then Beth lay down and returned his steady gaze, her bottom lip caught between her teeth, her eyes conflicting pools of desire and fear. She lifted her arms, bidding him to come to her.

A fierce protectiveness surged through Alex, as strong as the pent-up longings that held him hostage. He must be gentle with her. He must not cause her any more pain than absolutely necessary. He knew instinctively that it was the pain she feared, since pain was a happenstance of a woman's first experience, the tale of which she did not fail to pass on to following generations, sometimes with dramatic exaggeration.

"Patience, sweet Beth," he crooned. Then he began to remove his own clothing.

Beth lowered her arms and laid her hands, palm down, on her flat stomach. Mesmerized, she watched Alex pull his shirttail out of his trousers and tug the fine muslin up and over his head. Inch by inch his taut stomach, with its narrow swirl of dark hair that wickedly disappeared into the band of his breeches, was revealed. Then his chest, so sculpted, so brown. Ah, just as she remembered! Beth's heart beat a fervid, fluttering tempo. Her breath was ragged and erratic.

Alex pared off his boots and stockings, then stood up to remove his pants. Beth's eyes widened when he unbuttoned his trousers, drew them down, and kicked them effortlessly off, leaving them in a pool at his feet. Beth's pulse increased in volume to thunder in her ears. She did not remember that particular part of his body being so very large, so firm and . . .

He bent and lay down beside her, taking her gently into his arms. She could feel his manhood pressing against her stomach, heavy and hot. She whimpered, but not from fear.

The power of it, the pure male strength of it, made her weak with yearning.

"Don't be afraid, Beth," he soothed. "I'll prepare you. Trust me."

Beth nodded and swallowed, from nervousness or excitement, she knew not which. Then he kissed her again, his mouth settling over hers with slow and purposeful intent, his tongue delving, deepening. His hands glided over her body, every secret, sensitive nerve aquiver from his masterful touch. Beth was aware of so many feelings, so many tactile impressions. Cool night air against damp skin, especially where he'd last kissed her. The smell of him—so richly masculine, a mix of sandalwood and salt. The taste of his mouth—brandy-laced.

When he took her nipple into his mouth, without the cambric gown as a barrier between, she thought she might die. While he tugged and nibbled, sucked and tantalized with swirling motions, spears of pleasure radiated outward, downward, coiling in her stomach, making her legs limp and languorous. The tension in that most private, sensitive part of her built and blossomed. Agony. Ecstasy. They were one and the same. She felt his hand slide into the dip of her waist, over her hip and down between her thighs, tangling in the curls there. Pleasure shuddered through her.

"Alex! Oh, please . . . What's happening to me?" Beth cried, clasping his shoulders and arching against him.

"I'm loving you, Beth," he answered caressively. Then she felt him slide one long finger into the tight channel of her womanhood. She bit her lip. His touch was so intimate, so personal, yet felt so good. And so right. It was right because Alex was doing it.

"I'm making you mine, Beth. Mine," he whispered hoarsely as he moved his finger inside her, probing, stretching, preparing her for their joining. After a time, she needed more.

"Alex, don't . . . Please stop. I want . . . I want . . ."

"What do you want, my Beth? Tell me," he urged. "Tell me what you want."

"I want you to love me, Alex. To fill me . . . To make me yours. Please, Alex, now!" she begged, near delirious with a need she didn't understand, a need she'd never experienced before in her life. She just knew that Alex was the only one who could satisfy the hunger that raged through her body like a storm.

Alex let loose a deep, ragged sigh and rose to ease himself between her thighs. Beth parted her legs willingly, trustingly, and he settled his narrow hips against her pelvis, the hard arc of his manhood hot against her skin. He braced his hands on the ground on either side of her head, and she curled her fingers around his forearms. Their eyes met and locked, never wavering as he positioned himself and entered her. Slowly, slowly . . .

Beth's eyes fluttered shut, and she dug her nails into Alex's arms as pleasure was replaced by pain, sharp and tearing.

"'Tis only for a moment, my Beth," Alex whispered as he clenched his jaw. "Bear it for a moment and I'll make it up to you, I promise."

Beth believed him, trusted him, even before the pain abated. And when it went away, a new urgency blossomed within her. She instinctively lifted her hips. Responding to her obvious readiness, Alex moaned low in his throat and thrust deep within her. Oh, so deep. He was filling her, filling her. Filling the emptiness, sating the hunger, assuaging the need.

But it wasn't over, this sweet madness. It had just begun. Alex began to move within her, plunging deep, then pulling back. Again and again, setting a rhythm Beth mindlessly, wantonly met need for need. A tear trickled down Beth's cheek, which Alex kissed away. She was losing herself in this man, losing every thought, every dream except those

that centered in him. All she felt, all she knew was Alex.
Alex . . .

Fragmented. She was shattering into a million shards of
glass, diamond-bright, brilliant, piercing. She was drifting
heavenward, cradled in love's embrace. Alex cried her
name and strained against her, and she against him while
ripple after ripple of staggering pleasure debilitated her,
conquered her. Then her whole being exploded, pieces
scattering on the wind and finally raining down to settle on
the cool ground. Anchored to earth. Wrapped in a sweet
tangle of arms and legs. Alex's arms and legs.

Silence, except for their quick, shallow breathing and
the night voices. Crickets and toads, rustling leaves and the
soughing wind. The distant warbling of a nightingale. The
gurgle and slosh of the creek. Movement and sound. Life.

"I love you, Alex," she said, then nestled her head in the
crook of his arm and slept.

Alex carefully reached for his shirt and threw it over
Beth's shoulders, then gathered her close, lending her
warmth. He kissed her forehead and listened to her soft,
even breathing. "I love you, too, Beth," he whispered.
Then he stared at the sky, vacant-eyed, while a heavy,
soul-withering sadness enveloped him.

Beth awoke to the sound of a rooster crowing. She was
lying on her back and was confused at first to be staring up
at a star-dusted velvet sky instead of the gilded cornices and
rose-patterned wall coverings of her bedchamber. The moon
shone as bright as ever, but hovered close to the horizon,
skimming the edge of night.

She became suddenly conscious of Alex's body pressed
against hers. His bare arm was draped across her waist, his
leg angled over hers, his face buried in her hair, his breath
warm against her cheek. A tremor purled through Beth as
memories of last night flooded her with pleasurable sensations. It had not been a dream!

She was covered with Alex's shirt, and sometime during the night he had put on his breeches and boots. She ought to have felt cold, but she didn't. Alex had kept her warm as they'd slept on the bed of pliant grass with only her night rail beneath them. But, though it was still dark, dawn approached—or so said the trumpeting rooster—and with it would come the morning dew.

The cock crowed again, and Beth felt Alex stir. She turned her head to peer into his shadowy face. "Are you awake?"

Alex shifted and rose up on one elbow, supporting his chin with a curved palm. Emerged from the shade of the tall grass, Alex's face was illuminated by moonlight. As she looked into his eyes, Beth's heart thudded painfully. Mingled with a tender lover's expression, which Beth collected and cuddled to her heart's core, was a bone-chilling weariness. His look clearly reflected the anguish of a guilty soul, a riddled conscience, a tired spirit.

"Yes, Beth," he answered at last. "I'm awake."

"I'll wager you've not slept at all."

"No, I haven't. How could I?"

Pain sluiced over Beth like an Arctic Ocean wave, cold and numbing. "Then you regret it that much? I've brought you only trouble and turmoil?"

Alex groaned and gathered Beth to his warm bare chest in a fierce embrace. "Never say such words again, Beth. You've brought the healing balm of true love to my heart. You have revived in me a sure belief—a belief I clung to through years of dissatisfying alliances with women, only to finally, cynically discard—that some souls are meant to meet and join on earth. But why must the acknowledgment of our love, the consummation of it, bring such pain to the only other person in this world I love beyond life itself?"

Beth had heard and felt every word Alex said, but above the anguish and frustration the word "love" had rung out loud and clear. She pulled back and lifted her face to his. "You . . . you love me, then?"

Alex's features, whittled by pain to sharp angles and harsh shadows, melted into tenderness. "I told you so last night, but you were asleep already, I suspect." Beth's chest constricted with joy. He smiled then. "Was I such a dull dog, my Beth, that you had no recourse but to nod off while the night was still young?"

She knew he teased her, but she was too flustered to find words for a clever reply. Tonight she could speak only the truth. "I . . . fear you loved me to such a satisfying degree, Alex, that I had little inclination to do anything but curl up like a kitten sated with mother's milk. You were . . . magnificent."

Alex's smile slid away. Beneath her palms she felt his chest heave with quicker, deeper breaths. Her own breath responded in like manner. Her hands, seemingly of their own volition, began to roam across his broad chest, her fingertips tangling in the soft coils of hair.

He stayed her errant, eager wanderings by grasping her shoulders firmly. Startled, she raised her eyes to his. The dark Gypsy orbs were lustrous in the moonlight. "Are you still satisfied, Beth?" Alex's voice grated with need.

Though nothing but a green girl only hours past her first experience with love, she recognized the need as surely as she acknowledged her own aching emptiness. Heat eddied in the moist secret folds at her woman's core. "No. And the memory of it taunts me," she answered bluntly.

His hands began to caress her shoulders. The shirt, wedged between them as they embraced, fell away, exposing her breasts. She heard his gulp of breath as he looked at her. His adoring gaze inflamed her. She wanted him—oh, so much!—to touch her there, to do all the wicked, wonderful things he'd done before.

She moaned as his hands slid around her rib cage, then slowly progressed upward till they cupped both breasts.

Then he stroked her nipples with the hard pads of his thumbs. "It's late, Beth. Time to go inside." His voice lowered to a dark, rough timbre. "Time to return to our rooms before the servants are up."

"The cock crowed only twice," she whispered, bending toward him, teasing his own nipples between her thumb and forefinger. "There's time enough for us to find satisfaction once more, isn't there?" She settled her mouth on his and brazenly slipped her tongue inside, darting, dipping.

He broke away a moment, but their mouths were only fractionally separated. "Not perhaps the way you want it, Beth. Not slow and easy." The cock crowed again.

"I want you any way I can have you, Alex."

With a groan Alex pulled Beth onto his lap, setting her bottom against the heated swell of his manhood, his legs sprawled in front of him, his knees bent. She straddled him, her legs curled about his waist. "But what of regrets, my Beth? What of Zach?" he murmured against her hungry mouth.

"There's always time for regrets. Let tomorrow lend the hours for such indulgences. This night belongs to us!"

Goaded beyond human endurance, Alex lifted Beth slightly so that he could undo his trouser buttons and free his hips. Released, his manhood fell, heavy and hot, against her. She remembered how good he felt moving inside her, but the memory paled as he entered her, the actuality of it so much more satisfying than the memory. With his hands at her waist and her arms banded about his shoulders, he guided her and set the rhythm, a hard, swift tempo that jarred Beth to sensual heights she'd never dreamed of. Splintering the eerie predawn dark, she cried out . . . her voice melding, blending with the night sounds.

Beth watched her night rail burn in the grate, an almost symbolic act. The stain of blood on it had been proof of her lost virginity. She did not regret loving Alex, but she did regret hurting Zach, and the orange flames lapping at the withering, red-blotched nightgown seemed to accuse her.

She and Alex had returned stealthily to the house just as the sky lightened to a gray opalescence. Alex had left her at the top of the stairs, and they'd moved down opposite galleries to their bedchambers. She prayed God neither of them had been heard or seen. But Beth had not noticed any movement belowstairs or above for at least a half hour after they'd returned to the house. Now the house bustled with the sounds and smells of morning. In the interim, she'd bathed in cool water from the pitcher at her washstand and wrapped herself in a blanket. Sadie would bring yesterday's clothes to her, brushed and cleaned, but until then Beth had nothing to wear.

Now the night rail was no more than a shriveled clump of char. Just looking at the spent heat of it made gooseflesh rise on Beth's arms and legs. She slipped the blanket from around her shoulders and laid it on the end of the bed, then slid under the white Marseilles counterpane and pulled the warm coverlets up to her chin.

She shivered. Odd that she should be so cold in a fire-heated chamber, cuddled beneath a plethora of blankets, when last night she'd lain naked with only Alex to keep her warm and hadn't felt chilly for a moment. She smiled and rolled over on her back. Just thinking of him warmed her considerably. She eased her hand down the length of her, imagining him stroking her. Now she knew exactly how it felt to be loved, thoroughly loved, by the right man. Alex. The only man.

Beth's smile fell away as she anticipated the coming confrontation with Zach. She and Alex had discussed the problem briefly while on their way back to the house, agreeing that Zach must be told of their attachment as soon as possible. Of course, they would not tell him of their lovemaking, for that would be too harsh a blow. Neither Beth nor Alex wished to confess such a breach of fidelity.

No matter how much they loved each other, no matter how hard they'd tried to avoid what was apparently unavoidable, they both felt guilty about what had happened. And they were both consumed with worry over Zach's reaction. It was too sad that such a beautiful experience must be tainted by guilt and regret and worry. It was like her white nightdress with the red stain—colored by pain.

In the last few weeks, as Beth worried about her attraction to Alex, she'd thought of confiding in her mother and asking for advice. She'd even once or twice hinted at the subject, hoping that her mother might confess that she'd noticed the attraction. But Mrs. Tavistock seemed completely oblivious to anything of a subtle nature going on about her. While she loved her daughters very much, she lacked the depth of understanding that would help her recognize their need for counsel when they were too shy or unsure to ask for it.

Now that her relationship had progressed so far, Beth dared not tell her mother, for Mrs. Tavistock would probably be shocked and worried and rendered incapable of offering Beth any sort of advice anyway. Naturally Mrs. Tavistock would have to be told eventually, but to tell her so soon after Gabby's near tragedy did not seem wise to Beth.

Besides, what could Beth tell her mother that would be reassuring? She could not counter the bad news that she *wasn't* going to marry Zach with the good news that she *was* going to marry Alex, because he hadn't asked her! No, she was going to have to wait until all was settled before she told her mother anything.

The door creaked open, and Sadie peeked through the crack before entering. Beth feigned sleep. It was too early to look wide awake. She heard Sadie's shoes scuffle across the carpet, back and forth, and then the door closing quietly behind her. Beth opened her eyes and saw her clothes laid out on the purple wing chair by the fireplace. Eager to face the day, whatever it might hold, Beth swung one leg over the side of the bed as she prepared to sit up.

Suddenly the door opened again. Again it was Sadie, with kindling tucked under one arm and carrying a bucket of hot water. She stopped short when she saw Beth about to climb out of bed, saying, all in a breath, "What are ye doin' out o' bed already, miss? I didn't wake ye, did I? Lor', child, are ye naked under there?"

Beth quickly covered herself and scooted down beneath the blankets. "In answer to all your questions, Sadie, yes, I am attempting to leave my bed, though it is early. No, you didn't awaken me; I awoke of my own volition. And, yes, I am quite naked."

Sadie raised a disapproving brow. "There's a night rail in the bottom drawer of the wardrobe, miss. I thought I told ye last night."

Beth watched as Sadie laid the log on the tiles by the fireplace, stepped around the tub still filled with last night's bathwater, and then placed the bucket on the floor by the washstand. "Yes, you told me. Of course you did, Sadie," she said. "But, though I loathe to refute you, there was no night rail in the drawer when I sought it out after my bath last night. I must have taken it home." Beth hoped she looked and sounded much more convincing than she felt.

Sadie merely pursed her lips and moved toward the wardrobe, obviously intent on proving herself correct. She opened the drawer and stood gawking into it for a few seconds of patent disbelief. Then she opened all of the other drawers, systematically rifling the contents of each. "Well, I'll be snabbled," she said at last. "I could have sworn there was a night rail in that bottom drawer. I laundered it not more than a week ago."

"Well, sometimes our memories are not quite so precise as we'd wish them to be, eh, Sadie?" Beth said, forcing a bright smile. "But don't cudgel your brain over it. Today's much too splendid a day to worry over trifles. We have so much to be thankful for, don't we?"

"Aye, Miss Elizabeth, we do," Sadie responded, smiling

genuinely and complacently folding her hands over her stomach. "I never thought t' see Miss Gabrielle again. She'd flung herself well and good into the briars this time. Truth t' tell, I was sure they'd never find her in that mine once she'd wandered around a bit." Sadie turned, stooped to pick up the kindling, then placed it on the grate. "Thank the good Lord the master found 'er like he did. Without him, I fear she'd have stayed lost."

A sickening shudder convulsed through Beth at this bluntly spoken reminder of just how close they'd come to losing Gabby, and how much they all owed Zach because he'd been the one to find her. Beth revived herself a little with the thought that Alex had helped both Zach and Gabby to safety. A combined effort had saved them all from the wretched necessity of planning another funeral on this bright July day.

"Did ye have a fire already this mornin', miss?" Sadie asked as she poked at the ashes in the grate and stirred up a few hot embers.

"Why, yes, I did!" Beth said. "Due to the necessity of sleeping in the altogether, I was cold."

"What did ye burn, miss?" Sadie turned innocently curious eyes to her. "There waren't no kindling."

Beth bit her lip. She had not expected Sadie to be so very inquisitive. Yet the woman was intimately familiar with every detail and every routine, however minuscule, of the household. She would notice such things.

"I fetched some wood from the kitchen," she lied. Then, before Sadie could do something so outrageous as to study the ashes and comment that wood ashes looked quite different from those that presently reposed on the grate, Beth slipped out of bed and stood naked before her. "Help me dress, Sadie. Right now, before I catch my death, if you please."

Sadie dropped the poker, tsk-tsked, and grabbed Beth's

shift from off the chair. "Lor', miss, you're a brazen one this mornin', ain't ye?"

As Sadie pulled the undergarment over her head, Beth wondered how Sadie would react if she knew just how brazen she'd been in the wee dark hours of the night. Curtailing her small womanly smile at those delicious memories, she sobered herself with thoughts of Zach. "Is anyone downstairs yet?"

Sadie's lips straightened to a grim line. She nodded her head dourly. "I never thought t' see anybody up till nearly midmornin', what with all the goin's-on yesterday, but the master is in the breakfast room, miss, pushin' his food about on his plate and not eatin' a bit of it."

Beth's eyes fixed intently on Sadie's face. "What is his expression, Sadie? He doesn't looked vexed, does he? Do you suppose he's simply sober from last night or troubled about something else?"

Sadie picked up Beth's yellow walking gown and lowered it so Beth could step into the skirt. Then she pulled it up to slip it over her outstretched arms. Sadie sighed heavily. "It's not my place to speculate 'bout the feelin's of my betters, miss. But, nay, he didn't look vexed. He looked like he was makin' resolutions, so t' speak. I think Miss Gabby nearly turnin' up her toes scared 'im. I hope he's makin' plans to board up those dangerous mines, at least."

Beth sucked in her breath as Sadie tied up the back of her bodice. She hoped with all her heart that Zach was indeed making resolutions. She also hoped he would not be so distressed by the ending of their betrothal that all his good intentions would go by the wayside.

But there was more to worry about than a delay in estate business. The main worry, of course, was the survival of Alex's and Zach's closeness once the truth was told. When Zach discovered that Beth had finally recognized her love of him for what it was—a strong, sisterly affection—would he be able to accept her as his brother's wife? Beth's brows furrowed. There it was again! The fact was, though Alex had said he loved her, he'd never mentioned marriage. Love and marriage. The one went with the other, didn't it? She had to believe this was true.

''There, miss. Ye're as pretty and fresh as a daisy!'' said Sadie, offering Beth a rare compliment. Beth turned to look in the mirror above the dressing table. Even with her hair sleep-mussed, she did look fresh and glowing. Her cheeks fairly bloomed with delicate color, and her eyes sparkled. Ah, what love can do! she thought to herself, reaching for the brush to tame her tumble of hair into something like neatness. If only her love for Alex weren't about to hurt someone so very dear to her, she'd have been the happiest girl on the great island of England.

CHAPTER
eleven

ALEX STOOD AT the bottom of the stairs, one hand resting on the oak newel post that curved upward to form an ornamental trefoil. His gaze swept over the mulberry and peacock blue Axminster carpet at his feet, then shifted to the paneled door that led into the breakfast parlor. His eyes darted nervously back to the carpet and up to the heavy chandelier, brilliantly lucent in the early morning sunshine that beamed from a high window.

An hour earlier, when he could no longer delude himself into believing that sleep was possible, he had sent Dudley to inquire on the whereabouts of Zach. He'd been surprised, and a little alarmed, to be told that his brother was already dressed and having his breakfast. Or, as Dudley told it, Zach was *looking at* his breakfast. Then, since Dudley was such a good judge of mood and countenance, Alex had asked him to offer an opinion on Zach's present state of mind.

"Humbled, my lord. He's sorry about what happened to the little girl," Dudley had said with conviction. "He's determining to mend his ways, I think." Then Dudley got a rather pensive look about him and muttered, "Blue-deviled about some of the choices he's making, I'll wager."

"What do you mean, Dudley?" Alex had pressed him.

After subjecting his master to a penetrating look that implied he was pondering the wisdom of speaking the undiluted truth, Dudley had stated flatly, "I mean the girl—Tessy, as she's called. He'll serve the girl her congé."

Taken unawares by this prediction, Alex could not collect
himself immediately to hide his surprise and dismay. Now
was not the time for Zachary to become inclined to devote
himself to Beth! And Zach would have need of the
comforting arms of his mistress in the coming days and
weeks. "How do you come by this conclusion, Dudley?"
Alex had asked with an assumed calm he did not feel.

"That female intuition I'm cursed with, I suppose,"
Dudley answered briskly. "Call it what you will. It's just a
feeling I have. Now, my lord, shall we wear the Spanish
blue jacket or the Manila brown?" he'd finished, managing
to be both obsequious and uncompromising in the same
breath. Alex knew that Dudley had done with speaking on
the subject and had his reasons for keeping mum. Alex had
not pressed him further. Besides, he was deuced uncomfortable in Dudley's company, having a most unsettling impression that his manservant's intuition had also divulged to him
Alex's midnight meeting with Beth. A stupid idea, perhaps,
but still unsettling.

Now Alex was resolving to enter the breakfast parlor and
empty his budget. Honor demanded that he tell Zach of his
feelings and intentions toward Beth as soon as possible, but
he dreaded the encounter. He was already mourning the
death of the wondrously satisfying friendship he'd nurtured
with his brother over the past few weeks. Zach would be
surprised, hurt, angry—all of these things and more. The
closeness between them would flounder and dissolve for a
time; but Alex was determined that matters would not
endure for long in such a state. They had overcome
seventeen years of estrangement, so perhaps anything was
possible after that. But Zach would probably suspect, too,
just how strenuously Alex had resisted Beth's attractions.
With Alex's rakish reputation, Zach would wonder how
deep and honorable his intentions were.

Alex was surprised again and again whenever he realized
just how pure and unpolluted his intentions toward Beth

really were—as pure as the crystalline trumpets of the
Madonna lily newly opened to the first dewy dusk of
summer. He regarded these feelings with something akin to
reverence. He was going to marry her. But Zach's trust and
love might be the sacrifice required for finding such a
perfect mate with whom to wend his way through life's
fateful twists and turns.

Fate. Alex was prodded from his deep thoughts by a sharp
pain that radiated from his left wrist to his shoulder. He
looked down at the hand that gripped the newel post and
observed the knuckles stretched white and taut, the veins
blue and bulging from the pressure of his hold on the
unyielding piece of wood. It was almost as though the post
represented that illusory tyrant called fate, and Alex was
trying to strangle the very breath out of it as punishment for
playing so cruel a trick as to make him his beloved brother's
rival.

The breakfast parlor door opened, and a servant passed
through with a covered tray. The smell of bacon, coffee, and
kippers drifted into the hall, sending Alex's stomach into
churning revolt. He knew he had to go in straightaway and
speak the truth—at least as much truth as he and Beth
had decided upon. Anything was better than this wretched
suspense. He released his stranglehold on the railing,
tugged at the hem of his blue jacket, and trod purposefully
toward the dreaded door.

Upon entering, Alex discovered that the French doors
were partly open to a small enclosed courtyard with
terra-cotta walls and a climbing herb garden. Through the
uncurtained glass, he could see Zach's blond head cocked
thoughtfully to one side and both elbows propped on the
low wall, beyond which there was a charming vista of lawn
and moor. Alex walked past the servants standing sentinel at
either end of the heavily laden sideboard, and past Zach's
untouched plate of food. The plate was piled high with eggs

and thickly sliced bacon, as if Zach had had good intentions about eating a hearty breakfast, but had failed.

Alex turned to the servants and, with a flick of his wrist and a jerk of his head, dismissed them. Then he soundlessly slipped outside and stood gathering his courage amid the mingled fragrances of thyme, pungent Corsican mint, pennyroyal, and marjoram.

"Zach?"

Zach jerked and turned in a startled fashion, taken so by surprise that he had no time to erase the distraught expression he wore. Alex's heart twisted at such a look on the face of his younger brother. It was too much like the look he'd worn that day when he was thrust into the carriage and driven away by their grandfather. Then a smile suddenly appeared, but it did not reach his eyes.

"Alex," he said, stepping forward to clap him on the back, "you're up early. After such a night as you had, I thought you'd sleep till noon."

Alex registered the unintended irony of the comment, but only said, "I couldn't sleep. I need to talk to you, Zach."

Zach raised a knowing brow. "Indeed, brother, I can well imagine the things you wish to say to me this day—the day after, as it were. But I can assure you it's quite unnecessary." Zach pressed one boot-clad ankle neatly against the other and bowed at the waist. "I'm your most humble, most repentant servant. I have seen the folly of my ways and am determined to mend them."

His address was playful, but Alex could see anguish in the depths of his brother's golden eyes and the purple shadows of sleeplessness beneath. Alex frowned and watched as Zach straightened and walked to a chair, his hands loosely circling the bulbous carvings at the top. "You look skeptical, brother. But you shall see that I'm quite firm and resolved about this. I've arranged to meet with my steward directly after breakfast. Boarding up of the tin mines will commence today. I've decided to hire extra men from town to expedite the work, and I will not rest till the task is done. I will personally inspect each job, making sure that not even the smallest moor hare could creep between the boards!''

"I'm pleased, Zach," Alex said. And he *was* pleased— genuinely. But it was hard for him to muster up the sort of heartfelt smile that ought to have accompanied this praise. Even the praise was much too mild, however, much too lukewarm for the pride Alex felt in Zach's mature acceptance of responsibility. If only it did not have to be followed by the revelation Alex was about to impart.

"You don't look pleased," Zach said, a comment that did not take Alex by surprise. A complete dunderhead could have seen that he was suffering from acute agitation. He could feel the sweat beading on his upper lip even as he formed his next words.

"It's nothing more than I expected from you," Alex offered, stalling for time as he tried to construct a pleasing way to tell his brother that he was in love with his betrothed, and she with him.

"Ah, but it was something you expected from me much sooner than I delivered," Zach replied with self-directed sarcasm. "It only took the near entombment of an innocent child to awaken my slumberous sense of responsibility. A child, by the by, whom I placed in danger by my own vain refusal to listen to reason." Zach's returning smile was bittersweet. "Reason packaged so prettily in the shape of my wise little Beth."

The gentle way Zach breathed Beth's name—like a prayer—the possessive way he referred to her as *his* Beth, tore at Alex's heart like the fangs of a beast. Jealousy. Tearing, gouging jealousy. And guilt. Beth belonged to Zach first.

"You've had second thoughts, then, about your treatment of Beth lately?" he questioned in a tone as deceptively calm as Zach's had been. "I gather you're prepared to make amends?'' Was Dudley's prediction correct? Was Zach planning to leave his mistress?

Zach released his hold on the chair and walked slowly to the French doors, his hands clasped behind him. He gazed out a long moment, then said, ''You think about a lot of things when you face death. And sometimes you're surprised by the thoughts that are uppermost in your mind, the feelings that claim your heart most forcefully.''

Alex strove for composure. ''In what you supposed were your final moments on earth, your thoughts were of Beth?'' *His* had been, and those thoughts had been the impetus behind his surrender to desire last night.

Zach swiveled and faced Alex squarely. ''No, they were not. And that's the sting, brother.'' His voice lowered and hardened. ''That's what nettles me the most. God, Alex, I thought of Tessy! I thought of my mistress—my whore.''

Alex was astonished by the vehemence of Zach's tone. ''You've always spoken so tenderly of Tess. You said you had a strong affection for her.''

Zach paced up and down, clutching at his hair. ''Damnation, don't you understand? I can't allow myself to feel that strongly about Tessy. She's just a chit I keep for pleasuring, for bedding. I can't . . . I *don't* love her. I can't marry her, for Christ's sake!''

''Does she expect you to marry her?''

''No, of course not. She's never spoken of it, though I know it hurts her to hear of Beth. But what does she expect? What can a girl like her hope for beyond what I've given her? And I've given her a lot, Alex! I took her away from that crusty old witch, Mrs. Turley, who worked Tessy's fingers to the bone day after day. It was a wretched existence. She's been happy with me. I've been good to her.''

''Brother, thou dost protest too much,'' Alex chided him softly. ''Whether she is grateful, or whether you are kind and generous, is not the issue. I think you are more concerned about the strength of feeling you have for a girl who is socially inferior to you. What are you afraid of, Zach? Are you afraid of hurting Tess or of hurting yourself?''

"Mostly myself, I suppose. Yes, isn't that a lowering admission to make? But I don't want to end up like my friend, Charlie.''

"The fellow who married his mistress?''

"Yes, and him a viscount, no less. He caused a great scandal. His family never forgave him. Though he was still socially acceptable, except to the high-sticklers, *she* was never welcome anywhere! Then, to cap it all, he fell out of love with her within a year's time and regretted it so passionately he took to tipping brews and playing high and fast at every gaming hell in town. Lost his fortune as well as his respectability.''

"This is an alarming picture you paint, but it need not apply to you, or to every man and his mistress.''

"No, I realize that. But can't you see why I'm so appalled by those feelings I had in the mine? Lord, Alex, Beth is such a darling girl. I've known her, I've *loved* her, since I was in short pants. I ought to have been thinking of *her*. You've told me yourself that I've been neglecting her, and I've decided to heed your advice and pay her the attention she deserves. By breaking off with Tess, I'll be better able to do that. Sometimes I think the only reason I thought of Tessy instead of Beth is because I've been . . . you know . . . intimate with her and not with Beth.''

"You're not contemplating bedding Beth before you're married, are you?'' A sharp edge had crept into Alex's voice, but he could hardly help it. The beast inside, the jealousy that had been tearing at his organs for the past few minutes, was threatening to split him wide open.

An amused glint appeared in Zach's eyes, crowding out the pain for a moment. "Taking some brotherly interest in her, are you? Feeling a tad protective? Do not fear. She won't let me bed her till we're shackled well and good. But your concern is touching, to be sure. I don't suppose *you* made any resolutions whilst we were trying to escape that collapsing crypt? Are you going to give up your bits of muslin and find yourself a respectable girl? Or is that too much to ask of Wicked Wickham?''

Wicked Wickham. The sobriquet taunted him. The last thing Alex wished to be at the moment was wicked. But that was how he felt. That was what he imagined he personified, flesh and bone, heart and soul—wickedness. What had he done? How could he tell his brother—his *brother*—that last night he'd taken the innocence of the girl Zach had loved since he was in short pants? And she'd loved him, too.

Alex's thoughts and feelings were in turmoil. If he had never come to Pencarrow, the wedding would have gone off without a hitch. Beth would still be a virgin, still eagerly awaiting her nuptials. Maybe if he left, everything could go back to the way it was. No one would be hurt—except Beth, and she only for a short time. She'd forget him. Zach would be happy, as he deserved to be.

''There's something else, Alex.'' The tone of Zach's voice, gone abruptly from teasing to Sabbath-day sober, riveted Alex's attention. Zach's eyes, dark amber and glistening, were full of pain again.

''What is it?''

Zach leaned a hip against the edge of the table and toyed with the cutlery, fussily, nervously arranging the knives, forks, and spoons in precise juxtaposition. ''It may seem silly to you. I don't know if I should even mention it. . . .''

Alex could hear the tightness in Zach's throat. Whatever he wished to confide was very difficult for him. Alex's brotherly instincts came rushing to the surface, crowding out all other personal feelings.

''Just tell me what's bothering you, Zach.''

''Well, it's about our mother.''

''Yes?''

"The mine accident has made me think of her, too.
I . . . I feel responsible for Gabby running off and nearly
getting killed. Even you and some of the men might have
been killed because of my irresponsibility—"

"Zach, don't—"

"—and it made me think of Mother. I killed *her* and
made my father hate me. I never want to be responsible for
anyone's death again, Alex."

"You weren't responsible for Mother's death!"

"Common sense tells me that's true, but in my
heart . . ." Zach's voice broke as he viciously and repeatedly poked his chest with an accusing forefinger. "In my
heart I've always felt so desperately guilty."

Zach's tortured words slammed against Alex's heart like
a battering ram. "Ah, Zach—"

"Goodness, what Friday-faces the two of you are. No
more moping. Today's a day of celebration and thanksgiving!"

Mrs. Tavistock's voice broke into Alex's tumble of
tender sympathy, disjointed regrets, and grasping remedies
for his sins against Zach. He turned and watched Beth's
mother glide into the room, her face wreathed in a smile that
he suspected was a trifle false, like the forced gaiety he'd
detected in her voice. She was followed by a pale, unnaturally subdued Gabby and . . . Beth. Beth, in the yellow
dress she'd worn on the beach when she first touched him.
Beth of the passionate kisses and rosy breasts. Beth, *his*
Beth. Not Zach's. No, not Zach's anymore, no matter how
much he wished to spare his brother further pain. They
could never go back to the way things were before. The
sight of Beth made that crystal clear.

Their eyes met and held, hers eager and questioning,
while he was quite sure his own gaze spoke of guilt, doubt,
and a mute apology. Instead of giving him a recriminatory
response, Beth seemed to understand Alex's dilemma and
sympathize with him. He was grateful to her for accepting

his failure to tell Zach about the two of them, even though she couldn't have begun to know all the reasons behind his hesitation. He loved her all the more for understanding without knowing. All of this passed between them in the space of a moment.

"If Friday-faces are to be banished from Pencarrow, this must also apply to Gabby," said Zach, assuming his former playful air. He walked to Gabby and hefted her onto his hip, smiling into her sober little face. "What's wrong with your lip, sweeting?" he teased, tapping the pouty lower lip with his forefinger. "It's sticking out much too far. You're apt to trip on it if you don't pull it in."

"I'm just a stupid child," Gabby muttered, her lip protruding even farther. "I made a muddle of everything yesterday and might have killed us all." Her gaze dropped, and a tear trickled down her cheek.

"Stuff and nonsense," scolded Mrs. Tavistock, still smiling determinedly. "You simply made a small error in judgment. We're just happy to have you safe, dearest."

"Don't beat yourself, Gabby," advised Zach, lifting her chin so that she was compelled to look at him. "I made a mistake, too." He looked at Alex and then at Beth— tenderly at Beth. "I've made a lot of mistakes in my life. We must be thankful that our friends and family are willing to forgive us and to help us do better."

Beth and Alex exchanged anguished looks. Zach, in the form of a sincerely repentant, openly loving brother and fiancé, was a formidable discouragement to telling the truth.

"But what about the knackers, Zach?" Gabby blurted out, perhaps coming to the most painful source of her unhappiness—her disillusionment. "I believed Mr. Thatcher. Like a silly puddinghead, I believed there were knackers in the tin mines!" Now the tears streamed down her cheeks, her chin trembling with the effort to quell her childish grief. "Why does he tell those lies? Mama says it's wrong to spin whiskers. Are only grown-up people allowed to tell lies, Zach?''

Zach crooned soft words and wiped away Gabby's tears with the pad of his thumb. ''There, there, Gabby. Don't turn into a watering pot on your good friend's best green coat! You're not a puddinghead. And furthermore, I *still* believe there are knackers in the tin mines.''

Gabby raised wide, hopeful eyes to his. ''You do?''

Zach nodded his head.

''Then why didn't I see any? Have *you* seen knackers, Zach?''

Zach avoided answering Gabby's questions directly. ''Knackers are contrary creatures,'' he said. ''Like piskies and spriggans and other fairy folk, they appear only when they're least expected. Perhaps you didn't see the knackers because you'd gone into the mine expressly to find them.''

''Oh, do you think so?'' Gabby seemed struck by the wisdom of Zach's words.

''Yes, particularly since the mines are such a dangerous place for children. Fairy folk like children—they're of much the same height and disposition, you know—and they'd never encourage them to do dangerous things. If word got about among your play chums that you'd seen knackers in the old tin mines, children would flock to them in herds, you see. And they'd probably get lost, just as you did.''

''Oh, yes. I *do* see. That wouldn't be at all the thing, would it?''

''Now, do you promise to tell your mama exactly where you're going from now on and promise to be careful?''

''I do, Zach,'' said Gabby, nodding solemnly. ''I do promise, with all my heart.''

''There's a good girl.'' He pulled her fast against him, and she twined her arms about his neck in a close embrace. It was heartwarming to see the trust and caring so obviously in abundance between Zach and Gabby. Zach had a way with the child that Alex couldn't help but admire. But it

disturbed him, too. In fact, he resented it. Here was yet
further proof of Zach's greater claim to Beth's love, Beth's
hand in marriage. Zach was intimately entangled in Beth's
family. They all loved him—damn 'em to hell.

"I'm famished," Beth said, breaking into the tender
moment, which, in Alex's bitter opinion, was fast becoming
maudlin. "Why don't we all sit down and eat?" She darted
a worried look toward Alex, which he tried to ignore. Much
as he hated to admit it, he was feeling downright sulky.

They all did sit down, but only Gabby ate a good
breakfast. Restored to her usual animated self, she carried
the conversation, effectively centering it around childish
concerns and interests. Everyone else seemed too preoccupied, too tired, or too miserable to do justice to Cook's
hearty victuals, or to begin an adult conversation until Zach
began to talk of his plans concerning the tin mines and other
estate renovations. As he spoke, turning frequently to Beth
as if to gain her approval, as if her coming status as mistress
of Pencarrow required her inclusion in every minute detail
of his plans, his face fairly beamed with pleasure born of
good intentions.

Beth listened and smiled encouragingly. Alex knew she
was impressed by Zach's changed attitude, just as he was.
She did not know precisely how much Zach intended to
reform, however, thought Alex with a resentment that he
hated in himself. Beth still didn't know about Tess, and
Alex couldn't tell her, even though knowledge of Zach's
relationship with Tess would most probably wedge antipa-
thy between the lifelong friends. But Alex would not sink so
low as to use Zach's mistress to separate his brother from
Beth. He had to be fair.

Beth sat directly across the table from him. He watched
her as she listened to Zach. She fairly glowed with life
today, and a prideful masculine part of him exulted in the
knowledge that he'd given her that womanly glow. He
wanted to touch her—so badly. Just a few inches separated

his hand from hers on the table between them. It seemed cruel and unnatural that he had no right to touch her now in the sunlit routine of day, when last night by moonlight he'd made her his by every natural law attached to the loving sacrament between a man and a woman.

She must have felt his scrutiny. She turned. Their gazes met, meshed, and lovingly caressed. Alex swallowed hard. He had to find an opportunity to tell Zach the truth soon. But not, perhaps, till Zach had concluded the flurry of business he was about to arrange with his steward. To throw onto his brother's teeth such unsettling news at such a crucial time would not be prudent or kind. Let him board up his tin mines; then Alex would tell him all. Meanwhile, the more distance he could keep between himself and Beth, the better. Only by denying himself the sweet intoxicant of her delectable body could he keep from shouting his love for her from the steepletop of the parish church.

Two weeks passed like the slow, crushing turn of a gristmill—heavy and grinding. Beth had seen little of Zach and less of Alex. One day, however, she and Alex found themselves unexpectedly alone in the Pencarrow drawing room, everyone else having gone out for a moment on some errand or other. She demanded to know why he'd been avoiding her, and he succinctly informed her that it was all he could do to refrain from throwing her onto the floor for wicked purposes. This urge frequently came upon him even while the room was inhabited by numerous people. If he was alone with her for more than half a minute, he'd surely ravish her quite thoroughly. Even as they spoke, he was mad with desire.

He said all this as he sat quietly in a chair, one leg crossed over the other in casual repose. But the burning intensity of his eyes told all. He wanted her with the same fervor that had kept her tossing and turning in her bed all night, remembering. . . . Remembering how moonbeams bathed the supple, rippling muscles of his chest and stomach in creamy luminescence. Remembering how his broad back and firm buttocks felt beneath her questing hands. Remembering how his mouth fit perfectly against and into hers. Remembering . . .

"But why can't we be together?" she said. "How soon will you tell him?"

"We can't be together because if I make love to you one more time, I won't be able to stop myself from telling Zach. And we can't tell Zach till he's done with all this estate business."

"Must you help him? Must you be gone all day inspecting the tin mines, too?" she returned petulantly.

"If I help him, the work will be done sooner. If I'm busy and away from you, I'm more likely to be able to control myself." Alex sighed. "We can be grateful that Zach's zeal to speedily dispatch his most pressing estate responsibilities is giving him practically no time to play devoted fiancé to you. Every time he touches you, I—"

"I know," Beth said soothingly. "But he has been nothing if not a true gentleman. He does not press me for intimacies beyond the peck on the cheek I've allowed him. In fact, he's been so sweet, so repentant, that I feel an absolute villainess by comparison."

"It would be best if you stayed at Brookmoor till all of this is settled," Alex said tersely.

"Then I'd *never* see you. Zach would come to Brookmoor, and you would not be about to act as chaperon. No, I shan't take your advice in this instance, Alex."

Alex's mouth quirked in a small grin. "You're a determined baggage, Beth. You'd never have made Zach a biddable wife."

Beth's brows rose slightly. She was about to retort that she wouldn't make *him* a biddable wife, either; then she remembered that he still hadn't asked her to marry him. He would, wouldn't he?

"Now what, love?" he said, cocking his head to one side. "Have I made you angry by calling you a determined baggage?" His voice grew lower, softer. "But look at you! If you don't suck in that lower lip this moment, I'm coming over there to nibble on it till it bleeds. Are protruding lower lips a family trait?"

Coquettishly she thrust out her chin and stuck out her lip even further. She saw his whole body tighten like a spring about to uncoil and fling itself across the room. His black eyes flashed a warning, a plea. In a moment he'd be next to her on the sofa, nibbling said lip, regardless of the imminent interruption. The crossed leg slid to the floor, and he had leaned ever so slightly forward when the door opened and Zach came in. They'd been saved by Zach's unintended good timing, but what of the next temptation?

Frustrating days after this close encounter with passion, after which Alex had extracted a reluctant promise from her to help him resist making love to her, Beth was on her way to St. Teath to while away an hour or two at Mrs. Turley's dress shop. She was driving the cabriolet, a lightly sprung pearl-gray equipage her father had given her as a gift shortly before he died. A glossy mare the same shade as the carriage pranced before it. One of the smaller stable lads stood on the back platform serving as tiger.

It was the first week of August, and the weather was as hot and steamy as Sadie's plum pudding when it was freshly unwrapped from its cloth on Christmas Day. Generally Beth did not suffer from the heat, but though it was only midmorning, even she was feeling a bit wilted by the time the outskirts of town came into view.

St. Teath was a charming, bustling little village perched on a cliff above Port Isaac Bay. The cobbled main road of town was steep as it wound down to the small cove and stone pier below. Shops and cottages were crammed together tightly, their sturdy walls and shutters a defense against the many storms that blew in from the Sea.

Beth halted the cabriolet in front of Mrs. Turley's shop, and the tiger jumped down from the back of the rig and took the ribbons from her while simultaneously helping her to alight from the carriage.

Beth smiled her thanks and instructed the boy to return for her at half past the hour of noon, allowing herself two hours to peruse through *La Belle Assemblée* and some of the other fashion magazines Mrs. Turley kept in the shop for reference as well as for choosing patterns, colors, and fabrics for gowns. Then, if she had time left, she would browse through some of the other shops and perhaps pick up some peppermint drops at the confectioner's for Gabby.

Beth watched the lad drive the carriage away to find a watering trough for the horse and a shady tree under which he might take a snooze. She should have brought a female servant with her to lend her countenance, she supposed. But she was feeling tetchy today and not of a mind for company, even if the company remained silent. The only company Beth wanted—needed—was Alex's, and he continued to honorably fulfill his role as supportive brother and tramp about the mine-infested moors with Zach. It seemed their business would never be done. It did not help that Zach continually promised to be her most devoted and humble servant when the work was finished.

Beth wavered back and forth these days between guilt and desire, sympathy and frustration, helplessness and anger, a sisterly love for Zach and an all-consuming, not-to-be-ignored passionate devotion to Alex. All she really knew for sure was that she would go mad if her predicament did not culminate soon.

In the meantime she would order a dress made. Something rose pink. Next to nothing at all, Alex preferred her in pink. Those had been his precise and very satisfying words. A womanly smile curved her lips as she smoothed her willow-green morning gown and straightened her straw bonnet preparatory to entering the shop.

Just as she stepped forward, however, she spied a familiar figure from out of the corner of her eye. She turned and observed Dudley strolling down the street in her direction, his lank form looming taller than anybody standing near him, his bright thatch of carrot-colored hair gleaming in the sunshine, his thumbs hooked in the waist of his white breeches. He did not see her; he was studying the different wares on display in shop windows and did not seem in a hurry to arrive at any particular destination. She supposed that Alex had given him permission to enjoy a day in town. Certainly he was not much needed at Pencarrow when Alex was gone nearly all day every day.

Although Beth was disinclined to seek company, somehow the idea of a friendly chat with Dudley was cheering. She liked him. And he was Alex's valet, intimately involved in all those rituals of dress and grooming that enhanced Alex's innate attractiveness. Like a romantical miss who foolishly treasured objects and people attached in some way to her beloved, Beth found herself drawn to Dudley. Perhaps she could contrive to turn the conversation toward Alex. It would be a pleasure to at least speak of him.

She walked toward Dudley and raised her hand in greeting. When he did not see her, she was about to call out his name, but a young woman stepped up from the road to intercept him just then. Dudley halted and gave the girl his complete attention. Beth stopped and watched. She was but a few feet away now and could see both of them clearly, but she could not hear their conversation. She hesitated to interrupt them, though she was burning with curiosity as to who the young woman was.

The girl was beautiful. Beth thought she'd seen her about town before. Indeed, she was the sort of person one couldn't help but notice. She was petite, a bit shorter than Beth. Her hair was butter yellow but had a sheen like fine silk. Braids adorned her temples, pulling her hair away from her face to fall in a mass of waves down her back. Her profile was fair

and finely hewn; her skin—at least from a distance—looked
as clear and smooth as marble but with a blush to it. Her
ivory gown was as fine as Beth's own, which piqued her
curiosity further. The girl couldn't be a servant because she
was too well dressed. But if she were gentry, Beth should
have known her from the social gatherings hosted by the
local upper crust. Possibly she was a rich merchant's
daughter.

Beth's forehead creased in puzzlement. No longer caring
whether it was polite to interrupt them or not, she started to
walk toward the pair. She had to know who the girl was. She
had a strong feeling that if she didn't know her, she ought
to.

As she approached the absorbed couple, she noticed that
the girl had draped a Venetian lace shawl about her in such
a way that it fell low about her waist and stomach. Beth
wondered why anyone would feel the need for a wrap on
such a hot day. The girl fingered the goffered edging of the
shawl with small nervous fingers.

"He's well, then?" Beth heard the girl say wistfully as
she stepped up to them. As they both realized that someone
had joined them, they looked up simultaneously. Beth
smiled first at Dudley, then at the girl.

"Good morning, Dudley," she said cheerily. "Are you
doing errands for Lord Roth or are you having a holiday?"

Beth did not know what she expected in the way of a
greeting, but certainly she expected some sort of reaction.
Dudley seemed chipped out of stone. He stood as motionless as a statue, his freckles in harsh relief against the
suddenly pale color of his skin. The girl's reaction to seeing
Beth was identical. She did not move, and the pretty blush
in her cheeks fled, leaving her as white as a corpse. Beth
was instantly chagrined. Indeed she had been amiss to
interrupt them. She could only conclude that there was some
sort of an understanding between the pair. But who was the
girl inquiring after?

"Miss Tavistock!" Dudley blurted out at last. "Fancy meeting you. I had no notion that you meant to come to town today."

"How could you, Dudley? I've not been to Pencarrow today, and I hardly endeavor to keep you appraised of *all* my activities," Beth returned teasingly. The playful remark elicited only a forced chuckle from Dudley and nothing at all from the girl, who had fixed her gaze to a spot on the ground and was biting her lower lip. There was a pause, during which an introduction between the two women ought to have been made if one was going to be made at all. But no introduction was forthcoming. This surprised Beth, since Dudley was usually so polite.

"Well, I had better get on with my business." Beth was acutely uncomfortable but still exceedingly curious. "I've come to see Mrs. Turley to order a new gown."

"It was delightful to see you, miss," Dudley said, bowing. "If I can assist you with packages, I would be pleased to meet you wherever and whenever you wish."

"That won't be necessary, Dudley." Then, with a sudden inspiration, she turned to the girl and said, "That's a lovely gown you're wearing. Did you have it made at Mrs. Turley's shop?"

The girl looked up, apparently startled to be spoken to. Beth decided she must be shy and smiled warmly at her. The girl was not put at ease by Beth's friendliness, however. In fact, she looked uncomfortably hot and agitated, as though she might swoon. Beth observed damp wisps of flyaway golden hair sticking to the girl's slender neck. Her lips were bled of color, lifeless.

"I . . . I made it myself, miss," the girl replied in a defferential tone, as if speaking to a superior. The voice was sweet, but there was a slight roughness in the accent, as though she had not had the benefit of an education.

"You look very much heated," Beth commented kindly.

"Perhaps you should sit down in the shade somewhere, and Dudley can fetch you a drink of water."

"No," she answered quickly. "I'm quite well. Don't trouble yourself about me, miss."

Indeed, her manner and address suggested that she was a servant, but Beth couldn't imagine anyone managing to dress so well on a servant's wages. Even though the girl had said she'd made the dress herself, the fabric was worth several pounds. Not to mention the Venetian lace shawl and the cameo brooch nestled in the gathered material of her bodice. That brooch . . . It was pale peach and ivory, with a delicate lacing of gold all around it, framing the silhouette inside most charmingly. It was very like the one Zach had described to her.

"What a lovely brooch," said Beth with genuine admiration. "My fiancé bought me one just like it, but he lost it before he got home to—"

"I . . . I must go!" the girl exclaimed, a patch of hectic color appearing on each cheek. "I'm meeting someone. Pardon me, sir, m-miss. I *must* go." Then she turned and stepped hurriedly into the road, not looking either way despite the clatter of hooves on the cobbles and the jingling traces of two large horses pulling a fast-approaching hay wagon.

"Watch out!" Beth called, her heartbeat paralyzed by the possibility of a dreadful accident.

"Tessy, watch out for the wagon! Tessy!" yelled Dudley, but the girl seemed deaf and blind to everything around her as she continued to move into the center of the thoroughfare while the wagon closed in upon her. As if in slow motion, Beth turned to look at the driver of the vehicle. He was a coarse, hard-looking fellow, occupied in the process of lighting a cheroot. He did not see Tessy, nor would he have been able to stop in time even if he'd looked up at that very instant.

Beth's instinct was to rush into the road and pull or push

the girl out of harm's way. But before she could act on this urge, Dudley bounded past her, dashed onto the cobbled pavement, grabbed Tessy by the arms, and hauled her to the opposite side of the road in the very nick of time.

The two horses reared up and whinnied, and the driver delivered a string of curses that would have made the devil himself wince. Then, having vented his wrath, he continued on his way as if nothing had happened. Chaos broke out on the walkway as Tess fell into the swoon that had been threatening to occur for some time. Dudley, who had not let loose his hold upon her arms, lowered the both of them to the ground and gently cradled her head against his thigh. Beth crossed the road and nudged through the knot of people gathered around them.

"Stand back. Stand back, please!" she ordered in her most authoritative manner. "The poor girl needs some air. Don't crowd her."

At Beth's admonitions, most of the people moved away and went about their business. The few who remained murmured sympathetically and hovered at a more discreet distance.

"Is she all right, Dudley? Did she swoon from fright? Is she ill, or is she just too hot?" Beth asked with a characteristic flurry of questions as she got down on her knees next to the unconscious girl. She reached into her reticule and found a fan, snapped it open, and began to ply it through the air next to Tessy's pale face.

"I think she'll be all right in a moment, miss," Dudley muttered, his expression grim. He looked up, spied a young boy in the crowd of curious onlookers, and said, "You there, lad. Fetch this girl a drink of water and I'll pay you a penny."

"Aye, sir," said the boy, rushing off to do his bidding.

"You know her, Dudley. You called her Tessy," said Beth. "Who is she?"

CHAPTER
twelve

DUDLEY HAD NEVER imagined that during a family visit to the rusticated shire of Cornwall he would find himself faced with so many damnable dilemmas. Encountering Beth at just the same moment as Tess seemed too unlikely a coincidence. The blackest sort of foul luck was the only explanation for it. Now Beth was demanding to know who Tess was.

"Well, Dudley?" Beth prompted. "I did not press for an introduction before, though I thought it ill-mannered of you not to offer one. And so unlike you, Dudley. But now I must know who this poor child is. Are you . . . very good friends?"

Dudley was alarmed by the implication of Beth's words. "No, miss. I hardly know her," he said truthfully, wishing he could speak the truth in saying he knew nothing of her at all.

"But you do know her a little," Beth said impatiently. "You know her name. And she asked you about someone. Whom did she ask about?"

Dudley hated telling lies. He was an honest man, but he was a practical man as well. He knew that sometimes the consequences of truth-telling were worse than those of lying. "She's acquainted with one of the servants at Pencarrow."

"Oh? Which one?"

"I don't know which one, miss."

"But she knew *you* were staying at Pencarrow. How did she come to know that, I wonder?"

"In a small village the manservant of a visiting peer is always taken note of, so to speak."

"Even by a girl like this? Dudley, I confess myself befuddled. She speaks like someone of the serving or working class, and yet she's dressed so very well. Do you think she's a merchant's daughter?"

Lord, how could he even begin to explain Tess's expensive toggery to a delicate female like Beth? Wouldn't things come to daggers drawn if he told her how Tess earned her blunt, and with whom she earned it? "Perhaps she's independent," Dudley muttered.

"Aye, she's independen' awright," said a sneering male voice from behind Dudley. "If bein' kept by a flash cove kin be called independen'."

"Be off with you," Dudley growled, twisting around to glare at the man. "All of you, leave. We aren't in need of any further assistance, thank you." The small group dispersed.

Dudley turned back to find Beth staring at him with wide eyes. "Oh, dear, you're not telling me that this sweet-looking girl is some man's mistress, are you? Why, she looks to be younger than I am."

"I'm not telling you anything, miss," said Dudley, taking refuge in a stiff, disapproving tone. "I don't like speaking of indelicate matters with females of your gentle upbringing."

"Posh!" Beth said scornfully. "It doesn't matter, anyway. The important thing is to help her. I thought she'd revive before now."

"I thought so, too," Dudley admitted worriedly. "Do you have any sal volatile in your reticule, Miss Tavistock?"

"Perhaps I do," Beth said, setting down the fan to rummage through her bag again. "I never know what I have in here. My abigail keeps it tidy for me, and I've never used salts in my life. I'm a very unnatural female, for I never swoon. Oh, here it is.'' She pulled out a small vial of milky liquid.

"With your permission, miss, I'll administer it. I've revived swooning ladies before.''

"How so, Dudley?''

"My mother was a midwife,'' he explained, uncorking the vial and waving the bottle beneath Tessy's nose. In a matter of seconds Tessy came to, choking and gasping from the pungent smell of the restorative. "Ah, success. But where's that lad with the water?'' Dudley craned his neck and looked up and down the street. Now people slowed down as they passed, but they did not stop to ogle. Perhaps on such a hot day, prostrate ladies on the main thoroughfare of town were not so uncommon a sight.

Tessy moaned and lifted the back of her hand to her forehead. She stared up at Dudley and Beth in a dazed way; then she clutched her stomach and turned on her side. Dudley's eyes were riveted to Tessy's arm clasped protectively about her middle. He knew then, as surely as he knew his own name, that Tessy was with child.

Now that he was made aware of the condition, and with the way the gown lay close against her without a shawl to disguise her shape, his keen eyes could detect the thickness through her middle in variance with the slenderness of her arms and the trim ankles peeking out at the bottom of the flounced dress. An untrained eye would not immediately have recognized that Tessy was breeding. She carried the child low and flat. But he'd seen other women built the same way. They were usually small through the pelvis, too, and had the devil of a time delivering a babe. Some of them died.

"Here's your water, sir!'' said the boy, panting from his run up the hilly road. "Had to go a mite farther than I figured. Where's my coin?''

"In a minute. First we'll quench the lady's thirst, if you

don't mind." Dudley gently raised Tessy's head and helped her to a drink of water from the rough tin cup while Beth continued to look worried as she plied the fan energetically through the torpid air.

When Tessy had regained a little color in her cheeks, Dudley dug into a breeches pocket, pulled out a penny, and flipped it to the boy. The boy caught it neatly, held it up to the morning sun to admire its glint, and finally tested its metal between his teeth. Satisfied, he said, "Thank ye, sir," and swaggered away as if he owned the town.

Though Tessy had been revived physically, her embarrassment and emotional discomfort became more and more acute. When Beth had first joined them, Dudley could see that Tessy recognized her. He was sure she was horrified to be receiving such kind and sympathetic treatment from a woman who was, in essence, her rival. They both shared the same man, though in vastly different ways and with vastly different expectations. Judging by the way things were developing between his master and Beth, however, Dudley expected things to get a lot more complicated. And with this babe coming into the picture . . .

"Are you all right, Tessy?" Beth asked.

Tessy gasped when she heard her name on Beth's lips. She turned to Dudley, a mute question in her frightened gaze.

"Tessy, this is Miss Tavistock of Brookmoor Manor," he said evenly, trying to convey assurances with a speaking look. "You may have seen her about town before. She, however, doesn't know you and, in fact, has been chastising me for not introducing you earlier. I told her you were acquainted with a servant at Pencarrow and that you had heard I was staying there as valet to Lord Roth. That's why you stopped me, wasn't it, to send a greeting to your acquaintance? But I must confess, I've quite forgotten who it is you know. Is it Jem? Or perhaps it's Henry?"

Fortunately Tessy was not a thimble-wit and quickly

followed Dudley's lead. "It's Jem I know, sir. He's acquainted with my family." Then she raised her eyes briefly to Beth's. "Thank you, miss, for your kindness. But please don't let me keep you from your business any longer. I'm just a little overcome by the heat." Then before Beth could reply, she turned to Dudley. "Will you help me up, please, sir?"

Dudley pulled Tessy to her feet, lending her time to regain her balance with a firm hand at her elbow. Tessy swayed a little and bit her lip, giving the distinct impression that she was not yet recovered from her fainting spell.

Beth apparently shared Dudley's opinion in this, for she cried, "Look at you! You're still weak and unsteady. You must allow us to escort you home."

"I'll see her home, miss," Dudley quickly interjected. "I'm sure the young lady would not wish to inconvenience you further," he added pointedly. This time he was trying to relay an unspoken message to Beth. Balancing between the two women, trying to keep the most painful facts secret, he felt as if he were walking a tightrope at Astley's Circus.

"Very well, then, I'll say good morning, Tessy," said Beth, comprehending Dudley's hint, though she seemed reluctant to go. Dudley supposed that Beth was concerned about Tessy because she was fragile-looking, because she was unwell at the moment, and because she imagined Tessy to be at the mercy of some dastardly man. She probably felt for Tessy in that intrinsic, empathetic way one woman feels for another, especially when a man is involved. She would have felt all the more empathetic had she known Tessy was breeding. Yet how would Beth react if she knew Zach had fathered the child?

"Thank you again, miss," said Tessy over her shoulder as Dudley walked alongside her, supporting her light frame with little effort by tucking her arm inside the crook of his elbow.

"You remember where I live?" she asked him as they progressed slowly up the hill, leaving Beth behind.

"Indeed, that night is deeply etched upon my memory. I could probably find your cottage blindfolded!"

Tessy smiled but sobered quickly, saying, "She's very nice, isn't she?"

"Very nice."

"I wish she weren't," Tessy disclosed wistfully.

"I'm sure you do. Makes it all the harder, doesn't it?"

There was a long pause. Then Tessy said, "You never had a chance to tell me how Zach is. I know he's busy. But is he well? Is he happy?"

"You haven't seen him at all in the last three weeks?"

"No."

"Perhaps you should wait till he visits you next and ask him these questions yourself."

Tessy sighed. "His next visit will be a trying one."

"You're going to tell him about the child?"

Tessy halted and looked searchingly at Dudley. "Is it so obvious?"

"No. Your shawl and the cut of your dress disguise your condition quite nicely. But not for long. How far along are you?"

"Going on to six months, three weeks, as far as I can tell. But if I'm so well disguised, Dudley, how did you know?"

"As you lay on the walkway, your shape was clearly defined. And the manner in which you held your stomach when you awakened was . . . telling."

Tessy suddenly clutched his arm. "Beth . . . Miss Tavistock doesn't know, does she?"

"No."

"Then how is it that *you* know, Dudley, and nobody else?"

"I'm unique, Tessy," he said with a sigh and a smile, though the smile was more like a grimace. "Although I am a man, I see things from a remarkably feminine viewpoint.

I think my upbringing, playing helpmate to my mum's midwifery duties in London, contributed to this affinity I feel for womankind.''

"I wish more men were like you, Dudley," Tess declared with fervor. "You'd think Zach, of all people, would have guessed by now that I'm breeding. Then I wouldn't be faced with the daunting prospect of telling him about the babe at a time when he's least apt to be pleased about it.''

"What do you mean?"

"I'm not a fool, Dudley."

"Far from it, Tessy!"

"I've had a feeling for some time that Zach's going to leave me. Ever since his brother came to Pencarrow, nothing's been the same." Tessy looked Dudley straight in the eye. "I'm right, aren't I? He's going to leave me."

"I don't know what he'll do, especially now, what with the babe coming and all," Dudley said evasively. "Which fact, by the by, you won't need to tell him. Unless Zach's blind or a complete loggerhead, on his next visit I'm sure he'll finally realize how the land lies, so to speak."

"Yes, he'll know then. And I'll know, too," Tessy said as if to herself and with a faraway look in her eye.

Dudley felt a shiver of premonition shimmy down his spine. That look in Tessy's eyes did not bode well. He was afraid she loved Zach too much for her own good. He didn't want her to feel desperate if Zach did not meet her expectations. And though Tessy was no fool, her expectations concerning Zach and their relationship together were naive and rose-colored, viewed through the myopic eyes of love.

Dudley stopped and turned to Tessy, took her hands in his and chafed them softly. He looked not at her but rather at their hands pressed together. "Tessy, I want you to know that if you ever need someone, if you need anything— anything at all—you can always send word to me. I know what it's like to be alone and needful." He lifted his eyes and looked into Tessy's worried face.

"Do you think I'll be alone and needful, Dudley?" she asked.

Dudley could have kicked himself. He tried again. "No, dear. I've known Zach since he was no higher than my boot tops, and he'll do right by you and the child. Though he may initially be upset, Zach will never let you and the babe want for anything."

"I had wished for more." Tessy's eyes grew misty. "'Tis not the money, the security, I want. I want Zach. And I'm willing to share him with his wife. I still have hope, Dudley, that he'll love the child enough that we might become his second family."

Rose-colored vision, indeed, thought Dudley. He shook his head grimly. "Most wives won't stand for that sort of situation. Nor would you if you were married to Zachary. Especially since you live so near to each other, it would be difficult for Beth to turn a blind eye to the arrangements. And people can be cruel. You wouldn't want your child to suffer from the sort of vicious gossip people are capable of, would you?"

Tessy bowed her head. "No. I don't wish our child to suffer anything. I wish her to have the best life any girl could ever have. Much better than mine."

Dudley raised Tessy's chin with a forefinger and looked into her glistening eyes with a teasing smile. "You think it's a girl, do you?"

"I know it is," she said firmly, smiling through her tears. "A golden-haired beauty, just like her father."

"With a sweet, loving spirit, just like her mother," Dudley added. They stood there for a moment, just smiling at each other, till all of a sudden Dudley seemed to shake himself before saying briskly, "Now we had best get you home and out of this heat." He tucked her arm neatly against his side as before and gently urged her forward.

"Did I tell you I have some wonderful herbal remedies we can mix up that will help that dreadful ache in the lower back you pregnant ladies endure? And as for puffy ankles, it's simply a matter of putting one's feet up every morning and afternoon for at least an hour."

"Oh, Dudley, you *are* unique," said Tess, laughing.

Beth stared after the couple until they disappeared over the summit of the road. Despite the heat, she was oddly disinclined to move. After the rather dramatic events of the last half hour, choosing a pattern and fabric for a new gown seemed a trivial occupation.

Finally, as she became conscious of people staring at her curiously, she crossed the road and entered the dress shop. She was greeted there by one of Mrs. Turley's employees, a smartly dressed young woman with an ingratiating smile and a French accent, both of which were false. Once the woman had ascertained Beth's reasons for being there, she led her to an elegant little table and chair and invited her to look at fashion plates. Beth thanked her, sat down, and tried hard to concentrate on the task before her. But in every sketch that portrayed a fair-haired woman modeling an evening gown, a walking gown, or any sort of gown at all, she saw the girl, Tessy.

Beth knew that women sold themselves for money, for security, sometimes even for love. She had known for many years that such women existed, whether they went by the name of doxy, mistress, or fancy piece. She had never made the acquaintance of women who had earned such labels, but Beth had never supposed that one of them would look like Tessy. Meeting her that morning had changed forever Beth's heretofore fixed ideas about mistresses. She had always pictured them hard, brassy, buxom, and crude, not delicate with a gentle manner and a sweet countenance, like Tessy.

Beth sighed. She couldn't even imagine the circum-

stances that had precipitated Tessy's decision to accept a
man's protection in exchange for sexual favors. She wondered if this was Tessy's first liaison with a man or if there
had been others. She was so young, yet she had probably
dealt with far more of life's grim realities than Beth ever
would.

Beth's life had been easy and delightful, full of love and
laughter, comfort and stability. Her greatest trials had
occurred in the last two months, since Alex came to
Pencarrow. The mining incident and her realization of her
love for Alex had been the most emotionally harrowing
experiences she'd dealt with since her father's death. Since
she and Alex had made love, it was agony having to keep
him at arm's length; but the hardest part was yet to come.
They still had to tell Zach.

"Mademoiselle? Have you found something you would
like us to sew for you?"

Beth's attention was claimed by the simpering dressmaker's
assistant. Since Beth hadn't turned the page of the magazine
for several minutes while she pondered heavy thoughts, the
woman probably thought she had decided on the pattern in
front of her and was mentally envisioning it in different
fabrics and colors.

Beth looked down at the pattern. The sketch was of a
golden-haired woman in a gown the soft ivory of clotted
cream with butter-yellow trimmings at the bodice, sleeves,
and hem. The pale, delicate colors made her think of the
blossoms of honeysuckle, and honeysuckle made her think
of Tessy. A hint of a scent had clung to Tessy, and Beth
realized now that it was honeysuckle she'd smelled. Beth's
brows furrowed in puzzlement. Hanging on the perimeter of
her memory was another connection to honeysuckle, but she
couldn't quite grasp it. . . .

"Mademoiselle? Have you made a decision?"

When Beth looked at the assistant, she saw controlled
impatience behind the carmined smile. She stood abruptly.

Suddenly the little shop with all its dainty gilded furniture and calculated elegance seemed oppressive.

"I'm wasting your time," she confessed with an apologetic smile. "I can't decide. I shall have to come back another day."

"As you wish, mademoiselle." The answer was stiff, but the smile remained intact, as bright and false as paste diamonds.

Outside, Beth welcomed the heat of the sun on her shoulders, the press of humid air against her skin. Her life was good. This fact was made forcefully clear by a comparison with Tessy. She didn't know particulars about the girl, but she felt an instant liking, an instant sympathy, for her. She wished she could help her, yet there was no outward indication that Tessy needed or wanted help. Even if they were destined never to meet again, Beth felt as though she'd been touched by Tessy and reminded of her own good fortune.

Beth stepped onto the walkway and began to climb the hill in the direction the tiger had driven her carriage. She thought of Alex, and her spirit soared. Stirred by this exhilaration, every nerve in her body was sensitized, every sense keenly awakened to the sights, sounds, and scents all around her. The azure blue of the cloudless sky. The quaint stucco and brick of the squat little houses and shops with tidy yards no bigger than a square of calico and just as riotous of color. Gold-dusted snapdragons, granny's bonnets, columbines, and larkspur, all in blooming profusion.

Beth welcomed even the fishy smell of the sea. Passing the bakery, she breathed the aroma of fresh-from-the-oven bread and cakes. Strolling by the Nag's Head Inn just as someone came out, she caught a glimpse of men sitting around a long table, eating and drinking and making merry. Their loud, deep laughter made her smile.

The pull and flex of muscle felt good, too, as did the fall of soft muslin against her legs as she walked along. Beth felt blessed to be alive, blessed to be in love. If only everyone could be as lucky as she!

Sweat trickled down Alex's neck and inside his collar. His hair slanted across his forehead in damp waves. He had long ago shed his coat and wrapped it around the saddle pommel. His horse was so heated and thirsty that the poor beast was lathering at the mouth. It was just past noon and the hottest day he could remember since coming to Cornwall.

"The creek is just ahead," said Zach, wiping his arm across his perspiring upper lip. "We can water the horses, then cross at that narrow spot closest to the house."

Alex nodded. If he understood Zach correctly, the spot where they would cross was exactly where he and Beth had made love in the tall grass near the oak tree. He had avoided that particular section of the estate for the last two weeks. He'd wanted no reminders of that glorious night, for he had needed to keep a tight rein on his desire till he deemed it an appropriate time to tell Zach about himself and Beth.

Presently the shrubs and trees that followed the meandering creek came into view. He and Zach guided their horses through and around the foliage, stopped at the creek beneath the shade of a clump of overgrown juniper, and dismounted. The horses immediately bent to drink. Alex and Zach stooped by the pebbly shore and cupped water to splash over their faces and necks.

"Hotter than Hades," commented Zach.

"Hotter even than that," Alex returned, easing himself down on the grass by the bank, one leg tucked under him and the other bent at the knee. He rested one arm on the raised knee and tore fistfuls of grass with his free hand.

Zach sat down near him, his legs crossed Turkish style. "What's hotter than Hades, brother?" he asked lazily.

"Cornwall in August," Alex answered, throwing a wad

of grass into the creek and watching the water sweep it away.

Zach chuckled, then fell silent, his eyes seeming to rest on the rippling stream, but Alex suspected that Zach was thinking about Tess. He hadn't been to see her since the mine episode. Alex knew this for a certainty, since he and Zach had been together almost constantly.

Alex hadn't discussed Zach's decision to leave his mistress since that first time Zach had brought it up. He was hoping that Zach would change his mind. There would be no need to terminate the arrangement once Zach and Beth's engagement was broken. But today they'd seen to conclusion the most pressing tasks on the estate, and there was no reason why Zach couldn't visit his mistress for the purpose of saying good-bye.

There was also no reason why Alex couldn't tell Zach about himself and Beth. He was tempted to bring up the subject immediately, but the grim set of Zach's mouth indicated that he was not in the mood for such a revelation. After dinner, when they were both refreshed from a bath and some good claret, he would do the deed. God, how he dreaded it! But worse than his dread of telling Zach was the torment of wanting Beth and living without her.

"Alex, did you know that posies made out of honey-suckle have a special significance?" Zach asked abruptly.

"What do you mean?"

"According to Granny Harker, our local witch-apothecary, the exquisite fragrance of the honeysuckle stands for the sweet nature of the one who gives it."

"Oh?" Alex turned and watched Zach intently.

"Yes. You see, if the ribbon that ties the posy is to the left, the flowers speak of the sender. If the knot is to the right, the sweetness of the recipient is paid tribute to."

"Who's giving you posies, Zach?"

Zach's mouth twitched, then stretched to a stern line. "No one. Tessy used to, and I used to give them to her."

"Do you miss her?"

If possible, Zach looked even grimmer. "Yes. But it doesn't matter. I'll forget her, as she'll forget me."

When Alex did not reply, Zach turned to him with a penetrating look. "I wonder you haven't been urging me to pay her my farewell visit. You don't seem to care anymore whether or not I keep her."

"I probably shouldn't have tried to advise you before," Alex replied dismissively. "Why don't we return to the house now? I need a bath." Alex stood up, walked to his horse, and stroked the stallion's damp black coat with a soothing hand.

Zach stood, too, and caught his own horse's bridle. "A capital idea. Talking in this curst heat is too fatiguing anyway."

"I would like to talk to you after dinner tonight, though," Alex told him with a serious look.

Zach raised a brow. "Certainly, brother. I shall save my breath to cool my broth, as they say. Or I'll save it till after dinner when you may turn into a regular jaw-me-dead and lecture me thoroughly about my duties, after which I shall have to defend myself. I'm quite certain you've been saving up a lecture or two over the past weeks, since you've been uncharacteristically quiet. Are you coming?" He mounted his dapple gray and waded the horse into the creek.

Alex patted his horse. "Go ahead. This fellow's not ready to move just yet. I'll be along shortly."

"As you wish," said Zach, and he crossed the creek and headed for the gates of Pencarrow.

Alex watched till his brother was inside the gates and out of sight; then he mounted his stallion and crossed the creek, immediately dismounting on the other side. He tethered the horse to a branch near enough to the creek so that the beast could drink, if he felt the inclination, as well as enjoy the expansive shade of the large tree.

Alex wasn't sure why, but he needed to see the spot

where he and Beth had made love. Perhaps he needed to relive the experience to fortify himself for the ordeal of facing Zach. He leaned against the tree and gazed toward Pencarrow, remembering how she'd looked as she'd crossed the field of tall grass. All in white, her rich brown hair tumbling about her shoulders and down her back, she'd seemed more the substance of dreams and visions than reality. At first he thought he'd gone mad and conjured up the image out of his intense desire to placate the sweet-creeping madness. But she'd been real.

He pushed away from the tree and turned, reaching out to touch the bark, remembering how he'd pressed her against the trunk in a frenzy of passion. His pulse leaped and quickened at the memory.

Then he walked toward where they'd lain in the grass, looking for an indentation. Weeks had passed. Wind and rain, as well as animals that stalked and scampered through the grass daily, had made it impossible to determine exactly where they'd made love. There was no evidence, no proof, that they had ever been there. Perhaps it had been a dream after all.

Then he saw them. First one, then another, like cats' eyes winking in the night, the pearly buttons of Beth's night rail caught and reflected back the sunlight. He reached down and plucked one from the grass, examined it, and rolled it between his fingertips as if it were a precious gem. Then he picked up all the others he could find and deposited them in his breeches pocket.

He turned and walked to his horse, mounted, and headed back to the house, well fortified for the evening ahead. After all, dreams and visions did not lose buttons in the grass.

CHAPTER
thirteen

AS BETH TOOLED her cabriolet through the gates of Pencarrow, she reached for her watch locket to observe the time. It was two o'clock. Alex and Zach usually returned home for a nuncheon in the middle of the day, and she was hoping that, by an odd chance, they'd still be there. Driving along the main road from St. Teath, she'd turned impetuously onto the lane that circled around by Pencarrow. She had intended to go straight home, but the urge to see Alex was overwhelming. And the sweltering day provided her with a perfect excuse to stop for a cooling drink of cider.

Beth did not pull up decorously in front of the house, but instead took the carriage around by the stables and left it and her horse in the care of the tiger before walking into the house through the kitchen garden. All the neat crops of lush vegetation and plots of flowers, girdled by a brick wall, looked wilted and bowed from the heat. Inside the kitchen she discovered the scullery maid sitting at the long, knife-scarred preparation table lethargically scraping potatoes.

"Hello, Kathy," Beth greeted her.

Kathy pulled up from her slump and smiled wanly. "Good afternoon, miss," she said. "What brings ye here in the middle of such a hot day? If ye've come t' see the master, I'm sorry t' tell ye I just seen 'im ride off not more'n ten minutes ago."

Beth's shoulders drooped with disappointment. "I see. He and Lord Roth have resumed their estate business for the

225

afternoon, I suppose?'' She pulled off her bonnet and pushed back the frizzed tendrils of hair that fell across her damp forehead. That morning her abigail had swept Beth's hair atop her head and secured it with oystershell combs, but now most of it fell loose about her neck and face. The humidity gave her hair twice its usual curl and thickness, and it was already quite hard to tame without the added volume pulling it down.

"No, miss. Lord Roth never left with 'im. I believe his lordship's still in the house. One o' the lads just took up buckets o' water fer a bath fer 'im.'' Kathy grinned. "Though I 'spect I ought not t' be mentionin' such things to a lady.''

Beth returned Kathy's smile, but the corners of her mouth twitched with the effort. A strong mental image of Alex bathing had disordered her thoughts and weakened her limbs, not to mention weakening her resolve to keep her promise to stay away. Visions of long muscular legs barely fitting inside the close confines of a copper tub caused aching knots of desire to form in her stomach.

"S-so Lord Roth is here, but Master Wickham isn't?'' she said, trying to appear nonchalant as she picked up a piece of peeled potato and took a bite. She swallowed and discovered that her throat had become exceedingly tight, making the lump of barely chewed raw potato stick and scrape all the way down.

"Aye, miss, the place is as quiet as a tomb t'day. Sadie's at the widow Beeny's, makin' her monthly charity visit. Bound t' be gone all afternoon till time fer dinner. Too hot to stir out o' the house leastways. If ye're fixed in one spot, I say stay fixed till eventide cools the air and makes it fit fer travelin'.''

"My sentiments exactly,'' Beth readily agreed, a deliciously wicked idea forming in her head. "But what of Stibbs? I should think he'd still be stalking about the house issuing orders, the heat notwithstanding.''

Kathy smiled impishly. "Stibbs is sleepin' in the cellar 'tween the wine racks, miss. Coolest place in the house, 'tis." Then Kathy suddenly sobered, adding, "Don't tell no one I tol' ye that, will ye? Stibbs'd have my hide!"

"Don't worry, I shan't tattle. Besides, I don't blame the old griffin for snoozing away such a dreadfully hot afternoon. But where's Dudley? I saw him in town this morning. Has he returned?"

"Mr. Dudley said he'd be out o' the house till dinner at least. He was in here this mornin', crowin' that his master had give 'im the whole day off t' do as he pleased. Wisht I had the easy life of a valet." Kathy pronounced "valet" in a sarcastic singsong and with a wrinkled nose.

"I doubt Dudley meant to brag," said Beth, automatically rising to Dudley's defense, though her thoughts were elsewhere. "Won't you fetch me a tumbler of cider, Kathy? I'm absolutely parched."

"Aye, miss," Kathy replied promptly as she stood up and wiped her hands on her apron. "Where will I serve it to ye?"

"Pour it now, and I'll take it with me upstairs. I believe I'm going to heed your advice and rest in my usual chamber till the afternoon heat has subsided somewhat. And will you also send some refreshment out to my servant who attended me here? He's watering the horse. Tell him I won't be going home for a while."

"Aye, miss." Kathy bobbed her head and walked into the larder, returning in a moment with a heavy crockery pitcher. She poured a brimming glassful of cider and handed it to Beth.

"Thank you, Kathy," Beth said in what she hoped was a calm manner, since her insides felt like a bowl of quivering blancmange. Then she smiled and walked sedately from the room, her glass of cider in one hand and her bonnet ribbons clutched in the other. She ascended the stairs, progressed down the gallery to her chamber, entered the room, and closed the door softly behind her.

Now in secret she could give vent to the rising tide of emotion that was threatening to wash out to sea every vestige of her common sense. She set the glass of cider and her bonnet on the dressing table and sat down on the edge of the bed, pressing her hands together and squeezing them between her knees in the hope that it might help her to stop trembling.

It didn't. She trembled all the more. She'd seen and pitied some man's mistress that morning, but what she was contemplating doing was as brazen and reckless as anything a fancy piece would do.

The house was virtually empty, except for a few servants who were probably sapped of all their energy and curiosity by the excessive heat. Many, like Stibbs, might be snatching a nap in a cool corner while the upper servants were absent from their posts. And there she sat in one bedchamber, aching for Alex, while he was in another bedchamber, probably stark naked.

Beth's hands flew to her hot face. She propped her elbows on her knees and held her head in her hands in an agony of indecision. She knew what she wanted to do. She wanted to go to Alex's bedchamber this very moment and throw herself into his arms, the risk of discovery be damned. But the prudent thing to do would be to drink her cider, bathe her flushed face, rest for a few moments, and then return home without ever allowing Alex to know she'd been there.

He'd told her quite clearly that he wanted to refrain from making love to her till he'd told Zach about them. She supposed this decision was based on a need to reestablish a code of honor and loyalty toward his brother, which she was sure Alex felt had been severely compromised. Perhaps by denying himself, and her, he was also inflicting a sort of punishment on the two of them, which made him feel better.

"Oh, I don't care," Beth muttered between her fingers. "Denying my need for you doesn't make me feel one jot better, Alex. I'm a selfish creature, and unrepentant, too, I suppose." She lifted her face from her hands and found her gaze had settled on the plump figure of a cupid embroidered on the fire screen. She'd never paid much attention to the playful stitchery picture of a naughty, naked cherub poised with quill and arrow in the midst of a garden paradise. But today it leaped out at her, seeming to imply that love was as fanciful as a myth and came to people as unpredictably as an errant arrow sent flying through the air by an aimless cupid.

Beth did not believe such a stupid theory for a moment. She stood up, resolution filling her heart. She and Alex were meant to be together, and their need for each other was as natural and blameless as a babe's need to suckle at its mother's breast. Before she lost her newfound courage, she lifted the glass of cider and took a bracing drink. She snatched a look at herself in the mirror and saw a wild-eyed woman with heated cheeks and hair in a tumble about her face, but she had no patience to stay and tidy herself, for every second she spent at her toilette was time spent away from Alex.

She opened the door and scanned the gallery for signs of life. There were no discernible sounds, no footfalls, no distant conversations hanging indistinct on the heavy air. She crept out and closed the door behind her, releasing the latch with the self-consciousness of a house burglar. She tiptoed down the hall and around the corner till she was in the gallery in which Alex's bedchamber was located.

Lord, if someone saw her now, it would be well nigh impossible to explain why she happened to be where she was, since no common apartments where people congregated could be found in that section of the house. Then, having reached the door she meant to enter, she stretched forth a hand to open it. What would he do? Would he shout with surprise and overset the tub, alerting the entire household to her shameless foray into a bachelor's bedchamber?

No, he was much too cool and clever for that sort of behavior, she decided, though her heart beat like hard rain on a tin roof, fierce and loud. But what if Shadow was inside? He might bark. Then she remembered that she had seen Shadow in the mews, asleep in the hay, when she'd left her rig at the stables. She turned the knob . . . silently, thankful that Stibbs made sure the knobs and hinges were kept oiled. As she slowly opened the door, her view of the room widened. First she saw the scarlet swags of moreen curtains pulled back from the open windows to admit whatever capricious breeze might come along, the mammoth bed set on a dais and covered with a red silk counterpane, and finally, the black marble Adam fireplace, a fairly recent addition to the largely Tudor-style house. And there on the tiles in front of the fireplace was the copper tub, and inside it . . . Alex.

He was immersed in water up to his neck, his knees seeming to float like smooth brown-beached islands in the foamy water. His eyes were shut, the ebony lashes a slash of kohl against his cheeks. But he'd apparently detected the soft scuff of her slippers on the polished wood floor and felt the slight stirring of air as she shut the door noiselessly behind her, because, though his eyes remained shut, a fissure of irritation marred his tranquil expression.

"Lad, I said I'd enough water and was quite capable of bathing myself. I don't need mollycoddling. Thank you for your assiduous care, but please leave me alone."

He sounded authoritative and more than a little exasperated. Perhaps his nerves were just as raw and his emotions just as tumbled and needful as Beth's. She hoped that meant he'd be as happy to see her as she was to see him. Even his voice produced tremors of electric awareness through her, sending her blood pulsing through her veins.

"Dudley, is that you? Well, speak up! Damnation, I've had just about enough of this."

Alex peeked grudgingly through half-closed eyes. No doubt he had intended to look daggers at the chucklehead who insisted on disturbing his bath, but he didn't know quite how to react to finding Beth in his bedchamber. Sliding one bare, wet arm over the lip of the tub for support, he pulled himself up. As his upper torso rose out of the water, soapsuds slipped down the beautifully sculpted contours of his chest, sliding around the dark wine-colored nipples, catching in shiny knots of bubbles where the water-slicked black hair was the thickest.

Beth stood with her back to the door, her hands clasped behind her. The bodice of her willow-green muslin stretched taut across her breasts as she breathed deep and fast. When his eyes locked with hers, she felt a jolt of pure, undiluted pleasure surge through her.

"God, Beth, what are you doing here?" His reaction appeared to match the intensity of her own. His expression was equal portions of shock and elation.

She was entranced with looking at him, but she wanted to see more. More than that, she wanted to touch him. She took a step closer and said in a rush, "Nobody's home, Alex. Zach is gone. Dudley and Sadie are gone. Even Stibbs is napping in the cellar between the wine racks." She clapped a hand over her mouth. "Oh, dear, I wasn't supposed to tell anybody that."

Alex laughed, then stopped and looked disconcerted, as if he hadn't expected to laugh, or thought it inappropriate given the circumstances. "What are you talking about, my Beth? Old hatchet face is lying between the wine racks? Foxed, I suppose. But Lord, Beth, what are you *doing* in here?"

Beth took another step forward, hands clasped demurely behind her, but with anything but demure thoughts possessing her mind and motivating her behavior. "I told you, Alex. Nobody's here. The maid saw Zach leave and then told me where everybody else is. We're . . . we're quite alone, you see, except for a few sleepy servants." She took another step.

"Zach's gone?" Alex's brows dipped in a frown. "I suppose he's gone to—" He stopped abruptly and shifted his eyes about the room, resting here, there, then back to Beth. "I suppose he's gone to town. I was going to tell him about us after dinner."

"Perhaps he plans to return for dinner," Beth suggested with an uninterested shrug of her shoulders, all the while looking at Alex in a most interested fashion. "But there are several hours before dinner, you know."

Alex laughed again, but this time there was an underlying tension that was palpable, that hung, teasing and tempting, in the still, damp air between them. Beth liked the smell of his soap. It made her think of ferny dales and musky herb gardens, with a tang of spice. She liked the way his hair curled above his forehead, the dark coils plumped and shiny with water.

Alex let loose a hissing breath. "Beth, I don't think this is particularly wise. We might be found out. And, worse even than that, this is Zach's house. I'd feel like an absolute scoundrel making love to you under Zach's very roof."

Beth felt the genesis of anger and hurt pushing its way through the haze of passion. "Alex, are you ashamed of us?" she demanded to know. "If we love each other and are committed to each other, there's no shame in it. Would you feel better about this, more *noble*, if I married Zach? Then there'd be no guilt to deal with, just a few decades of loneliness and wretched remorse—at least for me."

"Ah, Beth, for me, too!" Alex assured her, his eyes darkening with swiftly building emotion. He braced his hands on the sides of the tub and seemed about to stand up, then stopped abruptly, looking almost sheepish.

Beth tried to cloak the eager look she was sure was evident in her eyes by dropping her gaze to the floor, but she couldn't help the small smile that tilted her lips. "If you're feeling a tad modest, Alex, I won't look. I know it was dark before.''

"Which time are you talking about, my Beth?'' he retorted softly. "The sun was shining full and bright that day at Dozmary Cove when first you saw me naked.''

Beth's eyes flitted upward to meet his highly amused expression. "You knew I was there? You've known all along that I saw you that day? Why didn't you say something?''

"Indeed, Beth, what could I say? 'Oh, Miss Tavistock, I chanced to see you yesterday at Dozmary Cove. So rude of me not to greet you with a bow, but I felt a trifle too informal in my state of dishabille. I hope you will forgive me. By the by, did you like what you saw?' ''

Beth giggled, her cheeks exploding with heat, and she reached up to hide the increased color that she knew had blossomed there. "I'd have died if you'd spoken so to me. I felt so guilty about watching you, especially since I *did* like what I saw *ever* so much!''

Alex settled back into the water. He drew his knees up and leaned his folded arms atop them. Over this quickly constructed plateau of beautiful crisscrossed male arms, he looked at her. His teasing smile was gone. He was dead serious. "Why are you so honest, Beth? You devastate me with your honesty. You humble me with your honesty. Lord, you *seduce* me with it!''

Beth rolled a shoulder. "I can't seem to be anything but honest with you, Alex. Lying to you would be like lying to myself, which I don't like above half, I can tell you. I'd been lying to myself ever since you came to Pencarrow, telling myself I didn't want you. I've never felt so truly myself, so liberated, as I did that night by the creek. Since then it's been hard . . .'' She took another step forward.

He watched her intently. "Would you like me to tell you something—honestly—about that day at the cove?''

She nodded, her throat dry, every nerve vibrant with expectation.

"I knew you were watching me and I liked it. I liked it excessively." His lips twisted ruefully. "I wanted to strut before you like a puffed-up peacock with all my colorful plumes spread for inspection."

She returned his smile. "Why didn't you? As I recall, you jumped into the ocean, disturbing Shadow from his slumber. I was compelled to leave."

"I was compelled to hide my arousal from your fascinated virginal gaze. I did not wish to surprise and alarm you with the . . . er . . . changes that come about when a man is aroused."

He was alarming her now. Oh, how he was alarming her, and oh, how she enjoyed being thus alarmed. "You did not frighten me by the creek. Since we made love, I've come to appreciate the importance of . . . arousal. I don't think I shall ever again dislike being . . . alarmed."

Alex's grin slackened and disappeared. His eyes were piercing, as black as Judas's soul. "Beth, you take my breath away with your words, as if Gentleman Jackson himself had plowed a huge fist into my belly. You must have been born a seductress, an enchantress like the sirens who mesmerize sailors and dash their ships against rocky shores. I wonder you do not leave in your wake a similar spoil of male bodies."

"I was no seductress till I met you, Alex," she replied. "'Tis only you I wish to mesmerize, as you've mesmerized me."

For a long moment they simply stared at each other, hearts beating wildly, breathing allocated to a secondary necessity of life, next to their need for each other.

Alex broke the charged silence. "There's a key on the chest by the wardrobe."

Beth walked unhesitatingly to the chest, found the key, and locked the door. She turned and looked at Alex, as if waiting for further instruction. In the school of love she was happy to be a most biddable student.

"Now, Beth, take off all your clothes, and do it slowly. You've seen me in the bright light of day, yet I've enjoyed your delectable little body only by moonlight." He rested his chin on his folded arms, a bemused smile on his lips, as if he anticipated a leisurely tryst with pleasure.

"Are you complaining, my lord?" Beth quipped, licking her upper lip nervously. She hoped he'd like what he saw by sunlight.

"Are you stalling, my Beth?" he shot back.

She wrinkled her nose in reply and proceeded, with shaky fingers, to untie her gown at the back. The gown was simply made, overlapping and fastened with only two lengths of ribbon. This swiftly accomplished, she nudged down the short puffed sleeves till her arms were free. The bodice fell in billows about her waist. She hooked her thumbs in the soft material and eased the dress down past her hips and to the floor. She stepped out of the gown and stood in her white cambric shift. She was thrilled and reassured to know that her inexperience in such matters was not off-putting to Alex; the ardent, soft-hard look in his eyes had intensified.

Alex was glad to be immersed in a cloudy camouflage of tepid water. His body had quickened the moment he set eyes on Beth, but now his loins were achingly engorged with desire. Sensuality incarnate, an innocent temptress, was his Beth. Circles of perspiration had collected on her shift, beneath her arms, in the valley between her breasts, at the dip of her navel. Even where it wasn't wet, the shift gave a collective impression of molded liquid, clinging loverlike to every swell and hollow of her body. He watched as a trickle of sweat rolled down her chest from the base of her throat, sliding into the dark, moist cleavage.

His eyes returned to bore into hers. "Well then, Beth?" he rasped, deploring his own eagerness. This was too exquisite an experience to hurry.

She smiled crookedly, the dimple in her right cheek showing like a crescent moon against a dusky pink sky. "You said to go slowly."

"Not so slowly that you drive me insane. Or is that your intention, Delilah?"

"A mad lord with a lascivious smile on his lips as they trundle him off to Bedlam would be satisfying scandal-broth for the ton to sip," she suggested playfully.

"Beth!"

She pushed down one small capped sleeve of her shift, then the other, baring both smooth, rounded shoulders. Then she did a sort of wiggle and thrust, wiggle and thrust, till the cambric fabric clung with teasing precariousness to both erect nipples before dropping at last to catch on the womanly swell of her hips. She seemed to be about to shake her hips and dislodge the undergarment, allowing it to fall about her feet, when Alex stopped her.

"Not yet, Beth," he said, his voice husky and low. "Let me look at you."

Aphrodite could not possibly have been more alluring, he thought. Beth's breasts were milky mounds, firm and upright, the nipples as richly tinted as damask roses. Her waist curved perfectly into a flat stomach. The shift still clung to her slim hips, but just barely.

"Now?" she asked, the eagerness in her eyes a reflection of his own impatience. He nodded. She rotated her hips, and the shift fell to the floor.

The sight of legs as long as a lazy summer day increased Alex's internal temperature to match the simmering heat outside. The rounded thighs and calves and trim ankles looked satin-smooth. Ah, yes, how well he remembered. They'd felt like a skein of exotic silk slipping between his own hair-dusted legs, twining round his waist. . . .

"Now it's your turn," Beth informed him with a tilt to her chin, a wicked look in her aqua-blue eyes.

"I'm already undressed," he retorted. "Or hadn't you noticed?"

"Yes, you appear to be unclothed," she conceded, "but unless you stand up, I won't know for sure, will I?"

Alex chuckled nervously. "You minx! You shameless baggage! Join me. Come! The water's refreshing."

"I'll come only if you stand up and make room for me. The tub is small, and you are quite large, my lord."

Alex knew not how to respond to Beth's assertiveness. It had been dark when they'd made love. And earlier, when she saw him on the beach, he was not aroused. He felt a trifle reluctant to show himself now, since he knew himself to be hard and swollen to the point where he might indeed alarm her, despite her brave and brazen words. The extent to which he wanted her made him feel vulnerable, too.

"Come, Alex," she coaxed. "Here is your opportunity to strut like a peacock. I believe I would exceedingly enjoy such a sight."

With a slight moue of reserved uncertainty, Alex finally complied. Beth watched as he straightened himself, braced his hands on the sides of the tub and slowly stood.

He was like Neptune rising from the foamy sea, but even that mythological ideal could not surpass the beauty of Alex's naked body. His wide chest narrowed to a spare waist and hips, a flat stomach, and long—ever so long— legs. All of him glistened like a merman, water-sheened, sensually slippery. And that part of him, which he referred to with modesty as his arousal, was proud, erect, the epitome of manhood.

"Beth?"

Alex's voice was a little uncertain, as if he was afraid he'd frightened her. But when his gaze searched hers, his concern disappeared under the blatant, unflinching admiration reflected there. "Well, come, then," he said gruffly, his arms extended in invitation.

Beth went. Later she could not recall those few seconds

as she crossed the floor to step into the tub. Perhaps the journey was lost in the confusion while her brain busily registered all of the delicious, delirious sensations being transmitted from every nerve as their bodies made contact.

Beth was immersed to the knees in lukewarm water. Alex has placed his large hands at the indentation of her waist and pulled her against his water-slicked body, at the same moment capturing her mouth in a hard, urgent kiss. Teeth and tongues, satin-moist corners, were rediscovered. So many sensations, so many aching points of connection. Tender nipples against wet, hair-textured chest. Belly against belly, his rigid arousal pressed between them, carnally enticing.

Beth's hands roamed over his shoulders and down his muscled back. She broke the kiss and dipped her head to nibble his shoulder, her tongue pleasuring itself in the moistness of his warm skin. Then her hands slid down to cup and knead his firm buttocks, as she bent her head to find his nipple, which she took between her lips and suckled greedily.

A growl of pleasure rumbled from Alex; his hand on her shoulders bit almost painfully into her flesh. "Let go, you water nymph, or I'll take you—now!—in the tub. The resulting tidal wave will leak through the floorboards and alert the household. Come." He pulled her upright with his hands tucked under her arms, his thumbs grazing the outsides of her breasts.

In accord, they stepped out of the tub and moved to the bed, heedless of the water dripping on the floor. They stepped on the dais and sank onto the crimson counterpane, instantly enfolded in each other's embrace, arms and legs already entwined in a body poem of beautiful physical prose.

Beth lay on her back with the cool silk beneath her and Alex above her, her nerves aquiver with a calliope of sensations—wet and dry fillips of roughness, sleek caresses, fire and ice.

He touched her; he worshiped every inch of her body with his hands and his mouth—a clever mouth so adept at making her murmur and softly exclaim with unexpected pleasure. When she was near crazed with need, she wrapped her legs around his waist and pushed her pelvis hard against his. She took his face in her hands and looked at him beseechingly. "Alex, love me."

Mingled perspiration and scented water beaded dewlike on Alex's face, his chest and arms. He held between his teeth the inside corner edge of his bottom lip, and his eyelids drooped, giving the incongruous image of an ardent grimace. He, too, had only a tenuous hold on his urge to consummate their lovemaking immediately.

"No," he rasped. "If I must go to the devil for my sins or be posted off to Bedlam in a restraining gown because you—witch!—have driven me mad, I will prolong the damning process as long as possible." Then, with one fluid movement, he rolled over on his back and pulled Beth atop him.

Beth trembled and thrilled at Alex's provocative threat. Her breasts were flush against his chest, her arms supporting her on either side. Her legs were parted, slightly straddling him, though she still reclined. She looked at him, wide-eyed. "What should I do now, Alex?"

Alex laughed, his black Gypsy eyes glimmering. He raised his arms above his head and linked his hands under his neck. "There are no 'shoulds' or 'shouldn'ts' in lovemaking, gosling. Do with me as you feel inclined. I assure you, it's all been done before, yet has never lost its allure over the centuries."

Beth believed him. She couldn't imagine ever tiring of bedding with Alex. Then she did as he bade her to do—she followed her instincts.

Beth pushed herself up till she was fully astride him, her

knees on either side of his hips, the smooth, hot tip of his
manhood nudging the insides of her thighs. She feathered
her fingers along his shoulders, his chest, his stomach, while
her eyes lovingly followed each caress. Her woman's pride
rejoiced when she noticed his responding quiver or flush or
cluster of gooseflesh. She looked up and saw that his eyes
were closed, as if in an ecstatic dream.

Spurred on by this proof of her own feminine power, she
pulled her legs up and over his and eased between his
thighs. She placed her hands, palms down, on his chest
and bent to kiss him there, lingering over each nipple with
the savoring delight of a confirmed gourmet. She liked his
nipples, she decided, best of all.

Now she closed her eyes and brushed her breasts across
his chest and stomach, back and forth, back and forth,
rhythmically, as if she were in a trance. The wet, teasing
spirals of chest hair tantalized Beth's rigid nipples. She went
lower and lower, alternately nuzzling him with her open
mouth and brushing his body with her breasts. She kissed
his firm stomach.

Suddenly she felt his hands tangle in her hair and heard
him moan with a deep resonating shudder. It thrilled her to
the core to give him so much pleasure. His hips rose
slightly, and she felt his manhood press against the under-
side of her chin. Instinctively, wantonly, she dropped her
chin and took him full in her mouth.

Alex's hands clutched her hair, then swiftly reached
down to grasp her shoulders and pull her up to face him. She
was surprised and mortified. "Oh, I'm so sorry, Alex! Did
I do something wrong?"

"No, my Beth," Alex said, a ragged, constrained edge to
his voice. "You did something very right, but so very
unexpected that it almost finished our lovemaking on the
spot."

Beth was confused but pleased by Alex's words of
reassurance, and quite willing to wait for further explana-

tions at a later time. Besides, Alex did not seem in the mood for an instructional conversation.

Suddenly she was on her back again, and Alex was on top of her. He reached down between her thighs and caressed the downy mound that seemed to be the center of all Beth's most urgent yearnings. He inserted a finger and plunged deep. Beth gasped as a spasm of pleasure unfurled in her lower stomach.

"Aye, you're ready," Alex whispered. "As am I."

Then Alex parted her legs and positioned himself between them. Beth drew her knees up to more fully accommodate Alex, wanting only to be as close as possible.

He entered her slowly, taking care not to hurt her. But there was no pain, no discomfort. And when he had buried himself inside her as deep as possible, they just held each other and looked into each other's eyes for a long moment. Beth knew that Alex shared her thoughts, just as he shared her pleasure. Together they were complete, gratifyingly complete and fulfilled. Apart they would only be a fragment of themselves, struggling through life, forever missing that wholeness of spirit that was confirmed symbolically through their physical joining.

As he began to move inside her, Beth knew not which part of herself—the physical or the spiritual—was more thrilled and stirred. In wonder she felt her eyes fill with tears, just as they had that first night by the creek. She felt so much for this man, and no act short of a total giving of herself could adequately express the strength of her love.

The exquisite tension built as Beth met Alex's increasingly powerful thrusts with equal force. The sunlight from the window dappled his skin, his hair. His eyes adored her, desired her, mastered her. The curve of his neck, the way he held the inside corner of his mouth between his teeth, a small birthmark on his left shoulder the color of moor bracken, were all revealed to her in the sunlight—in the pure light, where their love belonged.

Their short, harsh pants of breath commingled. Their hearts beat as one, her breasts stroked by the rhythmic motions of his chest. The tension sharpened, expanded, became all-consuming. Mindless, desperate need held her in its silken shackles, and she struggled for release. It came in a plummeting blindness, a burst of sensation that radiated from her womanly core to every fiber of her being. Her head fell back against the pillow, her neck arched, and she breathed an ecstatic benediction as her muscles shuddered and convulsed with unspeakable force.

Somewhere on the frayed edge of her consciousness she heard Alex's responding cry of repletion. She felt him relax against her, his body falling to one side of her, but he held her fast against him, their passion-damp bodies still connected. A languorous, molasses-sweet drowsiness invaded her body, and she slept.

CHAPTER
fourteen

ZACH RODE SLOWLY along the rough country lane, guiding his horse around the wheel ruts from farmers' carts and over the muddy pattern of cattle tracks. Picking his way along at a snail's pace, Zach brooded. He'd chosen to take this meandering, indirect way through the moor because he needed time to think.

During the past three weeks Zach had avoided thinking and was glad of the work that had kept him busy and exhausted, grateful at the end of day when his body embraced sleep in a kind of desperate forgetfulness. Now there was nothing for it but to think. He was going to face Tessy soon. He needed to find fitting words to ease her disappointment.

Zach smiled mirthlessly. And what of his own disappointment? His usually ebullient spirit had never felt so melancholy. He couldn't imagine not having Tessy to go to when the irritations of life, even just the occasional boredom of it, galled him so. Her sweet, uncritical conversation calmed him, and her tender smile warmed him. Her eager, passionate lovemaking brought him the most exquisite pleasure.

The sun beat on Zach's shoulders. He had shed his royal blue jacket and pale blue striped vest. His white shirt glared in the sunshine. He was sweaty and hot and damned unhappy, and he knew he ought to ride swiftly to do the deed, to get it over with so he could go on with his life—a life that Tessy, by the dubious fault of being too easily beloved, could not be a part of.

His mouth straightened to a grim line. His jaw lifted and hardened. He couldn't afford to love a doxy so well. It was unnatural and inconvenient. He wanted to come and go as he pleased and not have some ridiculous surge of emotion leap out to surprise him at every unexpected opportunity, as had happened to him in the mine. Mistresses had their place, and Tessy was definitely stretching those limitations. Not purposely, he supposed. He didn't think she had a conniving bone in her body, but she was insinuating herself into his heart to the point where it would become more and more painful to extract her from that retentive organ. Better now than later.

Zach ran his fingers through the thick hair above his ear, where the sweat collected and trickled, now and then, down his neck and inside his collar. He would have been wise to wait till the evening cool had risen from the sea and the loamy earth to settle over the moor, but impatience had seized him and fretted him till he could do naught but respond with action. Seeing Tessy and purging his life of her complicating presence seemed the most logical thing to do first. Then, on the morrow, he'd see to Beth.

Thinking of Beth brought Zach a modicum of comfort, even the beginnings of a relieved smile. In Beth there was safety and peace. His wise, fiery, generous Beth was exactly what he needed. With her he'd stumbled through childhood and green, embarrassing young adulthood when, as an unlicked cub, he'd made an ass of himself on a regular basis. She'd always forgiven him, just as she'd forgiven him for thoughtlessly endangering Gabby.

Beth was a gentlewoman, but not so prim and proper that he didn't have hope of turning her into a passionate bed partner in due time. He knew from past flirtations with gently bred women, however, that prudery was dutifully taught to them by their mothers and therefore ran rampant

among their privileged ranks. His brow furrowed. He'd
never thought of Beth as a prude, but she'd been skittish
lately, and he fervently hoped that such behavior wasn't a
sign of things to come. Certainly Tessy wasn't a prude, but
he supposed that mistresses were immune to that genteel
condition called frigidity.

He skirted town and came to the edge of Tessy's
property—really his property. But he was going to give her
the cottage and a substantial amount of money, at least
enough to take care of her needs till another *parti* came
along to protect her. Zach's insides tossed and twisted, like
a sapling in a storm, at the thought of another man touching
his Tess. But having someone to look after her would be
better than going back to work for that harridan, Mrs.
Turley.

Tess would manage very well, he told himself. Probably
she would suffer less than he would at the ending of their
relationship. Indeed, her sort were taught to make the best of
their opportunities, weren't they? She'd done well by him.
She was getting a permanent place to live, or a property to
sell if she chose to. And he'd been good to her. Hell, he was
going to miss her.

Zach took his horse to the stable, tethered him next to
Tessy's white mare, watered him, then walked toward the
kitchen door, which was his usual passage of entry into the
house. He expected Tessy's gaggle of geese and chickens to
announce his arrival, but even they seemed stupefied by the
heat; not a hiss or a cackle issued forth from the coop.

He stopped suddenly, deciding to make his visit more
formal and thereby set the mood from the beginning of a
business relationship being officially terminated. He would
go to the front door. His vest and jacket were properly back
in place, the added clothing, though quite hot and uncomfortable, serving as more armor in the battle against his own
natural inclinations.

He walked through the gate, along the cobbled walkway

that snaked through the delightful snarl of flowers and herb
plants, grass-green cucumbers shining in the sun and . . .
honeysuckle. Honeysuckle everywhere, most beautifully
arranged in the trellised arbor that arched over the front
door. Honeysuckle would make him think of Tessy, he
supposed, even to the grave. The sweet, romantic fragrance
would always bring him a pang, a tiny portion of the pain
and dread that were building in him now. But it must be.

There was no knocker, so he rapped softly with his
knuckles. He waited for a few minutes, then reached for the
doorknob, an absurd notion having entered his head that she
might not be alone. He thought he detected muffled voices,
but told himself she could be talking to her cat or to herself.
She'd admitted once in a shy voice that she did such things
out of loneliness. Perhaps he'd left Tessy alone too much.
Perhaps in this way he hadn't been so good to her after all.
He felt a surge of remorse.

The door was locked. Loneliness made people do unchar-
acteristic things, things they'd never do if they'd had the
pleasure of congenial company. He wondered if Tessy had
been driven to seek comfort elsewhere, to betray him with
another man. He knocked hard on the door with a closed
fist. It was confusing to feel so much wrenching jealousy for
a woman he was about to willingly set free of all her
obligations to him.

Finally Tessy opened the door. His gaze was riveted to
her face. His heart flip-flopped most alarmingly. He'd
forgotten how blue her eyes were and how good they made
him feel when they rested on him so lovingly, as they did
now. Obviously there was no other man with her.

"Zach! Oh, how glad I am at the sight of you!" She
threw the door wide, as wide as the smile that stretched her
rose-tinted lips. She'd been pale and wan when she opened
the door, but now her cheeks bloomed with color. Zach
viciously suppressed his urge to kiss her. He stiffened his
back—indeed, his whole demeanor stiffened—and smiled

with polite vacuity. "Hello, Tessy," he said. Then he walked in and moved to a reed-backed rocker by the fireplace and sat down.

Tessy stood, irresolute, at the door. He was sure she felt awkward, since he had not responded to her happy greeting in his usual style, with a kiss and an embrace. There had even been times when upon his arrival he'd swept her off her feet and taken her directly to bed, conversation postponed till the glowing aftermath of their lovemaking. The Lord knew he wanted to sweep her up right now and make love to her with all the pent-up fervor of three weeks' absence and the wretched awareness of their permanent separation coming up. But that would not have been fair.

She was dressed in a cream-colored muslin gown, loose-fitting and flowing about her feet. She wore a lace shawl, too, very pretty but an odd vanity on such a steamy day.

She closed the door and walked timidly toward him, her eyes fixed nervously to the floor. She sat down in a chair opposite him, the very chair they'd made love in a few weeks ago. He forced the image of the two of them together on that chair to the furthest corner of his brain.

"Would you like some tea, Zach?"

"Lord, no, Tessy. It's too hot for tea."

Her head bobbed up, then down again. Her fingers twined and untwined; she clasped and unclasped her hands in her lap. "You're right. How stupid of me. Would you like a drink of water?"

Zach sighed. Already he was hurting her. "Yes, love. That would be refreshing."

Tessy stood up quickly, as if grateful to busy herself, to leave the room to play hostess in lieu of facing her out-of-sorts lover. But she'd apparently risen too fast. On her way to the kitchen she stopped and steadied herself against the wall with an outstretched hand.

"Tessy, are you all right?" He half stood, surprised and concerned.

She straightened immediately and flashed him a beaming smile. "Of course I am. It's just too hot for me."

He sat back down. "Then why don't you take off that shawl?"

She responded to this suggestion by pulling the lacy thing more securely about her. "I just got back from town. I hadn't thought to take it off yet. I'll be back in a moment." Then she disappeared into the kitchen.

Zach tried to relax by rocking to and fro, the creak of wood punctuating the silence with a soft and intermittent squeak-squeak. He looked about for the cat, lest he rock on the lazy feline's outstretched tail. Tom was nowhere to be seen. In fact, the room had an eerie stillness that unsettled him. He was probably missing it already. He scanned the room, trying to memorize every detail, like a bereaved man staring into an open coffin at the face of his departed loved one. So sad, so dismal, this leave-taking.

Tessy returned, wearing a voluminous apron and carrying a tray on which sat two glasses of water and a plate of biscuits. He wondered that she thought it necessary to don the apron for so simple a task as conveying refreshments into the room that served as parlor and bedchamber. Perhaps she was responding to his own formality with corresponding decorousness.

She pulled a small serving table between them and set the tray down on it, then pulled her own chair nearer. They reached for their glasses at the same moment, and the backs of their hands brushed. Both pairs of eyes flew up to collide like Indian rubber balls, then bounced away, revealing distress, embarrassment . . . arousal. God, how he wanted her.

His hand shook as he took a sip of water, but he willed it to stop. He set down the glass and leaned back in the chair. "Tessy, you must know that I'm here today for a particular reason."

He thought he saw her tremble, as though a sudden spasm

of fear had coursed through her. "What can you mean, Zach?"

He hardened his heart, his resolve, and his voice. Somehow he had to get through this. "Surely you've noticed that I haven't kissed you. I've been distant. All of this is for a reason."

She did not respond. Her features seemed cut from fine bone china, immobile, unspeakably fragile.

"I've decided to sever our relationship, you see."

Still Tess said nothing. Her eyes were fixed on the table and all its accoutrements—the glasses of water, the biscuits, and two gaily flowered, bright yellow serviettes.

"You do understand what I'm saying, don't you?"

After a long pause Tessy nodded her head.

Zach hated this mute acquiescence. It seemed unnatural and somehow frightening. He wished she would upbraid him passionately, beat him on the chest with her fists, or cry, giving him an excuse to shout back his own defense, allow her to pummel him till she felt better, or comfort her by telling her of his generous parting gifts and of how very fondly he would remember their time together. Wasn't that how the severing of this sort of liaison was handled? In his heart, however, none of this seemed true or natural or right.

"You knew from the beginning that this wouldn't last," he began, feeling the need to explain, wanting her to understand, wishing to be reasonable. "It was our agreement, plainly set out from the start. Now that I'm marrying Beth, I don't . . ."

Suddenly she lifted her head. Her eyes, so intensely blue before, had dimmed to a dull gray, like a blanket of somber clouds snuffing out a sunny sky. "You told me it wouldn't make any difference when you married Beth," she said softly, earnestly. She bowed her head again. "But I suppose you have the right to change your mind."

"Yes, I do. But it has nothing to do with you, Tessy," he added honestly. "You've been . . . wonderful." He dared not tell her she'd been too wonderful, so wonderful that he thought obsessively of her and was afraid of doing something quite foolish if he continued to visit her.

He reached inside his jacket pocket and pulled out a bulging purse. He dropped it on the table, the heavy chink of coins sounding vulgar, degrading. He saw Tess wince. "I've made provisions for your security. I'm giving you the cottage and enough money to keep you going till . . ."

She lifted her head again. This time her eyes reflected hurt and shame. "Till what, Zach? Till someone else takes me as his whore?"

This time Zach winced. "Tessy . . ."

In a quiet voice she continued. "Won't it displease you even a little that I'll be in someone else's arms? You're the only man I've ever known."

Zach rubbed his eyes with the thumb and ring finger of one hand. Hell, yes, it displeased him mightily to imagine her in another man's arms. But he could not admit such a thing. "I knew you were a virgin. But you knew what you were about when you took up with me. And I assumed that when we'd had our time together, you'd find someone else."

Tessy looked thoughtful. "Yes, I suppose I assumed the same thing. My mother told me I'd find my fortune in my beauty," she added with candid unself-consciousness. "But somehow I never imagined that I'd feel the way I do about you, Zach." She paused, trying to find the words to sum up her feelings. She shrugged her shoulders and said simply, "I love you. I feel as though I belong to you. I don't know if I can ever let another man touch me as long as I live."

Zach remained motionless, striving to keep any reaction to her words from showing in his expression, but he was profoundly stirred. An answering conviction rose in his own breast, and a voice within him shouted, *I love you, too, Tessy. More than you'll ever know.* But he suppressed the urge to tell her because he was still determined to whisk away, like a delicate spiderweb, this intricate tangle of emotions that had so neatly ensnared them both.

When he did not respond, she lowered her eyes to the purse that lay on the table between them. She reached out to touch the soft tanned leather with a forefinger, running fingertip and nail along a seam to the puckered closure, which was secured tightly with a cord. Then, as if she'd found the texture displeasing, she pulled back her hand abruptly. She looked up at Zach, her mouth curved in a bittersweet smile. "Funny how all we've shared and all we've been to each other can somehow be consigned in value to a pouch full of golden sovereigns. So businesslike, so impersonal. So very cold." She shivered and folded her arms across her chest.

That shiver, that protective self-hug, shredded through Zach's determined reserve like a farmer's scythe through a field of grain. Love swelled in him and overpowered all other considerations. He rocked forward and stood up, nearly oversetting the table in his eagerness to reach across to Tessy, to touch her, to hold her against him. Somehow he managed to maneuver his way around the table, pull her up from the chair, and take her in his arms before surprise had even registered on her face.

"Tessy, Tessy!" he groaned as he buried his face in the thick waves of hair that fell around her neck and shoulders. "I don't want to leave you. Truly I don't! But I'm afraid . . ."

Tessy pulled back and cupped his jaw in her small fingers, her thumbs pressing into the laugh lines on either side of his mouth. Her eyes glistened with compassion and renewed hope. "What are you afraid of, Zach? Surely whatever it is can be worked out between the two of us. You know I'd do anything for you. Anything!"

"Ah, Tessy," he whispered, her loving words melting him, her soft, pliant nearness exciting him. He had to have her. He needed her. He wanted to make her sigh and gasp and shudder.

Rationalization wrapped him in its soothing embrace. Maybe he'd been overly concerned about his strong affection for Tessy. Some men kept the same mistress for years and carried on their public and family lives with nary a problem. Perhaps he'd overreacted. Perhaps they could continue as they were.

He bent his head and kissed her, her mouth open and yielding. He took possession of her lips and plundered the warm, moist recesses beyond with overt greediness. He rejoiced in the pleasure of her, made especially sweet and intoxicating by having so nearly lost her because of his own cowardliness.

He was impatient. Now was not the time for conversation or wooing foreplay. He wanted her. And judging by Tessy's own rasping breaths and seeking, caressing hands, she wanted him equally as much. He ran his hands down her back, across the swell of her buttocks and around to the sides of her gown, grabbing a wad of fabric in each fist. Then he lifted her skirt, the muslin heaping at his elbows till her bare legs pressed against his. His control tilted, slipped away completely. He was mad for her.

Tessy wedged her hands between them and pressed her palms against Zach's chest. "Zach, wait. I need to tell you something. I—"

"No talking now, Tessy. Later, love. Later," he crooned, as he worked at the buttons on his trousers with one hand and held her fast against him with the other.

"But I must—"

When he had freed himself from the tight confines of his trousers, he took hold of her hips, piles of fabric billowing about his chest, wisping under his chin, framing Tessy's face in a wreath of cream-colored muslin. He positioned himself to enter her.

"Zach—"

Then he knew. When they were hip to hip, belly to belly, he knew. Tessy's stomach was swollen and hard. Zach's mind reeled in disbelief. She had seemed plumper the last time he'd been with her, but he had attributed that to the fact that she was eating regularly and was happy. But she was breeding. Good God in heaven, she was carrying his child!

The revelation was like a blast of winter, withering his passion, numbing him, sheeting him with a thin veneer of ice. His hands dropped from Tessy's waist. Her gown drifted down like a veil of secrecy, like the curtain of concealment she'd used it for, with its full, flowing lines. The shawl and the apron, too, had been meant to disguise her pregnancy.

Like an automaton, Zach buttoned his trousers, never looking at Tessy, though he could see her convulsive shivering at the periphery of his vision. Finally he lifted his eyes to her face. She was pressing her hands, one on top of the other, against her mouth, as if to hold back a sob or a cry. Her eyes were swallowed up by their enormous dark pupils, leaving only a pale circlet of blue around.

But Zach remained strangely unmoved. She had nearly caught him, caught him well and good in her silken web.

"Why?" he asked her. "You knew I didn't want any little bastards. How did this happen?"

Tessy stumbled backwards to sit on the bed. She stretched one hand behind her to support herself, the other hand still clapped tightly over her mouth. Finally she removed her hand and whispered brokenly, "I never meant it to happen. I . . . I used the creams Granny Harker sold me, but sometimes they don't work."

"Apparently," said Zach, careful, cool detachment in his voice. But he was angry, so damned angry he could have screamed.

"Zach, I'm sorry. So very sorry. But I truly didn't mean this to happen."

"Why didn't you tell me sooner? Or were you waiting for

a time such as this? It is a convenient thing to have to say
to a man who's on the point of leaving you: 'Oh, by the by,
Zach, I'm with child. I don't suppose you'll go now.' ''

Tessy jerked as if Zach had struck her, then bowed her
head, the golden drape of hair eclipsing her face. He stood
there watching her. He knew she would speak eventually,
and he was full of bitter patience, morbidly curious to hear
what she had to say. She did not move. Every moment or so
a single tear would drop down from behind the fall of gilded
hair and onto the white apron.

Zach was at leisure to think. Black, turbid thoughts. A
child. His and Tessy's. He supposed he ought to feel
something besides danger, something besides this humiliating conviction that he'd been duped into parenthood. He
loved Tessy, but right now her love, her swelling belly, felt
like the wooden restraints of a pillory. The shame of this
new development would be as public as a pillory sentenc-
ing, because, though he'd somehow managed to keep
Tessy's existence secret from Beth so far, a by-blow would
be additional fodder for the gossip mill. His only hope was
that Beth would forgive him—once again.

There was nothing for it, it seemed, but to take care of the
child as well as its mother. But he would not visit it once it
slid and squalled its way into the world. Nor would he visit
Tessy. The money would be delivered through a solicitor.
He had finally learned his lesson. He would never again take
his pleasure with a woman at the risk of losing his heart.

Still Tessy sat, and still he watched her. Somewhere
beyond the anger, the shock, the resigned disappointment,
Zach pitied her—loved her. But any movement or expression betokening sympathy or affection would be fatal to his
irreversible determination to sever his ties with her, child or
no. Life, he thought on a sudden dark inspiration, was as
unfair as a fixed game at the wheel at Pigeon's Hole, that
infamous gaming hell at St. James's Square. Nobody ever
won.

Suddenly Tess brushed back that glorious thick hair of hers, and he saw the brooch. He wasn't sure how the sight of it had escaped him before, except that he'd been consumed with myriad emotions from the moment he'd set foot inside the door, from regret to passion to anger and back to regret. But seeing Beth's brooch affixed to Tessy's gown was the last straw. It did not belong to her, and she had withheld her knowledge of it from him for these many weeks. This was yet more proof that things had gone too far with Tessy.

"Tessy."

She lifted her head fractionally.

"Why are you wearing that brooch? Have you had it all along?"

Tessy's hand darted up guiltily to touch the brooch.

"Well? Are you going to tell me about it or not?"

"I found it that night after you left."

"Why didn't you tell me during my next visit that you'd found it?"

Tessy fondled the brooch, running her thumb along the filigreed edging. "It was so beautiful. I knew you'd bought it for Beth, but I felt a keen pleasure in wearing it."

"I have bought you many pretty things, Tessy. I would have bought you a brooch had I thought you wanted one so desperately."

She looked up. Her lashes were thick with tears. Her cheeks were pink and damp. "It was your engagement present to her."

Zach waited for further explanation. He raised his brows. "So?"

"I knew I'd never receive an engagement present from you. I think I valued it for that and not so much for its beauty." She looked down at the brooch. "Though it is beautiful."

"Give it to me." Zach stretched forth his hand. It was

wrong of her to have kept Beth's brooch. He no longer cared whether he hurt her or not.

Tessy's heart felt as cold and hollow as a stone crypt. She took off the brooch and handed it to Zach, taking care that their fingers did not touch. It felt rather good to give it to him. She'd always felt like a thief, though she'd intended all along to return it to him. She just had not been able to so far. Now she hadn't the slightest idea how to respond to Zach's accusations about the baby, for though she had not tried to conceive a child, she *had* hoped it would somehow bind him to her.

Zach, her lover and friend over the past months, the man whose mere being had justified her every breath and given shape and purpose to the fleeting shadows of each passing day, stood before her as a stranger, out of reach forever. She had made fatal, irredeemable mistakes. The finality of it crept over her like a mud slide, suffocating, impenetrable to the brightest beam of light. It was over.

Tessy lifted her head slowly and fixed her gaze on the knot of Zach's cravat, which was wilted by the heat and mussed by their embrace. "I don't expect you to continue our arrangement because of the child. I won't lie. I did hope you'd want to see me and . . . her now and then." Her lips twitched into what she knew must be an awkward, tragic smile. "Sort of like a second family for you."

She met Zach's cold, unyielding stare and recoiled from it, shifting her gaze to the floor and finding a warmer aspect in the lifeless planks beneath her feet.

"I'll arrange to have my solicitor meet with you this week," he said. "I'll provide a comfortable living for you and the child. But I will not support offspring bred by other men." There was a pause. "I'm sorry it must all end like this, Tessy. But I cannot have in my life such a complication as you've become. Good-bye."

She heard his heel swivel on the floor, heard his even

march toward the door. She heard the door open and close behind him. She lifted her stinging eyes to the window that faced the front of the house and waited. Through the filmy curtains she watched him ride past, a blur of dapple-gray stallion, blue coattails, and hair as bright as a new guinea. Then she was alone.

Tess ought to have been used to being alone. But this time the silence was deafening, and she was frightened. Her eyes darted about the room, settling here and there, observing each piece of furniture as if she'd never seen it before. These would be her only constant companions in the weeks and months ahead. A chair, a stool, a small sideboard cluttered with pretty blue and white crockery. And settled over it all, a quiet dust.

Tess stood up abruptly and began to pace the floor—quickly, restlessly, back and forth, back and forth—as terror gripped her. She could not bear it. She could not lose him like this and go on living as if nothing had happened. A sob collected in her throat. She bit her fist to keep it from spilling out in a cry of anguish. Tears—impotent, useless feminine tears—streamed down her face. Rage against her lot in life, rage against a society that denied her Zach's love because she was not conceived into the proper sort of family, tore at her till she felt she might split in two.

Her gaze, darting desperately about the still room as if the answers to her anguished questions hid in the growing afternoon shadows, finally alighted on the purse of coins. Its bulging shape repulsed her. To Tess it personified every hateful, prideful human failing. She moved to the table, grabbed the purse, and flung it against the hearth. The cord that secured it broke, and coins flew in all directions, then descended to the floor in a shower of golden confetti.

Then, as Tess stood in the midst of this mess, breathing hard, a pain came that nearly doubled her over. She felt as though she were splitting in two or as if a giant hand had clutched her abdomen and squeezed. She gasped. Her knees buckled. She stumbled to the bed and sat down. God, what was happening to her?

The baby kicked hard. Tess realized that the pain must have something to do with the child, but it wasn't time for the baby to come. She had two more months left. Tess laid her hands against her swollen belly. "There, there. Don't fret, little one. Your mum's just a little agitated," she whispered, rotating her open palms over her stomach and striving to calm herself. The rest of the world could go to hades, Zach included, she thought. She had her babe to consider, and she would calm herself for that reason.

It seemed to be working. The pain was gone. Her stomach, which had pulled up and hardened like a muscle in spasm, had relaxed. She breathed a little easier, though the tears still fell and the pain of Zach's callous departure still twisted in her chest like a knife.

Just as she was about to rise and bathe her face, the pain came again. This time it was even harder, almost debilitating. All she wanted to do was curl up in a ball till it passed, as she prayed it would do. It did pass, but with innate female wisdom, Tess knew it would come again. Regardless of when it was due, the baby was coming, too.

Tess was afraid. She'd planned to have a young village girl stay with her to help her about the cottage when her time grew near and she became too cumbersome to move about. More important, she wanted someone nearby to fetch Granny Harker when her lying-in began. Now there was no one to rely upon but herself. Zach was beyond shouting distance, and Dudley had left through the back entrance when Zach knocked at the front door.

Dudley! He would be the perfect person to help her. In fact, he'd offered to help her and told her to fetch him if ever she needed him. She needed him now, but she had no way to convey such a message. Before he left the cottage, he'd said he was going back to Pencarrow after he collected his horse from Mr. Smith's stable where he'd boarded the animal for the day. He could not have progressed far in his journey; maybe she'd be able to catch up with him.

Another pain seized her. She waited it out, gritting her teeth for the duration. When it was over, she stood, removed the apron, and tied on a wide-brimmed bonnet. Before the pain could come again, she hurried outside to the stable. While she was saddling the slope-backed white mare, the pain came again. She crouched in the straw and squeezed her eyes shut as sweat trickled down her forehead and clung to her lashes. When the pain had passed, she finished saddling the horse and pulled herself atop it.

She rode through town, watching for Dudley's tall figure and ginger-cropped head in the steady trickle of humanity that trod the walkways. She stopped at Mr. Smith's stable and discovered that Dudley was only ten minutes ahead of her. She took the southern road to Pencarrow, praying that she would catch up with him quickly.

For a moment she considered going to Granny Harker instead. But she wanted Dudley. He'd been so kind to her, and she felt that if anyone could see her through this childbirth ordeal, it would be Dudley. She needed a friend, not just a midwife. And Granny Harker had failed her already. In the birthing of her daughter, Tessy wanted to feel secure for once in her life and in the hands of someone who truly cared. She hardly knew Dudley, but somehow she felt certain he was exactly the person she needed.

She doubled over with another pain. It was so intense she nearly fell off the horse. She felt close to passing out. When the pain subsided to the crampy achiness that hung on in between the hard stomach contractions, she pulled herself upright again and spurred her horse to a brisker trot. She stared down the road, hoping at each turn to see Dudley just ahead.

The sun glowered down on her unmercifully. Tess was

sick and exhausted and more frightened than she'd ever been in her life.

"Why, Zach?" she whispered. "Why must you leave me now?"

CHAPTER
fifteen

BETH DREAMED OF a beach with white sand as fine as salt, with rolling, gentle waves lapping at the shore. She and Alex swam naked in the shallow water, coming together to kiss and embrace, then separating to float and dip in the sea. It was paradise. But then she looked toward the shore, and her dream world dissolved. Zach was there. Zach was watching them, his face contorted with anger and hurt. "No!"

Beth sat up abruptly, consciousness returning with the subtlety of a horse kick between the eyes. Her confused gaze darted from one unfamiliar object to another. There was a cherrywood chiffonier with a man's watch stand among the porcelain figurines and other items scattered atop it. A marble bust of Socrates. Red moreen curtains. A half-filled copper tub.

"Beth? Did you have a bad dream?"

Beth's hammering heart slowed as relief came to her along with returning memory. Alex shifted beside her on the bed and slid a warm hand along her shoulder in a loving caress. She turned to look at him. His hair was a wild tumble of curls, a disarming style created when Beth tousled his damp hair with impassioned fingers, then further disarrayed by deep sleep. His black eyes held a concerned expression.

She reached up and placed her hand over his and released a long, cleansing breath. "Yes, I did have a bad dream, though it started out rather nicely.'' She smiled. ''You were wet. I was wet, too.''

Alex smiled back. ''A delicious thought, prompted, no doubt, by our mutual affinity for water.'' They still lay atop the red silk counterpane, naked. Late afternoon shadows stretched rubberlike across the room, dark and elongated. Alex's hand moved from her shoulder, down her arm, and around to her breast. He cupped it and flicked the nipple softly, teasingly.

Beth gasped and closed her eyes. She never stopped marveling at how easily Alex excited her. ''The time.''

''Hmmm?'' His voice was lazily seductive.

''What time is it? Soon the house will be abuzz with people again. I ought to return to my room.''

She heard him sigh. ''You're right.'' He removed his hand and pushed himself to a sitting position, peering across the shadowy room toward the mantel clock. ''It's nearly five o'clock. I wouldn't be surprised if Sadie's back, and Stibbs will be about the house by now. Dress quickly, love. I'll dress, too, and before you leave, I'll walk down to the end of the gallery to watch for people who might be coming up the stairs or down the hall.'' He caught her chin between his thumb and forefinger, then kissed her lightly on the lips. ''When I indicate that it's safe, you may leave this room, but not before.''

''Of course, Alex,'' she answered demurely. ''I always do as you bid me, don't I?''

He made a scoffing noise with a soft hiss of breath, swung his legs over the side of the bed, and stood up. For a minute Beth was unwilling to rise and scoop her own clothes off the floor to get dressed. It was too pleasurable watching Alex. Did he have the slightest notion how finely made he was? she wondered. His back was to her. He pulled his pantaloons up and over his slim flanks, then buttoned the waistband.

He looked over his shoulder, one brow raised, an amused, aroused tilt at the corner of his sensuous mouth. ''Don't look at me like that. You know we haven't the time, or the privacy, anymore. Get dressed, Beth. I'm going to tell Zach about us tonight. There'll be no more sneaking about the house for us, I promise you.''

''Well, I hope not,'' Beth mumbled, scooting to the edge of the bed and dangling her feet above the dais. ''I feel like a criminal. But I'd do it again, you know,'' she finished bluntly.

''Yes, I do know it,'' Alex answered wryly, buttoning his shirt. ''All the more reason to come to the point with Zach.'' Alex frowned. ''How I wish he didn't love you. How I wish I didn't love him as I do!''

''And as *I* do,'' Beth agreed with a shake of her head. Then she stood up and walked to the pile of clothes she'd heaped on the floor. She stooped to retrieve her shift and petticoat while Alex walked past her to the door.

''Look out into the hall in a minute or two and watch for my signal that all is clear, but do it carefully,'' he said as he inserted the key in the lock and turned the knob. He opened the door just far enough to see through to the gallery beyond. Beth was directly behind him, in a straight visual line with the door. She and Alex saw Zach at the same moment. A glimpse of golden hair, a blue jacket, and curved fingers poised to rap on the door.

''Alex, I need to talk to you,'' she heard him say, the tone of his voice indicating that he was very upset. Beth clutched her petticoat against her chest. Between the door casing and Alex's jaw she had a narrow view of one of Zach's eyes. It shifted slightly and fixed on her.

Time stood still. Beth knew the scene would be seared into her memory forever. Zach's eye pinned her to the spot, paralyzing her, the very blood in her veins coagulating to the sluggish consistency of thick mud. Alex stood just as motionless, his broad, white-shirted back held rigid, his hand grasping the doorknob with taut-knuckled strength. The golden eye continued to stare, unblinking for what seemed an eternity but was probably a matter of seconds in actual passage of time. Then it narrowed and flashed with fiery emotion.

The door burst open, sending Alex staggering backwards. Beth lurched violently. The door slammed against the wall and swung back, nearly closing again, but Zach had already stepped into the room. He shoved the door closed behind him with a tap of his heel and stood with his arms crossed and his legs spread. He and Alex were separated by perhaps three feet. Zach's gaze slid back and forth between the two of them, then settled on Beth with her mussed hair, her nakedness barely concealed behind the flimsy wad of fabric she held against her.

Alex moved slightly, placing himself between Zach and Beth. "Don't blame her, Zach. I—"

"Don't try to explain," Zach interrupted, much too calmly. Beth had imagined how he would look, what he'd say when he found out that she loved Alex and he loved her. But she had never imagined that his eyes could look like cold coins, hard and copper-colored, yet as dull as dross. "It's perfectly obvious what's been going on here."

"There's certainly more to it than you see, Zach," Alex began in a reasoning tone.

"Undoubtedly," Zach replied coolly. "Yet I suppose you require privacy for the 'more' that you refer to!"

"That's not what I meant," growled Alex. "I love her."

Zach's mouth twisted into a sneer. "How wonderful for you. When may I wish you happy?" He turned his chilling glare on Beth. "Were you going to wait to tell me on our wedding day, Beth, so that Alex could simply take my place at the altar? So much easier than canceling one wedding, then planning yet another! We don't want to confuse our guests, do we? I can just hear them. 'Now, which brother is it she's marrying? Bloody hell, I just don't know!' "

Beth felt her knees weakening. She backed away to the bed and sat down, pulling the silk counterpane about her, curling up like a wounded animal.

Alex watched her, his expression tortured, apologetic. Then he turned back to Zach. He raised his hands, palms up, in a supplicating gesture. "Cruel sarcasm is unnecessary, brother. Both Beth and I tried to resist the growing affection between us. We didn't want to hurt you. We just—"

"I see how bloody much you tried to resist!" Zach spat, the dull copper of his eyes kindling to a fiery bronze. "And don't call me brother again!" He raked a hand through his hair and took two quick steps to the side and back again. He flung out his arm and pointed at Alex. "As for trying not to hurt me, that's goddamn decent of you. If you really didn't want to hurt me, you'd damn well not have bedded my fiancée!"

"Zach, you mustn't blame Alex." Beth's plea sounded as feeble as she felt. Then, deploring her henheartedness at a time when Alex most needed her support, she gathered all her courage. "I came to Alex's room of my own accord. He did not ask me to come here. He did not want to make love, but I . . . coaxed him."

For the first time, Zach's hard-edged facade of control slipped. Betrayal and pain showed plainly on his strained features. He dropped his head into his hands and Beth's heart ached for him. "I can't help how I feel about Alex, Zach. I never meant to hurt you. I'm so sorry."

Zach's head reared up. "Don't feel sorry for me. I ought to thank the infamous Wicked Wickham for coming to our dull little corner of England to expose you for what you are, Beth. A trollop!" Beth flinched. "Nothing but a trollop! And despite what I said before, if you think he's got the slightest notion of marrying you, you've been pathetically misled."

Alex stepped up to Zach and faced him squarely. In an

even and icy tone, he said, "Apologize to Beth right now, Zachary, or I'll—"

"What will you do?" Zach interrupted, glaring back at him and speaking just as icily. "Whatever it is, you might as well do it now because I'd sooner go to hell than apologize to *her*."

Alex hit him. Zach seemed completely unprepared. The hard blow to his jaw sent him reeling backwards against the door and falling to the floor with an "Oomph!"

Beth was horrified. She pressed one hand against her mouth to keep from screaming. Zach sat there a moment, breathing hard, rubbing his jaw, the expression in his eyes fulminating with anger. Alex stood, stony and implacable, waiting. Zach twisted sideways and slid his shoulder up the wall as he slowly stood up.

There was a soft rap at the door. "Lord Roth? Lord Roth? Is everything all right?" It was Stibbs.

The intense glare between Alex and Zach never wavered. "Everything is just fine, Stibbs," Alex called back in a perfectly ordinary voice. "Go away."

"But, my lord—"

"Do not, under any inducement, open that door, Stibbs!" Alex warned him.

There was no response, and Beth could well imagine Stibbs's irritated and unbelieving grimace as he hesitated on the other side of the door. The several other servants who might have gathered there as well would be all agog. She cared nothing about the resultant gossip if she should be discovered in Alex's room in the middle of a brawl between two brothers, but she cared very much that neither of them get seriously hurt. She sent a desperate prayer heavenward that Zach would not try to avenge himself.

Her prayers went unheeded this time. Zach lunged forward, grabbing Alex about the waist and sending them both plummeting to the floor. Zach straddled Alex and lifted his fist in the air, ready to strike. Alex caught Zach's arm midway and held it there. Zach grunted with frustration and grabbed Alex around the throat with his other hand.

Beth could hear Alex making little gasping chokes. He was pulling at Zach's hand, trying to pry loose the strangling fingers. She rose up with the intention of throwing herself on Zach's back to pull him off Alex, but just then Alex ripped Zach's hand away. He rolled up from the floor and pushed Zach backwards, sending him in a tumble against the chiffonier. The porcelain figures shook and toppled, one of them clipping Zach's ear on its descent to the floor where it crashed into small powdery pieces. Zach growled and reared up again, lurching toward Alex.

"Stop it!" Beth cried, unable to contain her terror any longer. "You're going to hurt each other! Please stop!"

Beth's cry must have given Stibbs the excuse he desired to enter the room. He came in, followed by Sadie. Two footmen stood gawking in at the door.

"Saints preserve us!" shrieked Sadie, plastering herself against the wall as the two brothers collided with the force of charging bulls. Stibbs stood back, too, apparently feeling unequal to putting an end to the quarrel. Beth could not blame him. The two men were large, strong, and very angry, though it was obvious to Beth that Alex was merely staving off Zach's blows and not trying to execute any hits himself. Zach was wild, thrashing and struggling like a mad dog. It was evident, too, that Alex was the stronger man. She thanked God for that, because it seemed as though Zach *did* want to kill his older brother, and it would not have boded well for the outcome if he'd been the stronger of the two. Beth could only trust in Alex to end the fight before mortal wounds could be inflicted.

The men continued to struggle, their grunts and hissing oaths, the scrape of heavy furniture against the wood floor, and the smack and thud of flesh against flesh in desperate battle creating a terrifying cacophony that filled the room. It seemed endless. Beth pushed back a strand of hair that had fallen forward into her eyes and she realized that her cheeks were wet with tears. The sobs that added to the general discord were hers.

She had done this. She had brought about this dreadful fight because she could not stay away from Alex. Zach would have been angry and hurt when Alex told him about their affection for each other, but finding them together after they'd made love had infuriated him. He seemed so vicious and violent that she thought he must have been troubled already when he came to the door. She remembered his tone of voice. He had been upset about something even before he'd found them out.

Suddenly Dudley appeared at the door, and Beth had never been so relieved to see anyone in her life. Though Dudley was not a well-muscled man, he had influence with both brothers, and Beth thought he might be able to bring an end to the fight. His horrified gaze took in the scene with a sweeping glance.

Dudley looked at Beth, bundled up to the neck in the crimson counterpane, then at the two sweating men, clawing and staggering about the room, and came to the only logical conclusion: Zachary had caught Alex with Beth in a most compromising situation. It was inevitable, he supposed, that it would come to this.

Too bad, however, that Zach's discovery of Beth's and Alex's love for each other had come so speedily on the heels of his interview with Tessy, and in such a cruelly obvious manner. Apparently the meeting with his pregnant mistress had not gone well. Otherwise Zach would not have returned so swiftly to Pencarrow in this blasted heat, actually arriving before Dudley, who'd had a bit of a head start. Subduing a twist of sympathy for poor Tessy, Dudley threw himself into the fray, seeing to the most pressing problem first.

"Stop it, both of you!" he yelled, keeping pace with them as they stumbled about the room, but taking care to avoid their flaying arms and jutting elbows. Neither of the men seemed to notice his presence.

Dudley took a deep breath and used the one weapon he hoped would be effective. "What would your mother say, I wonder? She would have given anything to have seen the two of you together through the past weeks, just as brothers should be. Now look at you! By God, Zachary, do you mean to *kill* him?"

The struggling stopped, but not all at once. Zachary just seemed to run down like a clock in need of winding. Then they stood together in the middle of the room, Zach's fists full of Alex's shirtfront, Alex's hands braced against Zach's forearms, both of them sucking in painful gulps of air.

Eye to eye, heart to heart, they stood, sweating, bleeding, staring, agonizing, repenting together. Zach's eyes slid away, his fists uncurled, and his arms fell limp to his sides. Without a backward glance, he moved haltingly to the door, bumping against the frame and walking through the servants as if they weren't even there.

After an awkward pause of deathly stillness, the observers of the shocking ordeal seemed to gather their wits about them and try to carry on in the manner expected of them. Sadie scolded the gawking servants and shut the door in their faces. Then she hurried to Beth and sat beside her on the bed, one arm thrown around her trembling shoulders.

Stibbs cleared his throat, announced that he would presently send a maid up to put the room in order, looked daggers at Alex, let his embarrassed gaze skitter past Beth, and left the room with as much offended dignity as he could muster. Dudley poured a glass of brandy for Alex and made him sit in a chair before allowing him to drink it.

"I'll be askin' ye to leave fer a few minutes, m'lord,"

Sadie said after a moment, waiting just long enough for
Alex to drink his brandy. "Miss Elizabeth needs to dress,
and while I can't help what went on before nor what will
happen on the morrow, as long as I'm here, I'll see that
things is done proper like."

Alex had been resting his forehead in his hand, his elbow
propped on the arm of the chair. He lifted his head and fixed
Sadie with a bone-weary gaze. A small trickle of blood
oozed down his chin from a split lip, and one eye appeared
to be forming a swelling bruise. "Of course, Sadie. I
wouldn't have it any other way." Then his gaze shifted to
Beth, and Dudley could see the pain and love reflected there
in equal portions. "I'll see you later, Beth. Don't fret, my
dear. All will be well in the end, I promise you."

Despite Alex's physical and spiritual depletion of energy,
a fervor that made one believe that he meant exactly what
he said underlay his words to Beth. It certainly engendered
at least *some* hope and faith in Dudley's doubting heart.
He was worried about Zach now. Where had he gone? He
looked toward the window that faced the back of the house
and the road to St. Teath. He perceived a distant rider on a
white horse—a woman, it appeared—but no Zachary. He
turned and followed Alex from the room.

Sadie cluck-clucked and crooned in a soothing undertone
as she helped Beth into her clothes, but Beth could not be
comforted. While she'd sat on the bed, safe the whole time,
it seemed as though she'd felt every blow and strangling
grip that occurred during the fight. She was bloodied and
bruised, not on the outside, but on the inside. Outwardly she
was numb.

When Beth was finally dressed and her hair brushed into
a respectable knot atop her head, Sadie seemed in a frantic
hurry to get her out of Alex's bedchamber, almost as though
the room itself had some sort of defiling effect upon what

was left of Beth's virtue. In the hall they came upon Stibbs, who had been waiting with two maids in possession of brooms and mops for the room to be vacant. Beth stopped and addressed him. "Stibbs, where is Lord Roth?"

Stibbs's upper lip lifted slightly. He stared at a point just beyond Beth's left ear. "I believe Mr. Dudley took him directly to the stillroom to dress his injuries, miss."

"And . . . Master Wickham?"

"He was seen mounting his horse and leaving through the southerly gate, miss."

Beth sighed. It was like Zachary to run away. He had been avoiding responsibility all of his life. She had thought that his recent experience dealing with the tin mine incident had cured him of the habit of ignoring what he considered drudging or unpleasant or . . . painful. But then, she knew she ought not to judge too harshly. It must have been a dreadful blow to find her in Alex's bedchamber.

"I think you'd best lie down fer a while, miss," Sadie advised her, nudging her elbow as if trying to urge her on. Apparently Beth had been standing in the hall, staring at the wallpaper in a rather vacant way.

Beth straightened her shoulders from their despondent slump and made herself smile at Sadie. "I'm all right. I'm not tired. I'm going to the stillroom to check on Lord Roth."

Sadie frowned. "Had ye ought to be hangin' about that man, miss?"

Beth sobered. "You mustn't think he did anything wrong, Sadie. Lord Roth and I are . . ." She knew not how to finish the sentence. She couldn't say they were betrothed, because he hadn't asked her. "He didn't do anything that I didn't fully encourage him to do," she finished.

Sadie clamped her mouth shut tight, causing her lips to disappear into a prim horizontal line. "Shall I send fer yer mother, miss?"

"No," Beth answered promptly and firmly. "Never fear, Sadie. I will tell her everything when I return home, where I will go as soon as I've spoken to Lord Roth. I hope the servants can keep mum that long."

Sadie did not reply but looked very grim. Beth supposed Sadie was thinking, just as she was, that the story would get bruited about no matter how much they threatened the servants with dismissal if they did not keep silent. Gossip was like candy—too delicious not to be shared. Sexual indiscretions were the richest chocolate comfits in the candy box. They were drooled over and savored the very longest.

Sadie followed Beth to the stillroom. Alex was seated inside on a simple wood chair, his head bent slightly back to accommodate Dudley's ministerings. His neck glowed with sweat, but his face had been wiped clean, his lip patted dry of blood, his eye now being covered with a thick slice of cucumber.

"Lor', Mr. Dudley, why're ye puttin' food on Lord Roth's face?" Sadie inquired, her curiosity overriding her disapproval of his lordship's misconduct.

"'Twill take out the puffiness. Perhaps it may even reduce the bruising a little," Dudley replied.

"I feel like a jackass," Alex stated flatly, "and not just because I've a cucumber on my face. Beth, are you there?" He reached out a hand.

Beth took the offered hand and squeezed tightly. "Yes, Alex."

"Where's Zach?"

"Stibbs said he was seen riding in a southerly direction."

"Gone to the cove, I suspect."

"Maybe he'll come back in a more comfortable state of mind," she said pensively. "I feel like a positive blackguard, Alex. Do you think he'll ever forgive us?"

Alex had no chance to reply because there came a sudden racket from the kitchen, which adjoined the still-room. Henry was shouting for Dudley as if the house were on fire.

Dudley left the room, followed immediately by Beth, Alex, and Sadie. In the kitchen, just inside the door, they discovered Henry supporting the limp figure of a young woman.

"Good heavens, it's Tessy!" exclaimed Beth, stopping in her tracks to stare at the girl. Tess's eyes rolled in her head, her face was glistening with perspiration, and the hem of her skirt appeared to have been dragged through a puddle.

Dudley ran to Tess and threw his arm around her waist, then caught her under the knees as she began to collapse. He lifted her and carried her into the morning room, which was the closest chamber containing a couch on which he could lay her down. Everyone followed and stood about, gazing down at Tess. She looked frightened by the multitude of curious stares and turned her head away from them toward Dudley, who was kneeling beside her. "Oh, Dudley, I'm so sorry. I didn't mean to come all the way here, but I had started to follow you and then I dared not go back. You said you'd help me if you could, and the babe—"

Suddenly Tess stiffened, her face creased, and she pulled her legs up against her stomach, as if she were experiencing excruciating pain.

"Lord, Tessy, it's not the baby coming, is it?" Dudley whispered. He reached down and patted the damp edge of her gown. "Your water broke, I gather."

"She's breeding?" Alex sounded incredulous. "Does he know?"

Beth lifted startled eyes to Alex's face. "Does *who* know? How do you know Tess, Alex?"

"Nay, how do *you* know her?" he countered.

"Miss Tavistock met Tessy quite accidentally in town today," Dudley supplied with an impatient edge to his voice. "But this is not the time to discuss who knows whom or who knows what. This girl is about to give birth two months early. Sadie, would you please help me by bringing a pillow and a blanket? I'll also need warm water and soap so that I can wash my hands. And a thick flannel sheet to put under her."

"Ye're birthin' the baby right here, Mr. Dudley?" Sadie blurted.

"I've no choice. The child's coming whether we're ready for it or not. Henry, leave the room, please. Stand just outside in the hall and stop anybody who tries to enter."

Henry immediately obeyed. Sadie left, too, muttering beneath her breath, leaving the three of them looking down at Tess, who was recovering from the last spasm of pain. Her eyes were closed, her face as white as hoarfrost and just as cold and damp.

"She's so small. Why, she hardly looks pregnant at all," Beth said.

"I never imagined her to be so young. And I certainly never knew she was with child," said Alex, concern etching a deep fissure in his brow.

Dudley looked grim. "He didn't know, either, till today, just before he discovered you and Miss Tavistock . . . together."

Abruptly Dudley and Alex darted a quick look at Beth, as if they realized that they'd said too much. Or maybe not enough.

"Perhaps you should take her outside and tell her everything," Dudley suggested.

Alex reached for Beth's arm, but she pulled away, her eyes fixed on Tess's bodice, remembering the brooch that had been pinned there earlier that day, the brooch that exactly fit Zach's description of her own engagement present. Suddenly everything began to fall into place. Tess's shy fear of her had had its source in something more cogent than natural bashfulness. Tess smelled of honeysuckle, just as Zach sometimes did when he had been to town. *Tess was Zach's mistress. The child was Zach's.*

The revelation wasn't earth-shattering, for the situation was too trite. Zach was a highly physical man and very attractive to the fair sex. Beth should have realized long ago that he had a mistress. The realization that Zach had been making love to this delicate, beautiful girl was not even especially damaging to Beth's pride. More than anything else, Beth felt a heavy, world-weary sadness. What would happen to Tess and the baby . . . Zach's baby?

"Where's the brooch, Tessy?" she asked softly. "He didn't take it back, did he?"

Tess opened her eyes. As the two women looked at each other, an understanding blossomed between them. Tess smiled wanly, her eyes drifting shut as she spoke. "I didn't mind, miss. It was yours really."

Beth reached down and squeezed Tess's hand. Dudley was holding the other hand and staring at Tess as if his heart would burst. She wondered how he had become involved in this hubble-bubble of unfortunate human blunderings. But he was obviously much in sympathy with Tess, as anyone with a heart would be.

Beth looked up at Alex, who had apparently been watching her rather closely. She thought she knew what he was thinking—that women were indecipherable creatures and that she was presenting him with a conundrum he would be hard-pressed to solve. But how did a woman explain to a man the bond women shared that sometimes transcended that notorious failing called jealousy? Under ordinary circumstances, and despite her love for Alex, she supposed she would have had a right to feel a little resentful and jealous toward Tess. But she didn't.

"Do you really think Zach went to the cove?" she asked him.

"I don't know. Why?"

"Because he ought to be here."

Alex accepted this statement with a frowning nod. "I can't fetch him, though. If he sees me, he's likely to go off in the opposite direction. I'll send a couple of the stableboys to try to find him." Alex left the room just as Tess curled up in another paroxysm of pain.

"Scream, Tess, if you want to," Dudley whispered into her ear, covering her hands with his and squeezing them tightly. "You don't have to be brave or dignified, or any such nonsense. You're bringing a small life into the world and enduring a great deal of pain in the process. You've every right to let loose—"

Dudley must have convinced her, or the pain did. She moaned loud, the sound piercing Beth's soul to strike a common chord of womanly feeling and imbuing her with both dread and wonder.

Sadie returned just then with the pillow and blanket, a maid following behind with a pewter basin of water, a basket of rags, and a bar of soap. Since Dudley was still holding Tess's hands, Beth hurried around to the end of the couch and lifted Tess's head so that Sadie could place the pillow underneath. As she pulled Tess's hair up from around her hot neck and arranged it on the pillow, she admired how silky and fragrant it was. It struck her again how young Tess was, and a knot of anger formed in her throat. How could Zach have stolen her innocence so selfishly for his own pleasure and then left her with child?

Sadie sent the maid out, then eased the flannel blanket beneath Tess's bottom and fanned it out over the end of the couch. "Birthin's a messy business," she stated flatly. She eyed Beth. "Ye ought to leave. Yer mother'd be thrown into high fidgets if she knew where ye was and what ye was doin', Miss Elizabeth."

"Dudley might have need of me. I'm going to stay," Beth answered firmly.

"I ain't experienced in such things, but I kin help Mr. Dudley if he tells me what to do," Sadie asserted. "A gently bred young woman hadn't ought to be witness to a birthin'."

"I'm not going, and that's final. Besides, Mama will be much more agitated by the other occurrences of this day. One more thing can't make much difference."

Sadie sighed and shook her head.

"All right, Tessy," said Dudley, freeing one hand from Tess's grip to stroke her forehead. "You've got to let go of my hands for a moment while I wash them. If there's one thing I learned from my mother, it's that your hands must be as clean as possible in order to avoid childbirth fever. Then I must take a look at you and see how much space you've allowed for that babe's head to squeeze through."

"Dudley, don't leave me," Tess whimpered, looking weaker than ever after the last pain.

"I have to, Tessy. I can't help you birth the babe from this position. Don't fret." But Dudley reasoned with Tess to no avail. She held fast to his hands. Judging by the color of Dudley's fingertips, her grip was surprisingly strong.

"Can Sadie or I see how she's coming along?" asked Beth. "Though I'm not quite sure what to look for."

"I don't know nothin' 'bout babes, Mr. Dudley," said Sadie, raising her hands in a gesture of helplessness. "I've never had any of my own ner helped with birthin' afore."

Dudley clicked his tongue against his teeth as if he felt exceedingly exasperated. "You must let go of me, Tessy. As you can see, I'm the only one who knows what to do."

Tess started to cry, bending her head to rest her brow against their joined hands. Dudley was throwing Beth a look of total despair when Alex returned.

"Thank God. You're just the person to do it!" said Dudley.

"To do what?" Alex stood at the foot of the couch, his fists resting on his hips.

"She won't let go of me. She wants to hold on to me while she bears the child. You're going to have to help it along. I certainly can't do it from here."

Tess bent into another pain, her head rolling back and forth on the pillow, her bottom lip viciously clamped between her teeth.

Alex watched and frowned. "You want me to deliver the baby? I admit I know a little about childbirth, since there were times during the war when one had to pitch in where one could. But you're so much better qualified to do it, Dudley!"

"I think I can serve best at Tessy's side," he said. "She needs someone here to hold her hand, and she evidently prefers that someone to be me. I can tell you exactly what to look for and what to do. But first, wash your hands."

Alex did as he was told after rolling his shirtsleeves up above his elbows. Beth washed her hands, too.

"Tessy, bend your knees and pull your legs up so that Lord Roth can examine you."

Tessy made a muffled protest and shook her head. Dudley sighed. "Tess, this is no time to be modest. If you won't let me do it, Lord Roth must. Next to me, he has the most experience in this sort of thing. We'll keep you covered so that only Lord Roth is able to see anything."

Beth moved to one side to show Tess that she would respect her modesty, too. Tess looked up at her and Lord Roth through teary eyes, then turned onto her back and did exactly as Dudley told her to do. Her grimaces indicated to Beth that Tess was pretty much in constant pain now, but with the intensity greatly increased during the stomach contractions.

Alex folded back the flounce of Tess's dress and the

blanket that covered her so that her lower legs were exposed. He gently pushed her knees apart and examined her.

"Pull open the curtains, Sadie. I need more light." Sadie obeyed, and Beth wrung out a rag in the basin, moved to the head of the couch, and bathed Tess's face.

"Is she increased sufficiently to accommodate the baby's head?" asked Dudley, while Tess reared back against the pillow as another pain claimed her.

"She's well stretched, and I can see the head. Since the child is premature and undoubtedly quite small, perhaps she'll not have any trouble pushing it out. I suspect it's time she started."

"Do you feel like bearing down, Tessy?" asked Dudley. Tess nodded.

"Good. When you feel the next pain coming on, you must try to push the baby out. The contraction of your muscles that's hurting so very much is your body's way of pushing the babe out. But sometimes the mother must help this process along. Do you understand, Tessy?"

"Yes. I've felt like pushing before, but I didn't know if I should."

"Now's the time, Tess," said Alex. "Do it with the next contraction."

They hadn't long to wait. Tess was immediately seized with another pain. "Grip my hands as hard as you need," Dudley encouraged. "And push, Tessy, push!"

Tess grunted, curled her neck, and pushed till her face turned red. Afterward she fell back against the pillow, panting and sweating.

"Did it do any good, my lord?" Dudley asked.

"Yes, a little. But it's going to take another two or three hard pushes, I think."

"I can't, Dudley," Tess whispered. "It hurts too much. Must I?"

"As his lordship said, Tessy, only two or three more

pushes and you'll have your baby in your arms. There's a brave girl. You can do it!''

Two hard contractions later, with Tess huffing and puffing and pushing as hard as she could, Alex cried, ''Success! I've got the head in my hands.'' Alex's face lit up, and a spontaneous smile curved his lips. ''Ah, and here comes the rest of it. Small as a whelp, but beautiful. Perfectly formed!''

''Is it a boy or a girl?'' asked Beth, tears springing to her eyes at the sheer miracle of it.

''A girl,'' Alex said, lifting his eyes to Beth for a moment of sharing, then dropping his gaze to Tess. ''You've a beautiful baby girl, Tess. Come, Beth. Help me for a moment while I cut the cord. Then we'll clean her up and show her off to her mother.''

''Make the baby cry first, Alex,'' Dudley expostulated. ''Get her to breathing, for heaven's sake!''

''It's too slippery to lift by the heels, Dudley. Beth, bring a rag and I'll wipe it off a bit.''

Beth grabbed a clean rag and held it out to Alex as she moved to the end of the couch. When her eyes first beheld the tiny form of Tessy's baby girl—Zach's baby—she was infused with wonder. As Alex had said, she was perfectly formed. Every feature, every finger and toe, was just as it should be. And beneath the bloody mucous covering, she was beautiful. Though her hair was slicked down, it promised to be as fair and golden as Zach's.

Alex laid the baby down on the flannel sheet between Tess's trembling legs. He wiped the child off with the rag, then lifted it by the heels, supporting its small squinty-eyed head with his other hand. ''Poke it or something, Beth,'' he said with a note of panic in his voice. ''Make it cry. It's not doing anything!''

''I don't wish to hurt her,'' Beth protested. ''Mayhap all we need to do is prime her sucking instinct.'' She reached out and stuck her forefinger between the baby's lips. This brought about the desired response. The baby opened her mouth, took in a gasp of air, and began flinging her arms about like the blades of a windmill. Then she screamed, filling the room with the wonderful discordant sound of new life.

CHAPTER
sixteen

ALEX LAUGHED. "WELCOME to the world, little one."

A grin spread across Dudley's face from one freckled ear to the other. "Sounds pluck to the backbone, Tess. Arriving early seems to have put the peppery little thing in a bit of a twit. Good lungs!"

Tess smiled and shook like a windowpane in a thunderstorm. Beth assisted Alex in cutting the cord, while Sadie watched from a distance and surreptitiously wiped her eyes with the hem of her apron.

Once the baby was detached from her mother and cleaned again quite thoroughly with a warm, damp cloth, Beth wrapped the squalling armful snugly in a square of flannel and gave her to Dudley. Dudley handled the baby with assiduous care, as if she were as fragile as the gossamer wings of a butterfly.

"I know, a babe is sturdier than it looks," he said, abashed, flashing Alex an embarrassed grin. "But a newborn child inspires something rather like awe in me whenever I hold one. Now, Tessy, here she is. All yours."

Tess looked half pleased, half frightened out of her wits. "Oh, I dare not. I'm shaking so hard I'll drop her!"

"I'll be at the ready in case you do," Dudley assured her. Tess took the baby and held it against her side, gazing into her daughter's small red face with a tender expression Beth wished Zach could see.

"I wonder if they've located Zach yet," she said.

Tess turned wide eyes to Beth. ''Why? You haven't told him about the baby coming, have you?''

''We sent some servants to look for him with that purpose in mind,'' Beth admitted, surprised by Tess's alarmed expression. ''You want him to know, don't you?''

Tess bent and kissed the baby's head, rocking her back and forth in that rhythmic motion mothers knew instinctively how to do. The baby quit crying and blinked open her eyes. ''He doesn't want her. He doesn't even want to see her,'' Tess said in a quiet voice.

''But why—''

''Beth, let's not get into a discussion that might upset Tess,'' said Alex, still poised at the end of the couch. ''She's not done with this birthing process yet. She has yet to purge the afterbirth.''

Dudley looked concerned. ''It hasn't come out yet?'' He turned to Tess. ''Are you still having pains?''

''Yes, small ones. Why? What's wrong? Aren't I doing something right, Dudley?''

''Tessy, you're as right as rain,'' he soothed her. ''The part that was attached to the baby's cord, which has also been attached to you on the inside, is always sloughed off by the mother's body once the babe is delivered. It's just a natural part of childbirth. But yours hasn't come yet. I'm afraid you're going to have to stay in this ridiculous position for a few more moments.''

Tess nodded, then turned her attention back to the baby, leaving Beth to ponder Zach and Tess's relationship. Even if Zach did not want the baby, he was certainly responsible for its existence and ought to feel some responsibility for it. Besides, she could not believe that Zach didn't have some affection for Tessy, so naturally he would feel some affection for the baby, no matter what he might have said in a fit of anger. How could he not be profoundly affected by the birth of a baby, especially one that belonged to him?

Beth already had a strong stirring of feeling for the child just because it was Zach's.

Beth, however, also admitted to knowing nothing about the unwritten rules and general customs practiced between a man and his mistress. All she could conclude in her own heart and mind was that it was unnatural to abandon one's own flesh and blood, no matter which side of the blanket it was born on.

"He was leaving me, miss." Beth looked down into Tess's pained yet earnest expression. "Even before he knew about the babe, he was leaving me. I can't fault him for that. It's the way for my kind. It's to be expected. He was looking forward to his marriage to you, miss, and he said he didn't need me anymore. He never wanted a baby, and I kept it secret from him for as long as I could. Don't be too angry with him. He loves you."

Apparently Tess had been too consumed with pain to have registered the comments earlier about Zach finding Beth and Alex together. She didn't know how very little Zach had to look forward to. An uncomfortable silence fell over the room as all of them were immersed in their own heavy thoughts.

"Dudley, you had better come and have a look," Alex said presently. Though he'd said it calmly, Beth thought she detected a thread of unease in his voice.

Dudley stood up immediately, just as attuned to the nuances of Alex's voice as Beth was. "Please sit by her, miss," he said to Beth, "just in case her arms grow weary of holding the baby."

Beth nodded and knelt down by Tess, who was still racked by strong shivers. "Are you cold, Tessy?"

"Very," Tess admitted.

This did not seem like an encouraging condition, considering how hot the day had been and still was. Beth turned to Sadie. "Fetch another blanket, won't you?"

Sadie left the room to do as Beth bade her. While they

waited for the blanket, Beth engaged Tess in conversation
about the baby, trying to divert her from hearing the men's
low-voiced exchange at the end of the couch. But Beth
listened and became exceedingly alarmed. It seemed that
Tess was bleeding much more than was generally expected
after the birth of a child. And the afterbirth still had not
appeared. She heard the phrases ''tearing on the inside'' and
''clinging to the wall of the uterus.'' Beth wasn't sure what
a uterus was, but apparently Dudley did, and he seemed
very worried about what was going on.

When Sadie returned with the blanket, Dudley immediately sent her out again for more clean rags. Beth covered
Tess with the blanket, but still Tess's shivering persisted.

''You'd better take the baby, miss. I'm dreadfully cold
and shaking so much I might drop her,'' said Tess.

Beth took the child and stood back a step or two,
watching the men. They appeared to be trying to stem the
flow of blood by packing Tess with rags.

By now Tess was beginning to be frightened as well. Her
face was completely devoid of color. ''What's wrong,
Dudley? What's happening to me? I'm so cold!''

Dudley moved to the side of the couch and stooped down
by Tess, taking her hands again. He smiled. ''You're losing
a bit of blood, love. I think it's because the afterbirth is
stubbornly clinging to the inside of you. Since the baby
came early, Mother Nature wasn't exactly ready in all
regards.''

''I'm going to be all right, aren't I? I want to be strong
and healthy for my baby. It would not do if I were to have
to lie abed for a long while. I'm going back to work at Mrs.
Turley's, you know. Zach left me some money, but I'm not
going to keep it.'' She sighed heavily. ''I'm suddenly so
very drowsy, Dudley.''

Beth saw the pained expression in Dudley's and Alex's
eyes as their gazes met. ''Close those beautiful peepers of
yours and rest, Tessy,'' Dudley gently advised her.

"But I'm shaking too hard to sleep," she whispered. "Goodness, I've never felt so strange in my life."

Her voice drifted off, and she closed her eyes. She appeared to be sleeping, though she was still racked by strong shivers.

"Damn it, Dudley," rasped Alex, one hand on Tess's knee and the other applying pressure to the rags between her legs. "Isn't there something else we can do?"

"I don't know what else to do," Dudley said hoarsely. "Keep checking for the afterbirth and keep applying pressure in the meantime. We can only try to stem the flow of blood till whatever's going on inside her resolves itself."

"What if it doesn't resolve itself, Dudley?" Beth asked him, her voice brittle with fear.

Dudley did not answer. She could see him clench his jaw with emotion. He looked down at Tess, probably agonized by their absolute impotence in the situation.

"These rags are saturated," Alex said tersely. "Bring me that basket, Sadie, and fetch some more rags."

Sadie carried the basket to Alex, and Beth watched numbly as he laid several rags soaked with bright red blood inside its shallow confines. Sadie looked distressed and almost as though she might swoon. She quickly set the basket on the floor next to Alex and left the room to fetch more rags, and probably to gather her composure.

Beth felt as though she were watching this drama unfold from the vantage point of another planet, horror suspended in a woozy, self-defensive detachment. She held the baby securely, rhythmically dipping her shoulders back and forth in a rocking motion, thereby lulling the child into a peaceful sleep. The baby had discovered her thumb and had slipped it inside her mouth to stave off the pangs of hunger. But aside from the comfort and security she was lending to this new, extremely tiny scrap of humanity, Beth felt completely helpless.

Tess wasn't shivering any longer, and Alex continued the

grim ritual of changing blood-soaked rags for clean ones. Dudley held Tess's hands and watched her devotedly, his usually neatly combed thatch of ginger hair a chaotic tumble, his white pantaloons smeared with blood.

"Why did she stop shivering?" asked Beth. "Does that mean she's stopped bleeding? Will she be all right?"

Neither of the men replied, and panic gripped Beth's heart. "She's not . . . ?"

"Not yet," Alex said in a resigned monotone. "But near enough."

"No!" cried Beth, starting forward, her eyes stinging with the start of tears. "It's not fair! She can't die. She's just a child herself."

"Take Miss Tavistock out, Sadie," said Dudley flatly. "She'll wake Tess and frighten her if she starts crying. I don't want Tessy to be frightened ever again."

"Come on, miss," said Sadie, gently taking hold of Beth's elbow and steering her toward the door.

"I won't cry, I promise," Beth beseeched in a quavery voice. "I want to stay with you, Alex." Beth dug her heels into the carpet and balked like a stubborn mule.

Sadie turned toward Alex for guidance, and he nodded his head, granting Beth permission to stay and giving Sadie permission to leave. Sadie then left without a backward glance. Alex stood up and moved to the basin of water, dipped his hands inside and washed away the blood, all the while looking at Beth, his eyes willing her to calm herself. Beth swallowed the huge lump in her throat time and again, but it kept coming back, threatening to spill out in a sob.

Finally Alex was beside her, his strong arm lending her strength. She slumped against him and looked down at the baby, the small thing so unaware that her whole world, her whole future, had changed in a matter of moments.

"I don't care what Lord Roth said, I'm going in!"

Zach's angry voice filtered through the thick panels of the door, and suddenly he was in the room. Behind him, Henry looked chagrined; evidently he had not been told that Dudley's stricture to keep everyone out did not apply to Zach. Alex nodded reassuringly at Henry, and the lad closed the door.

"What's this all about, Alex? By God, you've got my own servants hounding me, defying me . . ." Zach's voice trailed off as he took in the scene before him. First he saw Beth holding the small bundle of flannel, with Alex supporting her, their expressions pinched and drawn. His head jerked to the couch, and his eyes widened as his gaze was riveted to Tess's small figure reclining on the couch with Dudley kneeling, as if in prayer, beside her.

"Tessy?" His voice was barely audible and permeated with doubt and dread. He walked hesitantly to the couch and stood over Tess, his hands curled against his chest, spasmed by fear. He looked at her white face, her composed features, the basket of crimson rags, and dropped to his knees beside the couch.

"Tessy?" he said again, reaching out to touch her.

Tess stirred slightly, her eyes blinking open, shadowed by thick golden lashes. "Zach, is that you?"

Dudley turned to Zach and said in an almost savage voice, "I'll move, but don't you dare upset her, Master Zachary, or you'll have me to answer to." Then he gently disengaged his hand from Tess's now weak grip and moved to stand by the window, watching as the violet shadows of dusk moved irreversibly over the lawn, cooling, dimming, covering the green grass and colorful flowers in a shroud of darkness. In just the same way imminent death had crept stealthily over the bloom in Tess's cheeks, fixing her features in cold white perfection and turning her small, slender fingers icy and inflexible.

Zach bent close to Tess's face and clutched her hands between his two, devouring her with his anxious, loving gaze. "Tessy sweeting, I didn't know. . . . I never thought the babe was so near to coming."

"She was early. Too impatient by half," Tess said with a small, soft smile. Then her smile slipped away, and tears sheened in her fading eyes. Her words were halting and breathless. "I'm sorry, Zach. I never meant to make you angry. I only wanted to be a part of your life. I love you so much. I've been foolish—"

"Never say that again, Tessy!" Zach said fiercely, grabbing her by the shoulders. "*I* was foolish. Foolish and selfish. I do love you, Tessy, I do!" he cried, clutching her to him.

Tess sighed and lifted her hand to Zach's hair, sifting her fingers through the golden tresses in a last caress. Beth could see Tess's eyes just above Zach's shoulders as he rocked her back and forth, murmuring over and over again, "I love you, Tessy. I love you." Tess's eyes were filled with contentment, as if God had granted her a final, blessed benediction. She turned her face toward Zach, her cheek nuzzled against his neck. When her hand ceased stroking Zach's hair and fell limp to his shoulder, Beth knew she was gone.

The next few hours passed in a haze. The last Beth saw of Zach he was still clutching Tess's rag-doll form against his chest, still rocking her to and fro, still telling her—though she could no longer hear him—that he loved her, loved her, loved her. . . .

Beth had been guided to her chamber by Sadie, the baby taken gently from her by one of the maids. She remembered telling the maid to take good care of the baby, to find it a wet nurse as soon as possible, and in the meantime to feed it warm goat's milk and sugar. Somewhere she'd heard that advice given to a mother who'd had no milk of her own for her baby to suckle and no money to hire a wet nurse. Then Sadie helped Beth out of her gown so she was dressed only in her shift, and tucked her into bed where she immediately fell into an exhausted sleep.

When she awoke, Alex was there, sitting on the edge of

the bed, watching her intently. The room was dark except
for a three-tapered branch of candles on the bedside table,
the flickering light revealing dark shadows beneath Alex's
eyes. When he saw she was awake, he smiled and leaned
down to kiss her lightly on the lips.

Before Alex could straighten, Beth slipped her hands
around his shoulders and held him fast against her. His
hands tangled in her hair, and they clung to each other,
drawing strength from each other. He felt so warm, so solid.
He was her anchor to earth, a safe harbor in a turbulent
storm, her love, her life.

Finally Beth lay back against the pillows and looked up at
him. Their hands were clasped tightly together, resting on
the white counterpane that covered her. Despite the harrowing strain of the last few hours and the signs of fatigue in
deep lines about his mouth and the unnatural shadowing of
his Gypsy eyes, Alex had never looked so beautiful to Beth.
Against the backdrop of Zach's terrible loss of Tess, Beth
treasured Alex's love all the more.

"How is he?"

Alex's tender smile fell away, and his troubled gaze
dropped to their entwined fingers. He stroked the back of
her hand with his thumb. "He's suffering greatly. When I
was finally able to pull him away from Tess, I took him to
his room. I've checked on him twice since then, and he was
lying quietly on the bed. I didn't know whether he was
asleep or not, so I left him alone." Alex sighed heavily. "It
is time I roused him, however, whether from grief or from
sleep. Decisions must be made concerning Tess's funeral,
and only Zach can make them." Alex paused, then looked
at Beth. "He feels responsible for Tess's death, you know."

"I see how he might," said Beth.

"You blame him, then?"

"No, not really. He was stupid and selfish, but probably
behaved no differently than most men would have done in
the same situation, however wrong that behavior may be.

Zach made the mistake of considering Tessy unworthy of his most tender feelings. But he loved her; that was plain to see. And she loved him."

Alex nodded agreement. "I never knew she was so young. Or so innocent, in her way. I certainly understand better the conflict that he's been dealing with during the last few weeks."

"What do you mean, Alex?"

"After the mine incident he realized that he loved her too well. He felt that his love for you and his commitment to you had become secondary to his love for Tess. That troubled him, and a friend of his had made some blunders in his life that Zach was afraid of duplicating. He told me that he was going to leave Tess. But I planned to tell him about us before he went to see her. I thought he might not want to sever his ties with Tess once he knew that you weren't going to marry him after all. But he got anxious and left to see her this afternoon before I got a chance to explain things. He found out about her pregnancy today for the first time. It must have been a considerable shock. Obviously he had come to my room to discuss this new dilemma when he discovered us together." Alex shook his head soberly. "From there, things only got worse for him."

"Why didn't you tell me about Tessy, Alex?"

Alex shrugged and looked away. "I suppose I didn't want to hurt you. I didn't want to use Tess as a source of discord between you and Zach. I wanted you to break off your engagement to Zach for one reason only—your love for me. Any other means of separating you and Zach would have been dishonest." Alex's returning gaze searched Beth's face. "Are you angry with me, Beth? Are you angry with Zach? He never meant to—"

"No, I'm not angry with either of you. I understand your reluctance to speak to me of Tessy. And I suppose I understand why Zach had a mistress. He's very affectionate, very physical. I only wonder that I didn't realize what was going on long ago. Besides, I'm too tired and sick of the world's ways to waste my time being angry. Frankly, I'm afraid for Zach. I'm afraid he'll never forgive himself. This is too like what happened to his own mother, and he blamed himself for her death, too. He may be too hurt and angry with you and me to let us help him through this ordeal.'' Beth shook her head, her hair swishing against the soft linen pillowcase. ''Mayhap only God can help him now.''

''God must grant me a share in helping Zach recover from this tragedy, since I feel partly to blame. But Zach isn't the only person affected by Tess's death.''

''Do you mean Dudley? He seemed to care very much for her, though he didn't know her very long.''

''No, not Dudley, though he *is* suffering. I meant the babe. I wonder what Zach means to do with her.''

''Don't you think he'll keep her?''

''The child might be too painful a reminder of Tess and how she died. Knowing Zach, I think he might fear that he'd grow to hate the child, just as our father hated him.''

''I should think he'd do the exact opposite, Alex, since he knows how very unfair and illogical such a hatred would be. After suffering at his own father's hand, surely Zach would do better by this child.''

''Logic and raw emotion—the head and the heart—don't always lead to the same conclusions, my Beth. But no matter how Zach might feel about the child by and by, I'll wager he'd as soon not risk hating her and making her just as miserable as he was made by an unforgiving parent.''

''So what will he do with her? She mustn't go to a foundling home, Alex! If he cannot bear to keep her, he must give her to—''

Beth stopped herself, remembering abruptly that Alex still had not asked her to marry him. She did not want to seem presumptuous. But, truth to tell, she was becoming a little nervous about Alex's reputation as Wicked Wickham. She was secure in the knowledge that he loved her—she

knew that with her whole heart. But perhaps he was
reluctant to marry her. Perhaps he thought it would change
his style of living too much. Perhaps—

"Why don't you finish your sentence, love?" Alex
quizzed her, his head bent slightly to the side and one black
brow arched questioningly. "Why do you suddenly look as
if the world has tumbled about your ears? You must tell me.
Husbands and wives tell each other everything, you know.
Or at least in *our* marriage that will be the case."

Beth could hardly believe what she was hearing. She felt
deliriously happy, a relieved smile wreathing her face. "Oh,
Alex, you horrible, wonderful man! You've just now
reconstructed my tumbling world!"

Alex responded to Beth's joyous smile with a smile of his
own, but he also looked perplexed. "I don't understand,
Beth. Why am I a mixture of horrible and wonderful, and
how have I reconstructed your tumbling world?"

"Do you realize that this is the first reference you've ever
made to marriage in connection with you and me? Heavens,
I never really knew whether you wanted me as a wife or not.
I dared not assume—"

Alex's eyes widened in a horrified expression. "Lord,
Beth, how could you ever think I meant to offer you
anything other than marriage?" he said roughly. "You're
my better half, the half of me I've been looking for all my
life. You don't think I'd shackle you to me with anything
less binding than the irreversible bonds of matrimony, do
you? Whether you still love me or not by the time we've
grown old together, I intend to have you by my side. I love
you, Beth. Now have I made my intentions clear?"

Beth laughed softly. "Yes, yes. Delightfully, satisfyingly
clear. But what about my mother? Is she here? Does she
know . . . everything? Have you made your intentions
toward me clear to Mama?"

Alex grimaced, then smiled ruefully. "Yes, your mother
is here, and she knows all. And the miracle of it is, she does

not consider me a villain.'' He shifted slightly on the bed and continued in a more serious vein. ''She has agreed to our marriage. However, she has retired to the bedchamber across the hall to rest and, with the help of some laudanum, to restore her nerves to something like normalcy. I cannot blame her. Everything has changed in the last few hours. She must be given time to grow used to these new circumstances.''

Beth nodded and remained silent, hoping he'd reintroduce the topic of Zach's baby girl.

''You're thinking about the baby again, aren't you?'' he offered obligingly. ''I know what you're thinking. To finish your sentence from earlier, you think Zach should give the child to us to raise, don't you?''

Beth's heart swelled with hope. ''I do. I think it the most logical and at the same time the most emotionally satisfying alternative, next to Zach keeping her.'' She squeezed his hands hard and looked appealingly at him. ''Say you feel the same way, Alex. I could not bear it if that sweet baby wasn't given the chance for a happy, wonderful life just because of the circumstances of her birth. No one need ever know she isn't ours. We could marry here and go on an extended honeymoon. When we returned to England, we could subtract a few months from her actual age. I suspect she will always be rather small. She was premature, and Tess was petite. I think we could pull it off without a hitch, Alex.''

''Good God, Beth, but you're a sly cat, aren't you?'' Alex suggested teasingly. ''You seem to have thought this out quite thoroughly. But what about the gossip hereabouts? Somehow it will work its way to London, and everyone, from the lowliest stableboy at Tattersall's to the king himself, will know that the child we profess to be ours is, in reality, Zach's illegitimate offspring. It wouldn't come out at first, probably, and years would go by with the two of us feeling quite sanguine, thinking we'd fooled everyone. Then the truth would surface just as we were about to present her at court and give her a coming-out ball. That would be worse for the child than a more humble upbringing in an adoptive home nearby.''

Beth pondered this problem for a moment, then said, ''No one can claim she's Zach and Tessy's child if they think she died during the night and was buried with her mother.''

Alex raised both brows this time. ''Are you suggesting that we tell everyone she's in the coffin with Tess?''

Beth did not blink an eye. ''Yes.''

''Even the vicar?''

''Especially the vicar. He's the biggest tattle-tongue in all of Cornwall. If he consecrates the grave to receive both Tessy's body and the baby's, the story will be well spread that Zach's child died, too.'' When Alex continued to look sober and unconvinced, Beth added softly, ''God will forgive us. He'll see how we love and care for the child, giving her a life her mother was denied through no fault of her own. It will atone.''

Alex seemed to reflect on this suggestion for a few moments, then said, ''I hope it may atone. I'm not of a mind to cross God these days. I feel too grateful, too blessed.'' He lifted a hand to slide a caressing finger along the curve of Beth's cheek. ''We'll let Zach decide.''

CHAPTER
seventeen

ALEX STOOD OUTSIDE Zach's door, gathering his courage. It was nearing eleven o'clock, and Zach had been inside his bedchamber for several hours. The hot weather demanded that Tess's funeral take place the following day, and Zach had to make some decisions concerning arrangements, decisions that Alex did not feel entitled to take upon himself. Judging by the sultriness of the night, tomorrow would be just as hot as today had been, and Tess's body could not hold up for very long in such unremitting heat. Better to put her in the cool earth while she was still beautiful.

Alex slid his hand along his stubbled jaw and around to the back of his neck to massage the tight muscles there. It had been a damnable day, the likes of which he hoped never to repeat. He felt terrible about Tess's untimely death, though he had not met the girl till a scant couple of hours before he watched her die. As he'd told Beth, now he could understand Zach's obsession with her in the past weeks since he'd come to Cornwall. The trouble was, Zach hadn't realized that what he'd felt for Tess was true love—until it was too late.

Alex thanked God that he had found Beth and knew exactly what he felt for her. Beth. Alex closed his eyes and pictured her as he loved to keep her in his mind's eye. All in rose-pink, her hair loose and flowing down her back, her aqua-blue eyes fixed on him in unwavering love. Thinking of her gave him a temporary peace; she was his oasis in a vast desert of trouble and worry. Finally he recalled his purpose in standing outside Zach's door, and he raised his hand to rap sharply on the panels with his knuckles.

Zach did not answer the knock, but then, Alex hadn't expected him to. "Zach?" he called, his mouth close to the door. "I need to talk to you. I daresay you've wished me to the devil, but there are matters that must be settled tonight . . . about Tess."

Then, to Alex's surprise, he heard Zach call, "Come in." He let himself into the room, shut the door behind him, and found himself standing in utter darkness.

When his eyes adjusted, he could perceive varying shades of gray as illuminated by a three-quarter moon shining in through the one narrow window whose curtains had not been drawn. Positioned in front of the open window was a wing chair, and in it sat Zach. His profile was etched against the hazy background of the moon-bathed swell and dip of rolling moor, with its inky splotches of scrub and bracken and strangely candescent lichened stone. Zach sat motionless, his composed figure preternaturally still and eerie. Gloom hung over him like the pressing clouds of a bleak winter's day. Yet outside, the nightingale still sang in the trees by the creek, and the frogs and crickets still strummed their courting calls to the heavens.

"Do you mind if I get a candle? I'm likely to break my neck if I attempt to cross the room without a little light to find my way. Or would you rather I broke my neck?" He had tried to sound casual, playful, speaking to Zach in his old way, the way they'd spoken to each other before today's tragedies had taken their toll. But he realized how stupid he'd sounded, and that Zach might think he was implying something more than was meant.

"No, I'd rather you didn't break your neck," Zach replied in an expressionless voice. "I've no stomach for revenge, if that's what you're wondering. As God is my witness, never again shall I be responsible for another's death. By all means, brother, fetch a candle. There's a candelabrum on the mantel."

Considering a fitting reply to Zach's dismal words, Alex moved carefully past the looming shadows of scattered furniture to the mantel, locating the candelabrum and a tinderbox beside it. He had lit one candle and was about to light another when Zach said, "Just one, if you please. The dark suits me. It mirrors my soul."

Alex sighed at this self-loathing remark, cast his eyes about the room till he spied a chair pushed up against a far wall, fetched it, and placed it directly across from Zach. He sat down and placed the candle on the floor between them. He spread his legs, rested his elbows on his knees, twined his hands together, and leaned forward.

"Zach, you can accomplish nothing by sitting thus in the dark. As for your soul, it does not mirror this darkness you've pulled about you like a cloak. Perhaps it feels a bit tarnished, full of sorrow, wounded, but it will light again. You will recover. You will find happiness and give happiness, I promise you."

The low-angled candlelight cast strange, dancing shadows over Zach's face as he shook his head. "I don't deserve happiness. I've robbed yet another young woman of her life through childbirth. First my mother died. Then I got Tessy with child, and she died. I'm cursed, Alex."

"That's foolish talk—"

"I almost killed Gabby through my own irresponsibility, and then I tried to kill you. Lord, Alex, I wanted to strangle the very breath out of you! Don't you think that's indicative of a black soul?"

"You were angry, as you'd every right to be. I was wrong to take Beth to bed. In my heart's heart I knew that what we were doing was an injustice to you. Even though Beth and I are very much in love, we should have waited. We should have told you about us long ago—"

"You *are* going to marry her, aren't you?" Zach quickly interjected, showing for the first time a little interest in what Alex was saying.

Alex raised his brows. "Of course I am. There was never any question in my mind that that's what I'd do. Do you think me such a blackguard that I would trifle with Beth's affections and not offer her marriage? B'gad, even *she* asked me about my intentions!"

"Well, you never mentioned marriage in all your sincere efforts to explain things and to placate me this afternoon. You've a reputation to live down, Alex. After all, Wicked Wickham has avoided marriage all his life. No wonder Beth was insecure."

"I perceive I've been a bit remiss in my courting methods, but I assure you, brother, I've had some pretty troublesome thoughts filling my mind and heart these days. It seemed precipitate and disloyal to speak to Beth of our future together when we had not yet informed you of our affection for each other."

Zach chuckled softly, bitterly. "Yet making love to her did not strike you as equally precipitate and disloyal?"

"God, Zach, if you knew how I've suffered over this, how we've both suffered—"

Zach flicked his wrist in a dismissive gesture. "I know. It doesn't matter anymore. Everything is changed."

"But our friendship mustn't change, Zach," Alex said feelingly. "You don't know how much our reunion meant to me. I never dreamed we could truly be brothers again. I fought the feelings I had for Beth, ever so long, because I love you, Zach, and she loves you, too—"

"Like a brother," Zach finished quietly.

Alex paused, then said, "Yes, like a brother. And I would wager that you now realize your love for Beth is more appropriate for a sister than for a wife."

Zach turned his head toward the window. "Yes, the sort of love one feels for one's wife is . . . special. I loved

Tessy that way, you know. Like a wife. But I was a coward. I feared society's disdain. And in the end I feared the intensity of my own feelings." He did not speak for a moment or two, but Alex could see how his fingers fidgeted with the linen doily that rested on the chair arm. "I never told her I loved her before today. I didn't want to put myself at her mercy, you see. But I did love her, Alex, more than life."

Alex did not like the direction Zach's thoughts had taken. They were too morbid. "Yet life stretches before you, promising endless possibilities. You've a daughter now who requires your attention and concern. You must face life again, Zach, just as you've learned to face your responsibilities these past weeks. Tessy would want you to."

Zach released a long, slow hiss of breath. "And my first responsibility is to see to Tessy's burial. Would that I had never seen her that December evening last year. She would still be alive."

"Damnation, Zach, stop this!" cried Alex, growing impatient out of fear for Zach's self-condemning, melancholy state of mind. "I won't listen to your hateful remarks a minute longer. Even though they're not directed toward me, I find them abhorrent. When you deride yourself, you are speaking derisively of my beloved brother, in whom I have boundless faith and for whom I feel boundless love. It is self-indulgent and beneath you. Begin living *now*. Your life is painful now, and it will be painful for a long time, but you must live it."

Zach bent forward and rested his head in his hand. Long moments passed, and Alex sat quietly, allowing Zach this time to reach deep inside himself for the strength to carry on. Alex knew it would be a long, hard struggle, but he would not allow Zach to do anything but fight, to be anything but a survivor. He loved him; he needed him too much.

Finally Zach lifted his head, and Alex saw the tracks of

tears on his cheeks, but his expression was firm and full of resolve. Resolve to live, Alex hoped. Resolve to learn from the past and embrace the future. "I want Tessy buried here at Pencarrow." Zach seemed to be waiting for Alex's reaction.

"Of course you would," Alex agreed. "I don't see any problem with that. You are master of Pencarrow."

"And I don't give a blessed fig who might object to the fact that I've buried my mistress at Pencarrow. They would not allow her to rest among the quality at the parish cemetery, but would consign her to some beggars' corner. Even in death, society draws a line between the classes. But I'll not bury her close to Grandfather or any other of the priggish Hayles, for she would not be comfortable in their midst. There's a tall horse chestnut tree in the far corner, by that old family chapel we haven't used for services since King Henry was on the throne. It's green there and sheltered from the worst of the wind that blows over the moor. Tess will like it there."

"Then it is settled. Shall we have services in the morning?"

"She needs a proper casket. I'll not have her buried in a makeshift box, Alex."

"I put Dudley to work arranging for that and sent him to request the vicar's presence at the funeral, too. We have only to send word to the vicarage of the exact time and location at which we wish to hold services."

"Vicar Bradford did not object to presiding over Tessy's funeral?"

"He did not dare to. Dudley can be quite fierce when he feels strongly about something."

"Yes, I saw that in him today. And I suppose the good vicar would not dare to offend Lord Roth and his ramshackle brother. But I only want you and Beth, Dudley, and myself at the funeral. No one else knew her. I won't have a false or a pitying tear shed for Tessy."

"As you wish, brother." Alex leaned back in his chair and crossed his legs, left ankle over right knee. "Now what shall we do about the baby? Have you thought of that? For if you haven't, I've a suggestion."

"Oddly enough, I *have* thought of the baby. And I know exactly what I'd like to see happen to the little thing. She'll never have a chance if she stays in these parts. And I haven't the slightest notion how to be a father to her, especially since I haven't a woman to direct me. I won't marry merely to secure the child a mother. I want you to take her back to Surrey with you. I want you and Beth to raise her as your own."

Alex uncrossed his legs and leaned forward. "I must confess that that is exactly what Beth and I had hoped for. But are you sure about this, Zach? She's your own child. Tessy's child, too."

"All the more reason why I want the best for her. Tessy had to do without and was scorned for things she had no control over. Victoria must have the opportunities Tessy didn't!"

"Victoria?"

"I want you to christen her Victoria, if you will grant me that favor. I've always fancied the name."

"Victoria it is," Alex promptly acquiesced.

"But how are we to keep the child's true parentage a secret? I confess myself utterly befuddled as to how to accomplish that."

"Beth has a scheme of which you might or might not approve," Alex began cautiously. "Brother, lend me your ear." Then Alex briefly explained Beth's idea of announcing the child's death and telling everyone that she was inside the nailed coffin with her mother. Alex would then take Beth and Victoria to Italy for an extended honeymoon. When they returned to Surrey and reentered society, everyone would think the baby was theirs.

''Not even the vicar must know the truth. We will tell him that the child died, too,'' Zach added.

''Are we selling our souls here, Zach? Spinning whiskers to the vicar is most probably considered a monumental sin.''

''To put to right what's been terribly wrong, I'd tell lies to the king.''

''That's what we'll be doing when Beth and I present Victoria at court as our own daughter when she comes of age,'' Alex mused aloud.

Zach shrugged his shoulders. ''As I said, I don't care about that. I want her to have everything her mother should have had. I want her to have everything Tessy would want for her.''

''But do you think Tess would have wanted her daughter separated from you, her father? I'm sure that what Tess would have wanted above all else, above money or social standing, would be for Victoria to be loved and cherished within the circle of a family. You may not think so now, Zach, but someday you will marry. There'll be brothers and sisters for Victoria—''

''I shall never marry. But even if I did, there would always be a distinction drawn between Victoria and the other children, if not by me or my wife, by other people. No, I want only the very best for Victoria, and if that means I must give her up, so be it. Besides, I shall be her uncle Zachary and shall come regularly to Ockley Hall to see her. You will grant me that indulgence, won't you?''

''I wouldn't have it any other way, brother.'' Zach's hand was resting on the chair arm, and Alex reached across and covered it with his. Zach turned his hand, palm up, and clasped Alex's in a strong grip. ''God, Zach, I was afraid I'd lost you again.'' Alex choked out the words.

''Only wishful thinking, brother,'' Zach returned playfully, though his own voice was hoarse with emotion. ''You and I are shackled together for life.''

"And Beth? If you have forgiven me, I pray God you have forgiven her, too," Alex ventured.

A shadow crossed Zach's face for a moment. Then he said, "I've loved Beth forever and shall do so till I die, I suppose. I think I understand my feelings for her much better now. I truly wish her the very best life has to offer."

"Will you tell her that?" asked Alex.

"Yes."

"She's waiting in her room for your summons. Shall I go and get her now? Or would you rather wait till tomorrow to talk to her?"

Zach sighed softly. "No, I want to make my peace with Beth tonight."

Alex stood up to leave, but Zach stopped him. "Bring the baby, too. Let me see her before you take her away."

Alex nodded and left the room, returning in a few moments with Beth and the baby. Zach had roused himself sufficiently to light up the room to a reasonable brightness and had also made an attempt to straighten his disheveled clothes and hair. He had propped his shoulder against the mantelpiece and was waiting for them with a rather transparent air of ease, for Alex could tell that Zach's mind and heart were besieged with diverse and painful thoughts and feelings. Zach's eyes fixed first on Beth as she entered the room, then on the small bundle she held in her arms.

Beth appeared to feel timid in Zach's presence, a singular happenstance in their long friendship. But so much had changed between them. Alex watched from a distance as Beth walked slowly up to Zach, as all the while Zach stared at the flannel-wrapped scrap of humanity she cradled against her chest.

"Hello, Zach."

Zach lifted his gaze from the bundle to Beth's eyes—her softly pleading eyes. Without words being spoken, without the slightest movement made by either, forgiveness and love flowed between them. "Hello, Beth." He pushed away from the mantelpiece and stepped closer, his eyes once more drawn to the child. ''What have you there?''

Beth smiled and extended her arms. ''Why don't you hold her?''

Zach hesitated, agonized indecision written in his expression. ''I don't think I should.''

''Why not? She might as well get used to the feel of her uncle Zachary's arms about her. I've a feeling he's going to spoil her shamefully at every opportunity.''

The corners of Zach's mouth lifted in a tentative smile. He cast Beth a grateful look, then slowly, carefully, self-consciously, took the baby into his arms.

It was a sight Alex would not soon forget. Zach, all six feet two inches of him, was utterly captivated, completely enthralled by a small human being who couldn't have weighed more than five pounds. For Zach's sake, for Tessy's sake, and indeed for Victoria's sake, too, Alex knew then that he had irreversibly allotted a large portion of his heart to Zach's child. His protection, his name, and a father's commitment naturally were included in the portion that he willingly gave.

He caught Beth's gaze, knew she cherished identical feelings, and was glad.

Dudley had taken the baby in the dead of night to a small cottage across the moor in the opposite direction from St. Teath. A wet nurse awaited her there, as did another capable woman recommended by Sadie to tend her till Alex and Beth could pick her up on the way to Dover, from which port they would continue on to Italy. The two women were paid well to keep mum. All the servants at Pencarrow— except, of course, Sadie and Dudley—were told the following morning that the babe had died during the night and had been placed in her mother's arms inside the closed coffin.

It was a reasonable lie to tell and an easy one to believe. After all, the child was two months premature. Beth still feared that she might die suddenly from some quirk of nature despite her apparently hearty constitution. But the baby was a scrapper. Game for life, it seemed. She thanked God for that.

Zach pinned the cameo brooch to Tessy's bodice, and after one last tender, regretful look at her still-beautiful face, Zach had Dudley nail shut the coffin. While he was tempted to keep the coffin open so that he might look at Tess till the last possible moment, Zach was afraid one of the servants might wander into the antechamber just off the drawing room for a glimpse of Tess and discover that the babe did not lie with her mother.

Everyone—the vicar, the servants, and all the others who would hear the tale secondhand—must all believe that Tessy's baby had died and had been buried with her. This was the only way their plan for Victoria's salvation from her parents' indiscretions would succeed. Only by beginning her life in a masquerade as Beth's and Alex's child would Victoria stand a chance of not being branded as a merry-begotten, a child of the mist or any other euphemism for an illegitimate offspring.

As Beth, Alex, and Dudley gathered in the drawing room that morning, Beth reflected that so far the plan had come off as neat as wax. The vicar had arrived at the house promptly at nine, displaying an expected amount of barely concealed beatific revulsion to Tess's lamentable, sin-ridden life and nodding his head with a knowing, pious purse to his lips when he was told that God had taken the child as well.

"Poor wretched souls," he said, clicking his venerable tongue and implying quite ably that Tess and the child had received their just desserts. Beth was thankful that Zach had not been present to hear the vicar's sanctimonious expressions, but only came down the stairs in time to follow the coffin as it was taken out through the front door.

Beth and Alex walked on either side of Zach, their arms

locked with his. They glanced often at one another, their eyes conveying love, support, grief, and hope.

Dudley, walking just behind them with the vicar, had been nearly run off his legs accomplishing all of the tasks he was only too willing to do. The fact was, due to the necessary secrecy attached to many of the tasks, and also simply because he considered them a labor of love, Dudley would not allow anyone else to do much of anything. Besides, in character with his perfectionist personality, he did not think anyone would do them as well as he could, especially for Tessy. Today his features showed the strain of a sleepless night and the sure signs of a heart too tender for its own good.

Beth was dressed in the same black bombazine she'd worn for Chester Hayle's funeral, the dress she'd been wearing when she'd first laid eyes on Alex. That day had marked the end of a life and the beginning of Beth's future. Zach and Alex were dressed in black, too, as was Dudley. Beth considered the color quite oppressive and had been tempted to advise them all to wear gay colors, since she was convinced that Tess would have preferred a bright cortege following her coffin rather than such a sober one. But then she realized that they must convey the proper respect for Tess and not give the vicar any reason to suppose that she deserved anything less than a proper service.

They walked around and along the wall that enclosed the kitchen garden, past the espaliered apple trees, through the clipped box hedges that followed the cobbled walkway, past the tangled flower beds full of fragrant pinks—sops in wine, painted ladies, and nutmeg cloves. When they reached the trellised lych-gate that admitted them into the family cemetery and chapel grounds, Zach stopped and disengaged his arms from Beth's and Alex's. The trellis supported heavy vines of honeysuckle.

Zach judiciously picked three exquisite sprigs and arranged them in a posy, drawing a length of ivory ribbon from his jacket pocket to tie it together. He carefully positioned the knot to the right. Beth knew the saying that was attached to honeysuckle posies. Zach had explained it to her once. If the knot was to the right, it meant that the recipient of the posy had the sweet nature of the honeysuckle flower.

Now Zach continued on alone, with Beth and Alex falling in behind him, clinging to each other. The pain of lost love was poignantly displayed this bright, hot morning in August, and it made them all the more grateful for their own love for each other.

Now they were arranged around the open grave, which was situated in the lee of the tall horse chestnut. The smell of rich Cornwall dirt filled Beth's nostrils and reminded her of man's close kinship with the earth, both in life and in death. The servants who'd carried Tess's casket were preparing to lower it into the ground by securing it with two thick, sturdy straps that would slide through their firm grip as the casket descended.

Then, just as they were about to lower the coffin, Zach stepped forward and laid the honeysuckle posy on the wood surface, gently arranging the posy precisely so that the knot was on the right. He stood there for a moment, his fingers lightly stroking the tender stems, his face a mask of controlled devastation. Then he moved back to his former position next to Alex.

A breeze from the moor stirred the ribbons of Beth's plain black bonnet and toyed with the hem of her skirt. The smell of honeysuckle eddied around them. The servants lowered the casket and withdrew. As they walked back toward the house, the vicar opened his prayerbook. Without even looking at the pages, he began to speak.

"'Deliver our sister, Mary Teresa Kenpenny, and her unnamed child out of the miseries of this sinful world. The days of man are but as grass, for he flourisheth as a flower of the field. For as soon as the wind goeth over it, it is gone

and the place thereof shall know it no more. And the
merciful goodness of the Lord endureth forever and ever
upon them that fear Him, even upon such as keep His
covenant and think upon His commandments, and do
them.' ''

As Vicar Bradford's sonorous voice resonated through
the air, the birds chirped cheerfully, like a choir singing
joyous hymns. At that moment, more than ever before in her
life, Beth thought of heaven and prayed fervidly that Tessy
had been received there by a benevolent God.

" 'The Lord hath prepared His seat in heaven, and His
kingdom ruleth over all. For inasmuch as it hath pleased
Almighty God in His great mercy to take upon Himself the
soul of our sister, Mary Teresa Kenpenny, and her unnamed
child, we therefore commit their bodies to the ground.' ''

Henry, the only servant who had been allowed to remain,
threw the first clotted shovelful of dirt on Tess's coffin.

" 'Earth to earth. Ashes to ashes. Dust to dust. In sure and
certain hope of the resurrection to the eternal life through
our Lord Jesus Christ, who will change our vile body to be
like unto His glorious body, according to the mighty
workings whereby He is able to do all things unto Himself.' ''

When the service was over, the vicar left promptly and
was followed shortly thereafter by everyone but Zach and
Henry, the servant waiting for word that he might finish the
task he'd started with that first shovelful of dirt.

"Come on, Henry,'' Alex called from the lych-gate.
"Leave Master Wickham alone for a time. You may return
later to finish.''

Henry obeyed, and they all started back to the house. But
they had barely progressed a few feet past the gate when
they discovered Mrs. Tavistock and Gabby coming along
the walk. Mrs. Tavistock looked apologetic and more than a
little harassed. Gabby had hold of her hand and looked
almost to be dragging her mother.

"I'm so sorry," Mrs. Tavistock immediately began to explain. "I know Zachary didn't wish for Gabby and me to be at the funeral, but as soon as she saw the vicar return to the house, Gabby insisted that we had every right to join you now that the services were concluded. I'm not sure why she wanted to come. I don't think she even understands what's going on, but she's plagued me till I'm near distracted—"

"I want to see Zach," Gabby stated firmly. "He's very sad, and I want to help him."

"I don't know, Gabby," Beth demurred. "Sometimes people want to be alone, especially when they're sad."

"But I can make him feel better," Gabby insisted with a pleading look designed to soften the hardest heart this side of the Tamar. "Now that you're marrying Lord Roth, it will be up to me to be Zach's best friend. Beth, please."

After but a moment's reflection, she nodded her consent, and Gabby ran past them and through the lych-gate to Zach's side. Beth supposed that if he truly did not desire Gabby's company, he would think of some kind way to send her back to the house. She watched as Gabby stood there, looking up into Zach's face. He seemed absorbed in grief and hardly cognizant of his surroundings. Gabby reached up and slipped her hand into his. He looked down, and Beth was relieved and grateful to watch his grief-stricken features soften. He touched Gabby's cheek, then pulled her close with an arm about her shoulders.

"She has a way with him," said Alex.

"And he with her," agreed Beth. "Mayhap in time she'll help his heart to heal."

CHAPTER
eighteen

THE SPRING OF 1822 would always be remembered in the village of Positano, Italy, as especially warm and balmy, having come in like the proverbial lamb. Dudley watched from the veranda as Beth and Alex strolled arm in arm along the beach one fine morning in April, enjoying the sun's glint off the sapphire-blue waters of the Gulf of Salerno. Shadow ran along the shoreline, jumping at low-sweeping gulls and chasing the foamy waves that lapped at the sand.

Beth was dressed in a rose-colored muslin gown, her hair loose and flowing down her back, and she carried a frilled parasol to protect her freckle-prone nose from the strong Italian sun. Alex wore burgundy trousers and a blousy white shirt that was open at the throat, the full sleeves billowing softly in the breeze.

They were the image of wedded bliss, their two dark heads bent confidingly close in low-voiced conversation, the contented curve of his lordship's lips showing the pleasure he took in supporting the light pressure of his wife's leaning form. They were elegant and easy in their carriage and appeared as happy as ants in a sugar dish.

Now, although he hated to interrupt their morning promenade, Dudley was determined to catch their attention. "My lord? My lady?" he shouted, flailing his arms about till Beth turned and discovered his urgent gestures and spoke to Alex. Now they were both looking up at him, and Alex did not appear pleased. But despite Alex's annoyed expression, they bent their steps toward the villa.

"Dudley, if you have summoned us from such a delightful occupation for reasons similar to those you cited yesterday when, as you recall, you also interrupted our morning walk, I will be most displeased." Alex assisted Beth to a comfortable chair by a table laid out with fine china and small dishes filled with pastries and confections. A crystal vase in the center of the table held a bouquet of bright red poppies. Shadow joined them and stretched out in the sun at the top of the stone steps.

"My lord," Dudley began officiously, "by interrupting you two days in a row, I realize I've probably relegated myself quite permanently to your black book. Today, however, I hope you will forgive me, as I have something of great import to communicate to you."

Beth chuckled softly and reached for a scone and the jam crock. "Dudley, don't tease us. I assume this important communication has to do with Torie's nurse."

"Has Miss Brynne once again been bathing the baby in what you perceive as frigid water?" Alex drawled.

Dudley frowned. "I should hope not, my lord. But perhaps I *had* ought to stick my nose into the nursery in a few minutes just to make sure of it, you know. Thank you for reminding me."

Alex sat down in a chair he had pulled up next to his wife, then ran his palm along Beth's thigh till he cupped her knee. Dudley pretended not to notice. Indeed, by now he ought to have grown used to their open displays of affection. Truth to tell, he rather enjoyed seeing two people so completely in love. But now was not the time to ruminate on such romantical matters.

"A thank-you is unnecessary, Dudley, since I'm sure you would have remembered to check on the temperature of Torie's bathwater without my poor assistance," his lordship answered dryly, his annoyance with Dudley dissipating under the influence of his wife's radiant smile. "But, pray, what has Miss Brynne done *now*?"

"I do wish to speak to you about something that concerns Miss Brynne," Dudley admitted, "but at the moment I feel this other news I have is more important."

Alex raised a brow. "B'gad, what can possibly be more important to you than the well-being of that golden elf loaned to us by the fairy world to be raised among mortals?"

"I own myself equally curious," said Beth, licking a tiny dollop of jam from her pinky while Alex watched with avid interest.

"There's a letter from England, my lady," Dudley announced, his own excitement bubbling up in anticipation of theirs.

Beth's attention was captured completely, despite the eddies of desire swirling through her, which had been so easily created by her husband's admiring look and his warm fingers cupping her knee. She could feel Alex's response to Dudley's words in the increased pressure of those warm fingers.

"From Brookmoor?" questioned Alex.

Dudley shook his head.

"From Pencarrow, then?"

"Indeed, my lord," Dudley said with a sniff, "you don't think I'd make such a to-do over a missive from your solicitor, your agent, or even your dear aunt Saphrona, do you?"

Beth clapped her hands in delight. "It's from Zach! See, Alex, I told you it was just a matter of time. I knew he'd write eventually; he simply needed to recover a little from his grief."

Alex's black eyes snapped with emotion. "It's been nine months. It's about time he wrote. I've grown tired of hearing about him from others. It seems I've spent half my life waiting for letters from that rapscallion brother of mine. Well, where is it?''

Dudley gleefully produced the long-awaited letter from behind his back and handed it to Alex. Alex snatched the letter, opened the envelope, and unfolded a thin sheet of parchment covered with small, neat writing.

''It does not appear to be very long,'' Alex commented worriedly as he eyed the single sheet.

''But it begins encouragingly,'' Beth countered as she looked over Alex's shoulder. ''Read it aloud.''

Dudley shifted from one foot to the other. ''Perhaps I should leave.''

''No, stay, Dudley,'' said Alex. ''It's obvious you want to, and I can't think of anyone more entitled to listen than you. Sit down and quit fidgeting.''

Dudley readily obeyed, leaning on the table with his freckled chin supported by both freckled fists.

Alex began to read.

Dear brother and sister,

I hope you will forgive me for failing to write sooner, but I have traveled a rough road these past few months. The worst of it has been the necessity of coming face to face with my own blemished character. You have reprimanded me before for dwelling on my faults, so I will not. Let me just say that while I do not presume to suppose I will ever be perfect, I am striving to become a more sensitive, responsible, right-thinking man.

I still miss Tessy. That is an understatement, I might add, for the pain I've felt—and still feel—has been difficult to endure. As spring breaks over the moor, so does the new honeysuckle, its fragrance as sweet as Tessy's spirit.

But I will not wax morbid. And do not fear that I've become a hermit, either. I keep quite busy with estate business, and Beth's mama keeps me well supplied with letters of invitation to neighboring homes for dinners, soirees, musical evenings, and the like. It seems my recent disgrace has not discouraged the local marriage-minded mamas and their sweet, simpering daughters but has actually lent me a bit of rakish cachet. Such attention rather sickens me, but I suppose I shall have to put up with it till the scandal dies down. At least I am frequently in the company of others, which is preferable to sitting alone and brooding.

As for company, Gabby has been most dedicated in seeing that I don't brood, for hardly a day passes that the determined child doesn't ride over to while away an hour or two with me. She is, as Beth always was, a ray of sunshine in my sometimes dreary world.

Thank you both for your letters. They've been a source of support and joy as you've kept me informed of the excellent progress of Torie. If she truly is the golden waif you describe, the shortened version of her name exactly suits. Give her a kiss and a hug from her uncle Zachary. And pray tell Dudley that I do not mind if he behaves like a fusspot in matters concerning Torie. Tessy would have taken great delight in his interest in her child.

Enough said. I'm still not up to much writing, but I shall try to do better in future. I simply want you to know that I cherish your love and your friendship, and I pray God each night to bless you.

As ever,
Zachary

"Well, that was not precisely as cheerful as I might have wished," Alex said on a sigh as he refolded the letter.

"However, Master Zachary's words reflect quite a reasonable state of mind under the circumstances," Dudley suggested. "Indeed, I think he is coming along just as he ought."

"Dudley's right," Beth added gently. "If he had recov-

ered too suddenly from his megrims, I might have been
forced to conclude that he had suppressed the worst of his
feelings and was not truly dealing with his grief. It will take
time.''

"At least he does not seem to regret his decision to allow
us to raise Torie," said Alex. "I've worried about that."

"Yes, so have I," Beth admitted. "I've come to think of
her as mine." She reached over and laid her hand on Alex's.
"As *ours*. I don't think I could bear to give her up, even to
Zach.''

"You shall never have to, my lady," Dudley said with
conviction. "Mastery Zachary wants what's best for the
child, and what's best for Torie is, quite simply, contained
within these walls.''

"Despite Miss Brynne?" teased Alex.

"Which reminds me, my lord," Dudley said, standing up
and assuming the affronted air he wore whenever some
ineptitude was committed by one of the other servants.
"You'll never believe this, but I feel duty-bound to tell you
even though you may feel compelled to dismiss Miss
Brynne.''

"That would cause you a great deal of anguish, I make no
doubt," Alex commented, surreptitiously winking at Beth
when he thought Dudley wasn't looking.

"Don't mock me, my lord, I beg you," said Dudley,
arranging his face in a pained expression. "I'm sincerely
concerned about this matter.''

Beth reached up to thread her fingers through the thick
hair at the nape of Alex's neck. He had been wearing his
hair longer since they'd been in Italy. It curled over his
collar now. She loved it that way. "Do explain yourself,
Dudley," Beth said encouragingly, trying to pay Dudley the
attention he was seeking, though she knew his concern was
exaggerated because of his devotion to Torie.

"Miss Brynne has been feeding Torie''—Dudley paused
for effect—"*fish*!"

Much to Dudley's disappointment, this announcement did not faze his listeners in the least. Beth continued to twine her fingers lazily through Alex's hair, which, in Dudley's opinion, reduced his lordship's mental faculties to the level of an idiot. Beth finally said with composure, "Oh, is that supposed to be an unhealthful thing to do? I can't believe Miss Brynne would feed Torie anything that would be bad for the child. What do you think, Alex?"

Dudley observed his employer with skepticism. It was obvious what his lordship had on his mind, and it assuredly was not fish, babies, or incompetent nurses. "I think Torie has a remarkable appetite and a stomach like a cast-iron kettle," he said at last, his eyes fixed on his wife and not a bit on his valet-cum-nurse. "To my memory, Miss Brynne has never fed anything to Torie that the child did not find eminently digestible."

Dudley heaved an exasperated sigh. "She's only nine months of age. Despite Torie's obvious enjoyment of a wondrous variety of food, it has been my experience that children under the age of two do not digest fish."

Beth daintily wiped her mouth with a serviette and smiled at Dudley, her single dimple punctuating her rosy right cheek. "But you must admit that Torie is a special child and cannot, as a rule, be lumped into the same category with other, more average children."

Dudley knew Beth was appealing to his belief in Torie's inherent uniqueness, and her tactic was working. Torie *was* unique. She had proven that from the beginning as she consistently exceeded the expectations one might have for premature babies. She smiled, she turned over, she sat up, and she crawled sooner than most full-term babies, and at nine months she was walking, despite her small size. She was an extremely intelligent child, and fish *was* said to be food for the brain. . . .

"If Mr. Dudley is telling tales on me again," came a

disgruntled female voice from the French doors opening onto the veranda, "I shall have to offer my resignation."

Miss Brynne was angry. Her mobcap was askew, her white hair escaping from its pins to wreathe her flushed round face like spun sugar. In truth, she looked like Beth's idea of a fairy godmother, all soft and pink and rotund. And the golden-haired, golden-eyed child she held in her arms simply looked like a fairy, an ethereal waif plucked straight out of one of Pye Thatcher's drolls.

Beth sat back in her chair to watch Dudley and Miss Brynne spar. This was a daily occurrence and one that never failed to entertain. They both loved Torie so much they were constantly at odds with each other over the proper way to attend to her needs. Torie flourished under their care, seeming to sense that their frequent disagreements were just as harmless as they were. Beth felt Alex's arm ease around the back of her chair, his long fingers brushing her shoulder. Such a light touch, so gentle, so casual, yet just as exciting as it had been months earlier when he'd first touched her.

"I should be well pleased if you did resign, Miss Brynne," Dudley said stiffly. "Feeding fish to a baby, of all things!" He harrumphed disdainfully.

"Don't turn your nose up at me, Mr. Dudley," Miss Brynne retorted. "Fish is good for healthy babies like Torie. I ought to know—I'm the child's nurse, not you. Though you seem to think otherwise."

"She's right, Dudley." Alex reached for the baby, Miss Brynne handed her to him, and then the roly-poly nurse crossed her beefy arms and stared cockily at Dudley. "Though your interest in her is estimable," Alex continued, "and quite unobjectionable to Lady Roth and me, you're not Torie's nurse. And there would be a great deal more tranquillity about the house if only you would refrain from trying to run roughshod over Miss Brynne's authority."

"I interfere only when I see a problem, my lord," Dudley

coolly asserted. "It just so happens that I see problems on a daily basis."

"Oh, posh," hissed Miss Brynne, her face reddening to the bright tint of a ripe tomato.

"Oh, look, Alex!" Beth exclaimed, catching a glimpse of something she knew would be of interest to them all and might perhaps end the quarreling of Torie's two nurses. "I believe Torie has a new tooth on the bottom."

The delicately featured baby, dressed in a white flounced gown and knitted shoes, was perched on Alex's knee, secured by one of his large hands on her stomach and the other on her back. Miss Brynne had pulled Torie's fine baby hair atop her head in a decorative plume that looked remarkably like a rooster's comb. She was energetically kicking her legs and rotating her arms, her laughing mouth obligingly open to expose the new tooth.

Miss Brynne and Dudley immediately forgot their grievances to bend over and peer into the baby's mouth.

"A beautiful specimen!" Miss Brynne declared proudly.

"She'll have a dazzling set of ivories by the time she's ready to set London on its ear," Dudley concurred.

"It's undoubtedly the result of such a fine diet," Beth suggested demurely.

Dudley straightened and pulled at his chin with thoughtful fingers. "I don't know about *that*."

Miss Brynne also straightened and faced Dudley squarely—or perhaps roundly would have been a more appropriate description—her arms akimbo. "When are you going to admit, Mr. Dudley, that I know what I'm about when it comes to raising babies? I raised Lord Fabbersham's seven daughters and three sons with nary a peep of complaint from my employers. And certainly none of the other *servants* dared criticize me."

Now it was Dudley's turn to redden.

Alex interrupted the exchange. "While you—pardon the pun—*digest* Miss Brynne's latest piece of prickly pie,

Dudley, won't you take Torie to the nursery? She needs her napkin changed.''

"I should be pleased to, my lord," Dudley replied stoically, sending Miss Brynne a withering look. "Never let it be said that I shirked my duties because of a little unpleasant odor." He lifted Torie from Alex's knee and wedged her in the crook of one elbow, his free arm wrapped about her chest. "Come, sweeting," he crooned to the baby. "It's time for your bath."

Miss Brynne followed Dudley from the room, her short, pudgy legs barely keeping up with his long-legged stride. "Now, Mr. Dudley," she was saying breathlessly, "you know the water must be merely tepid, not overly warm. You'd best let me bathe the baby. You might get water in her ears, and that would never do."

Alex chuckled. "Those two are quite a pair. They couldn't be more devoted to the child. But then, she easily inspires devotion, the little charmer." He turned to Beth, his Gypsy eyes crinkling in a loving smile. "I hope there's no jealousy between the children. Torie is used to a great deal of attention, but she'll have to share Dudley and Miss Brynne when another child comes along."

"Which reminds me," said Beth, looking at him from beneath coyly lowered lashes, "it's been nine months since we married, time enough to have given birth to a child since our marriage in August." She ran a finger lightly along the seam of his trousers, from knee to mid-thigh.

"Just as we planned, my Beth," he said thickly, watching her intently. "Now no one can say Torie isn't ours. Surely when we return to England next year people will only look at Torie's small size and not take into account her abilities, which will assuredly be beyond those expected in a child of her purported age."

"We shall just say she is exceedingly bright," said Beth.

"Which she is," Alex agreed.

"But there is something else, my love." Beth leaned

forward and touched her lips lightly to Alex's chin, to his jaw, and lower, to his neck. She thrilled when she heard his sharp intake of breath.

"What is that, my Beth?" he rasped, gently grasping her shoulders and pulling her into his lap.

"Isn't it time we started another baby?" She snuggled against him.

Alex chuckled. "So soon? Everyone will think I've no consideration for you. People will call me a brute and look at you pityingly if we return from our honeymoon with two children within less than two years."

Beth slipped her hand inside Alex's open collar and spread her fingers over the warm, hair-dusted surface of his broad chest. "I'm quite sure I will not engender pity, Alex. Rather I will stir envy in the hearts of all women who look upon me, since I'll be glowing with satisfaction and happiness."

"Saucy baggage!" he murmured. "You are the most seductive creature I've ever known. Sweeting, if you want a baby, you shall have one."

"When, Alex?" she prompted brazenly, leaning over to bite him neatly on the ear.

Alex did not reply. He was a man of action who considered words unnecessary in this case. He lifted her and carried her into the house, up the stairs, and into her bedchamber, where he locked the door behind him.

Dudley had heard his lordship's booted footsteps on the stairs and down the hall, striding swiftly past the nursery. He poked his head into the gallery just in time to see Lady Roth's dainty slipper and the tip of Shadow's tail as they disappeared through the entrance to her chamber. A breathless silvery laugh of sheer delight commingled with the sound of a key turning in the lock.

Dudley smiled and returned to Torie and Miss Brynne, who were ensconced in a rocking chair by the window. The childish ditty the nurse was singing wafted on the soft breeze that blew in from the sapphire sea to imbue listeners with sleepy content. Miss Brynne *did* have a nice, soothing singing voice, Dudley admitted to himself.

As he watched Torie's golden eyes drift shut, Dudley leaned against the door casing and closed his own eyes. He thought of Tessy and felt the familiar ache in his throat that didn't seem to diminish no matter how much time passed. But he knew she'd be happy about the way things had worked out for Torie. He'd lied like Old Harry himself—to the vicar, to the other servants, to anyone who'd asked about the babe Tess had borne. But in his heart's heart—a heart too tender for his own good—Dudley knew he'd do it again in a pig's whisper.

epilogue

Ockley Hall, Surrey, England—December 1831

BETH NEVER TIRED of the view from her bedchamber window, and on this Christmas Eve it was a winter wonderland of pristine white. The clouds had been threatening all day, but in the last three hours the snow had fallen in earnest, just as though a plump pillow full of goose feathers had been split open and dumped by a playful God over the rolling Surrey countryside.

The river Eden, which wended its way through tall, winter-bare oak and ash trees, was an ice-flecked, chilling blue, and the road to the nearest village of South Godstone was piled high with downy mounds of new snow. As each hour passed, the ability of a coach and four to traverse the thoroughfare seemed more and more doubtful to Beth.

Though it was only six o'clock, dusk was upon them, and golden light spilled through the windows from the bright, lamplit interior of Ockley Hall onto the shadowed exterior of landscape and cobbled courtyard. The silvery pink of the outbuildings, made of the same weathered brick as the main house, melded with the muted colors of eventide. Snowflakes drifted against the many-paned chamfered windows, wedging in crescent designs in the corners.

Beth's brow furrowed. The scene was ideal. But she was viewing this beauty from the vantage point of her snug bedchamber. Those who were forced to travel in this

325

unusually severe snow storm would probably not appreciate its beauty so much as they would curse its inconvenience. Zach might be quite frozen when he arrived, but since he was already half a day overdue, Beth's main concern at this point was that he would arrive at all.

If the weather was worse to the west, Zach might decide to wait out the storm at an inn, and Torie and Jason and Cecily would be terribly disappointed to miss their uncle Zach this Christmas Eve. Truth to tell, so would Beth, and she knew that Alex felt the same way. Zach had been spending the holidays with them for the past four years.

Beth turned away from the window and moved to the dressing table, the top cluttered with perfume atomizers, a pretty variety of combs, a length of emerald green ribbon left over from her abigail's dressing of Beth's hair for the evening, and a small jewel casket. She picked up her brush and began to upwardly stroke the wisps of hair that had fallen from her chignon.

"Don't tidy them," came a low voice from the door. "You know how I love the way those dainty curls riot against your beautiful neck."

Beth not only felt the tremor that ran down her spine at the sound of her husband's deep, admiring voice, but since she was sitting in front of a mirror, she saw it, too. They had been married for ten years, and yet his mere presence—the sound of him, the look of him—still thrilled her. She set down the brush and turned toward the door, a ready smile at her lips. But the impact of seeing Alex, dressed fine as fivepence in evening black with a green brocade waistcoat and a sprig of holly pinned to his lapel, quite took away her ability to do anything but stare.

At forty years of age, the only thing that had changed in Alexander Wickham's appearance since they were wed was the devastatingly handsome addition of silver at his temples. His figure was still as splendid, still as strong and muscled and slim. His eyes were still as black as India ink and as hypnotizing to Beth's senses as an opiate.

An ebony brow winged upward. "I hope I'm deciphering that expression on your face correctly, my Beth. Do you find me as fetching as I find you?"

Alex shut the door behind him and crossed the blue and beige Aubusson rug to stand behind Beth at the dressing table. With his long, slender fingers curled around the bulbous carvings at the back of the chair, he bent and positioned his head just next to hers as they both looked into the mirror.

"I'm glad you wore green," he whispered close to her ear. "So festive a color. And now we match. But best of all, it makes your skin look so creamy and so . . . kissable." Alex dropped his head to place a lingering kiss on the slight swell of bosom that peeked above the white lace ruching of her gown.

Beth lifted her hand to thread eager fingers through the silky thickness of his black hair. Her voice was breathless as she said, "You rogue! Must you tease me so? You know the children are awaiting us in the drawing room, and dinner must not be late tonight, or Cook will blame us if the goose is dry."

Alex lifted his head, his face flushed and tender. "I don't care a whit about juicy goose when I've the most delectable little gosling right here to enjoy."

"Pooh!" Beth said with a laugh.

Alex smiled, kissed her soundly on the cheek, and straightened to his full imposing height. Then he walked to the window and stared out into the early evening shadows, just as Beth had done. "Besides," he said, "the guest of honor isn't here, and I'm afraid the children won't have an appetite to eat until he arrives."

"Only the children?" Beth suggested archly.

Alex flashed her a sheepish look. "Well, I admit to being

a little worried, too. This is a damnable night to be traveling. I hope he's not stuck in a snowbank somewhere."

"Zach is two and thirty, Alex," said Beth, "and quite a capable man. I believe that if he thinks himself unable to make it here safely tonight, he will stop at an inn. You and the children will just have to be patient and wait to see him on the morrow."

"That sort of reasoning might be helpful to ease an adult mind, but the children will be disappointed," Alex returned.

"I know they will," Beth agreed. "We must keep them occupied with parlor games. Jason loves to play Going to Jerusalem."

"That's because Jason always wins," Alex remarked with a hint of fatherly pride. "A quick one, that boy."

"The image of his father in every way," Beth said, grinning.

Alex's chest swelled perceptibly, and then he noticed Beth's impish expression. "You're roasting me," he accused.

"Not a bit, love," she assured him demurely, patting at her curls. But when she caught the mischievous glint in her husband's black eyes, Beth braced herself. Such a look was usually followed by some prank, like a pillow fight or passionate lovemaking. She knew they hadn't time for either, but if she had a choice. . . .

"Mama? Papa? Are you in there? May we come in?"

Beth let loose the breath she'd been holding and threw her husband a sly look. "Saved by Providence. Thanks to our children, we'll have tender goose tonight."

"And *I* will still have gosling later," he warned her.

Beth laughed and called, "Come in, children!"

In walked the Wickham children all in a row with Torie heading the queue, and with the devoted aging Shadow following spryly behind.

Torie was still small for her age, but with a needle-sharp intelligence and self-assured demeanor that made her seem much older. Coupled with these adult characteristics was an infectious enthusiasm that made her a sheer delight to be around. While her adventurous curiosity had led Jason and Cecily into many a scrape, she had also taught them to beg forgiveness with such angelic sincerity that they seldom received very harsh punishments from Miss Brynne or Dudley.

Torie was lovely, too, in an exotic sort of way. Beth recognized Tessy's delicate features in Torie's face, but the golden eyes and the unbiddable expression that twinkled there had definitely come from Zach.

Jason was eight and was, as Beth had said, the image of his father, whom he frankly adored. He was already taller than Torie, though she was nearly two years older. He was very slender—almost wiry-thin—but as sturdy as a battering ram, an analogy that Beth thought suited him well since he was frequently running into things. He was all boy, that was a certainty, but sensitive, too, having a strong protective tendency toward his sisters. This was demonstrated most forcefully when he planted a facer on the vicar's son when the rude child was so unwise as to call Cecily a pudding face.

Cecily, at four, was the baby. She was dark-haired and dark-eyed like Jason but had her mother's milky complexion. To sum up Cecily would have been to say she was a happy child, for Cecily never cried. She followed her beloved older sister and brother around like a devoted pet, taking part in all their activities with sweetly optimistic eagerness.

Still padded with baby fat, Cecily was eminently huggable and was constantly being drawn onto someone's lap for just that purpose. She sucked her thumb, a habit Miss Brynne and Dudley were constantly trying to curtail by some process or other, which processes Miss Brynne and Dudley were seldom in agreement upon.

The girls were dressed in pretty green gowns, identical

miniature versions of their mama's. Jason was outfitted like
his papa, but in short pants. Most festive of all, their faces
were wreathed in smiles.

Alex sat down in a wing chair next to the dressing table,
and Cecily immediately took possession of his lap, snuggled
her head against the silky smoothness of his vest, and placed
one chubby hand against his cheek. The other hand was
occupied with supplying herself with a thumb to suck. Torie
and Jason stood at attention, like soldiers at review, waiting
for permission to speak.

"Well, children, what is it?" prompted Beth. "You look
as though you might burst with this news, whatever it is. It
must be something quite remarkable if you could not wait
till Papa and I joined you in the drawing room."

"He came across Blindley Heath," Jason burst out as
Torie opened her mouth to speak. "He said the roads were
all mucked up, so he left his team in Godstone and crossed
the heath on horseback t' get here in time for dinner. A real
bruiser in the saddle is our uncle Zach. Almost as good as
Papa," Jason finished proudly.

"Zach is here?" Beth exchanged a relieved, delighted
look with Alex.

"Yes, Uncle Zachary has come," Torie said sedately,
obviously trying very hard not to look as childishly eager as
her brother. "He said you must hurry and join him in the
drawing room. He has some important news to tell you."

"Oh?" Alex looked surprised. "Is it good news or bad
news?"

Torie's mouth twisted in an expression of perplexity.
"I'm not sure, Papa. He didn't say. But as he was taking off
his wet boots in the entrance hall, he muttered something
about a letter from Aunt Gabby and that she's flung herself
into the briars again. What do you think he meant by that?"

Beth and Alex exchanged another look that was anything
but delighted. "I don't know, Torie," said Alex, standing

and hiking Cecily up to rest her on his hip. "But we shall find out. Did Zach go to his chamber to change clothes?"

"Yes," said Torie, glad to be able to offer information where she could. "But he said he would change in the twinkling of a bedpost and that you must come downstairs at once because he'd probably be waiting for you."

Alex and Beth were happy to comply, since they were exceedingly curious about Gabby's latest misadventure. Since Beth and Alex had married, they had been receiving letters from Brookmoor that frequently included Mrs. Tavistock's fretful descriptions of Gabby's antics. Most of Gabby's scrapes were fairly minor and fixable, such as the time she and her cousin locked themselves in the pantry and got bosky on the cooking wine. But sometimes—such as the day she put a pollywog in the vicar's tea and he nearly choked to death—the consequences of her actions were quite embarrassing and long-lasting. Vicar Bradford still had not forgiven the Tavistocks for the pollywog incident, though Gabby was only ten when it occurred.

The last Beth had heard from her mother, Gabrielle was visiting a chum in Edinburgh. Due to poor health, her mother had not accompanied Gabby on this trip, but trusted her to the care of her aunt Clarissa.

Clarissa was a dear lady, but hardly the stiff-rumped, ferret-nosed, eagle-eyed sort of dragon one could wish for in a chaperon, especially for a high-spirited young woman like Gabby. Beth had worried about Aunt Clarissa's chaperonage but was hoping that the Murray family in Edinburgh would be watchful and wise enough to make up for her aunt's deficiencies.

At nineteen years of age, having already enjoyed her come-out last spring, turned down several suitors for her hand, and been chastised for being too persnickety, Gabby had probably been eager to go to Scotland to escape Brookmoor Manor and a winter of recriminations from her mama. But what trouble had she attracted this time?

They entered the drawing room, which was festooned with fir boughs and smelled of warm wax and hot apple punch. There, toasting his backside at the briskly burning fire, was Zach. He was still tall, still lean, still a golden Adonis in buckskin breeches and a black coat, but the faint lines that stretched from his straight nose to the corners of his mouth bespoke a wisdom and maturity earned the hard way. Today his expression was troubled, annoyed. Yes, Gabby had done something to put him in a twit. They embraced and exchanged greetings, but they were somewhat subdued because of the tension that hung about Zach like a thundercloud.

"Dudley says I must send all you children to the kitchen," Zach said presently, bending down to straighten Jason's cravat, tweak Cecily on the nose, and run a tender finger along Torie's cheek.

"But we don't want to go to the kitchen, Uncle Zachary," Torie complained with a beseeching look at him from under her thick golden eyelashes. "You've only just come, and we want to visit with you."

"I promise we shall spend time visiting, Torie," Zach soothed in a hushed voice, cupping her shoulder and looking lovingly into her eyes. "But I must speak to your mother and father, and I don't want . . ." He inclined his head just slightly to indicate the other children. He winked conspiratorially. "Well, you know."

Torie beamed with pride. "Oh, I understand, Uncle Zachary. The conversation will not be suitable for children, I see. Come, Jason and Cecily. I believe Dudley's got some berry tarts in the kitchen for us. Perhaps after dinner we shall have a game of puss in the corner."

In this way the children were dispatched, Torie feeling quite grown up, Jason's mouth watering at the mention of tarts, and Cecily looking forward to the promised parlor game of puss in the corner. When they were gone, Alex and

Beth sat down on a sofa together and waited for Zach to speak.

"I can't sit down yet," Zach apologized. "I'm too cold and too upset."

"Good God, what's she done this time?" said Alex. "Is it so very bad?"

"It's bad enough that I must not stay and keep the holidays with you," Zach grumbled, "but must hie myself back to Godstone in the morning, then on to London to change horses and head for the border. I got a letter from Gabby yesterday, as did your mother. She's betrothed!"

"Betrothed?" Beth sat up and looked keenly at her brother-in-law. "I admit I'm surprised, but a betrothal is generally held to be good news, Zach. Why are you so upset? Is there something objectionable about the gentleman?"

"Rumor has it he's a gambler and a rake," Zach said disgustedly.

"Men of bad reputation *have* been known to reform," said Alex, sliding a sly look toward Beth.

"We—her own family—don't know this man from Adam. And you know how I feel about Aunt Clarissa's judgment. I rue the day I allowed your mother to send Gabby away with that buffle-headed sister of hers. Beg your pardon, Beth, but your aunt Clarissa hasn't the sense of a babe."

"I'm sure Mother expected the Murray family, whom she met and became well acquainted with in London, to make up for Aunt Clarissa's shortcomings," Beth soothed. "And Aunt Clarissa's not so bad as that, Zach. What do the Murrays say about the match? Have they written to Mama?"

"Yes, they wrote," Zach said gruffly. "Before you ask me, yes, they do approve of Gabby's choice. Their opinion seems to be all that your mother requires to be totally enamored of the fellow, though she's never met him!"

"But she will, of course," said Alex, eyeing his brother with interest. "A betrothal is not a marriage. There is time for all of us to meet him. Who is he?"

"His name is Rory Cameron, Marquess of Lorne. He has a castle in Perthshire."

"I've heard of the family," said Alex, rubbing his chin. "The late marquess was quite respectable. I *have* heard, though, that the present marquess is a bit wild."

"But what privileged, titled, rich young man isn't described in such a way in this day and age?" Beth countered optimistically. "Besides, as Alex said, we'll have an opportunity to meet the marquess before Gabby marries him. Then, if we discover he is unsuitable—"

"I hope to God we get a chance to meet him," Zach interrupted with an exasperated hiss of breath. "In Scotland all a body needs to do to tie the nuptial knot is exchange vows in the presence of two witnesses. No publishing of banns is required by law. If Gabby is really besotted with the fellow, she might marry him before any of us has had a chance to form an opinion and counsel the girl. The letter I got from Gabby reveals her to be in a most alarming condition of complete infatuation. What if he's gambled himself into a state of genteel poverty and is after Gabby's inheritance?"

"Calm down, Zach," Alex said. "Gabby may attract trouble, and she may be too curious for her own good, but she's not stupid or likely to be bamboozled easily by an opportunistic marquess with pockets to let. Give the girl a little credit. I'll wager she's being more sensible about this relationship than you suspect. In her letter she probably used exaggerated romantical terms that appealed to her sense of the dramatic."

"Well, I don't think my concern is unwarranted," Zach returned rather petulantly. "In any case, since Mrs. Tavistock is still too unwell for such an arduous journey, and you and Beth are busy with family matters, it seems most practical for me to go up to Scotland and meet the fellow. You know, make sure he's right for Gabby.'' Zach paced back and forth in front of the fireplace and ran lean fingers through his golden hair till it stood on end. ''Can't let the girl make a mistake she'll suffer from her entire life,'' he muttered. ''Pollywogs in the vicar's tea is one thing, but matrimony is quite another!''

Beth and Alex exchanged meaningful glances. Then Alex cleared his throat and addressed Zach in a carefully measured tone. ''You couldn't be more right about that, Zach. Matrimony is serious business. Beth and I often wondered when Gabby would take the plunge. She's had plenty of opportunities. If she truly wants to marry this Rory Cameron, I hope he is an honorable, worthy man. If he isn't, we'll have something to say about it. But it strikes me, Zach''— Alex shifted slightly in his seat—''that you seem as troubled by the fact that Gabby's finally consented to a proposal of marriage as you are by the slim possibility that the fellow might be a scoundrel.''

Beth's eyes were riveted to Zach. Alex was implying that Zach had feelings for Gabrielle that transcended brotherly interest. She and Alex had sometimes suspected—in fact, they'd hoped—that Beth's beautiful little sister could heal Zach's wounded heart, a heart that still suffered ten years after Tessy's death. But they'd never discerned a loverlike manner in Zach toward Gabby, though they sometimes speculated that Gabby might have feelings for Zach that could explain her lack of interest in the dashing beaux who groveled at her feet during the London Season. But the way Zach was acting today . . .

''I'm not sure what you're implying, Alex.''

''Yes, you are,'' Alex stated flatly.

''How I feel about Gabrielle is irrelevant,'' Zach snapped. ''The girl needs watching after. I only want to make sure she's thought this marriage business through. Does she even realize how far away from the rest of us she'll be clear up in Perthshire, Scotland?''

Zach turned his back to them to prop his hands against the mantelpiece and hang his head between his shoulders. Alex and Beth exchanged another look rife with meaning.

When Zach did not move for several moments, Beth stood up and placed a hand on his shoulder. ''Gabby is so lucky to have a friend like you, Zach. We're glad you're going to Scotland to meet her betrothed. I'm sure she would wish for your approval most of all. If you can be easy about the marquess after you've met him, the rest of us will be satisfied that all is well.''

Zach lifted a hand to place over Beth's. ''Thank you, Beth,'' he said. ''Don't worry. I'll see to it that Gabby doesn't make a dreadful mistake. I could not bear to think of her being unhappy.''

The rest of the evening passed pleasantly enough, though it was probably obvious, at least to Torie, that the adults were preoccupied. When Zach had retired to his room and the children were tucked into bed, Alex and Beth stood at her bedchamber window and looked out over the countryside. It had quit snowing during dinner, and they could hope that Zach would have a comfortable ride back to Godstone in the morning.

Beth leaned back into Alex's chest, his arms clasping her close to him, her head nestled in the hollow of his throat. ''I wish him godspeed,'' she said. ''I wonder how long it will take him to realize he's in love with Gabby? And once he's realized it, will he admit to it?''

''I pray to God he admits to it,'' Alex said on a sigh. ''He deserves some happiness. Do you think Gabby planned all this to bring Zach to his senses?''

Beth's brows furrowed. ''I don't know, but if her betrothal to another man doesn't make him face his own feelings and put the past behind him, I can't imagine anything else that would do the trick. You do think she's quite safe, don't you?''

"Yes, I've met the Murrays on more than one occasion— George is a member of White's and is frequently there when I visit—and I don't think your mother's trust in them is misplaced. Besides, Zach will be there in a couple of days to see that all is well."

Beth sighed and nestled closer to Alex. "You're right, you know. Zach deserves to be happy. Gabby, too."

"Yes. But we must all make our own happiness in the world. Zach and Gabrielle have to work this out for themselves, and I firmly believe they will." Alex turned Beth around in his arms and smiled down into her face. "You've made my happiness, Beth."

"And you mine, Alex," she whispered, returning his smile radiantly.

They kissed.